"If you ever need me, call."

She nodded. "I will."

"Promise."

The serious tone and eyes made JT's heart pound. "I promise."

He lifted his hand and ran a dark finger down her soft cheek. "I will kill the next person who hurts you."

"Reese?"

"They'll have to go through me."

This was a bonding moment and she knew from this day forward they'd be linked in ways both beautiful and new. The certainty thrilled her and scared her all at the same time. "When you court a woman, what should she expect?"

The question garnered a small smile. "That I'll buy her flowers and make love to her." He traced her cheek again. "That I'll take her to dinner and make love to her. That I'll take her to my place in Hawaii and make love to her on a black beach under the moon."

By Beverly Jenkins

DEADLY SEXY
SEXY/DANGEROUS
BLACK LACE
THE EDGE OF DAWN
THE EDGE OF MIDNIGHT

BEVERLY JENKINS

DEADLY SEXY

AVON

An Imprint of HarperCollinsPublishers

Permission granted to quote lyrics from "Reasons" written and composed by Frankie Beverly, Amazing Music.

AVON BOOKS
An Imprint of HarperCollins*Publishers*
10 East 53rd Street
New York, New York 10022-5299

Copyright © 2007 by Beverly Jenkins
ISBN: 978-0-06-124639-5
ISBN-10: 0-06-124639-5
www.avonromance.com

First Avon Books paperback printing: November 2007

Avon Trademark Reg. U.S. Pat. Off. and in Other Countries, Marca
Registrada, Hecho en U.S.A.
HarperCollins® is a registered trademark of HarperCollins Publishers.

Printed in the U.S.A.

10 9 8 7 6 5 4 3 2 1

Prologue

When sixty-three-year-old Gus Pennington got into his eight-year-old Dodge Ram and headed off to his janitorial job, he had no idea this would be his last night on earth. He drove the fifteen miles to the L.A. Grizzlies Stadium and parked his truck in the designated space, took out his keys, unlocked the door lettered MAINTENANCE—AUTHORIZED PERSONNEL ONLY, and went inside. He'd found out that afternoon that the young man who was supposed to have mopped the executive offices last night hadn't because he'd quit. Apparently the kid hadn't worked in three days, and Gus refused to let the floors be dirty even a minute longer. A contract service kept the floors of the stadium's luxury boxes clean, so Gus didn't have to worry about them, but he and his two-man operation were responsible for the floors in the offices of the president, the GM, and their secretaries.

Gus liked his job. He'd been a football fan all of his life, and during his thirty years of employment with the old L.A. Rams teams, he'd had a chance to meet and greet his heroes up close and personal; he'd also accumulated enough autographs to start his own hall of fame. Coming to work kept him active, and the job made him the envy of his buddies at Wilson's Barbershop.

Using the mop's long yellow handle to steer with, Gus pushed the heavy red bucket off the elevator. He was on the third floor, where the offices of the team executives and secretaries were located. Gus took pride in doing a good job no matter where, but up here he did his best work. The place was quiet, the computer screens filled with moving, hushed screensavers. Tiny lights on the fax machines and printers glowed at the ready.

Taking out his iPod, he put on the headphones and clicked on the tunes his grandson Christopher had downloaded into it. The small silver-colored player had been a birthday present—even had the word pops, Chris's name for him, engraved on the front.

Miles Davis came on first. Gus adjusted the volume to the blaring beauty of *Bitches Brew*, then went to work.

After taking care of the secretaries' offices, he pushed the mop bucket down the hall to the conference room. Because he was grooving with the music, Gus didn't see the four men standing around the long table until it was too late to run, back away, or even to pray. The gun fired and his world went black. Miles wailed on.

One

•

You've given me a reason to love one more time,
Came into my life and made up my mind.
I knew you were meant for me . . .
　　　　　　"Reasons" by Frankie Beverly and Maze

Seated behind the steering wheel of the big eighteen wheeler, Reese Anthony checked his outside mirrors for the traffic flowing behind him, then hit the button on the dash to change the CD. Seconds later the first signature notes of "The Golden Time of Day" by Frankie Beverly and Maze flowed sweetly through the cab's surroundsound speakers and Reese smiled. He was a big Maze fan, and this particular tune was one of his favorites, especially on a long road trip with the day winding down. He was driving north on California's I-5 on his way to San Francisco, over

150 miles away. It would be dark by the time he made it to the yard, but he didn't mind. He had Frankie B and a small mountain of CDs to keep him company.

Reese was singing along with the lyrics when the phone rang. Frowning at the interruption, he eased down the volume and engaged the speaker for the communication component also routed through the cab's high-tech dashboard. "This is Reese."

"Hey, brother man. How are you?"

The familiar sound of Taylor McNair's voice lifted Reese's lips into a smile. "Doing fine. How're things in Gotham City, Mr. Commissioner? How are Tara and the kids?" Six months ago Tay had been appointed the new commissioner of the World League of Football, but because of killer schedules, the two old friends hadn't talked in some time.

"Everybody's doing well," Tay replied. "How about you?"

"Can't complain. I'm in California road-testing a new solar engine for Brainiac Bryce." Bryce was Reese's thirty-three-year-old baby brother, a mechanical engineering genius and computer geek who'd graduated from MIT at the age of sixteen.

"He still churning out the designs?"

"Yep, and it's a wonder the boy's brain doesn't catch fire. He's bringing in more money than we can spend."

Tay laughed. "I wish I had that problem. How's your pops?"

"Good. Retired a few months back but he's still at the yard giving Bryce and Jamal fits." Jamal, sometimes known as Pinky, was Reese's thirty-five-year-old middle brother. If Bryce could design it, Jamal could build it.

"Make sure you tell Pops and Pinky and the Brain I said 'Hey.'"

"Will do." Reese took a moment to pass a small truck loaded down with mattresses, then swung the sparkling green cab with its unblemished silver trailer back into the right lane. "So Tay, you calling just to catch up, or is something on your mind?"

"Got a murder."

Reese frowned. "A murder? Who?"

"An older brother named Gus Pennington. Head janitor for the L.A. Grizzlies. His body was found a few mornings ago in his truck. Had a gun beside him on the seat."

"Sounds like suicide."

"LAPD thought so too, at first, but the gun was on the right side of his body. According to the family, he's left-handed."

"Where was the truck found?"

"Grizzlies Stadium parking lot. Police think it might have been a petty robbery, but the M.E.'s saying the body was placed in the truck after the murder. Something to do with blood loss or something. I'm not sure."

"Not a good way to start your new job."

"No kidding. I've been so busy hitting the ground running there hasn't been time to pull together an investigative office, but now I have to have one. Hoping you'll take the head job, at least temporarily."

Reese went still. Frankie Beverly sang softly against the silence. Reese had retired from the Detroit police force over a decade ago, swapping his Vice Squad badge for a law degree. Since passing the bar, he'd enjoyed a comfortable, albeit boring life coordinating the legal affairs for the family firm, Anthony Trucking International.

"You still there, Reese?"

"Yeah. I'm here. Thinking about your question." Reese didn't miss the day-to-day interaction with crackheads, dealers, and prostitutes, but after ten years of being cooped up in air-conditioned offices, he sometimes longed for the chaos and excitement of the good old days. For the last few months he'd felt restless, antsy. Would a change of pace help, even a temporary one? "The police don't usually like outsiders in the mix when they're running a case," he finally said.

"I know, but I've already talked to one of the captains. As long as you don't represent yourself as law enforcement to anybody you contact, the detectives don't have a problem with you asking questions on behalf of my office. For them, this isn't a high profile case. As I said earlier, they're pretty sure it was a petty robbery gone wrong, but as commissioner, I need to be satisfied that Pennington's death isn't tied to somebody involved with the league."

Reese thought that made sense, but did he want the job? Being away from his law office wouldn't present much of a problem. His staff was well-trained. If something came up that they couldn't handle, he'd only be a phone call away. Yeah, he needed a break from the corporate world, so why not? "Okay, Tay, I'm your man. Temporarily."

"Excellent. Let's go over some of the details."

Driving I-5 on her way back to her Oakland office, JT Blake snarled into the headset of her phone, "I could've killed him!"

Carole Marsh, her secretary, was on the other end of the line. JT was venting about the disastrous meeting she'd just had at the home of a potential new client, a young defensive back named Keith Owens, a recent graduate of USC who'd had the talent and the smarts to go pro. "I was under the impression that the kid and I would be meeting one on one. Nobody said anything about Mr. G3 being invited too."

Robert L. Garrett the Third—or Bobby G3, as he preferred to be called—had worked for her agency a few years back, but she'd fired him after only six months for a litany of sins. Among them: insubordination, getting in her face, and generally being a pain in the ass. He had his own shop now, and was doing his best to be the best, but because his clients were the selfish coddled young men who passed for superstar athletes these days, he was having trouble getting to the top and staying there.

While Carole asked questions about the meeting, JT reached down and adjusted the air-conditioning. It was a warm, early May evening. She'd dumped the jacket to her gold suit in the backseat and was wearing the slinky but tasteful yellow silk camisole she'd had on underneath. The silver Lexus she was driving was sleek, powerful, and fresh out of the box. She'd picked it up from the dealership yesterday, and it handled like a dream. The smooth ride was almost enough to cool her anger. Almost. "No," JT replied to the question in her ear. "The parents looked as surprised as I did when Bobby strolled in skinning and grinning and trying to work his way into the mix, but this Owens kid's future is too bright to turn it over to a demon. I'll shoot Garrett myself if it comes down to that."

The car began shaking and howling. A surprised JT fought with the steering. "What the hell!"

"What's wrong?"

"Car's messing up. Trying to keep it on the road." The front end was bucking like a steer at the Texas State Fair, and the noise filling the plush interior was deafening. "I'm going to pull over. Stay with me girl!"

Reese Anthony and Taylor McNair were still talking on the phone when Reese saw a car pull over on the side of the road up ahead. Looked brand new. He hoped it hadn't broken down. There was nothing on this stretch of road but miles of brown hills topped by sea after sea of white-winged wind turbines. Then the woman stepped out of the car and into view. At first he thought she was a mirage, but when he blinked, she was still there, striding to the front of the car, and all he could see were the sexy stilettos and the sleek brown legs that seemed to reach to China from beneath the short but tasteful gold skirt.

He let out an awed whispered, "Wow." Her arms and shoulders, bared by the soft yellow camisole, looked as sleek as her legs.

"What are you wowing at?" Taylor asked.

Reese saw the car's hood go up, and he instinctively slowed and began downshifting. "Coming up on a sister with car trouble. I'm going to stop and see if I can help."

"Okay, man. Call me back when you can and we'll tighten up the rest of the details."

"Sounds good. Later."

When the semi blew by her on the highway, JT swore she saw a brother driving. She probably should have flagged him down, but for the moment she was more concerned with what was going on with her car. With the hood raised and anchored, she looked around inside. It didn't take her long to spot the problem. A broken drive belt was hard to miss. She picked up the ends of split rubber and stared at them grimly. Belts on new cars just didn't pop, and this one hadn't either. The break looked too clean to have occurred spontaneously. "Carole, that bastard cut my belt," she steamed into the mouthpiece.

"What belt?"

"The drive belt."

"You sure it didn't just break?"

"I grew up with cars, Carole. This was no accident."

"You don't know that G3 did it."

"No, but if it stinks like a skunk and smells like a skunk, guess what?"

"Where are you?"

"On I-5, just north of 41."

"You're in the middle of nowhere."

"No kidding."

"Need some help?"

JT jumped. He was walking toward her with a slow measured stride that could only be described as mesmerizing. Tall, he was wearing a blue T-shirt that showed off hard ebony guns. The jeans were tight and the tan work boots worn. He was dark-skinned and fine. She definitely liked what she saw, but as her mind reminded her, fine men could be axe murders, too, so she grabbed hold of herself, took her eyes off that fluid walk and met his eyes. "Busted belt."

"Who's that?"

"A brother trucker," she told Carole, then said to him, "I'm talking to my secretary."

He nodded. "Belts don't usually break on new cars. Let me take a look and see if we can find the real problem."

It vexed JT to no end to have a man assume she didn't know what the hell she was talking about, but rather than setting him straight, she coolly gestured for him to make his own diagnosis.

He leaned in, peered around for a moment, then looked up at her.

"Belt's busted, right?" she asked.

He gave her a ghost of a smile then backed out and straightened up to his full height. JT was five feet eight inches tall, but this trucker man with his beautiful mahogany arms and thigh-hugging jeans loomed above her like the Colossus of Rhodes.

"Looks like the belt's been cut. Who'd you piss off? Husband? Boyfriend? An ex?"

JT wasn't pleased by his assumption that she was somehow at fault. "Ex-employee."

He closed the hood. "Nice person wanting you to be stuck way out here."

"Yeah, he's a real piece of work."

"What do you do?"

"Athlete representation."

His surprise was plain. "What kind of athletes?"

"Professional. Where you heading?"

"San Fran. You?"

"Oakland."

For a moment neither spoke. Reese noted how smoothly she'd cut off more questions about her job. He could respect that; he rarely talked about his clients either. Meanwhile, he'd never seen so much beauty in one woman before in his life. He was doing his best not to gawk at her fine lines like a country boy at his first truck show. "I doubt any garages will have a belt for a car like this way out here, but there should be a gas station about ten miles north. If you want, I can give you a ride and you can ask around when you get there."

JT studied him, then into her mouthpiece said, "He's going to give me a ride to a gas station."

"Are you sure it's safe. Does he have a name?"

"What's your name?"

"Reese . . . Reese Anthony."

"Reese Anthony," she told Carole, but what she didn't say was that he had an aura about him strong enough to be felt by sisters in Boston.

"He as fine as his name?"

"Oh, yeah."

"Get me a tag number. If Reese the Fine turns out to be a serial killer, I'll be able to sic the popo on him."

JT met his assessing eyes and smiled. "Okay. The tag number on your truck?"

Reese didn't mind her wanting to be safe, so he gave it to her easily. JT repeated it for Carole.

"Good. I'll call the dealership and have them pick up the Lexus. I'll play the dumb woman and tell them we don't know why it stopped. Do you want me to send a car for you at this gas station? It's late, so it may take a few hours to get there."

"Hold on." She focused her attention on the trucker. "Can I hitch a ride? I'll pay. Say three hundred, to cover your gas and the inconvenience?"

Reese didn't need money. Helping her out was something his pops had raised all of his sons to do, no matter the situation. "You don't have to pay me."

"Sure I do. Gas isn't cheap."

He assumed she assumed he was a trucker. He saw no harm in letting her think that. He also figured her paying him might make her feel safer. They were strangers, after all, and he could always donate the money." Okay. Three hundred sounds good."

"Thanks. Carole, Mr. Anthony's going to give me a ride back to the office. Have a rental waiting and I'll pick it up when I get there."

"Sounds good. Stay safe. Scream if you need me."

"Will do. 'Bye."

JT cut the connection but kept the earpiece in: one, because Carole might call back; and two, although she didn't feel threatened by Reese the Fine, if she needed to make a call in a hurry, she could do so.

Reese took in the flawless face framed by the bone-straight, shoulder-length, auburn highlighted hair, and then the expensive-looking gold chains hanging from the alluring sweep of her neck. Being male, he knew that a lot of times beautiful women turned out to be self-centered and crazy. Would she fit the mold? "Ready to ride?"

JT forced herself to look away from the power emanating from his assessing dark eyes. "Let me grab my stuff." Shaking off the instant vibe she was getting from him, she opened the back door of the Lex to retrieve her briefcase and jacket, slid into the front seat to grab her CD case, and then got her title and registration papers from the glove box. If jackers happened upon the Lexus before the dealer's people arrived, anything else that might be inside could be replaced. She locked the doors with her clicker. "I'm ready."

"You going to be okay walking in those shoes?" The rig was a ways up the road.

JT looked down at the $250 Italian stilettos on her feet, then back up into his skeptical but still fine face. "I'll be okay."

He didn't look convinced but began the walk to the truck.

Reese was sure she'd have trouble keeping up in the killer shoes, but the gravel shoulder didn't seem to be an issue. She was striding beside him as confidently as a woman in sneakers and looking damn good doing it. The silky looking camisole and the hoops in her ears looked as expensive as the rest of her. She didn't fit his image of a sports agent though. "What's your name? If you don't mind me asking."

"JT." She turned his way. "Blake."

Reese knew the name right away and fought to keep the awe from showing on his face. The Lady Blake. The damsel in distress was one of the toughest and baddest sports agents around. She'd negotiated multi-million-dollar contracts for players in football and basketball. Being a big sports fan himself, he'd come across references to her in sports magazines and in articles on the sports pages, but had never seen a picture. Who knew she'd be a brown-skinned goddess? Wait until he told Pinky and the Brain. They were going to be too impressed. "Like I said, I'm Reese Anthony. Nice meeting you."

A few cars and trucks whizzed by on the road. "Same here. You're a lifesaver." And he was, JT realized. There was no telling how long she might have been stuck on the side of the road had he not stopped. Granted, she'd had Carole on the line, but help would still have been a long ways away. Instead, she was going to get to ride in an eighteen wheeler driven by a good-looking Sir Galahad.

They finally reached the truck. He opened the passenger side door. "Hand me your things. You're going to need both hands to climb up."

She took one look at the height of the running

board and without a word handed everything over. She grabbed hold of the rails on each side and as gracefully as she could climbed up to the step.

As she maneuvered herself, Reese tried hard not to stare at the sweet curve of her behind and the long brown legs, but it was futile. All he could say in response to all that beauty was, *Damn!*

Once she was settled in the seat, the bright smile she gave him went straight to his groin. He closed the door. Mentally reeling, he shook off the aftershock, then walked around to the driver's door and got in.

As her rescuer eased the big rig back onto the highway and slowly built up speed, JT looked around the interior. It was plush and way more modern than she'd imagined. Her high-backed seat was made like a recliner, and the soft leather was the color of dark caramel. Matching leather panels were inset into the doors. The same leather was wrapped stylishly around the steering wheel and accented the beautiful interior. The dashboard looked like something taken from a space shuttle. Above her head was an open tinted glass sunroof. "This is very nice."

Reese was pleased by her praise. "Top of the line. In the back is an eighty-six-inch foldout sleeper, a built-in TV, a fridge, and a table that folds down when there's paperwork to do. Got some reading lights, a couple of spotlights on the floor, and a skylight in the roof."

JT was turned around in her seat checking out the amenities. "This is sweet. How long have you been driving?"

"Since I was eighteen."

"Do you enjoy it?"

"I do. It can be a pain if you're in city traffic, but out here on the open road, nothing's better."

"I've never ridden in a semi before. It's way more fancy than I thought. Didn't expect it to ride this smooth either."

"Trucks have come a long way."

She peered down at the dash. "You have GPS too?"

He nodded. "The technology's pretty standard these days. Even truckers get lost occasionally."

JT looked out of the windshield at the road spread out before them and felt like a little kid.

Seeing her excitement made Reese reevaluate her yet again. He hadn't expected her to be this down to earth. He'd always associated high-powered women with attitude. Not that he doubted her ability to turn it on, but at this moment she appeared relaxed and open. "If you're thirsty, there's pop in the fridge."

She angled her head his way. "Pop? You must be from the Midwest."

He couldn't deny it. "Detroit. Soda is a drink we put ice cream in."

She tossed back playfully, "We Texans, and the rest of the country, say soda."

"Texas, huh?"

He met her eyes, and JT could feel herself responding again to their silent power. "Yep. Little town outside of Austin."

"If you call pop soda, what do you call ice cream and pop?"

"Parfait."

"We call it that too."

JT thought he was even more handsome when he smiled. Everyday brothers weren't usually comfortable with women like her because of their different worlds, but something about him made her want to know more about who he was. Needing to collect herself, she undid her seat belt and made her way to the back. Up close it was even more spacious than his description. The leather bed was folded up and ran the width of the cab. The trim above it was done in brown mud cloth. "I like the mud cloth."

Reese was again pleased. "Nice touch, huh?"

"Real nice." With the truck still rolling beneath her feet, JT moved to the small refrigerator nestled in a niche in the wall near the bed. She opened it and saw chilled bottles of water, cola, and fruit juice. There were also a couple of apples and a Ziploc bag holding some of the blackest cherries she'd ever seen. They immediately called her name. She loved cherries, but because it seemed she'd already imposed on the man enough, she didn't ask for any. Instead, she grabbed a water. "Do you want anything to drink?"

"Yeah, bring me a water. There's some cherries too. Do you like cherries?"

She wondered if he was a mind reader. "I do."

"Then bring the bag and we'll share. They've already been washed."

She grabbed another bottle of water, and with the cherries in hand, closed the door and moved back to the front of the cab.

Reese took his eyes off the road just long enough to be bewitched by her golden behind as she retook her seat. Reminding himself that he was a gentleman, or was at least trying to be, he checked the traffic through his mirrors while she undid the cap on one of the bottles.

When JT handed over the bottle of water, her hand accidentally brushed against his and a shard of heat shot up her arm. Outwardly she gave nothing away, but inside she was resonating like a kalimba.

Reese felt the heat too, and like her, pretended he hadn't. "Thanks." Taking a long drink to cool himself down, he placed the bottle in the holder beside him and forced himself not to look her way.

Very aware of Reese the Fine, JT checked out the cherries through the transparent Ziploc bag. "Do you have a trash bag or something for these cherry pits?"

"There's a receptacle built into the door. Just pull it down."

JT did and was again impressed with the truck's efficient design. "Do you have one on your side too?"

"Yep."

"Here." Holding the bag open and careful to keep her hand from touching his again, she moved it close so he could reach in. He grabbed a few, and she took out a few for herself and bit into one. That first taste was so wonderful, succulent, and firm, she moaned before she could stop herself.

He grinned. "That good?"

"Oh hell, yeah. Where'd you buy these?"

"Traverse City."

She ran through a mental map of the state of California but drew a blank. "Where's Traverse City?"

"Michigan. Western side of the state."

"Michigan? They grow cherries in Michigan?"

"Yep. One of country's biggest producers."

"Learn something new every day." She bit into another big fat one, and this time silently savored the flesh and the juice. "I could eat these 24/7. Did you have them shipped or can you buy them here?"

"Brought them with me when I came west."

JT stared. "You drove this truck all the way from Michigan?"

"Yep. Drove it down to Dallas first."

"Damn," she said, awed.

Reese chuckled. Yes, he liked the Lady Blake with her bling, her tall svelte curves, and her blunt speech.

"I thought you were local," she told him.

"Nope. As the kids say, I'm from the D."

She cut him a playful look. "D stands for Dallas."

"No, Dallas is the *Big* D. Detroit doesn't need a qualifier."

She liked this man. She studied his hands on the steering wheel. They looked capable and strong. The fact that he didn't wear a wedding ring meant nothing these days, but she wondered if he was married. "What's your wife say about you driving cross-country."

He met her eyes. "Divorced."

"Ah."

"You?"

She shook her head. "Single all my life."

Reese found that hard to believe. Was she a lesbian? He didn't have the nerve to ask that. "Pass me some more of those cherries before you kill the bag."

She hung her head in embarrassment, then gave him a chagrined smile. "I'm sorry."

He reached into the bag. "It's okay, I can get more."

She bit into another one and delicately licked at the juice on her lips. "If I give you the money, will you get me some? I'll pay whatever they cost. These are the best cherries I've ever had. In my life."

It was the second time she'd offered him money, and Reese wondered if that was how her world worked. "I'll send you some but they'll be my gift for being such a good shotgun."

"Thanks, but I'd rather pay you. You didn't have to offer me a ride, and with the price of gas and everything, this has to be costing you good money."

"Even a truck driver can afford cherries, Ms. Blake."

JT winced. "I wasn't trying to offend a brother. Sorry."

"You didn't, but there are men in the world who aren't looking to be paid."

"Not in my life there aren't. Everybody's chasing dead presidents."

"Must be rough being a woman doing what you do for a living."

She took another sip of water. "It was worse when I first got started. Now, its not so bad. There's still a lot of stupid gender stuff, but less of it."

Reese could only imagine what she must have faced having to deal with not only the gender issues, but being a Black woman as well. The lady had to be tough. "Tell me about the person you think cut your belt."

"I'll keep his name to myself to protect the guilty."

"That's your right."

She saw the concern in his face and that touched her too. "He used to work for me. Had to fire him, though, because he thought the name on the office door was his instead of mine. Has his own agency now and considers himself my competition."

"He's playing hardball if he's jamming your ride."

"I know, but he's having cash flow issues and thinks that if he gets rid of my shop he'll be able to rise to the top. Jerk."

The cop in Reese wasn't happy knowing she was being harassed. "Are you going to file a police report when you get home?"

"No, because without tangible proof, the police will just tell me to go home."

He knew that was true, but still. "Do you have any security?"

"Yep. A bunch of six-foot-four-, -five-, and -six-inch linebackers who'd stomp him like grapes if they ever find out."

"Good." That made him feel better.

"Do you like football?"

"As much as you like those cherries."

Her smile seemed to light up the cab. "Then let's talk some ball."

Their grins met, and Reese was sure he'd died and gone to heaven. A beautiful woman who could talk football? When they reached Oakland, he just might keep driving so he wouldn't have to let her out of the truck.

Two

With the top down on his red Mercedes convertible and a sharklike smile on his egg-shaped light brown face, Robert L. Garrett the Third, aka Bobby G3, drove toward L.A. He was pretty sure Bitch Blake's new Lex had broken down on the 5 by now and he hoped she was out in the middle of nowhere. He'd been stealing cars since middle school, so bypassing her sorry-ass, factory-installed alarm system had been a snap. Hiking the hood and slashing the belt took two minutes, max. He hadn't even gotten his hands dirty. If she figured him for the perp, so what? She had no proof, and the only witnesses were the cows and corn in the Owens's family pastures.

Garrett's grin spread, showing off crisp white teeth. Sooner or later she was going to have to recognize. The fresh-faced intern she'd fired without cause three years ago had his own agency now, one with a decent stable of clients even if a few had turned out whack, like running back Jermaine Crane, who instead of setting records for most carries in a season was sitting in state prison for betting on his own games. The conviction let the league void Jermaine's multi-million-dollar contract, causing him serious cash flow problems, but that wasn't at issue at the moment. All he wanted to do was gloat. He hoped she'd get jacked by some crazy trucker and never be heard from again.

Reese was rolling up I-5 enjoying the company of the most remarkable woman he'd ever met. Not only could she talk sports, she knew stats, tendencies, and it didn't matter whether the athletes or teams played basketball, baseball, football, or soccer. She even threw in hockey, something few Black men were into, let alone Black women. But she knew her Original Six from her blue line, and he wanted to propose marriage right there and then.

"Any more cherries?" he asked.

They'd been riding for nearly an hour.

She held out the bag so he could reach in. As he did, he used the moment to feast on the gorgeous lines of her face, lingering for a second over the curves of her cherry-stained lips before turning back to the road. "How'd you get into sports negotiations?" But what he really wanted to know was if her mouth would taste as luscious as it appeared.

"A woman from my mother's church. Her son was drafted in the first round. She knew I was a lawyer, so she asked me to handle his first contract."

"Football or basketball?"

"Football."

Reese didn't ask for a name. Being a lawyer himself, he didn't expect her to divulge the identity of her clients. "Did the owner try to jam you because you were a rookie?"

"Oh yeah, and for being female. The first contract was so insulting I tossed it back across the table and walked out. Told them to call me when they were ready to be serious."

"And did they?"

"The next day. Their team finished dead last the season before so they needed my player, bad. We eventually got the contract done and my guy reported for training camp. On time."

"Has to be pretty wild being around the athletes."

"Most times they're a lot of fun. There are a few idiots, but every profession has those."

"I suppose you get to go to all the big sporting events?"

"Oh yeah. Super Bowl. NBA Finals. You name it, I get tickets."

"Must be nice."

"Every fan's dream. I can send you a couple of tickets if you like. Maybe not the Super Bowl, but I can get you into the all-star weekends. I'll even hook you up a stadium suite for coming to my rescue."

"Nah. That's okay." Now that he'd agreed to Tay's offer, more than likely he would be able to swing his own suite and tickets. He didn't tell her about the new job, though. He'd been enjoying her company. If she found out he worked for the league, she'd shut down immediately. Everything he'd read said no

agent worth her salt would be caught dead fraterniz-
ing with someone tied to the league office. Not only
did it look bad, but it could impact her credibility
with her clients.

"You don't want to go?"

"No, I'm okay."

JT studied him. "No strings attached."

He smiled. "I know, but thanks anyway."

She hoped she hadn't offended him. Some men
found it hard to accept gifts from a woman, but he
hadn't impressed her as the type. Was she afraid of not
fitting in because of his profession? Not being a mind
reader, she didn't have an answer. In the awkward
silence that followed, Frankie B sang softly about a
southern girl. She turned to the window, sipped from
her bottled water and watched the night roll by.

Reese wasn't happy with the change in the cab's
atmosphere. As she sat looking out of the window, he
could see the distance settling over her manner. The
nice easy time they'd been having seemed on the verge
of slipping away. "The reason I turned you down is
because I'm not sure what I'll be doing for work that
weekend." Which was technically the truth. He had
no idea what he might be doing for the commissioner's office. It crossed his mind that when they met
again—and he was sure they would—he'd have some
explaining to do.

"No problem. I understand." She faced him in the
faint glow thrown off by the small lights beneath
their seats. "Thought I'd offended you."

"No."

Their gazes held. JT sensed time slowing, a sensation she'd never experienced before. Beneath all that chocolate fineness was a man she was becoming more and more curious about.

Suddenly, the cab began to shake violently, and whatever they were about to say was lost.

"What the hell!" Reese fought with the steering to keep the semi from leaving the road. "Hold on!"

The truck had taken on a life of its own, stubbornly resisting his efforts to bring it back under control. In his side mirror he could see headlights of the traffic behind him swerving wildly as cars tried to avoid rear-ending the truck or being totaled by it. Reese downshifted, working the clutch and the brake until the big eighteen-wheeler slowed enough for him to safely pull onto the road's shoulder and stop.

Braced with her hand on the door, JT blew out a breath of grateful relief. "Lord."

Reese's adrenaline began to ebb. "You okay?"

"Yeah. Déjà vu."

"Let's hope not." He reached beneath his seat and pulled out a flat tool chest and a flashlight. He checked his outside mirror for oncoming traffic before opening his door. "Be right back."

JT sat in the quiet for a few moments, then decided to get out and join him. He might need help.

Mindful of her training under the steely eyes of Old Man Bowman, her high school automotive teacher, JT walked up but stayed silent. When a mechanic had his or her head under a raised hood, being surprised by another person's presence was not a good thing.

That wasn't the case here, however. He wasn't under the hood. He was on the passenger side of the truck's trailer crouched down beside an open panel that held the oddest looking engine she'd ever seen. He acknowledged her with a grim nod, then went back to peering into the works with the flashlight. A yellow lantern on the ground beside him added extra illumination.

"Thought you might need some help."

He turned to her. "What do you know about engines?"

She wanted to smack him for the sexist question, but instead drawled, "I know that isn't your standard Big Three issue."

The surprise on his face almost made up for the crack.

"Took automotive shop in high school."

Wonder filled his eyes.

JT smiled sweetly and asked, "So what kind of engine is it?"

"If I tell you, I'll have to kill you," he said, grinning, and took out his phone.

Amused, she shook her head.

His bad mood banished by their banter, Reese stood and spoke into the phone, but kept his vision on her. Lord, she was beautiful. Even in the dark. "Bryce. Pick up. I know you're there."

When Bryce did pick up, he wasn't happy. "You caught me in the middle of someone. You and that damn truck better be on fire!"

"Sorry," Reese laughed. Bryce was a genius, but he liked the honeys as much as he did equations. "No fire, but I'm having steering issues. Need you to figure out what it is."

"Shit."

"My sentiments too, but that's not going to get me and the lady back to the Bay area."

"What lady?"

"Never mind that, just tell me what to do."

When the eavesdropping JT smiled in response, Reese met it with one of his own.

Following Bryce's instructions, Reese pushed a button on the palm-sized computer docked on top of the engine then waited while Bryce ran a diagnostic from the laptop in his bedroom.

A fascinated JT was sure Old Man Bowman had never seen anything this high tech, and neither had she. "Where's your brother?" she asked.

"Detroit."

"Wow."

"We call him Bryce the Brain. Graduated from MIT at sixteen. This is his baby."

"He built the engine?"

"Yeah. It's a prototype. Some kind of melding of solar components and computer chips. I don't understand half the things he says, but he's got a brain the size of Lake Michigan."

"How old is he now?"

"Thirty-three."

"Any other siblings?"

"Brother named Jamal."

"He an egghead too?"

"In his own way. He builds what Bryce designs."

JT blinked. A family of geniuses. "Are you as brainy as they are?"

"In my own way."

The tone of his voice and the playfulness in his eyes made JT's insides tingle, but she played it off by gazing up at the moon overhead. "Nice night."

Reese grinned, then switched gears as Bryce's voice came over the phone. The diagnostic had pinpointed the problem. One of the chips had burned out. Bryce was in the process of rerouting the system to bypass it. Once that was achieved he said, "Okay. You're set. Let her sit for thirty minutes so everything can reboot. There shouldn't be any more problems."

"Thanks, man. My apologies to your guest."

"Just hang up."

Chucking, Reese ended the call. "Thirty minutes and we can roll," he said to her.

"Good." JT's job involved dealing with drop dead gorgeous hunks on a regular basis, so she considered herself pretty much immune to men like Reese the Fine, but he was something. On the ride, they'd discussed sports, politics, music, and movies. He'd shown himself to be intelligent, funny, and so good to look at that as far as she was concerned he didn't have to utter another word. But within the sexy, well-built trucker's body beat the heart of a man with a good mind, and she liked that. This morning, if someone had told her that by nightfall she'd be mesmerized by a sweet walking trucker with eyes that were even now teasing her, she'd've asked to see their crack pipe.

Reese knew they should be getting back to the cab, but he couldn't seem to move. The wind had come up, and under his silent scrutiny she brushed her hair

Deadly Sexy 31

back from her face. She was beautiful enough to light up the night, but her intelligence was the draw. He'd always had a thing for smart women, and the Lady Blake definitely qualified. "Sorry about the delay. I know you're probably wanting to get home."

"It's okay. Stuff happens, and as I said, I'm enjoying the company." The sounds of the traffic roaring by on the road could be heard, but JT paid it scant attention.

"Let me set some flares so we don't get rear-ended."

"Probably a good idea." Their gazes were still locked, and for a breath of a second, and the first time in her life, JT wondered what it might be like to be someone else. Were she a nurse or a teacher, or a woman with a regular job, she didn't think he'd have a problem pursuing whatever was bubbling up between them. She could almost envision herself as the woman he came home to after being out on the road; the woman who had his dinner waiting; the one he called late at night to let her know where he was and when he'd be returning. Grabbing hold of herself, she shook off the vision, mainly because it scared her to death. She didn't have a Suzy Homemaker bone in her body. "I'll wait for you in the truck."

As she turned and strode away, Reese mused on Ms. JT Blake. The vibe flowing between them was sparking like a downed power line. Being a gentleman, he turned the beam of the flashlight in her direction, ostensibly to light her way back to the cab. In reality, he just wanted to watch the sister walk.

In the cab, JT told herself there was nothing wrong with being attracted to a man she'd just met. The problem came when she started fantasizing about something that would never materialize. She'd never had a man affect her this way, and she wasn't sure what her response was supposed to be. Men like him didn't hook up with women like herself, and vice versa. She made a lot of money, and in the few relationships she'd had, the size of her bank accounts eventually became an issue; even with the men whose finances matched hers. If those men couldn't handle her for whatever reason, survey says a blue collar brother would have issues, too. But lord, the man was fine.

He reentered the cab a few moments later, and as he settled in, she asked, "All set?"

Reese nodded. Normally, he would have considered the thirty-minute wait a pain in the butt, but not this evening. Until the truck rebooted he'd be able to give her his undivided attention. He slid the toolbox and flashlight back under his seat. "My brothers are going to fall out when I tell them I had you in my cab."

"Why?"

"Because you're famous."

"I'm just me."

"I like just you."

The timbre in his voice shook JT's insides again, and in a tone far more nonchalant than she felt, she said, "You're not so bad yourself. Your cherries aren't too bad either."

"I'll make sure you get more."

He seemed reluctant to break the contact but eventually turned his eyes to his mirror to check out the traffic. She continued to watch him. Who would have ever thought she'd feel a connection to a truck driver? In the middle of that mental question, her earpiece beeped. She answered, "Hey, Carole."

"Everything okay? Where are you now?"

JT relayed their approximate location based on the last visible road sign. "We had engine trouble, but it's been fixed."

"Reese the Fine being a gentleman?"

"Completely." JT turned his way and checked out the chiseled lines of his mahogany face. "I couldn't be in better company."

He graciously bowed his head.

"He's kinda silly too."

Showing a grin of his own, he took a sip from his bottled water.

"I won't keep you," Carole said. "Just wanted to let you know that the rental's hooked up and waiting for you at the office. The dealership has picked up the Lex."

"Good. Thanks for all the help. I'll see you in the morning."

"Stay safe."

In the quiet after the call, Reese wanted to tell her the truth about what he did for a living, but his doubts remained. He'd been having too nice a time to risk riding the rest of the way to Oakland with an angry, icy sister upset by his revelation, so he kept his mouth shut. "Do you have any siblings?" he asked her.

"A younger sister named Max."

"She represent athletes too?"

"No. She works for the government."

"You're the oldest, then. So am I."

"Being the oldest is okay, but it sucked sometimes when Max and I were young and my mother would say, 'You're the oldest. You should know better.' Max was always getting us in trouble. Always."

"Pinky and the Brain weren't easy to have around either."

She laughed. "'Pinky and the Brain'? Is that what you call Jamal?"

"Yep. Hates the name, but he's been called that for so long, not much he can do about it at this point."

"That's terrible."

"He's a big boy. He can handle it."

"How old is he?"

"Thirty-five. He and Bryce are two years apart."

JT found the story amusing. "Your mother must have had her hands full raising three boys."

"She died when we were young."

"I'm sorry."

"Thanks." Even though Veronica Anthony had passed away almost two decades ago, Reese still missed her.

"I didn't mean to bring up sad memories."

"I'm okay. My pops raised us. He'd love you."

Surprise showed on her face. "Why?"

"He appreciates a lady with a brain."

"And his oldest son?"

Reese ran appreciative eyes over her angular face

and deep brown eyes and said, more softly than he'd intended, "Like father, like son."

The vibe arched again.

JT found it hard to keep her voice casual. "Sounds like a family of very smart men. Maybe I'll get to meet the rest one day."

"Maybe. Ever been to Michigan?"

"I try and stay away from places where stuff freezes."

He laughed. "It's not too bad. You learn to deal with it. Never been cross-country skiing, then?"

"No."

"You'd like it."

"Probably not the cold, but I'm up for anything once."

"I'm going to hold you to that."

Gazes were locked. Reese wanted to tease a finger down the flawless skin of her cheek, but he beat down the urge. In spite of the shared adventure, they were still strangers. The last thing he wanted to do was scare her or make her feel uncomfortable. To distract himself, he checked his watch. "We'll give the engine another five minutes, then start her up. You want fresh water?"

JT's bottle was just about empty. "Sure."

He got up and went into the back, giving her the opportunity to check out the tight fit of his jeans as he moved by. Shaking her head with female appreciation, JT smiled and looked out at the night.

The patch Bryce had programmed into the engine held up nicely, allowing them to cover the rest of the miles without incident. She kept sneaking eyes at him, and he did the same. They talked, they laughed, and by the time the big rig slowed to a stop outside JT's office in the Jack London Square area of Oakland, neither wanted the night to end.

JT slowly gathered her belongings. "Thank you so much."

"You're welcome." He knew that the penalty for kidnapping was nothing to play with, but he wanted her to stay so bad, he amusingly considered it. He took the card she handed him.

"You can send the cherries to that address, and call me if you like." She meant it, but doubted he'd take her up on the offer. Two different worlds.

He slipped the card into the console beside him. "I may just do that."

As if wanting to commit these last parting moments to memory, they drank in the sight of each other.

Though Reese knew he was flirting with a traffic ticket if he didn't get the rig moving, he tried to delay her leaving. "You need me to go in with you?"

She shook her head. "I should be okay."

He wanted her to be careful. The cop in him knew that the man responsible for sabotaging her car would probably make another attempt. People like that were rarely satisfied with one shot. "If you have any more trouble with that ex-employee, call the cops."

"I will."

Resigned to the inevitable, he said with feeling, "Been nice riding with you."

"Same here." She scooted over and placed a soft kiss on his dark cheek. "Thanks again."

She was illuminated by the headlights as Reese watched her walk the short distance to the door of a gentrified storefront that butted up against a small soul food restaurant. She stuck keys into the locks, then opened the door. She went in and he saw lights go on. A few seconds later she stepped back out to wave good-bye. He gave her a few blasts from the horn and was rewarded with her smile. He waited until she went back inside before driving away. The sweet sting of her kiss was still fresh on his cheek. Unable to help himself, he touched the spot with all the happiness of a high school kid and grinned.

The CD player was bumping loud enough to be heard in San Diego as Bobby G3 reached his home in the Valley. The sight of Kelly's beat-up black Chevy Cavalier parked out front curled his lip. Another bitch he wanted to pimp slap. She was his babymama, and he was not in the mood for her drama. He drove up the driveway to the garage. A glance in the mirror showed her walking to meet him. The jeans were too tight, the top too small, the stilettos too high. He sighed, cut the engine and got out.

"Your check bounced," was the first thing out of her mouth. Back in the day, that mouth used to do anything he asked, and gladly. Now all it did was piss him off.

"I'll fix it tomorrow."

"That's what you said last month."

"Look," he told her coldly, "I'm having cash flow issues. The check will be good by the end of business tomorrow."

She scanned his face by the light of the halogens attached to the garage. "What kind of trouble you in now, Bobby?"

He had to admit she knew him well, but he wasn't telling her a damn thing. "Just take your ass home, Kelly. I don't need you in my business."

"Apparently you need somebody in it if your support check is bouncing. Aren't you the one with the million-dollar clients?"

"Go home to your grease monkey, Kelly. He's calling."

"Don't you dare dis him!" she shot back angrily. "He's making an honest living at the garage. He's also clothing and feeding your son, or have you forgotten that?"

Bobby began walking to the house.

"Send me my money by the end of the week or I'm dragging your ass to court. See how your clients like that!" She stormed off.

He went inside and slammed the door.

Preparing for bed, Matt Wenzel stared at himself in the mirror. The idea that the truth about what happened a few nights back could somehow come to light and drag him down to hell scared him to death. His hands shook as he reached for his toothbrush, and it took a couple of tries to place the glob of toothpaste on the bristles. He'd be the first to admit that he'd never had much of a spine. His father, Big Bo, had kept those genes to himself, or so it seemed. Matt had just enough spine to walk upright, Big Bo often pointed out. In the past, Matt failed to see the humor in the dig, but in this instance it proved true. How does a person sleep at night after seeing a person's head blown away? Every time he closed his eyes, he saw blood. Everywhere. The police were calling the incident a botched robbery, but he knew better. His hands still shaking, he finished brushing, then padded back into the bedroom.

"Are you okay?" Melissa asked. They'd been married ten years. She was the only joy in his life. "You were in there quite a while."

He slid under the bedding. "I'm okay. Just stressing about the job."

She snuggled back against him, her hips warm against his thighs. He placed a protective arm around her and wished he could tell her the truth.

She twisted around and looked up into his thin face. "Is it something you want to talk about?"

He savored the familiar sight of her. "No."

She didn't appear convinced but nodded and turned over. He reached back to turn off the lamp on the nightstand. In the dark, he resettled himself, kissed the top of her brown hair, and prayed he didn't dream.

After driving the rental car home, JT took a shower then slipped into a slinky black nightgown that brushed her toes. Seated now on the balcony of her waterfront condo and surrounded by the darkness and the sounds of the water, she sipped from a goblet of red wine. The memory of Reese Anthony hummed inside her like a song. She wondered where he was, what he was doing, where he'd be sleeping tonight. Would she ever see him again? Men who promised to call most times didn't. Not that she hadn't done the same thing over the years, but Reese the Fine had left a memorable impression. Although it hadn't come up, she was sure a man as gorgeous and as smart as he was had a steady lady somewhere, probably one he took cross-country skiing and who didn't mind the cold.

Sighing, she took another sip and turned her thoughts to a less likable man. Bobby Garrett. She was going to have to do something about him eventually. Since there was no proof that he'd sabotaged her car, she'd have to cede him this round, but if he caused her any more grief, she would have to get him straight, otherwise this little war he was intent upon waging was going to escalate into something ugly.

She put Garrett out of her mind and her thoughts slipped back to Reese. Raising her glass in a toast, she said against the breeze, "Sleep well."

Reese turned the rig over to the night crew at Anthony Trucking's San Francisco facility and took a cab to the Le Meridien Hotel. After the long truck ride from Dallas to San Francisco, the glamour and glitz of the five-star establishment seemed over the top, but the amenities in the pricey suite were just what he needed. He had a bracing shower, ordered some dinner, and flopped tiredly onto the plush cream-colored sofa to await its arrival. JT filled his mind. He was certain there was not a woman like her anywhere on the planet. Smart. Sassy. Sexy. A perfect package. Would their next meeting be good, or would she blast him for not telling her the truth about himself? In truth, it didn't matter. He'd never had a woman work her way into his psyche with so much impact before, and whether she was mad at him or not, he planned to pursue her and let the sparks lead where they would.

To that end, he grabbed his phone and made a call. His old college friend Carl Carlyle grew the Traverse City cherries JT had loved so much. Carl answered the phone on the fifth ring and sounded groggy with sleep. "Hello."

"Hey Carl. Reese."

"Man, do you know what effing time it is? You better be needing bail money."

"No bail money. Cherries. Need you to ship a couple of pounds to Oakland, California, in the morning."

"What! You call me at three in the damn morning to order two pounds of cherries? What's her name?"

Reese laughed and told him.

"Send me an e-mail with the address, and you will be getting the bill for whatever the same day shipping costs. Now, good-bye!"

It was the second testy phone conversation of the evening, but he didn't care. Grinning, he tossed the phone onto the sofa, picked up the remote and clicked on the TV.

Three

Big Bo Wenzel kissed his mistress good-bye, slid beneath the steering wheel of his gold Escalade, and drove toward his office at the Grizzlies Stadium. It was 6 A.M., and the sky was gray with the early morning smog that passed for sunrise in L.A. Better smog in L.A. than hogs in Mississippi where he grew up, he thought. Back then, he'd been expected to follow in his daddy's shit-filled footsteps and take over the family's hog farm, but in 1969 a football scholarship to Ole Miss saved him from a life of stink and slaughter, and he never looked back. He was fifty-five now. Over the years, he'd put on some weight and maybe his blond hair wasn't as thick as it had been back at Ole Miss, but thanks to the wonders of modern pharmaceuticals, he was still a stud, or at least that's what he told himself, and so did the women drawn to his bed by the scent of money and power. He liked them young, big breasted, and blond. It didn't matter if they were dumb as artificial turf as long as they had IQ enough to spread their legs.

He'd owned the L.A. Grizzlies for five years and had yet to see a profit. Owning a football team was every sports fan's dream, but as his granny often said, be careful what you wish for. The first season, the combined costs of salaries, uniforms, equipment, and a thousand other expenses might have sent him to the poor house had he not had his fingers in other pies. A less confident man might have sold the team, but he stuck it out, convinced the fledgling league would be worth millions one day because they played good old-fashioned, back in the day, smash mouth football. Not that lethargic, rule-bound sorriness the older league passed off as sport. In the new league there were no half-assed rules like "in the grasp" or spiking the ball by the quarterbacks. End zone celebrations were encouraged, and the fans loved it. The only things outlawed were chop blocks, leg whips, and helmet-to-helmet contact. There was also no instant replay—if the officials got it wrong, cry in your beer. The human element had been returned to the game, as had the weather, because the eight teams played outdoors.

All in all, Big Bo Wenzel knew he should be happy. And he would have been if the league would hurry up and start paying off. The newly signed agreement between the league and one of the cable giants to televise the games helped his bottom line, but it wasn't enough. With the losses he'd incurred, his other pies were no longer able to keep him afloat. The cash flow problems were keeping him awake at night. His four ex-wives were hounding him about their alimony, he'd gotten a foreclosure notice on the condo he kept in Vegas, and a few days ago he'd watched an old man get blown away not ten feet in front of him.

The memory of that haunted a man even as jaded as himself. In hindsight, he should have known better than to get mixed up in what he had, but the broker had promised big profits in exchange for a small investment, and no businessman, no matter how ethical, would turn down a 150 percent return. With that in mind, he'd thrown in on the deal, thinking it would be easy, and it had been until the janitor Gus Pennington showed up. The pressure of being linked to this mess was even greater than having to face the grand jury in Texas twelve years ago. He'd beaten that rap thanks to friends in high places, but if he was brought up on murder charges now, he knew that friends were going to be as scarce as a hog with a condom.

At the stadium, Big Bo parked the Escalade in the space reserved for the owner, then walked across the empty lot to the entrance. With any luck, he thought, the whole thing would disappear. The police seemed to think the janitor's death was tied to a robbery gone bad. He hoped they stuck with that theory—he couldn't afford the truth.

JT felt good when she walked into work that morning. On the drive in from her condo in San Francisco, the rolling fog covering the bay had burned off to reveal a sunny, blue sky day. She felt light, buoyant and apparently it showed.

"You look awful happy this morning," Carole said from behind her desk.

JT met the smile on her dark-skinned face. "And I am. Don't know why, but the sun seems brighter, the air sweeter."

"Sound like an overdose of trucker to me."

JT grinned. "You could be right. I haven't had that much fun with a man in my life. Lord, he was fine." And the first thing on her mind when she opened her eyes in bed this morning: Was he still in California? Was he having breakfast with a woman?

"Planning on seeing him again?"

JT shrugged her lean shoulders, encased in a fire engine red, Italian designer suit. "He said he'd call, but who knows?"

"Well, while you're waiting on yon knight to pick up the phone, one of your court jesters is in your office."

JT glanced over at the closed door. She'd been so dazzled by Reese last night, she'd forgotten about this morning's appointment with basketball superstar Deuce Watson. His team, Charlotte, was in town to play the local club that evening, so they'd arranged to get together that day. "Coffee first," she said. She liked Deuce. He was one of her oldest clients, but like most of her guys, he had issues. She poured a cup of the brew Carole kept hot and fresh, all day, every day, and strode into her office.

While playing in Dallas, Deuce Watson had the distinction of being named the league's Defensive Player of the Year, four of the last seven seasons. He'd also earned back-to-back championship rings and would probably be in line for a third had he not asked to be traded at the end of his contract last year.

"Mornin', Deuce."

"Hey, Lady B."

JT placed her briefcase on top of her desk, then took a seat. "How are you?" she asked, sipping from her coffee and studying him. He was a big old country boy from Alabama.

"Miserable."

"I hear you and Coach Palmer aren't getting along."

"You heard right. I want to go back to Dallas."

JT shook her head. She'd tried to tell him to stay put, but he'd been so dazzled by the extra thirty million Charlotte offered, he chose to take the cash and leave behind the team he'd taken to the championship and a city that loved him.

"I'll give Charlotte their money back," he offered. "Hell, I'll play for Dallas for free if they'll have me."

"You know that isn't possible. Trading deadline was back in February. Playoffs will be starting soon."

"And I'm going to be home watching it for the first time in seven years."

"Tried to warn you."

The sadness on his face was evident. He could have passed for a homesick fifth grader if it weren't for his six-eleven height. "I miss my boys in Dallas, too."

The members of the Dallas team had been as close as brothers. JT allowed herself a sympathetic smile. "Let's talk about this at the end of the season. Maybe

Charlotte will be as sick of you as you are of them and want to do something about it. No guarantee, though."

He sighed with resignation.

"What time is shoot-around?" she asked.

"Four."

"You want to have lunch?"

"No, Coach wants me on the court at one to work on my free throws."

JT thought that an excellent idea. His stats were terrible. The only players with worse free throw percentages were Shaq and Ben Wallace of the Bulls. "You know, you could make that team into a contender if you wanted to."

"You sound like my wife."

"Lisa is a very smart woman, so I'll take that as a compliment. You're just homesick, Deuce. You were with Dallas seven years. You've been with Charlotte one. Give yourself time to settle in before you talk about throwing in the towel. They paid a lot of money for you, my man."

"Will I make incentive money?"

Incentive clauses were common in pro athletes' contracts and were tied to productivity. In Deuce's case, he got bonus money for pulling down ten or more rebounds in a game. "I'll have Charlotte fax the stats over and let you know."

That seemed to satisfy him, but he still looked glum as he rose to his feet and filled the office with his girth. "Thanks, JT. Lisa said I was homesick, too, so maybe there's something to it."

"Maybe." Over the years, JT had learned that sometimes hand holding was the most important aspect of her job. "Have a good game tonight and think about what Lisa said. You could make that team fly."

He didn't appear convinced, but JT didn't press him. Sooner or later Deuce would realize that if he played his game instead of acting like a little boy wanting to come home from summer camp, he'd enjoy himself and his new team much more.

She walked him out. "I'll call you with your numbers as soon as Charlotte gets them to me."

"Thanks."

She watched him fit his big frame into his navy blue Maybach, and when he drove off, she stepped back inside.

She spent the rest of the morning poring over paperwork and calling various team execs on behalf of her clients. It was a busy time for her. The 2006 NFL draft had been held a few weeks ago, and training camp would be opening soon, not to mention the NBA playoffs just getting under way. Every now and then her thoughts slipped back to last night, and Reese's face would rise in her mind's eye. She'd linger there for a few moments enjoying the memory of his smile, then, after reminding herself that she had work to do, return to the job at hand. By noon her eyes were blurring from all the clauses, contract addendums, and reports, so when Carole beeped her on the intercom, she was grateful for the break. "What's up?" She'd hired Carole five years ago. It was the best personnel move she'd ever made.

"You should probably come out here."

Puzzled, JT got up and walked out to see what was going on. The first thing she saw were the beautiful long-stemmed calla lilies standing so elegantly in a stylish glass vase on top of Carole's desk. Some were gold and the rest a soft ivory. "These were just delivered," Carole explained.

"They're gorgeous. Brad sent you flowers?"

"No. They're for you."

Confused, wondering why Carole's husband Brad would be sending her flowers, JT took the florist card Carole handed her and read: *Thank you. Reese.* She couldn't contain her grin, but before she could say anything, Carole told her, "And this box came by FedEx about an hour ago but I didn't want to interrupt you."

JT wanted to marvel at the flowers but forced herself to scan the shipping label attached to the top of the box for a clue to the sender. "Carlyle Farms in Traverse City, Michigan?" Then as the memory rose of where she'd heard the city's name before, excitement grabbed her. "Give me something to open this with. Quick."

Carole dug around in a desk drawer and handed her a box cutter. The blade split the tape. There was a smaller box inside. After opening it, JT grinned. Cherries. Big, fat, deep red berries that appeared to be just as succulent as those she'd eaten in the cab of Reese's truck filled the cardboard interior. She couldn't believe he'd managed to have the cherries shipped to her so quickly. First the callas, and now this. "Carol, I think I'm in love."

The secretary grinned. "Oh really?" But after JT washed up a handful in the office's small kitchenette, Carole was in love as well. "Oh, these are good."

"Like butter. Oh, my."

"These are from Michigan?" Carole asked, eating a couple more. The handful JT had washed weren't going to be enough.

"Yeah." They were just as sweet and delicious as the ones last night. "I didn't know they grew cherries either."

"If you don't want Reese the Fine, I will definitely take him. Callas and cherries like this?"

"Back off. I saw him first. You already have a man, remember?"

Carole and Brad were high school sweethearts. They'd been married seventeen years. "If Brad can get me cherries like this, I'll stay with him another seventeen years."

Carole bit into more red flesh and declared, "Reese the Fine could be a keeper, Jess."

"Don't start looking at bridesmaid dresses yet. I may never see him again."

"Any man sending you goodies like this—same day, overnight? He'll show. Don't worry."

JT wiped her hands on some toweling then picked up the vase of callas. "We'll see. In the meantime, these babies are coming with me." She carried the gold and ivory beauties into her office and set the vase on the small glass coffee table by the sofa so she could enjoy them to her heart's content. JT couldn't remember the last time she'd gotten flowers that weren't from clients or that she hadn't purchased for herself. Reese's face floated into her mind again and she smiled. The truck driving man had definitely scored on this one. Big-time. Where was he? she wondered. She knew better than to read anything into his gift other than the thank-you he'd written on the card, but he was proving to be just as nice as he'd seemed last night, and what woman wouldn't appreciate that? Feeling even more buoyant than she had at the start of her day, JT floated back to her desk to work.

Reese's flight from San Francisco touched down at Detroit Metro Airport at 9 A.M. local time. The long drive in the truck from Texas to California coupled with the predawn flight had left him dead on his feet. Seeing his Pops waiting for him in the baggage claim evoked a tired but affectionate smile. They hadn't seen each other in a few weeks, and so embraced like the close family they were.

"How was the flight?" Pops asked while they walked over to the carousel. Tall dark-skinned Richard Anthony was glad to have all of his sons with him again.

"Long. I had to be at LAX at 4 a.m. to make the six o'clock flight. I want to sleep for a week."

"Bryce told me about the call you two had last night."

The bags from Reese's flight were just coming out of the chute and down onto the carousel when they walked up. "Except for that glitch, the engine performed pretty."

"Who was the lady?"

He froze. Seeing the humor and curiosity in his father's eyes, Reese shook his head. "You're as nosy as Bryce."

"True. Answer the question."

Reese lifted the handle on his wheeled bag and pulled it behind him as they walked to the exits and outside to the parking structure. "She had car trouble. I gave her a ride to Oakland. That's it."

"Nothing else?"

He shrugged and lied. "Nope."

Richard Anthony was sixty-three and still a formidable man. If the truth be told, Reese and his brothers were still half afraid of the old man, who back in the day busted chops as a defensive lineman for the Chicago Bears before retiring and founding his trucking firm. When the three of them were young, they did their best not to cross their father. They loved him as much as he loved them, but nobody wanted to go to the woodshed with Pops. Nobody.

Reese put his bag in the backseat. Once they were ready, Pops drove out of the structure and headed for the freeway. Merging into the traffic, he said easily, "Carl Carlyle called me this morning."

"Oh really?" Reese said, hoping he sounded nonchalant and that Carl hadn't told his father about the cherries. But when he saw the amusement on Pops's face, he knew he was busted.

"Sent her cherries, huh, son? Okay, spill it. You know I live vicariously through the three of you."

Reese wiped his hands across his face, then smiled. "I'm going to shoot him."

"Funny. Same thing Carl said about you. Three in the morning?"

"Yeah."

"She must have been something." It was a statement, not a question.

JT's face rose and filled Reese's mind's eye. For a moment he drifted back, then turned to his father and asked, "Do you believe in love at first sight?"

"Sure. First time I saw your mother, I knew she was the one. Didn't matter to me that she was the daughter of some elite Chicago doctor and I was a poor kid from Detroit at Illinois on a football scholarship. The moment she walked by, I told my boys, 'That's the one.' They laughed at me, but I wasn't playing."

Over the years, Pops had told many stories about the past, but Reese had never heard this one before. "Had your nose open, huh?"

Pops's eyes twinkled. "Wide enough for the proverbial train to roll through. If I hadn't had to go to football practice all day every day, I would have followed that girl around campus like a lovesick puppy. My boys thought I was pitiful enough as it was."

Reese laughed. "I'm nowhere near that but I might like to see her again."

"Might?"

"No. *Would* like to see her again. Soon."

"Glad to hear it."

"Why?"

"You're getting old, boy. Time for some sons. Only way I'll get any grandsons from Pinky and the Brain is if they build them. You're my only hope."

Reese laughed so hard he thought he was going to hurt himself. "Pops, you're crazy."

"No. I'm serious."

Shaking his head, Reese chuckled the rest of the way home.

Reese slept until late afternoon. At dinner he told his father and brothers about the new job offer.

His father said, "Change of pace might be good for you."

He was glad for the support. "I think so too. Been feeling hemmed in lately. This is only temporary, for now. We'll see how it goes."

Bryce, with his dreads and the movie star good looks inherited from their mother, Veronica, asked, "That means you'd get tickets for games?"

"Probably."

Jamal raised his fork. "That's what I'm talking about."

Talk of tickets and games made Reese think about JT. He wondered if she'd gotten the cherries.

Jamal asked, "So who's the honey you sent the cherries to?"

Reese checked out the smiling faces around the table and replied, "Does everybody know my business?"

Bryce made a show of thinking for a moment, then replied, "Just about."

Pops chuckled.

Jamal asked, "Is she tall? Short?

Bryce added, "Fine? Butt ugly?"

Reese cut them a look.

"Just asking," they said in unison.

"Her name's JT Blake."

Jamal froze.

Bryce froze too.

The pleased smile on Pops's face was sunny and bright.

A satisfied Reese eyed his speechless siblings and drawled drolly, "Thought that might shut you up."

Bryce and Jamal shared a look of wonder, then Bryce asked with whispered awe, "*The* JT Blake? The sports agent?"

Reese nodded, adding, "Could be tight when I meet her again, though. She thinks I'm a truck driver."

Pops looked confused. "But you are."

"I know, but not really. She just assumed I drove for a living, and we were having such a good time, I thought telling her the truth might crush the vibe. She is an agent, after all. Not sure how she'd react to me being tied to the commissioner's office."

"So you didn't tell her you're joint owner of a multinational corporation and that you're the head legal beagle either?" Bryce asked.

"No, Bryce. I didn't."

"That was probably a good move."

"I thought so too, but I'm glad to get the approval of the Einstein playa."

Bryce nodded regally in response. "Always here to help an old guy."

"Watch it," Reese warned, amusement lifting his lips.

Jamal said, "Never known you to worry about

what a woman thinks or to send cherries at three in the morning. She must be special."

Reese nodded. Again her face shimmered in his mind's eye. "She is."

The other men around the table shared a look, then Jamal raised his glass of red Kool-Aid. "To tickets to the NBA Finals!"

"Hear! Hear!" They shouted, and all Reese could do was shake his head in response to the antics of his crazy family.

Later that evening, as he sat in his bedroom watching the Pistons whip the Bulls, he pulled out his phone. With JT's card in hand, he keyed in her number and listened as it rang. He wanted to hear her voice and tell her the truth about himself.

JT was shutting down the office for the day when the phone rang. Carole had already left for home, so she grabbed it. "This is JT."

"Hey."

She melted at the sound of Reese's voice. "Hey yourself. How are you?" She sat down on the sofa, swung her feet up and got comfortable.

"I'm okay. Did you get the cherries?"

"I did, and the beautiful lilies. Thank you."

"You're welcome. Just wanted to check. How was your day?"

"Fine. Yours?"

"Not bad. The 6 a.m. flight almost killed me, but I'm home."

"In Michigan?"

"Yeah. Where are you?"

"Office, getting ready to head out." She conjured up his face, noting that she'd gone all gooey inside from just the low timbre of his voice.

"I'd like to see you again."

Her heart pounded. "Like to see you too."

"So how do we make it happen?"

"Will you be back in California any time soon?" JT turned over on her belly.

"Next week probably, and there's something I need to tell you."

Before she could ask what that meant, her phone beeped, alerting her to an incoming call. "Hold on a minute. I have another call."

JT clicked over, and when she clicked back to Reese a short while later, she wasn't happy. "One of my clients just choked his coach."

"What?" he said, and chuckled, unable to help himself.

"Not funny." She rose from the couch and walked angrily back to her desk. "I have to catch the next flight to Philly and hope I can keep his dumb butt out of jail. I'm sorry. Can I call you back?"

"Yeah."

"Thanks." She sighed over the lost opportunity, adding genuinely, "Thanks again for the cherries and the lilies."

"You're welcome."

She ended the call, then shouted, "Reason number 216 why I don't have a man!"

In Michigan, Reese, smiling, set the phone aside. What a job she had. Being a sports fan, he couldn't help but wonder who the player and the choked coach might be. Being a man, he was disappointed they hadn't talked longer. Her sultry Texas voice made him realize how much he was looking forward to knowing all there was to know about her. Telling her the truth about his identity would have to wait, but doing it face-to-face might work out better in the long run.

Still thinking about her, he raised the volume with the remote and settled in to watch the rest of the game. Jamal was right about him. Since divorcing his first wife, Suzanne, he hadn't let himself get emotionally involved with any woman. When he and Suzanne met as students at Western Michigan University in Kalamazoo, he was twenty years old and the biggest baller on campus. They'd married eighteen months later, but when he tore up his knee senior year and the media hype and accolades died, his potential to be her personal cash cow turned to dust. She stayed with him long enough to realize that being the wife of a policeman wasn't her calling, so when she presented him with divorce papers, he'd signed them. Last he heard, she was married to a land developer with enough money to keep her in the style she wanted to become accustomed to, and he wished her well.

Since the divorce, he'd kept his feelings on lockdown because he never wanted to be torn up that way again. Men didn't like pain, especially pain of the heart, and he was no exception. To keep that from happening again, he made a point of staying emotionally aloof. With his looks and money, the ladies came easy, and over the years he'd been with some fine ones, but none were fine enough or interesting enough to make him change his M.O. Until now. It was his hope that her choking client wasn't an athlete in the league he'd just agreed to work for. Meeting her again for the first time in his new role as head of security was not going to go well, and he didn't need Bryce's big brain to figure that out.

The fates were against him, however. At eleven o clock that evening he received a call from his old buddy the commissioner. One of the players had choked a coach. He needed to be in Philadelphia by noon.

It was midnight eastern time when JT stepped off the plane in Philly. The usually bustling airport was all but empty of travelers and many of the shops were closed. When she reached the baggage claim, one of her clients, Turo Rodriguez, an all-star cornerback for Philadelphia's World League of Football team was there signing an autograph for an airline employee. Looking up, he greeted JT with a smile and handed the signed piece of paper back to the employee. "Hey, Lady B."

"Hey Turo. Thanks for meeting me."

"Any time."

They shared a hug, he grabbed her luggage, and they walked out to his car. The silver Porsche was new and shone like a star beneath the lights of the parking structure. He opened the door and helped her in. After putting her bags in the trunk, he got in, secured his seat belt, and drove toward her downtown hotel.

"So what happened," she asked.

Turo, built like Machu Picchu and with a face as beautifully chiseled as an Inca god, shrugged and grinned. "I'm not sure. I think Quise just snapped. Took three of us to pull him off. He was shaking coach like a rot with a rat."

Quise was Marquise Chambers—star wide receiver and star of the choking incident. Coach was second-year head coach Scott Walker, aka the chokee. "Did Walker say something, do something?"

"Nope. Just being the dickhead he always is. There's not a person on the team who didn't want to choke him, but Quise actually did it. After the dust settled, they took coach to the E.R. and the GM sent Quise home."

A grim JT shook her head. This was not Quise's first incident. He'd had a few DUIs, babymama drama that hit the papers when he was picked up by Dade County for nonsupport, and now this. His temper was infamous, but in her eyes it was more a show of how spoiled and pampered he was. She took out her phone and called him. "I'm on my way, and yes I know what time it is. Do you?"

He gave her some guff about being asleep, but she wasn't having any. "Be up when I get there. Get rid of the hos and start drinking coffee because if you're drunk I'm going right back to L.A. and you can handle the commish's office on your own."

She snapped the phone closed and met Turo's sparkling eyes. "I'm through playing with him."

"Glad it's not me."

"Just drive."

The size of Quise's place was indicative of the million-dollar contracts she'd been negotiating on his behalf. The palatial estate had enough bedrooms and bathrooms to house a team of players. Also on the property were two guest houses, a garage filled with a fleet of expensive pimped-out rides, and a swimming pool that doubled as a skating rink in winter. As she got out of Turo's car and strode up the long, winding, coachlight-lined walk, she decided that someone else would have to do the negotiating next time. She was done representing him. Marquise Chambers brought way more drama into her life than she needed.

Four

"Why do I have to apologize?" grumbled Marquise Chambers to JT as they sat in the backseat of the car she'd hired to take them to their meeting with the commissioner. "The man's whack."

"He's your boss, Marquise. We went over this last night. Whack or not, you can't put your hands on him. You know that." She could feel a headache coming on. It had taken her most of the morning just to convince him to wear a suit and tie. Now, all he wanted to do was whine.

"But he dissed me." The catalyst for the confrontation had been Marquise's late arrival for a 2 pm practice. He claimed to have overslept.

"You were late for your job. What was he supposed to do, clap?"

In response he mumbled something unintelligible then stated, "He can't be dissing me. He did the same thing last week."

That she hadn't heard before. "You were late last week too?"

"Yeah. I told him I had car trouble."

She threw up her hands. "You have what, nine cars? That's a sorry ass excuse, Quise. Real sorry."

"Yeah, well, that's what he said too. He tried to make me run laps, but I told him I'd file a grievance and he backed off."

She didn't believe this. Of the fifty athletes she represented, Marquise was the biggest pain in the butt. She couldn't wait to walk away. "Expect a fine and a suspension."

"Why?"

"Why do you think?" she asked in incredulous tones. "You choked your coach! And you'd better hope he's been talked out of pressing charges."

Again he mumbled, but she ignored him.

The meeting was to be held in a conference suite at one of the city's swankier hotels. When she and Marquise entered the fancy lobby with its crystal chandeliers and blue-uniformed bellmen, she was pleased to see no signs of the press. Her hope was to get in and out of the meeting without being detected, but as soon as they stepped off the elevator they were swarmed by a microphone-wielding horde. A din of questions were shouted at them, but because she'd told Marquise to keep his mouth shut, he didn't respond. On the other hand, she must have called out "No comment" a hundred times on the walk to the door of the suite; a walk that took an inordinate amount of time because of the crush of cameras and scribes.

Inside, the silence was a blessing. The new commissioner, Taylor McNair, flanked by two men in suits turned at her entrance. He was of medium height and had just a touch of gray in his hair. She'd never met him before, but knew his face from the bio the league sent around after he was hired, and from subsequent newspaper articles written about him. According to the bio, he was in his mid-forties. A confident JT stepped forward and extended a manicured hand. "Commissioner McNair, I'm JT Blake. Pleased to meet you."

Smiling, he shook her hand. "Ms. Blake. Thanks for coming. Marquise."

The surly-faced Quise nodded, but McNair didn't seem bothered by the athlete's mood. Instead he took a moment to introduce her to the other two men in the room. League lawyers.

JT was just about to start the standard chitchat that always preceded meetings of this sort when out of a back room walked Reese Anthony. She blinked. *What the hell?*

The face was the same but gone were the cutoff T-shirt and the snug-fitting jeans. This Reese had on a dark GQ suit over an equally expensive looking turtleneck, and damn if he didn't look good enough to eat. Maybe better. The dark powerful eyes she re-membered most were subdued, but she swore she saw a sparkle of humor hidden there.

The commissioner did the introductions. "Ms. Blake, I'd like you to meet Reese Anthony, new head of the league's investigative unit. Reese, JT Blake."

JT nodded coolly. "Mr. Anthony."

"Ms. Blake."

She felt like she'd been played, but she'd deal

with that and Mr. Investigative Unit later. At the moment she had a job to do. "Shall we get started, gentlemen?"

After everyone was seated, JT opened her navy snakeskin briefcase and withdrew some papers. "This is the apology Marquise will read to the press after we're done here. Note that he accepts full responsibility for his actions. Hopefully, it meets with your approval."

While the men around the table took a few moments to scan the statement, JT forced herself not to look at Reese. There were nine hundred questions screaming in her head, but she beat them down. Add to that the fact that he was so damn distracting, and she was doing good remembering why she was even in the room.

Reese, on the other hand, couldn't take his eyes off her. He read the statement, but she was his main focus. She was as gorgeous as he remembered, even more so dressed in a navy power suit, a silky camisole that drew a man's eyes to the tasteful but feminine neckline, and a pair of killer heels that matched the exotic briefcase. His mind floated back to the cherry-stained mouth while he discreetly assessed that same mouth now. The tastefully applied gloss made it appear even more lush. It came to him that he had to have this woman or die trying.

McNair finished reading the statement then set it down. "This is fine, Ms. Blake. I've talked to Coach Walker and he's agreed not to initiate any court action as long as Marquise is suspended and takes anger management classes."

JT sensed Marquise tighten beside her, so she placed a warning hand on his arm. "Just hold up. How many games?"

"Ten," Reese stated, entering the conversation for the first time.

Marquise exploded to his feet. "That's bullshit!"

JT snapped, "Sit down!" Her flashing eyes dared him to keep standing.

For a moment they battled silently, then he sat. "I'm not doing ten games. Y'all can kiss my ass."

"You don't have a choice," Reese replied tightly. "The new commissioner has zero tolerance for violence. First-time offenders, ten games. Second time, twenty."

"This is my livelihood!" Quise yelled angrily.

"You should have thought about that before you laid hands on your coach," Reese tossed out, then sat back and folded his arms.

Quise shot him a look of fury.

JT offered, "How about we cut it to seven and call it a deal?"

Reese shook his head. "No deal on this one, Ms. Blake. Ten games or your client can take his chances with Walker's lawyers and a jury."

"You're really going to play hardball?" she asked, meeting the eyes of the man who a couple of nights ago had been someone else, or so she thought.

"On instances like this, always."

She knew she didn't have a leg to stand on. Were this Quise's first run-in, she might have some wiggle room, but because of his past sins, there was no getting around the suspension. Finally turning away from Reese, she said to Quise. "Take the deal."

"But—"

"Take it." Marquise wouldn't fare well if this went to trial. Trouble-causing highly paid athletes weren't well liked by Mr. and Mrs. Middle America. For choking his coach, a jury would send a man like Marquise Chambers to the Bastille given half a chance.

Quise wasn't happy. "You're my agent, Lady B. Fix this."

She gave him a look but didn't respond verbally because she'd told him last night there'd be consequences to pay, and that more than likely his past behavior would earn him way more than a quick slap on the wrist. There'd be no fixing this. "Commissioner McNair, do you have something drawn up that we can sign, or will you be faxing it to me later?"

Reese took a document out of the folder lying in front of him and held it out for her. When she took it, their hands accidentally brushed and the spark affected them both, though neither gave any indication that it had.

He and the others waited silently while she read. Reese's assumption that he'd have some explaining to do when they met again was more accurate than he could have imagined. Meeting her this way was going to make it extremely difficult to reconnect.

Purposefully ignoring Reese, JT looked up into the commissioner's face. "This is fine." She turned to Quise and handed him a pen. His eyes battled hers for a long moment, then he took the pen. Snarling, he signed in the places the lawyers indicated, then angrily pushed the agreement back across the table. "Bet Bobby G3 woulda done something to fix this."

She held onto her temper. She'd never called out a client in front of the enemy, but Quise was tap dancing on her last nerve by bringing Bobby Garrett's name into this mess. "Are we done here, gentlemen?"

They nodded.

Still avoiding Reese's eyes, JT gathered up her personal effects and rose to her feet. She nodded at her opponents. "Thank you."

McNair said, "Nice meeting you, Ms. Blake."

"Same here." Only then did she face Reese. "Nice meeting you, Mr. Anthony."

"You too."

"Let's go, Quise." Handing him the prepared statement he was to read to the press, she led him from the room without a look back.

Once she left, Tay McNair let out an awed, "Wow!"

"No kidding," Reese agreed. His eyes still on the closed door and his previous memory of that familiar feline walk.

"I'd heard a lot about her," Tay said, "but she was way more than I expected. Damn!"

"The Lady Blake is all that." And would probably never speak to him again, given the choice, Reese guessed by her iciness. "I'll touch base with her in a couple days and make sure Marquise is signed up for the classes." The call would be a legitimate way to approach her again, and serve to get her to talk to him, whether she wanted to or not.

"Sounds good," Tay replied. "Now, let's talk about the Pennington killing."

Reese cleared his mind of the tall sultry JT Blake to concentrate on the job at hand. "Police find anything new?"

"A little. They're pretty sure he was shot in the executive wing of the team's offices. Forensics turned up traces of blood and cocaine on the floor and a tabletop in one of the conference rooms."

"Cocaine?"

Tay nodded.

Reese's instincts told him there was more to this than a simple robbery. "Was there coke in Pennington's system?"

"No. Autopsy said he was clean. So my question is, how'd the coke get in the offices and how was Pennington connected, if at all?"

"If the autopsy said he was clean, then he wasn't using. Maybe he was with some folks who were. Nephew, grandson, maybe? A fight started over something or other?"

Tay shrugged.

"I take it there were no answers on the surveillance tapes?"

"System had been down all week for maintenance," one of the lawyers explained.

"Sounds pretty convenient."

"According to the GM, they take it off line twice a year for service."

"How many people knew that?"

"No idea," Tay replied, "but I told the LAPD captain handling the case that you'd make contact tomorrow. I had the secretaries book you into a hotel near the airport and arrange for a car rental. Your flight's at five this evening."

Reese could feel the cop inside himself coming to life. It had been a long time since he'd done an investigation, but in truth he was looking forward to getting back into the saddle. "Okay. I'll touch base with my Detroit office, let them know I'm going on to L.A., and I'll call you as soon as I get in."

Tay nodded. The meeting wrapped up an hour later, and at five o'clock Reese was on a nonstop flight bound for LAX.

JT stayed in Philly just long enough to tell Marquise Chambers to find another agent and for her to make it to the airport. An hour later she was on a plane back to the West Coast. Sitting in first class, she gazed out of the window beside her at the fluffy white clouds and the gorgeous blue sky and tried to let go of what had been a piss poor day.

Marquise Chamber's dumb behind was no longer her problem, and she was glad of that. Mr. Reese Anthony was another matter. The word *shocked* failed to describe how she felt seeing him at the meeting, of all places. Since the two of them were together only a few days ago, she assumed he'd been a member of the commissioner's team then. He hadn't volunteered that information, even after learning her identity. She was still trying to decide if she was mad, and if so, how mad? Truthfully, one part of her didn't care about the inner debate and was glad just to see him again, to hell with the circumstances; but on another level she felt like a fool for having fallen for the whole blue collar, let me buy you some gas, truck driver persona. She was mad about that for sure.

The smiling stewardess interrupted her reverie to hand her a small bag of peanuts. This being first class, the peanuts came with a bonus, an even smaller bag of pretzels. JT took them both, thanked the woman, then resumed her vigil at the window.

Upon landing, she grabbed her baggage, retrieved her rental car from the lot, and headed to the office. It was late afternoon, plenty of time left to pull out Quise's files and get them ready to fax over to his new agent. Once that was done, she'd be free of him at last.

The look on her tightly set face as she entered the office prompted Carole to ask, "Bad flight?"

"No, bad day." Only then did JT see the flowers on the counter behind Carole's desk. Tulips. Purple. Beautiful.

Carole grinned, "Guess who these are from?"

"Who?" JT asked suspiciously." And you'd better not say Reese."

"Okay I won't, but I'd be lying." Carole scanned her boss and friend. "Arrived about an hour ago."

"I'm going to smack him," JT gritted out. Pointedly attempting to ignore the gorgeous tulips and failing badly, she walked over to the vase and snatched free the small florist card. She read: *Sincerely, Reese*. She didn't know whether to melt or curse.

A confused Carole watched her closely. "Want to tell me what's going on?"

"How about Reese the Fine works for the World League commissioner."

"What?"

JT told her the tale, and when she finished, Carole's brown eyes were sparkling with mirth. "When do tickets go on sale? I want a front row seat, you hear me?"

"Shut up," JT tossed back, smiling.

"I'm not joking. He's with the commissioner's office? Doesn't he know you can't hang with the enemy?"

JT was sniffing the flowers, then caught herself. "Apparently not."

"They are beautiful. Think he knows you garden?"

She shrugged. "The man could be a florist too, for all we know."

"Feel like he played you, huh?"

"I do," JT replied emotionally. "And there I was offering him money for gas. Was he laughing at me the whole time?"

"My gut says no. Me, I want more cherries."

"You would," she accused with a laugh, and picked up the vase of tulips. "Gather up all Quise's stuff so we can forward it. I'm assuming he'll be represented by my archenemy from now on, but let's wait for a call."

"Yes, ma'am. Enjoy the tulips."

Seated at her desk, JT took in the sight of the two vases standing proudly on her glass coffee table. The lilies were still beautiful. The thick fragrant scent filled the office air. The purple tulips stood as a color counterpoint to the gold and ivory callas. But she was still undecided on where she stood. She reread the card from the tulips. The wording hadn't changed: *Sincerely, Reese.* Was she to assume he was apologizing? She'd assumed he was a truck driver, and look how that turned out. Sighing, she set the card aside and booted up her computer. She had work to do.

Reese tossed his suit bag over the arm of the sand-colored sofa then glanced around at the hotel suite that would be home for a while. It was spacious enough to keep him from feeling claustrophobic, offering a separate bedroom complete with a king-size bed. There was also an expansive bathroom with a six head shower. The sleek furniture and other fancy appointments were indicative of a pricey hotel. A walk over to the large door-sized windows showed he was facing one of the runways at LAX. As a big 767 rolled in, the noise was minimal because of the soundproof glass, another hotel amenity. He'd have to tell Tay to raise the pay of the administrative assistant responsible for booking the room. The view was perfect for a man who'd loved planes since childhood.

Taking out his phone, he placed a call to the LAPD captain heading the investigation into Gus Pennington's death. Voice mail answered, so he left a message and went to unpack.

Later, Reese had just finished his room service dinner and was going over the reports the detectives had shared with the commissioner's office when the call back came in. The captain's name was Luis Mendes. "Welcome to L.A., Mr. Anthony."

"Thanks, Captain, and thanks for returning my call."

"No problem. Commissioner McNair told me you're ex-Vice, Detroit?"

"Yeah. Left the force about ten years ago. Lawyer now."

"Pays a lot better, I bet?"

"You got that right."

They began discussing the case. Mendes said, "For the record, my detectives are still calling this a robbery, but the gun being found on the wrong side of the body and the coke moves it into another realm."

"McNair said the autopsy on the victim came back clean?"

"As a germaphobe's bathroom. The old man wasn't using. We're assuming he was there to clean the place because his company had the contract."

"Could the death and the coke be unrelated? Say, Pennington was shot in a robbery but the coke is tied to something else going on in that office? How fresh was the coke residue?"

"Forensics is still running tests. Something to do with the way the molecules dissipate when exposed to air. You know how techie the techies can get on you."

Reese did.

"But what you're suggesting is a possibility too. We're going to keep digging."

"Report says the detectives interviewed the GM?"

"Yeah. GM Wenzel was nervous, but no more than the average citizen would be. They took his statement and the info on the security cameras service records and left. They didn't say anything to him about the coke. We'll play that close to the vest for now. See what else turns up."

"The cameras being down seems a little too coincidental for my tastes."

"Ours too. It might not be related but it's another piece of the puzzle that's got my gut churning."

"And you don't mind me asking around on the league's behalf?"

"No. Budget cuts have us so low on manpower we're having problems handling our case loads. We could use the help. Maybe you'll see something we might have overlooked. When the commissioner called me and gave me your name, I reached out to your old captain. He said you were a good clean cop, so I'm taking him at his word."

Reese respected his old captain too. "Thanks."

"Commissioner told you the parameters?"

"Yep. I can't represent myself as law enforcement."

"Fine. Gotta go. Other line's flashing. Call me if something churns your gut."

"And you'll keep me in the loop?"

"As long and as legally as I can."

"Looking forward to working with you Captain Mendes."

"You too, Lieutenant Anthony. Watch your back."

And he was gone.

Reese was pleased to know that the locals weren't going to deal with him as an interloper. He turned his mind to the victim. Who shot Pennington and why? Cocaine didn't just magically appear in offices. Someone was either dealing or using or both, and from the autopsy report, it hadn't been Pennington. Reese made a mental note to talk to the man's family members. The police had already interviewed them, but as Mendes said, maybe he'd see something they'd missed.

He watched some TV, hoping to put off making his next call for as long as he could, but the draw of hearing her voice again was making it hard to hold off. God, she'd looked good at the meeting today in her lawyer suit with her long brown legs and her snakeskin heels. Her hair had been lustrous and light, framing that gorgeous face like a painting; the makeup stellar. The memories of their road trip together resonated so hard he was sure everyone in the room could hear his heart beating. Unable to stand it any longer, he picked up his phone, spoke her name into the speaker, and waited for her number to dial through.

JT was in the kitchen at the stove throwing together some shrimp stir fry when her earpiece buzzed. "This is JT."

"Hey."

She fought off the melting feeling and said coolly while stirring the stuff in the skillet, "Hello, Mr. Anthony. How may I help you?"

"How mad are you?"

She allowed herself a small smile, but kept her voice distant. "Mad enough to hang up unless this is official business."

"That mad, huh? Then consider this an official request to have dinner with me."

She shook her head. "This has to be *league* official business, Mr. Anthony. For the record, Marquise Chambers is no longer my client, so all subsequent issues pertaining to him should be directed to whomever his new agent turns out to be."

"Duly noted. Now, back to dinner."

"There isn't going to be a dinner."

"Why not?"

"Because you're with the commissioner's office, Mr. Anthony, and that makes you the enemy."

"Suppose I send over more cherries?"

"Now you're offering me bribes?"

"Baby, I'll offer you the Great Wall of China if that's what it'll take to see you again."

Her heart skipped and her knees wobbled. "You saw me in Philly."

"And it wasn't long enough."

Another skip. "You're good."

"Hoped you'd like it. Besides, I want to apologize in person."

JT was having trouble maintaining her distance from him on the phone; seeing him in person would be infinitely harder. "Okay. Next time you're in California, maybe we can work something out."

"I'm in L.A. now."

She blinked and her blood rushed madly.

"Working on something for Commissioner McNair."

She toyed with the idea of lying to him about leaving town in the morning for a month-long mythical meeting somewhere on the other side of the world, but the woman inside her who wanted to see him again, damn the torpedoes, wouldn't allow it. "I can't have a relationship with a man tied to the league office."

"Is that what we're starting here—a relationship?"

"No!" she countered quickly. Appalled by her choice of words, she grabbed hold of herself. "All we're doing is dinner and your apology."

He chuckled softly. "You sure?"

"Positive."

"Okay, then how about I come up Friday afternoon? I'll meet you at your office and we can take it from there."

Having never been so flustered by a man before, she tried for nonchalance. "Fine. See you then." And hung up.

She stood with her back against the edge of her brown granite counter thinking about the conversation for such a long time the smoke alarm went off. Her dinner was burning! Cursing, she snatched up a pot holder and grabbed the handle of the skillet with its blackened veggies and shrimp. Stepping quickly to the sink, she doused the mess. Fanning the smoke, she opened up the patio door, blaming Reese Anthony for making her so mindless she couldn't even cook dinner.

Bobby Garrett ended the late night call from Marquise Chambers and thanked the gods. Chambers had fired Bitch Blake and wanted to be represented by BG3. Chambers was big-time. He'd only been in the league a few years, which meant he'd be a cash cow for some time to come. Bobby couldn't be happier. He'd been waiting for her clients to wake up. With any luck, Quise would be the first of many to ask themselves what kind of man sent a bitch to handle his business. Who cared if she graduated near the top of her class in both undergrad and law school? A real man wanted a man guarding his back, not a pair of tits, and he planned to step into the breach. When he first formed his agency he'd tried to raid her clients, but they were loyal to her, to a man. In the years since, he'd managed to corner some of the second tier athletes coming out of college, but he didn't want to be second best. He wanted the cream.

Last year he'd snatched the Heisman Trophy winner right out from under her nose. By treating the much heralded University of Miami quarterback to all the women he could fuck, a shiny BMW, and a big new house for his babymama, Bobby made it next to impossible for the QB to say no, and he hadn't. The player signed with his agency on the day before the draft. Per his reputation, in order to squeeze every last cent out of the team during contract negotiations, Bobby kept him out of training camp. Economically, the tactic worked, but missing camp cost the quarterback in terms of learning the playbook and in bonding with other members of the team. As a result, he rode the bench during the summer exhibition games and rarely played more than a down or two during the regular season. Bobby didn't care. Of course he pretended that he did, and made noises on his client's behalf to the team's GM about the lack of playing time, but he didn't really. All he cared about was being paid. Period. And now he was on his way. The agent's cut of Quise's salary would help plug the holes in his bank account, get Kelly off his back, and give him room to breathe, at least for now.

"The new commish is sending the head of security to talk to you tomorrow," Big Bo announced, walking into Matt's office.

Seated at his desk, Matt's head shot up. "I already talked to the police."

"I know, but the league is conducting its own investigation."

"Can they do that? I mean, legally?"

"Yes, Matt. They can. For God's sake stop looking so damn scared."

"I've got reason to be scared." Memory of the murder rose again but he forced it away.

"Not if you stick to the script and keep your mouth shut."

His lips thinned. He thought about his wife and the prospect of spending the rest of his life in jail, or worse. California did have the death penalty. "I don't know how long I can do this."

"You'll do it for as long as we need to. So buck up. If you crumble, we all fall."

"You should never have gotten us involved in this mess in the first place."

Big Bo leaned down. "Boy, we're losing cash like water flowing over a damn. What was I supposed to do?"

"Take out a loan like every other legitimate businessman."

"And put us further into debt? Hell no. This is fast and painless."

"It wasn't painless for Gus Pennington."

His father's blue eyes blazed. "I took care of his family. What more do you want?"

"For you to stop trying to take the easy way out all the time. We could do life!"

"Not if you keep your damn mouth shut."

The eyes of father and son, so much alike, locked on each other, but as always, Matt looked away first.

Big Bo smiled. "I'm leaving. Got a date with a young woman who wants to be a team cheerleader. Hooters out to here." He gestured. "You just hold it together tomorrow. Another few deals and we can pull out."

Matt fumed silently. They were going straight to hell, and his father was driving.

Bo gave him a wave. "See you tomorrow afternoon. My love to Melissa."

Alone again, Matt put his head down on his desk. It was all he had.

Five

Reese drove his rental car to the Grizzlies Stadium and pulled into a parking space. Getting out, he scanned the area of the lot where the police report indicated Pennington's truck and body had been found. Studying the office buildings across the street and the early morning traffic flowing around the stadium, he spent a few moments trying to imagine the circumstances surrounding what went down that night, but because he had only a few tiny pieces of the puzzle, no images surfaced, so he walked around to the door leading to the team's offices.

Inside, he noted the red eyes of security cameras staring down as he stepped up to the desk marked information. Behind it sat a good-looking blonde who was all smiles.

Reese nodded. "Good morning. I'm here to see GM Wenzel. Name's Reese Anthony."

"Good morning, Mr. Anthony," she replied, looking him up and down like he was something she wanted to take home and try out. "I was told to expect you. Here's your visitor badge. Take that hallway to the left, then the elevator to the third floor. I'll call ahead and let Matt know you're on your way."

Reese pressed the white tag onto his black sport coat. "Thanks."

"No, thank you," she countered, still smiling.

The walk was a short one, and as the elevator doors closed and the car began its climb, he wondered if this was the elevator Pennington had taken the night of his death. Were the killers lying in wait when the old man stepped out, and if so, why? Nothing in the police report indicated Pennington to be anything other than the owner of a janitorial service. He had his family, his church, and his buddies at the barbershop. No drama in his life whatsoever. Yet he was dead.

Reese stepped off the elevator. The team's logo, the image of a snarling grizzly, dominated the walls of the executive wing. Mounted beside the glass doors of the GM's office was a huge snarling grizzly standing on his hind legs. It appeared to be eight feet tall and loomed so ferociously lifelike, an impressed Reese paused to check it out. The claws on the massive arms were awesome, the teeth no joke either. Then he saw the small gold plaque on the base of the stand: shot by big bo wenzel, 2003. Reese looked back up at the bear. "So you are real, or at least were." Pity. Alive, it would have been both magnificent and terrifying. He couldn't see himself shooting anything so primal unless it was trying to make him dinner.

"I see you're admiring Ursus."

Reese turned. The man was Matt Wenzel. Reese recognized him from the file. "Morning, Mr. Wenzel. I'm Reese Anthony."

The two shook hands.

Reese nodded toward Ursus. "Didn't know your mascot had a name."

"Can't have a mascot without one, Mr. Anthony. The fans expect it. Come on in. Would you care for coffee?"

Wenzel led him past a couple of desks manned by more pretty blondes who looked as if they had names like Bambi and Chrissi. The cop in Reese gave the place a slow, discreet study, still trying to connect the dots on the crime. The conference room where Pennington was allegedly killed would be around the corner from the main exec office Wenzel was escorting him into now.

"Have a seat."

"Thanks." Reese made himself comfortable in one of the cocoa brown leather chairs. The office was plush. The Grizzlies team colors of brown and gold were reflected in the carpeting and drapes. The stuffed head of another growling grizzly centered the wall behind Wenzel's cluttered desk. He wondered if Bo Wenzel had killed that one too.

Wenzel took a seat at his desk, then spoke into his intercom. "We'll have that coffee now, please."

A lilting female voice replied, "Be right there, Mr. Wenzel."

He then turned his attention to Reese. "Welcome

to Southern California, Mr. Anthony. This isn't your first trip, is it?"

"It is. Been in Michigan most of my life."

"I hear the weather there can get pretty fierce."

"We fry in the summer and freeze in the winter."

A blonde in a short but tasteful skirt came into the office pushing a cart topped with coffee and pastries. Her firm tanned legs were perched atop stiletto sandals made of clear acrylic. "Here you go, sirs." She gave Reese a deep look. "If there's anything else I can do for you, let me know."

Wenzel said coolly, "Thank you, Cami."

"No problem." She gave Reese a flirty little wink then switched out.

After her departure, Reese asked, "You running a cloning company on the side?"

Wenzel shook his head knowingly. "My father handles office personnel. Luckily, they're fairly competent if the task isn't real complicated."

He and Reese shared a grin, then Reese asked, "Is your father here?"

"I'm afraid he's out of town on business. He'll be back next week sometime."

Once they both had cups, Reese launched into the reason for his visit. "Commissioner McNair wants to make sure the team is cooperating with local law enforcement."

"And we are. When the detective was here, I told him everything I knew, which wasn't much, I'm afraid."

"Tell me about Gus Pennington."

"Like I told the detective, Pennington's company

had the cleaning contract for the offices. My father hired him, and since the cleaning crews work nights, I rarely saw them. I may have met Mr. Pennington once, twice, at the most. "

"No problems with the work not being done. Employees bringing friends in?"

"Nothing like that. The work was always done and on time. That's why we think it had to be a robbery."

Reese studied Wenzel's blue eyes for a moment before asking, "How do you think they got inside?"

Wenzel took a sip of his coffee and shrugged. "No idea. Our cameras were down for maintenance."

"Saw that in the police report. Was there anything stolen from any of the other offices on the floor? Computer equipment, drawers pried open?"

"No. Everything is where it should be."

Reese set his coffee cup on the tray. "Can I see the conference room?"

Wenzel seemed to hesitate for a moment, then said, "Sure," and stood. "I was shocked when the detective told me they think he was shot there. No one's wanted to use the room since."

Reese followed him out and into the conference room. It was pretty standard as conference rooms went. Long wooden table. Chairs around it. Mendes hadn't said where the coke traces had been found, but Reese guessed one place would have been the polished oak tabletop. Wood grain had a tendency to hold onto things like dust and minute particles of blood. The grout in the tiled floor was another good place for Forensics to look for evidence. Anyone with a bathroom knew how hard it was getting grout to come clean. And if it was blood, forget it.

Reese gave the space another slow scan, then asked, "Is the floor in here cleaned nightly? Every other night?"

"Nightly."

Reese made a note to ask Mendes what Forensics had found, if anything, in the mop bucket Reese assumed the old man must have had with him. He also wanted to know if the other offices on the floor had been mopped that night. "Okay, Mr. Wenzel. I think I'm done in here. Thanks."

"Will there be anything else?"

"Just a couple more questions then I'll let you get back to work. Who has keys if someone wants to get into the stadium after hours?"

"Besides my father and me, the coach, Mr. Pennington's people, of course, and that's about it."

"About it, or, it?"

Their eyes met. Wenzel showed a small smile. "It. The detective asked the very same question using your exact words. Are you sure you aren't a cop, Mr. Anthony?"

"In a former life I was. Worked vice in Detroit."

Wenzel paused. "Really?"

"Yes." Reese then stuck out his hand. "I'm going to head out. Thanks for taking the time. It was nice meeting you."

Wenzel returned the shake. "Same here. How long will you be in town?"

"Until the job's done."

"Then let's hope for a speedy resolution so you can get back to your office and family."

Reese nodded. "I'll be wanting to speak to your father, so let him know, if you would. I'll have the commissioner set up a time with his office. Thanks again."

"You're welcome."

Reese Anthony's visit resonated ominously with Matt Wenzel as he went back into his office. At the sound of the door opening that connected his office to his father's, he turned. "The commissioner's man is a cop. Vice cop from Detroit."

Big Bo didn't appear impressed. "So. He's not going to find anything. What's his name?"

"Reese Anthony."

"Could be bluffing, trying to make you think he's more important than he is."

"I don't think so. He was pleasant enough, but there was something about him . . . I couldn't quite put my finger on it until he told me what he used to do for a living. We need to back out of this deal right now, Dad."

"Too late. The wheels are already turning."

"Didn't you hear me? He's going to be trouble. I just know it."

"Just calm down. We're fine."

"I'm telling you right now, I'm not going to jail for you or anyone else."

"And I'm telling you that if you even think about ratting out I will kill you with my bare hands and stuff your yellow ass like Ursus!"

Matt's face was mutinous. Their eyes battled for a few tense moments, and then, as always, Matt looked away. "I have work to do."

"And if you want to keep having work to do, you'll play along until the game's done. I'm going to Acapulco for a few days. I'll call you when I get back. Try to grow some balls while I'm gone." Big Bo went into his office and slammed the door.

Furious, Matt forced himself to calm down. He was thirty-five years old and knew he should be used to his father's verbal backhands by now. After all, he'd been battered by them since childhood. But admittance didn't take the sting off his father's berating words. He reached out and clicked off the small digital recorder lying so innocently on top of his cluttered desk and placed it back in his briefcase. He didn't need balls. He had Big Bo's on tape.

JT spent the early part of the week making sure that everything in her office pertaining to Marquise Chambers was turned over to Bobby Garrett's agency. All contracts, negotiation notes, copies of his parking tickets, court orders for child support, arrest warrants, and audit information on his investment accounts were sent, and good riddance. The two men deserved one another. She hoped they'd be happy.

Thursday morning she'd just booted up her computer when her intercom buzzed. She hit the button that opened the speaker. "Yeah, Carole."

"Bobby Garrett's here."

She stared at the intercom. "Excuse me?"

"Mr. Garrett wishes to speak with you."

She sighed. She was not in the mood for little boys this morning, or any morning if the truth be told. "Send him in."

A minute later she stared coolly into the smug face of Bobby Garrett. As usual he was dressed as if he'd just stepped off a model shoot. Expensive suit, snow white shirt, Italian shoes. And as usual she couldn't stand the sight of him. "What can I do for you, Mr. Garrett?"

"Was in town. Thought I'd stop by and make sure you sent over all of Quise's documents."

"We did. Check with your office people. Anything else?"

"How's it feel to lose a big paycheck like Quise?"

"Much better than you're going to feel if you put your hands on my car again."

"No idea what you're talking about," he said innocently.

"Don't play with me, Bobby."

"Why would I want to play with you? I'm getting ready to turn your whole list."

"Only if they start doing crack. Anything else?"

"You're a bitch. You know that?"

"You make that sound like a bad thing. What else you got?"

The anger was evident. He'd always had a thin skin. "You just wait."

"Get out. I have work to do." With any other person, she would have simply turned to her computer and ignored their further presence, but not him; him you had to watch. "Out or I call the police."

"What, you that scared of me?" he asked with a hard arrogant smile in his eyes.

"No, Bobby. I'm not." She reached beneath her desk and smoothly drew out her Colt. "And neither is she."

He jumped a half foot in the air. She was glad to finally have his full attention. "I keep this because of Lamont Keel. Remember when he put me in the hospital?"

He nodded.

"Never going to happen again." Keel had been a disgruntled client who took out his anger on her. "Now say good-bye."

He didn't, but he did leave, and that's all that mattered.

Carole rushed in. "Are you okay?"

"Yeah." Carole knew about the gun that was again safely tucked away on the shelf hidden beneath the desk, but JT didn't mention its role in Bobby G3's hasty exit.

"He didn't look happy."

"Good. Jerk. Let's start the day over, shall we?"

Carole's concern was all over her face but she smiled. "Sounds like a plan."

Alone again, JT allowed herself a few minutes to be angry over Garrett's visit, then wished him to hell and went on with her morning. After making a note to call the Owens kid later to see where she stood on his choice of an agency for representing him, she picked up her coffee cup and turned her eyes to her computer screen. Every morning she started the day by scanning the Web for sports news. The process usually took an hour or two for her to scan the sports sections of the country's major newspapers, surf the official league sites, and scroll through the sites of sports media outlets like ESPN. The daily routine kept her abreast of last night's scores, along with any trade news, gossip, and more important, any troublesome off-court behavior by her clients that might have occurred while she was sleeping. She hated being blindsided by stuff like that.

Sometimes, however, the news made her smile, like a wedding announcement of an athlete or an article touting one of the many charities the players supported. What didn't make her smile were late night gun possession incidents, DUIs, or scandals of any kind. None of that was on the Web that morning, so she guessed it was safe to begin her day.

Or so she thought until a few moments later when Carole buzzed her on the intercom. "Ms. Blake. Marva Wingate is here."

JT ran her hands wearily over her eyes. *Lord.* "Send her in, would you, Carole?"

Marva Wingate was the athlete equivalent of a stage mother. She'd been guiding her son Marvin's basketball career since middle school. He'd been in the league five years, but only recently had he manned up and taken charge of his own affairs. As a result, Marva was having a hard time letting go of the reins.

"Good morning, JT. How are you?" As always, Marva Wingate was dressed well. No ghetto fabulous for her. From her handbag to her pumps to her designer suit, she was as classy and glamorous as a woman who'd inherited old money.

JT motioned her to a seat on the sofa by the windows. "Doing just fine, Marva. How about you? Can I get you some coffee, juice?"

"Coffee would be fabulous."

"Be right back."

JT hustled out to the outer office. As she poured coffee into the dainty china cups she kept around for such occasions, she met Carole's knowing eyes and acknowledged the look with a simple shake of the head. Marva was a class A pain in the butt, and JT knew why she'd come.

Once they both had cups of coffee, JT made herself comfortable on the copper-colored chair near the sofa where her visitor was sitting. "So what can I help you with, Marva?"

"Have you talked to my son lately?"

It was a loaded question and they both knew it. "A few weeks ago. Yes. Why?"

"I didn't get a look at his new contract and I want to review it."

Sighing inside, JT put down her cup. "Legally, I can't let you see it without his permission, Marva. I'm sorry."

Mrs. Wingate didn't seem pleased, but JT had no solutions for her. Marvin was in charge of his life now, and he'd been very specific about keeping his mother out of the loop.

"How much of an increase did you negotiate?" she asked, as if JT hadn't said what she had.

"Is there something else I can help you with, Marva?"

"Yes, you can tell me who is poisoning my son against me," she demanded, her voice cracking. Her hand shook as she placed her gold-rimmed cup and saucer on the glass-topped table. "He refuses to talk to me."

Marva had been a force to reckon with when her son graduated from the University of Indiana five years ago. Refusing to turn his basketball future over to a stranger, she'd eschewed all the high-powered agents who came calling and negotiated Marvin's first contract herself. Because of her razor sharp brain and take-charge attitude, the league powers had been scared to death of her, and as a result, whatever Marva wanted for her phenom son, Marva got. Now, things had changed. Three months ago Marvin had chosen JT's agency to negotiate his new contract, and his mother hadn't been happy.

"Your son's twenty-six years old, Marva," JT told her. "He's taking charge of his own life. No one is poisoning him against you. He just needs some space." What she didn't tell Marva was that in addition to wanting to control his own fate, Marvin was tired of being ribbed by his teammates. During his first two years in the league, he'd earned the balls-breaking nickname MB—for Mama's Boy.

"He's been my whole life all my life. What am I supposed to do?"

JT spoke as gently as she could, "Get your own life, Marva. You've walked through fire for him, and

I know how much he appreciates it, because he's told me so, but he's in charge now. Let him go. It's time for you to kick back and enjoy the fruits of your labors. You've earned it."

She could see that the perfectly made-up face and eyes were caught somewhere between anger and sadness.

"This is who you raised him to be. He's there, Marva. Let him call the shots."

"You don't have children. You can't possibly know how painful this is."

JT bit down on her temper. "No, I don't, but I do know that the more you push, the farther and faster your son is going to run. Is that what you want?"

There was no reaction at first, then Marva admitted softly, "No."

"You're his mother, always will be, just like he'll always be your son, but he's not your baby anymore. Marvin Wingate is a man. He needs you to accept that."

"He's not going to marry that hoochie, is he?"

JT grinned. The hoochie in question was Marvin's latest girl, Atria, a young woman who'd made her living sleeping with ballers and had been passed around by the players more times than a blunt at a rapper's ball. "I doubt it. You raised him better than that."

Marva seemed pleased. "Good to know." She then turned and asked sincerely, "Would you tell him to call me when you talk to him next, please?"

JT nodded. "But you'll have to promise not to stress him about his business."

She didn't respond right away. But then, as if finally resigning herself to the reality, she visibly sighed. "Okay. It's going to be hard."

"I know, but he'll let you back in his life if he feels you trust him to handle his own affairs."

"I'm just so accustomed to . . . " Her voice trailed off.

JT remained silent.

Marva gave her a bittersweet smile. "Thanks, JT. He picked a good agent and a good person when he chose you." She had tears standing in her eyes, and JT prayed Marva wouldn't start to cry; crying was *not* allowed in the JT Blake Agency.

Marva pulled it together. "Okay. I've taken up enough of your time. I'm flying back home this evening. Guess I'll try and start a life for myself."

"Sounds good."

Marva stood. "Thanks for everything."

"You're welcome."

JT walked her back to the outer office. "Have a good flight."

Once she was gone, Carole cracked, "Since I didn't hear any furniture breaking or glass shattering, must mean it went well."

"It did, surprisingly. I think she's finally getting it."

"No more calling you a thousand times a day telling you what to do at the negotiation table?"

"Nope."

"Hallelujah!"

"Call Marvin and tell him I said to send his mama some flowers."

"Will do."

Back in her office, JT sank down into her chair with relief. Speaking of flowers, her eyes strayed to the lone purple tulip sitting in a bud vase on her windowsill. It was the last of the two batches of flowers she'd received from Reese. She hadn't heard anything from Mr. Investigative Head since the evening she set off the fire alarm. Remembering the verbal faux pas about wanting a relationship with him still brought heat to her cheeks. Add to that the memory of the sound of the soft knowing chuckle he'd responded with made her heart beat fast. He had a voice like mahogany; deep, rich, strong. Like any woman in her situation, she wondered if he'd really show up on Friday.

The buzz of the intercom snapped her back to reality. "Yeah, Carole."

"Reese the Fine on line one."

JT froze.

When the silence lengthened, Carole asked, "You still there?"

She shook herself. "Uh, yeah. Thanks."

She took a deep breath to calm herself then hit the button. "Good morning, Mr. Anthony. How may I help you?"

"Morning, Ms. Blake. How are you?"

Mahogany. "Doing well. You?"

"Can't complain. Just wanted to make sure we're still on for Friday."

"Far as I know." She forced herself not to smile.

"Good. I'll be at your office around six."

"Do you remember how to get here?"

"No, but I have the address. I'll find it."

There was silence after that. Enthralled by his voice, she asked, "How're your brothers, Pinky and the Brain? Did they fix that engine chip?"

"They're still working on it. They'll freak when I tell them you asked. Jamal is already talking tickets to the NBA Finals."

"So, you told them about me?"

"I did," he said softly. "Had to. Once word got out about my sending you the cherries, everybody and their brother was in my business."

"The price we pay for having family."

"Tell me about it."

"Let Jamal know I got his back. He can be my guest. You, however, Mr. Commissioner's Man, will have to procure your own."

"You're a cold woman."

"You have no idea. See you Friday. 'Bye, Mr. Anthony."

His voice rippled with amusement. "'Bye, Lady Blake."

With the call ended, a smiling JT sank back against the chair again. It was so unlike her to be blown away by anything, let alone a man she barely knew, but she was honest enough with herself to admit that she was looking forward to seeing him again, even if this would be their one and only dinner together. Technically he was out of bounds. She couldn't afford gossip, not even for a man with a voice like mahogany. She'd worked hard to get to where she was in life. If word got around that she was sleeping with the enemy, she'd have no cred whatsoever; not that any sleeping would be going on, but she had a reputation to maintain. So one dinner. That's it.

But she was uncharacteristically nervous Friday evening while waiting at her office for Reese to show up. The black silk kimonolike dress she was wearing had been custom made in Chinatown last fall. It was exotic, classy, and fit her curves like a glove. Her hair and makeup were tight, as were the heels her sister Max had sent from Italy last year. Her mama Michele had raised her and Max not to be afraid of their height, so both sisters wore high heels proudly and without guilt. JT couldn't remember the last time she'd gone to dinner with a man that didn't involve work, but she didn't know why she was so nervous. *Maybe because you like him,* said the voice in her head, *or maybe because he's made it plain that he likes you.* Whatever the reason, she was as antsy as a cat in a pen of pit bulls.

He arrived a short while later, carrying lilies. He had a suit coat over his arm, was wearing a black silk tee that showed off his killer build, and well-tailored gray pants. His smile of greeting brought back memories of the truck ride, making her forget he was here to beg her pardon. "Hey JT."

"Hey Reese."

He handed her the paper-wrapped flowers. She was glad she'd already sent Carole home. "They're lovely. Thank you." And she meant it sincerely. A woman could get real spoiled, real easy, being around him. "Let me put these in water."

While she went into the small kitchenette to retrieve a vase, Reese forced himself to calm down. The high-necked kimono with its glittering black jeweled buttons was a killer, and he was ready to die.

"Did you fly or drive?" she asked, returning with the flower-filled vase.

When she walked by him and into her inner office, he watched the sexy sway of her behind in the tight black silk. *Lord have mercy!* "Flew. Flight back to L.A. is Sunday. Thought I'd do some sightseeing while I'm here. Got a room at the airport."

"Really?" she asked, now standing framed in the doorway. She had no idea he'd be staying for the weekend.

"You sound suspicious." He ran appreciative eyes over the picture she presented and wondered how long she'd make him wait before he could brush his lips over her soft jawline.

"Should I be?"

"Maybe."

JT saw the playfulness in his eyes and she shook her head knowingly. "I'm going to leave that alone. Where would you like to eat?"

"You choose."

"Seafood?"

"Sounds good."

They were staring. As the silence lengthened, she noted that the air in the office seemed to warm and thicken.

He spoke first. "My apologies for not being truthful the day we met. I didn't know how you'd react if I told you I worked for McNair."

"I felt like you played me."

"I'm sorry for that too, but playing you wasn't my intent, believe me. I had this beautiful, beautiful lady in my truck, and I didn't want to mess it up."

Her heart skipped. "Are you always this truthful?"

"About things important to me, yes."

In her eyes he was a truly gorgeous man, both inside and out. "Let's go eat. I'll drive."

"No problem. I'll sightsee." And the best thing to see was the Lady Blake in her hot black kimono.

She drove them back across the bridge that connected Oakland to San Francisco and pulled up at the curb of a small jazz club downtown. The valet, a brother in a dark suit, hurried to assist with the driver's door, and he grinned as she stepped out. "Looking good, Lady B. How are you this evening?"

"Fine, Leo. How are you?"

"Seeing you just made life worth living."

JT chuckled, gave him a tip, and led Reese inside.

The interior was shadowy, and because it was just past 7:00 pm, early for the club, the place wasn't crowded yet. Even so, a young sax player was on stage playing like a musician with a gift.

"He's good." Reese noted, liking the intimacy of the place.

JT agreed. She came here often because the service was good, the music on jam, and she rarely ran into any of her players. The establishment's hostess, a middle-aged woman named Wanda, stepped up and picked up a couple of menus. "Evening, Lady B."

"Hey, Ms. Wanda, how are you?"

Wanda eyed Reese. "Be better if he was my date instead of yours."

JT saw that he was smiling. "He is kinda cute, isn't he?"

"Got that right. Regular spot?"

"Yes, ma'am."

They followed Wanda through the club, and Reese followed the seductive swing of JT's hips.

Once they were seated in JT's favorite booth, Wanda said, "Waitress will be right with you." She shot Reese a wink then left them alone.

In the silence that followed, Reese scanned his menu, but in fact he was checking out JT. He'd never seen a more perfectly put together woman. From her expertly arched brows to the sexy paint on her toes, she made a man want to roar. "So what's good here?"

"Everything. I'm having the catfish."

"Then I'll go with that too."

The menus were set aside and they turned their attention to the young sax player. He was covering Grover Washington's "Black Frost" and making it his own. The waitress came over, they gave her their orders, then settled back to wait for their food.

Reese asked the question he'd been wanting to ask since first meeting her. "What's JT stand for?"

"Jessi Teresa. I'm named after an aunt who lived back in the 1800s. She was a rancher."

"Really?"

"Yep, married an outlaw named Griffin Blake."

He stared, she grinned. "Legend says she could shoot the wings off a fly at fifty paces."

He smiled and shook his head. "Anyone call you Jessi?"

"Only my mother, and only when she's mad."

"I like the name. It's distinctive."

"It's old-fashioned."

"Mind if I call you Jessi?"

She assessed him for a moment. For as far back as she could remember, she'd always insisted on being called JT because growing up she hadn't particularly cared for her name, but hearing him ask to call her Jessi in that mahogany voice of his made her rethink things. Trying to play it off, she shrugged. "No, I don't mind."

"Good."

She had to look away from his eyes or drown. He made her feel female, and she wasn't sure she knew how to handle that because it had been such a long time since she'd had a man truly interested in what lay beneath the JT persona. When she faced him again, he was watching her with muted interest, so to keep her nerves from showing, she asked, "What else should I know about you?"

"That I used to be a cop and am now a lawyer. I'm also part owner of my pops's trucking company. We operate here in the states and in twelve countries overseas."

Now it was her turn to stare. "Twelve countries?"

He nodded confidently as he sipped at the water in his glass. "Working on numbers thirteen and fourteen."

JT scanned the chiseled features of his gorgeous face. "Anything else? No diamond mines? Working on a cure for cancer? Recipe for the perfect barbecue sauce?"

The low-voiced chuckle he responded with made her insides zing.

"I'm serious," she countered in an amused voice. "Lawyer, huh? Where'd you go to school?"

"Did my undergrad at Western Michigan University. Got my law degree from Northwestern outside Chicago."

"My sister was a cop in Detroit a few years back."

"When?"

They discussed that, and found that Max had joined the force after Reese's departure, so the two never met. Out of the corner of her eye JT saw their waitress approaching, loaded down with their dinner choices. "Here comes our food."

"Good. I'm hungry." But Reese was hungrier for more insight into the woman he now called Jessi.

Six

While they ate, they talked about his life as a cop and her life growing up in what she called Little Bitty Texas. "My mother was a cook in one of the state prisons. She didn't make a lot of money but it was steady. She retired a few years ago."

"Your father?"

"Died when Maxie and I were small. Construction accident."

"Sorry to hear that."

"Thanks. You and I have that in common, losing a parent."

He nodded. "My pops never remarried."

"Neither did my mother. Raised us by herself."

The club was starting to fill. Well-dressed patrons of all races took seats at the tables, in the booths, and along the long curved bar on the far side of the room. The sax man had been replaced by a Latina on keyboards who sang just as well as she played.

Reese was impressed. "Can't get over this great music."

"A lot of the big names play here. I try and get over here as often as I can. The owner wants to retire, so my sister and I are thinking about buying the place."

He couldn't hide his surprise.

She shrugged. "Have to have something to do when I decide to close my shop. I'm a big jazz fan." She glanced toward the door. Seeing two of her players enter, she groused, "Dammit."

"What's wrong?"

She sighed with frustration. "A couple of my clients just came in."

Reese knew that her being there with him might present problems. "Maybe they won't see you."

"No such luck." They'd already spotted her and were coming her way. Jason Grant and D'Angelo Nelson were two of the best linebackers in the league. On the field they were known as Shock and Awe, respectively.

When they reached her, both big men said in turn, "Hey Lady B," but their attention was coolly fixed on Reese.

"Hey, you two," she said in greeting. They were eyeing Reese like prey. "This is Reese Anthony. Reese—Jason Grant and D'Angelo Nelson."

Reese stuck out a hand. The men shook. "Nice to meet you," he said. "You play for the Oakland Earthquake."

The mountain-sized men nodded but their faces weren't any friendlier. JT knew an interrogation of Reese would be next. Her players were very protective. They seemed to think it was their job to scrutinize every man who even looked like he might be interested in her. She appreciated their concern but it was yet another reason why she had no love life to speak of. Their antics had sent more than a few of the men in her past scrambling for the exits.

Jason Grant, his trademark long blond hair flowing behind him like a Viking, asked, "Where'd you meet our lady?"

Reese noted the possessive emphasis. "On the 5 last week. She was having car trouble."

She added, "And because he was the perfect gentleman, I'm buying him dinner. So back off."

D'Angelo's dark face flashed a predatory smile, "Now JT, you know we have to check the brother out."

She dropped her head then raised it again. "Go play. I'm fine." She was glad that Reese appeared amused as opposed to offended by the encounter, at least so far.

D'Angelo said to his compadre. "I've seen him before. Just trying to remember where." D'Angelo was an all-pro linebacker with a Mensa card. Not only was he a certified genius, the brother had a photographic memory. Like the proverbial elephant, he never forgot anything he'd seen or read.

When his eyes brightened she knew he had the answer and her spirits sank. "You're with the commissioner's office. New head of Investigations. Saw your face in the team newsletter a few days ago."

The two men were now staring her way accusingly.

"What?" she asked. "We're having dinner. That's all. Would you leave us in peace, please?"

Jason warned, "Just so he knows—he hurts you, we kill him."

JT threw up her hands.

D'Angelo gave Reese one last steady look, then said, "Nice to meet you." Only then did they move on.

She sighed. "Sorry."

"They always so protective?"

"Always."

"The cop in me likes that. Lets me know you're safe when I'm not around."

The words were touching, but she'd been raised to look out for herself. "Their hearts are in the right place but they make me crazy sometimes."

His soft smile met hers. "They care about you."

"Or something."

"Did you tell them about what that ex-employee did to your car?"

"No, because I didn't want to have to bail them out of jail."

"Any more incidents?"

She shook her head.

"Good."

They finished their dinner. The saxophonist had returned and was filling the club's interior with sweet mellow sounds. Many couples took to the small dance floor in response.

In a voice that pierced her as sweetly as the notes of the sax, he invited, "Come dance with me."

His words went through her like heat through butter. She hesitated for a moment, then rising to her feet, walked with him to the floor. Jason and D'Angelo were watching but she didn't care, she'd deal with them some other time. When they found a spot on the dimly lit floor, she couldn't believe how nervous she was. Her heart was thumping so hard she was sure he could see it, but when he took her in his arms and held her close, all she wanted to do was sigh. Their bodies fit perfectly. His arm across her back was respectful but the weight was warm. He was a good dancer; smelled good too.

He asked against her ear, "Did I tell you how good you look tonight?"

She rippled. "No."

"Well, you do. I like the dress."

"Thank you."

Reese was enjoying finally getting to hold her close. He'd wanted to be near her this way since the truck ride. She was tall, soft, and fragrant. As they moved slowly to the music, he noted the displeasure on the faces of the two linebackers watching so intently, but he wasn't bothered or intimidated. He knew they had a prior claim, but he planned to make this woman his if she'd have him, and her players were just going to have to deal with his presence in her life. "Ever been courted?"

Humor twinkled in her eyes when she raised them to his. "No."

"Would you like to be?"

JT couldn't remember meeting a man quite like him. "I'm too old for games."

"So am I." His look was so intense she felt singed to her toes.

"And if I say, no?"

"I don't think you will."

"You're awfully confident."

"With you, I'll need to be." That said, he eased them back together.

JT was no prude. The heat slowly building between them made her want to invite him home and into her bed to find out once and for all if his mouth kissed as well as it promised. She sensed he'd be a good lover, a giving lover, and what woman wouldn't want that, even if it was only for one night?

"I want to kiss you," he whispered.

She trembled and swore she'd never breathe again. "Do it here and Jason and D'Angelo will put you in the hospital."

He grinned. "Then maybe we should leave."

Their gazes locked for a long moment. She nodded.

Ignoring the glowering linebackers, she followed him back to the booth. The check was taken care of, the car brought around, and then they were on their way. Night had fallen.

"Where are we headed?" he asked, watching her, wanting her.

"My place okay?"

He met her eyes in the dark car for a long moment. "Yeah, that's okay."

Neither of them spoke on the twenty-minute ride to her place. This is what they'd both wanted since meeting on the 5.

She pulled the car into her condo complex then turned the car over to the valet. The high-rise building overlooked the bay. Her place was on the top floor. As they entered the elevator, she shot him a quick glance and saw he was watching her. Feeling like a schoolgirl, she looked away.

"You don't do this often, I take it?"

"No." She'd been in her condo three years. He was the first man she'd ever invited back.

"Then I'm honored. And Jessi?"

She looked up.

"Make sure this is something you want to do. Yes, I'll be disappointed, but I can wait if you change your mind."

What a man. "Let's see how it goes."

He nodded.

They entered her condo and he ran his eyes over the warm cocoa-colored walls, the framed artwork, and the classy furniture. "Like your place."

"Thanks. Care for some wine?" she asked, walking into the kitchen. She was so nervous she didn't know who she was.

"Sure."

He joined her, making her very conscious of his presence as she moved around the well-lit kitchen with its granite countertops and sleek stainless appliances. *I want to kiss you,* continued to echo in her head.

Glasses in hand, they moved outside to the patio to enjoy the sound of the waves and the warm breezy night. "It's nice out here," he said, sipping and watching her.

"One of the reasons I bought this place. The sunsets are spectacular." Out on the bay were the distant lights of a few ships. He was standing beside her, and the heat of him played over her arms in concert with the soft wind.

Reese could tell she was nervous, and he found it both surprising and endearing. He knew her reputation as a hard-nosed, kick butt kind of girl, but out here with him she seemed almost unsure. He turned his head her way and found her looking up at him. Unable to hold himself back any longer, he leaned down and placed his lips against hers, slowly, wondrously, invitingly. Her mouth softened, and he moved closer to taste her better and heard her sigh of pleasure. The opening stanza was so sweet and powerful, the first strings of desire began to rise, and he pulled her closer. The kisses remained lazy, unhurried. They were exploring each other, teasing each other. His tongue found hers and his palm began to map the length of her spine, moving up and down the polished silk.

Neither remembered the goblets of wine in their hands until the sounds of glass shattering against the stone tiles at their feet caught their attention, but even then he continued kissing her, moving his lips over the shell of her ear. "Let's move before you cut your feet."

It was a good suggestion. Her strappy heels left most of her feet and toes bare, but she didn't want to turn his kisses loose, so they stood there for a few moments longer letting lust and desire flow, then he took her by the hand, walked her around the glass and led her back indoors.

JT felt like she'd entered another world. Everything was hazy: her vision, her hearing, her perception of where she was. The only thing substantial was Reese. Floating, she took his hand. "This way."

The bedroom was dark, and Reese had no idea what it looked like until she left him standing for a moment to light some of the candles spread around the space. Soon the room was ablaze with tea lights illuminating the space like a Tibetan temple and he saw the large silk-shrouded bed, the gauzy drapes lifted by the soft breeze playing in through the opened windows, and the sumptuous gold bedding. It was as if he'd been magically transported to the inner sanctum of an ancient queen. While she moved around lighting more candles, the man in him wondered how many other men had been there before. One? Three? No way of knowing, of course, and in reality it didn't matter because he planned on making himself and this night unforgettable for them both.

JT put down the lighter and turned to the man standing in the middle of her room. She had no regrets about inviting him. None. She walked back over. He slid an arm around her and eased her close. Without a word, he lowered his head and kissed her until the fires caught and blazed again.

His hands were roaming, sliding, exploring. Her nipples were hard, her hidden core damp and soft. "Thanks for the light," he rasped. "When I take this dress off you, I want to see." His voice was as potent as a caress and her body responded in kind.

He undid the top buttons on her dress to give his mouth access to the warm scented skin of her throat, while he moved a palm over her still covered nipples. More buttons were slowly undone, and the twinkling tea lights let him feast on the sight of the sexy purple bra she wore beneath. He brushed his lips over the twin soft rises and her head fell back in response.

Reese couldn't ever remember wanting a woman this bad. His manhood was hard and ready to be satisfied, but he forced himself to take this slow. She was a woman to be savored, not rushed as if this was nothing more than a booty call. Her skin was satiny, warm. He could spend the rest of his days touching her, kissing her, and it wouldn't be enough.

JT was accustomed to being in charge, but tonight she let herself be led. The few men she'd shared lust with in the past hadn't wasted much time on foreplay because they seemed more intent upon their own pleasure. They'd never eased her bra aside and gifted her with such prolonged finesse, but Reese was different, and so good that when he took her nipple into his mouth the pleasure made her groan aloud. His tongue and mouth teased and dallied and lingered until she swore she couldn't take any more. Feeling the orgasm gathering, she backed away from his dazzling caresses in order to keep from coming so quickly and to gather herself. Under his powerful candlelit eyes she rid herself of her dress and stood before him wearing nothing but her sexy purple underwear and her shoes.

"God, you're gorgeous," he husked out. "Gorgeous, beautiful, and hot."

The praise felt good. She watched as he removed

his sport coat and shirt, and her eyes moved hungrily over the fine lines of his bared brown physique. She ran a hand down the plane of his chest, liking the feel of the muscles against her palms, then flicked her tongue catlike over each flat nipple. He was gloriously made. While she kissed and licked her way across his skin, her hands explored the strength of his arms, the solid sweep of his shoulders, the trimness of his waist. When her hand moved down over his hard need, he sucked in a breath and she watched his eyes close. She smiled. Her adept fingers made short work of the closed belt and slowly pulled it free. His eyes burned down into hers, increasing her own desire. Stepping away for a moment, she silently, shamelessly, undid her bra and tossed it away, then removed her shoes. Her bared beauty came in for more of his magical touches and all she could do was stand there on shaking legs and let him have his way. She crooned as the hand exploring so sinuously between her panty-shrouded thighs filled with a spreading heat that took the shakes to a whole new level.

"You're wet," he whispered. Reese had no idea where she'd purchased the sexy little purple panties and the matching bra, but he hoped she had dozens of sets because they were as erotic to his eyes as they were to his touch. He liked the small sounds of pleasure she was responding with too, and knew that if he didn't have her soon he was going to come without her. "Let's move to the bed, Jessi . . . "

She thrilled at the sound of her name on his lips and the feel of his spellbinding hands; hands that were still teasing and tempting and making it hard for her to remember her name let alone walk to the bed. But she was laid down and pleasured as he kissed his way down her body, lingering here, licking there, then slowly peeled her lacy panties down and off. His fingers found her then, and she responded with uninhibited delight. While he kissed her passion-parted lips, he prepared her with touches that made her arch, coo, and greedily spread her legs for more.

Reese moved away for a moment to remove the rest of his clothing and to ease on a condom. Ready now, he knelt above the queen, teased a finger over the damp and swollen temple, then filled her slowly to the hilt.

JT came screaming.

Reese gritted his teeth to keep himself from tumbling after. Forcing himself to remain still, she rode her orgasm while he kissed her softly and kept her tight nipples damp and ripe. With lazy passes of his hand he reveled in the heat he'd brought to her skin and in the sound of her throaty cries piercing the candlelit silence. Although his manhood was demanding its turn, he hung on because he wanted to bring her to orgasm again with their bodies joined. This first one had been the result of the foreplay, the next one would be from his loving.

So he began to move. The male in him wanted to take her like there'd be no tomorrow, but he reminded himself again that this was no booty call. She was a woman he wanted more than any other, and his intent was to show her what that meant.

JT never had a man love her this way. In the past,

one orgasm was all she ever managed. But Reese? She sensed he could make her come 24/7 for years and she'd be ready for more, just like now. Even though the remnants of the first orgasm were still resonating, the size, girth, and rhythm of him were rekindling her again. She loved the feel of him and the strength of his hands lifting and guiding her hips. With her long legs wrapped around his waist, she gladly rode the strokes he invited her to take, and as the heat began to climb, she didn't care about anything in the world except Reese Anthony and the hard thick wizardry stroking so masterfully between her thighs. The bliss was too much, the pleasure too great, and she came again, twisting, bucking, and calling his name.

That was it for Reese. Hearing her cry out his name sent him over the edge and the orgasm shattered him like a pane of glass. The pace of his thrusts increased, his hold on her roughened, and he heard himself roaring as he was swept away.

They lay boneless and entwined in the silent aftermath. He lifted his head to look into her face. There was so much he wanted to talk to her about, so much he wished to say, but he kept it to himself as she reached up, cupped his cheek and whispered, "Thanks."

"You're welcome."

She cuddled back against him, he wrapped an arm around her, then they both slept.

JT awakened the next morning to the gray fog of dawn. Because the windows hadn't been closed overnight, the air in the room was chilly enough to cause shivers. She gently dragged the comforter to her shoulders and watched him sleep. Even asleep he was gorgeous. An urge to trace her finger along the strong lines of his jaw rose inside, but she forced it down because she didn't want to disturb his dreams. What would it be like to awaken with him beside her every morning? she wondered. What did he eat for breakfast? Did he prefer bacon with his eggs? Did he even eat eggs? So many questions and no time to learn the answers.

She still had no regrets about bringing him home. He was a magician in bed and he could make love to her for an eternity, but one performance was all she could allow herself. Loving so fine from such a magnificent man could make a girl question the future plans she'd laid out for herself; make her wonder about babies instead of contracts and acquiring a jazz club. He was a man dreams were made of, but not for a woman with an independent streak as wide as the state of Texas, plus she didn't do men real well. The ones in her past always wanted to corral her like she was some kind of wild filly in need of a saddle and a firm hand. Would Reese be the exception? A part of her wanted to find out, while a louder part asked if she'd lost her mind. Maybe she had because she was selfish enough to want his company and his full attention until he flew back to L.A. on Sunday, but she was enough of a realist to understand that any further involvement with Reese Anthony would bring drama she didn't need, even if he did kiss like a god.

Reese awakened to the smell of coffee. He opened

an eye but his location failed to register. A moment later it did, along with a lusty set of memories that made him smile. Lord, what a night. Just thinking about her made his manhood rise up and want to go to work. "Down boy," he chided. Getting up, he dragged the sheet off the bed, wrapped it around his waist, and set off to find the woman who'd cried out his name.

He found her out on the balcony, talking on the phone. She was dressed in a pair of sweats, a loose fitting halter top, and her face was clean and free of makeup. She looked younger but no less beautiful. Seeing him standing in the door, she gave him a smile that warmed him like sunshine, then pantomimed pouring coffee and pointed to the kitchen. The male in him was disappointed that her attention was else-where, but he didn't hold it against her and padded into the kitchen to get coffee.

She was still on the phone when he came back to the door with a cup of brew, and she didn't sound happy.

"Kimon, for the fifth time, there is nothing I can do. I'm not going to waste my time or yours suing a tattoo shop."

Reese could see her listening to the response, then she turned his way and threw up her hands.

He had no idea what the conversation was about, so he drank and waited. He wanted to shower, but settled for watching her and the sun as it burned the fog off the water.

"I don't care what it really says, Kimon. You should

have had somebody verify the translation before you got the tat done."

She listened for a few more seconds, her face set tersely, then stated, "Kimon, I'm hanging up. My breakfast is burning. Find somebody to laser the damn thing off. 'Bye!"

She sighed and turned to Reese. "Apparently, the Asian characters he had tattooed on his arm don't say, 'King of the Ballers.' "

The light of amusement in her eyes made Reese start grinning. "What's it really mean?"

"Hog fat."

Reese spit coffee, and a laughing JT fell into a chair and laughed until she cried. When she finally regained control, she told him, "Twenty-five players were bamboozled by the same tat shop. He wants me to file a class action lawsuit."

Reese shook his head. "You lead an interesting life."

"Whack is more like it. Good grief," she added, still chuckling. "Hog fat."

Reese wondered if all of her mornings began with calls from her clients. The day was Saturday and yet she was working. "Do they call you 24/7?"

"All day, every day."

"When was the last time you took a vacation?"

She thought back.

"If you have to think about it, it's been too long."

She shrugged. "Maybe, but I enjoy what I do."

Their eyes met. JT didn't want to talk about her workload. "What would you like for breakfast? I'm a pretty good cook."

"Really?"

"Yeah. Omelets okay?" She'd never had a sheet-wearing man in her house before. Just looking at his buffed brown body made her want a repeat of last night.

"Omelets are fine. I'd like a shower first, though."

"Oh shoot, I'm sorry." She walked to the open patio door, and he backed up so she could enter. She stopped. Looking up into his eyes, she said softly, "Good morning."

"Morning."

"Did you sleep well?"

"What little I got, yeah."

She grinned and led him to her guest bedroom with its connected bath. "Bathroom is through there. There are towels and soap. Toothbrush. I'll get you a robe."

He raised an eyebrow. He certainly didn't want to sit at her table dressed in one of her frilly robes.

She opened a closet door, looked through the garments hanging inside, and pulled out a robe that was black silk and by its size obviously made for a man. Thrown a bit by the idea of her having male robes waiting to be worn, he put his cup down and took the hanger. "Thanks," he said.

"My sister sent it to me from Hong Kong a few years ago. Said it might come in handy, so I guess she was right. You're the first person to wear it, so you can take it home if you like."

He viewed the robe in a whole new light. "Your sister has good taste."

"Yes, she does. I'll start breakfast."

Left alone, Reese stood in the silence, feeling the echoes of her vivid presence resonate, then dropped the sheet and went to shower.

JT found she liked making him breakfast. Of course if she had to do it for a living, she might not be as happy, but for that morning it was okay. The cracked and seasoned eggs were in the bowl waiting to be cooked, and a small plate held the veggies and cheese that would fill the omelets. The bacon was frying up nicely in the skillet, and Mary J was thumping on the kitchen's CD player. She and Ms. Blige were jamming so tough, she didn't notice him standing and watching until she turned. He looked freshly showered and the smile on his face warmed her to her toes. "Better?" she asked, lowering the volume on the music.

"Yeah, but I'd like to go back to my room and get some clean clothes." He'd had no choice but to put on what he'd taken off last night, and seeing her made him want to take them off again, along with the loose sweats she was wearing.

"We can run over there after we eat."

Reese nodded, then sat on one of the stools tucked under the counter. He watched her pour milk and a spoonful of water into the eggs and whip them up. "Not many women cook these days."

"Not many men either."

"Touché." Enjoying her, he sat silent while she poured the egg mixture into a hot skillet. When the bottom layer set she added the veggies, chilies, and cheese, then expertly folded it over. It slid from the skillet onto a plate, and he savored the mouth-watering sight and smells.

Plates were set out along with silverware. She pulled out a carton of orange juice from the fridge. They helped themselves to the offerings then moved out to the table on the patio to enjoy their meal.

He took a few bites of the flavorful omelet and groaned with delight.

She grinned. "That good?"

"Better."

"My mama made sure Maxie and I could cook."

"She did a good job."

She saluted him with her juice glass.

Reese studied her. Classy, sexy, and she could cook—what more could a man want besides making love to her on a regular basis? He hadn't gotten nearly enough of the fascinating Jessi Teresa Blake, and the more he was around her, the more he realized how multifaceted she was. "So, you've never been courted."

She eyed him for a moment. "I already told you, no. Nobody courts anymore anyway."

"Real men do."

"Oh, really?"

He took a draw on his juice and watched her over his glass. "Yep."

Amused by him, she shook her head. "Is that why you sent the flowers?"

He nodded.

"That's sweet but not necessary."

"I think it is. I'm old school, Jessi, and this is the way things are done where I come from."

"So you think this is going to get serious?" she asked skeptically.

He leaned forward. "You said it best. Relationship."

She looked away for a moment then back at him. She chose her words carefully, "As long as you work for the commissioner, I can't be with you and keep my cred. My players will jump ship faster than you can say 'collusion.' "

"Then let's see if we can find a way around that. I don't want whatever it is we're doing here to negatively affect you or your livelihood, but I do want you, Jessi. No sense lying about it. I want you, your kisses . . . "

Putting down his cup, he stood, walked around to her, and held out his hand. She accepted the offer and rose to her feet. He tilted her chin up gently, then brushed his lips across hers. "Especially your kisses."

And what kisses they were. The logic she'd been attempting to apply slid away, replaced by something far more sensual. He could bring a marble statue to life. No, she didn't want to be courted, but she did want this. "After this weekend, I can't see you again. Not like this," she told him, needing to let him know she was serious.

"I understand." He rubbed his palm over her bra-free nipples. "But your kisses and your body won't stop calling me."

To prove his point, he took a nipple in his mouth through her shirt, and arrows of delight flooded her senses. He pulled her shirt up, exposing a brown-tipped prize that he fondled, licked, and sucked until she groaned. He treated her other breast to the same magnificent conquering and JT's world grew hazy. She didn't protest when her sweats were slid down her hips, baring her and her black lace thong to the sunny morning, the warm wind off the bay, and his possessive hands. Even though in reality she barely knew him, he had the touch of a man who'd caressed her body down through time, and she wanted more.

Seven

Drowning in the eddy of his magic, she husked out, "Let's go inside." Lord knew she didn't want to stop, but she didn't want to give anyone who might be looking a show either.

With hands roaming and tongues mating, they blindly kissed their way indoors. Once there, she pulled his shirt up and off. He returned the favor and immediately transferred his mouth to her nipples. She gasped, arched and thrilled as he ran a roughly possessive hand over one bared hip to pull her closer. Last night's interlude had been an introduction. Now that they knew each other's measure, there was no holding back. Her sweats were down around her ankles and his fingers were creating sweet havoc between her thighs. God he's good, she thought, standing there while he plied her so expertly her first orgasm of the day rippled over her like sunshine. Shuddering, she dropped her head on his chest and melted with bliss.

Fingers dewed with her heat, Reese thrilled at the sight and feel of her response. She was so erotically tantalizing he was hard, ready, and wanted her then and there. Stepping away for a moment, he pulled a condom from his pocket and took off his pants.

Eyes closed, a boneless JT stood braced against the wall lost in a world filled with pulsing delight. The orgasm was still resonating. Her mouth was kiss-swollen, her nipples hard and damp.

Then she felt his kiss. A man's kiss; soft, solid, and strong. He drank as deeply from her as she did from him while their hands slowly explored and enticed. He touched the gates to her paradise and asked with a hot whisper, "Are you ready, Ms. I Don't Want to Be Courted?"

JT wanted to respond but he was slowly filling her and she couldn't have spoken had her life hung in the balance. *Damn he was good.* How she wound up off the floor with her legs wound around his naked waist, and her hips in his hands, she had no idea, but she didn't care. It was scandalous, delicious being made love to in the middle of her living room by a man tall enough and strong enough to support her and work her like she weighed nothing. She held onto his shoulders and let him do the rest. He played her like a bowed instrument, and the sensual music he wrung from her rose in the silence. "Reese . . . "

He grinned and kept stroking. "What, baby?"

She forgot what she'd planned to say. Her flesh sheltered him as if he'd been made just for her pleasure, and she returned his rhythm greedily while his big hands directed her hips how and where he wanted.

Soon, the orgasm grabbed her and her joy was plain. A few seconds later his climax exploded too, and he joined her in vocalizing his release. The passionate battle engulfed them both, and they fought for all they were worth until they had nothing left. Only then did he collapse with her onto the sofa.

Later, after their breathing and heartbeats slowed, JT was sheltered in his lap and braced against his arm. Sated, sweaty, and satisfied, she gave him a shy grin. "Never made love standing up before."

Humor flashed in his eyes. "Glad I could help a sister out."

"Bet you've done a lot of helping out in your time."

"I plead the Fifth."

She reached up and cupped his clean-shaven face. Her inner woman wanted to become attached to this man. Even though she knew it was not in her best interest, she couldn't seem to make it stop.

"What're you thinking?" he asked.

"That I can't become attached to you."

She had no idea how good that made him feel. "At least you're honest."

"Always."

"Well, stick to your guns."

She scanned his face. "You're not taking this seriously enough for me."

He traced a crescent over her cheek, "Sorry. I respect your worries, but I think whatever this is we're doing is already way past our control and that it's a lot deeper than just killer sex."

She dropped her head to hide her grin. When she raised it again, his eyes were waiting. She couldn't deny his words. There was something happening between them, she just didn't understand what. "So what do you propose we do?"

"Keep us a secret for as long as you need to and let the rest run its course."

She nodded. Lord knew she wanted him in her life, but would her need for him ruin her life? The answer was tied to the future.

He gave her a playful swat on the butt. "Up. We both need a shower. Wanta share?"

She stood. "Sure." Her legs were rubbery. "Are you going to behave?"

He shook his head. "Nope."

Laughing, she held out her hand, "Then come on."

True to his word, he didn't behave. He gifted her with a third bout of lovemaking in twenty-four hours, and she glorified in every throbbing inch of it.

They dried and dressed then headed for his airport hotel so he could grab a fresh change of clothing.

Bobby Garrett drove through Watts bobbing his head to the beat of Tupac rapping about California on the CD player. As a young blood, he had grown up here, snatching purses, jacking cars, and dealing weed. Ironically, an eighteen-month stint in jail for carjacking when he was seventeen placed him on the road to success. Her name was Priscilla Steele, a green-eyed, red-haired prisoners' rights advocate who saw something in him no one else had. With her help, he'd gotten his GED and while still incarcerated began taking college classes. Once he paid his debt to society and the courts kicked him free, she wrangled a partial scholarship to USC, known in the hood as the University of South Central, and he was on his way. He'd always been smart, but in his world, academic success was ridiculed, not celebrated. A man wasn't measured by his brain power, but by the colors he wore and the weapons in his trunk.

He'd had to bang Pris of course, but during his sophomore year she got engaged to a Stanford tax lawyer and exchanged her commitment to the poor and underprivileged for a mansion in Malibu and a membership in the local country club.

He hadn't cared. By then he knew how to work the system. By charming, bullshitting, and clawing, he went from USC to a Wharton degree in Economics, maintained his ties to his gang, as every righteous member did.

Bobby pulled up in front of the short, one-story white house and by habit scanned the street before getting out. He'd known Michael "Ham" Birmingham since he was ten and Ham twenty. Back then, Ham's mother, Doris, had been alive. Now, Ham lived in the white house with his woman Niki, a former gang queen. Both she and Ham were too old to rule the streets by force anymore, but they ruled in other ways.

Bobby checked the empty street one more time then got out. He visited Ham often enough that the young bloods on the block knew his ride and knew to leave it the hell alone or pay the price. Moving casually but keeping his eyes peeled, he stepped up onto the porch and knocked.

Niki answered the door. She was Spanish. Back in the day, she'd been the finest thing walking, but the years and the vices had taken their toll. She didn't say much, rarely did. Upon seeing it was him, she simply backed up and let him in. "Kitchen."

"Thanks."

Ham was seated at the kitchen table weighing up dimes of coke on a palm-sized digital scale. Two gallon-size plastic bags filled with white powder lay on the table. Ham looked up. He was Black, not particularly big in stature, but deadly just the same. The nose he'd broken in a fight years ago had healed fat and ugly like a boxer's, making his light brown face appear wider and flatter than it was. "What can I do for you, Bobby?"

"Just came by to make sure we're still cool."

Ham scrutinized him for a long moment then went back to his scale. "Killing that old man wasn't smart."

"I had to kill him."

"True, but you should have taken him somewhere else and offed him. The popos aren't stupid."

"We cleaned up everything. Not that you stayed to help."

"It was your mess. Not mine."

Bobby's lips thinned. It had been Bo Wenzel's idea to put the janitor's body in the truck. He'd wiped Bobby's unregistered gun clean, placed it in the dead man's hand to make sure his prints were found, then they went back inside to clean up. "So what about the next shipment?"

"What about it?"

Bobby held onto his temper. "Do I get it or not?"

Ham shrugged. "My guts says doing business with you will send me back to San Quentin, and I ain't going there again. You've lost your edge, Bobby. In the old days you wouldn't have panicked when that janitor walked in on us."

"I didn't panic."

"Yeah, you did. I saw your eyes, man. Big as saucers. You didn't think. All you did was reach in your coat and blow him away. Stupid," Ham added with disgust. "We had the perfect deal going. Perfect. Now?"

Bobby tried to defend himself and to explain. "Look, Ham—"

"No, you look. You need to decide which world you want to walk in because it's obvious you can't do both. It's cool that you kept in touch while you were off in college doing your thing, but I keep telling you, all that higher education and fancy living ain't a plus here."

"It was a plus back in the day when I was running weed for you with the frat boys, and it was a plus when I brought you this deal."

"True, but look where it's got me. The only thing standing between me and going down on an accessory to murder are two rich White men who'll give us both up in a heartbeat if it means saving their own asses."

"They're not going to say anything."

"Damn right, because if they do, you pay, Bobby. You."

He got the point. "I'll keep the lid on."

"You do that."

"So what about the next shipment?"

"Let's wait a week. If nothing jumps off we'll move."

Bobby wasn't happy about the delay, and he knew Bo Wenzel wouldn't be either, but there was no getting around it. Ham was the distributor. The operation couldn't run without him and his nationwide network of contacts. Bobby thought it might be in his best interest to try and hook up with one of Ham's competitors, but that could entail way more danger than he needed in his life right now if word got back to Ham, so he was stuck. "I'll call you next week."

"Yeah." Ham went back to weighing out the dimes. As the time lengthened and he didn't look up, Bobby knew he'd been dismissed. Keeping his anger in check, he left.

Driving back to his Wilshire Boulevard office, he seethed. Tupac was still blasting on the CD, but all he heard was Ham calling him soft. Yeah, he might have traded in his tats and colors for a fancy high rise office and designer suits, but he wasn't soft and he hadn't lost his edge. Achieving what he had proved as much, otherwise he'd have been a burned-out banger relegated to making a living dealing drugs, like Ham.

He stopped at the light and changed the CD. As it

went green, Fifty's voice filled the speakers. He reflected that he wasn't the first man in the history of the world to prefer the finer things in life. Just because Ham had never seen life outside of Watts and Compton didn't mean those who had were inferior. The sooner he could cut Ham out of the equation, he decided, the better off he and the Wenzels would be.

On the drive back to her place from the Point Reyes National Seashore, Reese was more content than he'd been in a while. She'd taken him to see whales, of all things, and he knew it would be a day he'd remember for many years. But even more memorable was the woman seated behind the wheel. "Thanks for the whales," he said.

"You're welcome. I don't get up here as much as I'd like, so thank you."

Her smile touched him in the way it always seemed to do.

JT had had a great time, too. She very rarely took time out to do something like this. Work usually ruled her life. Even now the agent in her wanted to stop and call the Owens kid to find out if he'd decided to let her represent him, but the woman inside didn't want anything to intrude. She and Reese had a wonderful day. Now, driving back across the Golden Gate, she felt as if she didn't have a care in the world. She could get used to this real quick. "Hungry?"

"Yeah."

By the teasing light in his eyes it was easy to see he wasn't necessarily talking about food. As if to prove her point, he said with half amusement, "Never been around a woman I wanted all day long."

Heat surged through her on the heels of that mahogany-voiced admission, and she had to pull in a deep breath to keep her hands steady on the steering wheel of the Lex. She hazarded a look his way and found him smiling. "Women probably melt in your mouth, don't they?"

"Those that I taste, yeah."

She jerked the car back into the lane. "Stop it!" she laughed.

"You asked," he tossed back with a shrug of his sculpted shoulders and the woman-melting smile. He was wearing a white tee and a pair of jeans.

"You are awful," she accused.

"That's not what you said last night or this morning."

"I think we should get some ribs," she said, pretending that his comments hadn't stroked her or made her nipples harden in shameless response. He was the most seductive man she'd ever met. Period.

"Ribs. Burgers. Whatever the lady wants."

What the lady wanted was another dose of his magic, but she was trying to fight it, and losing badly, of course. She called ahead and placed their orders.

In her kitchen, they took their dinners out of the two big white bags, then sat at the table on the patio to eat. The sun was setting in a red blaze of glory, and the sky was filled with floating calling gulls.

In the aftermath of their heated banter in the car, JT's awareness of Reese was as strong as it had ever been. His casual dress brought back the memories of their first meeting and the ride in his truck.

He asked, "Where do you see yourself five years from now?"

She pondered the question for a few moments. "Back home in Texas somewhere, chilling. Watching all the games as a fan and not as somebody counting assists or yards for the next contract."

"I thought you liked what you do?"

"I do, but I'm starting to burn out on all the hand-holding and arguing and worrying about injuries. Lord knows I don't need any more money." She looked over at him. "What about you? Where do you see yourself?"

He shrugged. "I don't know. Settled down. Maybe a wife and couple kids before I get too old to enjoy them. See if I can't make a marriage work this time."

"Do you see her? Your ex?"

He shook his head. "Not since the day she walked out with my autograph on the divorce papers. Put me off relationships for a long time."

"Ugly divorce?"

"Not particularly. She wanted out so I obliged her."

JT could only wonder about the true reason behind the breakup and how long ago it had been.

He asked, "You think about kids?"

"I do. I might like to do that somewhere down the road, before I get too old. My globe-trotting sister probably won't have any so somebody's gotta give my mother the grands she's been wanting. Right now my sister's rottweilers, Ruby and Ossie, are mama's granddogs, as she calls them."

"Granddogs? Named Ruby and Ossie?"

The humorous wonder in his voice made her smile. "Yep. They have a couple of sibs named Jessi and James."

"Named for you?"

She shook her head. "No. My sister's breeder was just trying to be cute."

They were staring again. The attraction between them was as solid as the breakers down on the beach yet as shimmery as fog.

He said to her, "This is something special."

She couldn't lie or pretend that she didn't know what he was talking about. "It is, so let's just enjoy. No commitments, no ties."

He leaned over and kissed her gently, "Whatever the lady wants . . . "

JT's entire body came alive. Like a jolt of caffeine or a dousing from a barrel of Gatorade, her senses were instantly engaged. The barbecue dinners were forgotten, the wine ignored. They were much hungrier for each other.

They wound up on her bed, and he treated her to a loving that was as slow as it was fiery. He made her feel worshipped, adored, hot. By the time he brought her to the third orgasm, she swore she'd never let him leave her side. It was as if they both knew it would be some time before they were together again this way, so the loving continued until dawn.

When JT awakened bleary-eyed around noon, she was in bed alone. She sat up listening for sounds of him, then saw the piece of paper on the pillow beside her. It read: *Called a cab. Didn't want to wake you. See you soon. Reese.*

She smiled, but inside, she felt bereft. She missed him already.

Meanwhile, on the flight back down to L.A., Reese decided that his memories of Jessi would have to hold him for the present. She'd said she didn't want a relationship, and he respected her honesty, or at least that's what he told himself. In reality, he didn't think she knew what she was up against. This thing happening between them seemed destined, fated, and if that were true, he'd been seeing her again, just like he'd written on the note, *soon.*

As it turned out, JT didn't have to call the Owens kid at all. When she walked into her office Monday morning, Keith and his parents, Ken and Patrice, were seated and waiting in the outer area with Carole. "I take it you all have good news for me?" she asked, smiling.

Keith nodded, and his mother said, "Yes, Ms. Blake, we do. Don't we, Ken?"

The father, Ken Owens, had played for USC back in the late seventies, and he still held some of the musculature that had made him such a great offensive lineman. In response to his wife's question, he nodded. "We'd like you to handle our son's career."

"Then let's go in my office and talk about it. Carole, hold my calls."

"Will do."

JT wanted to do cartwheels but instead calmly lead the family into her office and closed the door.

She spent the rest of the day with them. They talked about the team that had already drafted him in the first round and what he could expect in terms of salary and incentives. There were a multitude of papers to sign to make her representation of him legal. There were discussions about investment lawyers and tax issues, and she gave Mrs. Owens cards with the names of a few accounting firms many of her other clients used.

The father, Ken, asked pointedly, "You won't keep him out of camp?"

"No. We may have to take a bit less money but I want him to start out on the right foot. We'll make it up on the other end."

The parents and son nodded approvingly. By late afternoon most of the paperwork had been signed and JT asked Carole to send out a quick press release announcing Keith's decision to have her agency be his representative. She knew Bobby G3 would pitch a fit when he found out, but she couldn't be worried about him. With a promise to call them tomorrow to give them the date for the start of her negotiations with Keith's team, JT walked them back to their parked car, then waved good-bye as they drove off to return to their home in Bakersfield.

Back inside, she looked at Carole, let out a roof-raising scream of joy, then hurried to break open a bottle of champagne.

Later that evening, Bobby was at home looking over the paperwork surrounding the Chambers transfer to his agency and watching the sports news. When the anchor announced that Keith Owens had picked JT Blake's agency, he threw the glass of vodka in his hand angrily against the wall.

That bitch! Owens was supposed to be his! *Damn her!* He'd spent six weeks and cash he didn't have wining and dining the kid and his folks. While she'd bored Keith with talk of playbooks, minicamps, and tax brackets, he had introduced him to women, took him to parties and high-class strip joints so he could get a taste of the finer things in life. He was confident the contract settlement he'd promised to negotiate would be far and above what JT Blake planned to ask for, but it hadn't meant a thing. "Damn her!"

His world was starting to unravel like the threads on an old sweater. If any one of his clients were bright enough to call for an audit, the books presented would pass the test, but his real books showed him to be over $16 million short. His fee from Marquise had helped his bottom line, but the bitch had Quise's money invested in such a way that he couldn't access the accounts without Quise's signature and verbal okay. He'd been counting on the Owens money to make him solvent so he wouldn't have to continue cooking his books every quarter like he'd been doing for the past three years. The deal with Ham and the Wenzels would also have been a money-maker, but now that project was on hold too. "Damn that bitch!" he yelled again.

Although he pretended otherwise, the killing of

the old man had him looking over his shoulder. Just as Ham said, if push came to shove, the Wenzels would give him up faster than they could say "the Black guy did it!" But no way was he going to jail, not after the high life he'd been leading since getting his degrees. He was thirty-two, highly educated, and smart enough to know that even with his gang roots he'd be prey in prison, and he wasn't going down like that. He had to control his own fate by making sure the Wenzels kept their mouths shut and then finding a way to put JT Blake out of business. She had everything he needed, and he was going to have to take it, even if he had to get ugly.

JT spent the early morning hours at the gun range. Wearing ear protectors, a T-shirt, and a pair of jeans, she fired her first round. Her evenly balanced stance showed her training. The perfect score on the targets showed her skill. Both she and her sister Max were taught to shoot at an early age by their uncle Wheat, their late father's brother. He wanted them to be able to protect themselves, and taking lessons from him in both gun safety and maintenance was the only way their mother would let him buy her daughters the bb guns he wanted to give them for their birthdays.

JT walked to the next target and squeezed off another round. Unlike Max, a former cop and Marine, she had let her gun skills slide as she got older, and it had almost cost her her life when fullback Lamont Keel burst into her office and beat her so viciously she spent weeks in the hospital with three broken ribs, a busted clavicle, and so much facial bruising and swelling she couldn't look at herself in the mirror. As soon as she recovered, though, she did the paperwork for a CW permit, bought herself a 9mm, and went back to the range. She'd been a faithful attendee ever since.

Her gun practice done, she went home, showered, dressed, and drove to work. On the drive, she thought about Reese, and the memories of their weekend evoked a bittersweet smile. At this point in her life she knew that any relationship with him would bring drama, and even if the knots could be worked out, she wasn't sure she wanted a man. Yes, he was a lot of fun, and gave her such a good loving that just thinking about him made her nipples rise up and look for him. But she was accustomed to being her own woman. Unlike her married friends, she didn't have to compromise on the color of the bath towels, which car to purchase, or anything else. Her world was her own, and she enjoyed being the center of it. Granted, there were women who took on relationships for economic reasons, but there was nothing a man could buy her that she couldn't afford on her own. As for children, if she decided she wanted kids, there were sperm banks, and adoption was no longer off limits for singles like herself. So in reality, why did she need a man?

To have and to hold, the inner woman said.

She blew that off and focused her attention on the drive, but Reese's smile continued to shimmer in the far corners of her mind.

The first thing she did when she hit the office was

phone Pete Landers, the GM of the Oakland Earthquake, the team that had drafted Keith Owens. She didn't like Landers particularly well and he didn't like her that much either, but her Pro Bowl clients, linebackers D'Angelo Nelson and Jason Grant, played on the team too, so he had to deal with her and she with him.

The initial dollar amount Landers quoted her on the phone was below Keith's true value—not insultingly below, but low just the same. JT didn't fuss; negotiations had to start somewhere, so she politely told Landers she'd be in touch, ended the call, and opened her laptop to begin fashioning counterproposals. There'd be ample opportunity to yell at him later.

Reese spent the morning of his first day back from San Francisco talking to Captain Mendes about the Pennington investigation. There was nothing new. The traces of blood found in the Grizzlies conference room had been typed and matched. It was definitely Pennington's. The only prints found by the techs belonged to the Wenzels and their secretaries, which was to be expected since they all worked in the office.

"Have you had a chance to question, Bo Wenzel?" Reese asked Mendes as they sat in his office.

Mendes was brown-skinned and tall. The tailored suit belied the rumpled detective stereotype. "He's still out of town, according to his secretary. When he gets back, he's on the top of the list. What were you impressions of the son?"

Reese shrugged. "Seemed harmless enough. I didn't get any vibes one way or the other. Didn't strike me as a coke user, if that's your question, but as cops, we know not to assume."

"True, and my cop gut says somebody in that office knows something.

Reese agreed. "You think Big Bo is avoiding us?"

"Maybe. He's had some legal issues over the years."

Reese knew from the league files that Bo had wiggled out of a grand jury investigation over a decade ago. Word on the street back then had him guilty of selling fraudulent Texas oil stocks. Apparently a few of his high placed friends made the charges go away. Reese wished he knew the details about what happened to Gus Pennington in the conference room that night. Did he see something or do something that caused his demise? "I'm going to take a crack at Big Bo too when he gets back."

"Be my guest. I'm open to any and all suggestions. I don't want this to turn into a cold case. The victim's family deserves to know why he died and who killed him. My detectives are still canvassing, but I'm not happy with this no progress."

Reese wasn't either. "I'd like to talk to the Pennington family too, if that's okay."

Mendes nodded. "Family was pretty shook up when my detectives first interviewed them. Maybe they've remembered something that might help. Also, here's the paperwork for your state CW permit. You're legal now if you need to be."

Reese's weapons certification was up-to-date back

home, but he hadn't strapped on a holster in many years. He didn't see himself having to do that out here either, but it never hurt to be prepared. "Thanks." He stood and shook the captain's hand. "I'll let you know if anything turns up."

"I'll do the same."

Mendes nodded, and Reese left his office.

Eight

While Maze played on the CD, Reese let the GPS on his phone guide him to the Pennington home in Compton. He parked the car out front. The neighborhood was quiet, the houses well kept, as were the lawns. He'd called ahead to get Mrs. Pennington's permission to visit, and as he walked to the porch, a short round woman wearing jeans and an apron stepped out. "Mr. Anthony?"

"Yes, ma'am."

"Come on in."

Reese was led into the living room. The shades were drawn, keeping the room in shadows, and there was a silence in the air that seemed to settle into his bones. On the wall hung a collection of framed photos depicting her and a man he assumed was her late husband at various occasions and ages. "I'm sorry for your loss, Mrs. Pennington," he relayed genuinely as she gestured him to a seat on the rose-patterned couch.

"Thank you," she told him quietly as she sat in a matching armchair.

"I won't stay long. I just have a few questions, if you don't mind."

"Have the police found out anything?" she asked before he could begin.

He shook his head and watched pain rise in her eyes.

She said, "I already told the police everything I know. Gus went to work that night and the police called me that next morning saying he was dead."

"Did your husband have any altercations with the people who worked for him? Someone who might have done this?"

"No. Gus was good to his people and they were good to him They're as tore up about this as me and my grandson."

Reese's report said the young man was a college student. "Is your grandson at school now?"

"Yes. This is his junior year at UCLA. He wants to be a film director."

"How's he doing?"

"He's doing. Misses his grandfather a whole lot. He'd just given Gus one of those music player things for his birthday. Spent all night loading it up with Gus's kind of music. Said he wished the police had given it back."

Reese paused. "What do you mean?"

"It wasn't with the personal effects they brought over."

Reese pulled out his phone. "Excuse me a moment, Mrs. Pennington." His call to Mendes went right through. They talked for a moment then he ended the call. "The police didn't find a music player, Mrs.

Pennington," he said to her. "Are you sure he had it with him that night?"

"Positive. He was so excited. Said it made him feel like he was with the young crowd having one. Chris, my grandson, said the police probably kept it."

Reese hoped not. "I'll look into that for you."

"Thanks. You said on the phone that you work for the commissioner's office?"

"Yes. I used to be a cop back in Detroit too."

She studied him seriously for a moment. "Then you tell me, you think the police are doing all they can?"

Reese understood the question. "Yes, ma'am, I do. The captain's straight up and he's real frustrated that the investigation isn't moving faster."

She looked off into the distance for a few silent moments. "Sometimes the police don't care about us little folks."

"I know, but I promise you, the captain and I will do everything we can to get Mr. Pennington and your family justice."

Tears were sliding slowly down her cheeks now. She offered him a watery smile. "Thank you, Mr. Anthony."

Reese thought he'd imposed enough. Her grief was still fresh. He'd just wanted to meet her, relay his condolences, and try and get an idea of who the real Gus Pennington was. "Thank you for agreeing to talk to me." He took out a business card, wrote his cell number on it, then handed it to her. "If you need *anything*, you call, okay?"

Her graying head nodded.

"And I'll look into the missing player."

She walked him out to the porch.

As Reese drove away, he watched her in the mirror as she went back inside and closed the door. His heart was heavy. Having been a cop and seen a lot of death, he had special empathy for families suddenly losing a loved one to violence. According to the report, the Penningtons had been married over forty years. He shook his head sadly. He'd call her back later this evening to talk to the grandson. Hopefully the young man still had the receipts and serial numbers. Mendes might find it useful. Reese didn't own one of the devices, so he knew next to nothing about them. He called Bryce and put him on the speaker. "Hey, baby brother."

"What's up? How's La La land?"

"It's here. Talk to me about MP3 players."

"What do you want to know?"

"If I stole one, could I use it?"

"Depends on what kind it is. With some you'd need the real owner's password in order to download. Why, somebody steal one?"

"Possibly. If I call the manufacturer would they know if anyone tried to download on it?"

"Again, depends on the type, but probably. Everything else is tracked on the Net these days."

"Okay."

"How you coming on those Super Bowl tickets?"

Reese smiled. "Thanks for your help, Bryce. Be home in a few days."

After ending the call, his mind naturally settled on JT. He'd left her sleeping because he hadn't wanted to disturb her. Leaving while she slept also made for a less awkward good-bye. He wondered what she was doing. Did she think of him at all? He'd been away from her for only a day and admittedly found himself missing her bad. Because thinking about her was so distracting, he put it away for now and turned his mind to his next stop. His buddy the commissioner called last night to let him know that Marquise Chambers had yet to send the league any information on the anger management classes he'd agreed to take. Now that JT was no longer his agent, he had an appointment to meet the new representative, Bobby Garrett, and find out the cause of the delay.

The GPS guided him to Wilshire Boulevard. He parked and entered the tall fancy brick building where Garrett's fifth-floor office was housed.

The Garrett agency's suite wing was as fancy as the building: lots of glass, sleek modern furnishings, and plants. Hip hop music blasted the air. Framed black and white glossies of his athlete clients lined one wall. A heavily made-up woman was seated at a desk by the glass door. She looked him up and down approvingly. "May I help you?"

Accustomed to being looked over, Reese simply smiled. "Morning. Reese Anthony to see Mr. Garrett."

"He's in conference right now, but he should be done in a few minutes. Can I get you some coffee?"

Before he could respond, a young woman with gold-streaked hair stormed into the waiting area, shouting, "Have my money tomorrow, Bobby! Tomorrow!" Her dark brown face was contorted with anger as she strode past Reese and the receptionist, snatched open the glass doors and departed.

The receptionist shook her head, handed Reese a cup of coffee and explained quietly, "Babymama drama."

"Ah," Reese responded just as discreetly.

On the heels of the angry exit, a medium-size man in an expensive gray suit appeared. He didn't look happy, but upon seeing Reese, walked over and stuck out his hand. "Mr. Anthony?"

Reese stood and shook. "Yes. Thanks for seeing me."

"No problem. Come on in. Trina, hold my calls."

"Yes, Mr. Garrett."

Garrett took a seat behind a massive wood desk and motioned Reese to a chair. "Sorry about the disturbance. She's my ex. Wants more money."

Reese simply nodded.

"So, what brings the league to my humble abode?"

"Chambers. The anger management classes."

"What about them?"

"Where's he taking them and the name of the facilitator."

Garrett smiled faintly. "He's not taking them so there is no facilitator."

Reese studied him. "And his reasoning?"

"Now that I'm his rep, that agreement is null and void."

"Really?"

"I told him we'd revisit the issue and see if we can't get it resolved more to his satisfaction. His former agent has a history of not looking out for her clients' best interests, and this is just another example."

Reese found Garrett to be quite interesting. "This

is Ms. Blake you're referring to, I assume?" Reese asked, though he knew the answer.

Garrett nodded. "Used to work for her. I didn't agree with her capitulation tendencies, so I left her agency and formed my own."

"I see." What Reese also saw was probably the perp who'd sabotaged her car. This was getting even more intriguing. "Ms. Blake aside, your client doesn't get a do over on this. The commissioner's office isn't going to capitulate."

Garrett looked him up and down. "You're new on the job, I hear."

"Yes. And?"

"Nothing, just needed confirmation. I'd like to meet with Commissioner McNair at his earliest convenience."

Reese shook his head at the arrogance. "I don't think you understand. If Mr. Chambers decides to withdraw from the agreement, he'll be suspended for the remainder of the season, and will probably go to jail when Coach Walker files assault charges."

"We disagree."

"Then we'll leave it at that. You have twenty-four hours to fax the info on the anger classes to the league offices in New York. If you decide not to, consider your client out for the season." Reese set his cup on the edge of the desk and stood.

"You can't keep him from making a living, Anthony."

"No, I can't, but the league can. Thanks for your time, Garrett," he said, and walked out.

Back in his car, he asked himself if Garrett was really that arrogant. He knew the agent was posturing in an effort to impress his new client, but there was posturing and there was reality. He also hadn't liked hearing JT dissed. Unless she had a slew of disgruntled ex-employees, Garrett had to be the one who'd done her vehicle, and the cop in him wondered if the man had a record. His carriage, speech, and mannerisms said no, but the damage to JT's car said something else entirely, so he planned to check Garrett out. In the meantime, he hoped Garrett had a Plan B because if the coach choking incident went to court, Quise Chambers might as well be in hell wearing gasoline drawers. A jury would fry him. "Capitulation, my ass," he groused aloud, and headed the car back to his airport hotel room to file his report with McNair.

After Reese Anthony's exit, Bobby Garrett thought about what a shit morning he'd had so far. First Kelly with her ghetto self in his face about her checks still bouncing, and then the commissioner's man trying to tell him his business. All he needed to make his day even more whack was to have something go down with the Wenzels, so he got Matt on the phone.

Matt Wenzel's voice was cool. "What do you want, Garrett?"

"Just making sure you're holding up your end."

"I am. Anything else? I'm busy here."

"Yeah. You said a man from the commissioner's office stopped in to talk with you last week. What was his name?"

"Reese Anthony. Why?"

"He just left my office."

"What!"

"Calm down. We talked about a client. Had nothing to do with the other item."

Wenzel's sigh was audible, "Good. He's a former cop. He tell you that?"

Garrett stilled. "No."

"Vice cop. Detroit."

Bobby factored that into the mix, but decided he had more pressing issues at the moment. "We need to get together and talk about the next step."

"There isn't going to be a next step. Soon as my father gets back, we're out."

Bobby sat up angrily. "No, you're not. I've got too much riding on this, and so does Bo."

"Price is too high."

"How much do you love your wife?"

"What?"

"I asked how much do you love your wife? Would you want something to happen to her?"

There was silence on the connection for a moment, then Matt Wenzel asked in a voice cold with suspicion, "Are you threatening me, Garrett?"

"No. I just posed two simple questions."

"You come near my wife and I'll drop the ball so fast you won't know what hit you."

He wasn't moved. "You have your daddy call me when he gets back. I need to talk to the man of the house."

Outraged, Wenzel growled, "Did you hear me, Garrett?"

Bobby replied by ending the call. Matt was a weak link, and if the elder Wenzel didn't do something about it, he would.

Across town, Matt Wenzel sat fuming. His digital recorder had caught the whole conversation, but as he angrily shut off the recorder, the knowledge offered little solace. Would Garrett really harm his wife? He already knew the answer. Reaching over, he picked up the framed picture of Melissa sitting on his desk and for a few moments gazed down at her sunny smile. He had to get out, but how to do it and stay alive was now the question.

While munching on the turkey sub she was having for lunch, JT checked her e-mail and saw a message from Marquise Chambers. Wondering what he wanted, she clicked on it. The display on the monitor began to shimmy and sway. What appeared to be numerical code filled the screen. Line after line, faster and faster, moved up from bottom to the top until it seemed to be rolling at warp speed. Eyes wide, she yelled, "Carole!"

Carole was too busy yelling herself. Her screen was doing the same thing.

An hour later Misha, the young Nigerian woman who handled the agency's tech issues, looked up from JT's laptop and said, "You picked up a virus, JT. Pretty ugly one too. It managed to get past your firewalls and it ate everything, and I do mean everything. Files, address book, registry. Hope you've been backing up your stuff."

JT nodded.

Misha gave a sigh of relief. "Carole's virus was on her desktop and it's spread through the office network to your desktop too."

"So my laptop and all the computers in the office are dead."

"Yep. Probably two different versions of the same virus."

JT wasn't happy. "Where'd it come from?"

"Probably that e-mail you clicked on. As for Carole's?" She shrugged. "Hacked maybe?"

JT snatched up her phone and got Quise on the line. When he answered, she said through gritted teeth, "Hey Quise. Your e-mail wouldn't open. What did you want?"

"I didn't send you an e-mail."

"You sure?"

"Why the hell would I be sending you e-mail? I've moved on, remember?"

"Well somebody sent me an e-mail using your name and it fried my computer."

His laughter didn't endear him to her one bit. "Wasn't me, but if you find out who, tell them dinner's on me."

Angry, she ended the call. "He says it wasn't him."

Misha packed up her tools. "Sending viruses is a felony. What else was he going to say?"

"Let's suppose he's telling the truth. Is there a way to tell who did send it?"

"Stuff that deep is out of my league. You need a big brain for that. I know a guy. He's in Mexico right now, but he'll be back in a week."

JT shook her head. "I need this figured out asap because I don't want it happening again. Do you know anyone else?"

"Not anyone with those skills. You could call around to the colleges."

"That's an idea."

"In the meantime," Misha said, "I'll go online and order you some new equipment. Even if you find out who, none of these computers are going to work again."

JT sighed. "Okay."

After Misha left, JT said to Carole. "Good thing everything's backed up."

"I know. We'd've lost everything from contracts to phone numbers to Lord knows what else. People pick up viruses all the time. I just never thought we'd be one of them."

"Me either. We'll have Misha upgrade the firewalls and whatever else she needs to install to keep this from happening again."

"Sounds good."

"In the meantime, you may as well go home. With no computer, there's not much you can do. The answering machine can handle any calls."

"What are you going to do?"

She shrugged. "Go home too, I guess."

JT was rarely home during the day, and as she moved around her place it felt odd seeing sunlight streaming through the windows instead of the darkness that usually greeted her after a long day at the office. After going into her bedroom to remove her suit, she changed into a pair of shorts and a T-shirt, then sat on the couch and called her mother, Michele, in Texas. "Hey Mom."

"Hey, yourself," Michele answered. "How are you?"

They spent thirty minutes catching up. JT shook her head upon hearing about the young women at her mother's church throwing themselves at the new unmarried minister. "He is a cutie," her mother said. "And if I were thirty years younger I'd be acting just as silly, I suppose."

"Mom, we both know the only thing you'd get out of a marriage to a preacher is a divorce."

Her mother laughed. "You're probably right."

"Have you heard from Maxie?"

"She's in Michigan somewhere babysitting a big-brained scientist."

"Wonder if he does computers?"

"What?"

"Nothing, just some drama at work. How long has she been back in the States?"

"Not long. I heard from her a few weeks back, but not since."

Max did security work for the government and was likely to be anywhere in the world. JT and her mother worried constantly about her safety. Even though they knew she was highly trained and could take care of herself, they worried just the same. "Did Daddy court you, before you two got married?"

"Yes, he did in his own way—sent me flowers, took me to the movies. Why'd you ask? Somebody courting you?"

"I don't know. He says he wants to."

"Well now."

"Don't start buying clothes for your grandbabies yet," she laughed. "I told him no."

"Because?"

"Because its complicated, and I'm not even sure I want a man in my life."

"There is that. Men take up a lot of air."

"He's nice, though."

"Since I know you're not asking for advice, I'll just say keep me posted."

"If there's anything to post, I will."

They talked for a few more minutes, then said their good-byes. JT sat on the couch smiling like a daughter does when she loves her mama, then picked up her phone again.

When Reese's phone went off, he checked the number displayed on the caller ID, raised an eyebrow with surprise and answered, "Hey, Jessi. How are you?"

JT found it impossible to remain unmoved by his voice. "Fine. You?"

"Fine. How's the day going?"

"Rough. I need to pick your brain for a minute."

"Pick away."

She told him about her computer problem, then asked, "Do you think your brother knows anyone out here he could recommend? My techie says that kind of diagnosis is out of her sphere."

"I could ask him and call you back."

"Would you?"

"For dinner."

She paused, then smiled. "That's blackmail, my brother."

"And since I am a Black male . . . "

She rolled her eyes. "Okay, dinner."

"I miss you."

She fought through the dizziness that came over her all of a sudden. "I miss you too," she replied, even though she hadn't meant to.

"I'll call you back."

"Thanks." She closed the phone, and after a few moments of floating, yelled out into her silent condo, "JT! What are you doing!" In reality, she knew exactly what she was doing. She just didn't want to admit it.

True to his word, he called her back a short while later. "Bryce is going to fly out tomorrow and take a look at your computer."

"What?"

"Hey, we Anthony men are suckers for damsels in distress. What can I say?"

"Reese, I'm sure your brother is busy. All I wanted was a name."

"He doesn't have one, so he's coming himself."

She didn't believe this. "Is Pinky coming too?"

"No, he's in Montreal at a conference, and Pops is in Amsterdam touring a new plant we just opened. Otherwise he'd be on the plane too."

"What have you been telling them about me?"

"Only the truth. I swear."

"You are a mess. Do you know that?"

He laughed. "Bryce is going to fly into San Francisco. I told him I'd meet him at the airport."

"But you're in L.A."

"Now I am. At seven-thirty this evening, though, I'm hopping a flight to Frisco. Be there in less than an hour, according to the airlines. Can you meet me?"

Her heart pounded in the silence. "Yes."

He was impossible to miss, standing by the curb among all the other travelers waiting for friends, shuttles, and other modes of transportation to their destinations. Dressed in a black silk tee and black slacks, he looked devilishly handsome. She maneuvered the Lex to where he stood then popped the door locks so he could enter. He tossed his bag in the backseat then got in. She pulled out into the slow moving traffic and headed toward the streets. "How was the flight?" She hoped chitchat would help settle her nerves. It didn't.

"Not bad. Thanks for picking me up."

"No problem." She gave him a quick glance then swung her attention back to the road.

Reese sensed her nervousness, and rather than force a conversation, made himself comfortable against the plush leather seat and relaxed. "I booked rooms for Bryce and me at the Le Meridien. Do you know where it is?"

"Yep. Been there quite a few times for dinners and things. Pretty fancy place."

He soaked up the angular profile peeking out from behind the curtain of shoulder length brown hair. The long gold earrings graced her slender neck the way he wanted his kisses to do. She was casually dressed in a plain white shell and white pants, but from her gold-beaded, low-heeled mules, to the perfectly manicured nails, to the tasteful bling on her wrists, she looked like a million bucks. The girl would look good in a brown paper bag, he thought. Not a bad image, he mused further, then set the thoughts aside.

A red-uniformed valet met them at the hotel's grand entrance and opened her door.

Reese said to her, "Come on up. We'll order some dinner."

JT's eyes met his. The offer was innocent enough, and since she hadn't had dinner, she asked herself why not, all the while knowing there would be nothing innocent about the happenings that would probably take place later on.

The bellman didn't take them to the penthouse suite, but did take them to one luxurious and beautiful enough to be a cousin. The view was stellar, the furnishings lush and expensive. He spent a moment walking them through the amenities, like the flat screen TV, the wine rack, and the multihead shower and Jacuzzi tub, then graciously accepted his tip from Reese and departed. JT had stayed in five-star suites all over the country, but even she was impressed by the rich surroundings. "I knew they had killer rooms here but this is lethal." Stepping over to the windows, she looked out on the small stone porch. "You can see the Golden Gate."

Reese came up behind her and enjoyed the sight as well. "Should be great once it gets dark."

She turned and looked at him over her shoulder. "I'm not staying the night, Reese."

His eyes were dancing. "Whatever you say, Ms. Blake."

"I mean it."

"I'm sure you do."

Grinning, she turned back, and he moved in close and put his arms around her waist. The heat of their bodies merged and his lips against her hair felt so natural, it was as if he'd been holding her for a lifetime. "Missed you, woman, and it's only been a day."

She smiled. "Texas girls can be addictive."

"So I'm learning." He ran his hands languidly up and down her arms, liking the feel of her silky skin. Lips against her ear, he husked out, "Do Texas girls like to be kissed?"

She looked up and said heatedly, "You tell me."

To determine the truth, he kissed her, and in the slow, warm moments that followed, the answer became quite evident. She didn't remember turning in his arms, but as his lips burned down her throat, she realized she was facing him, her soft curves pressed against his hard chest. Their lower extremities were flush and the aroused state of his manhood was hard to ignore, so she didn't. Reaching down, she ran a palm slowly up and down. He sucked in a ragged breath, and she smiled at the power of her touch. "We Texas girls can be pretty fast sometimes too," she sultrily pointed out, her manicured hand still exploring, enticing.

Reese's eyes were closed. Her touch was so hot and sweet, he had trouble breathing. "You keep that up and you won't get dinner."

"No kidding. You Midwest men are pretty smart."

"Didn't know you were playful."

"I didn't either, till now."

Their eyes glittered with mutual desire. His mouth curved into a smile then descended on hers and kissed her with a possessive hunger that soon ruffled the silence with the sounds of heightened breathing. He filled his hands with her breasts and worked his thumbs expertly over the taut tips until she groaned her response. A beat later her top was raised, his head lowered, and his warm mouth moved over her bra-shrouded breasts. He drew the black demicups down and treated the dark nipples to his own brand of hello. She growled, he licked and slipped a hand between her thighs that lazily played and delighted. He thrilled at the heat his touch evoked. The warm passage and thoughts of the treasures it shrouded intensified his level of need. He wanted her now. He kissed his way back to her ear. "Either we find the bed or we do it right here."

JT didn't care where just so he didn't stop.

Nine

He didn't stop, and because he didn't they ended up on the large velour love seat with him seated and her riding his condom-shrouded manhood, her back to him. She'd never made love in such a scandalous position before but it allowed his magnificent hands to touch her everywhere she wanted to be touched while he brazenly guided her up and down. It didn't take long for the combined sensations to send her over the edge. She came with a hoarse cry. Her body stiffened and she lost herself in a pounding orgasm and in his equally pounding thrusts as he climaxed a beat later.

She came back to herself boneless and arched back against him. Her brain didn't want to move, and neither did she. She could feel the heat and dampness of her skin fused with his, and she reveled in the feel of his arms wrapped around her and holding her close. "Wow," she said softly, finally. She glanced up and met his soft smile. "You Midwest types are very talented."

"Given the right stimulation anything is possible."

She moved to make herself comfortable in his lap and he wrapped her in again. She placed her head on his bare shoulder. "What are we doing here, Reese?"

He kissed her brow. "I know what I'm doing," he told her softly. "The question is, what are you doing, Jessi?"

The eyes she met were serious. "I don't know. Can we keep taking it one day at a time while I try and figure it out?"

"Whatever the lady wants." Truthfully, Reese wanted her for his own to have and to hold from this day forward until the end of time, but he knew laying claim to her was not what she wanted to hear, at least not yet, so he gave her a soft pat on the butt. "Up. Let's go see what the shower looks like."

Back in L.A., dusk had settled and Matt Wenzel was driving home. As he turned into his driveway, Garrett's threats continued to weigh heavily, but he was determined to set them aside. Melissa had called him earlier and said she had a surprise. He had no idea what it was, but he was looking forward to whatever it might be. He didn't see her car, so he assumed she hadn't come home yet. He cut the engine and stepped out.

"Hey," a voice called.

Puzzled, he looked around and was startled by the sight of a man on the roof of his garage. He was dressed in all black and his face was covered by a ski mask.

"Who are you?"

"Not important. What is, though, is where's your wife?"

Matt froze.

"Knew that'd get your attention." The man chuckled softly. "Seriously, though, I'm just here to make sure you keep your word, Matty. In the scheme of things, a man's word is his bond. You know what I mean?"

Matt nodded like a puppet.

"Good. Here comes your old lady now."

Matt turned to the shine of the lights coming up the driveway and was so glad to see her he could have cried. He turned back to the roof. The visitor had vanished.

Melissa walked up and peered into his face with concern. "You look like you've seen a ghost. Are you okay?"

"Yeah, yeah. Not feeling good. Think I'm coming down with something."

"Well this ought to cheer you up. I had a doctor's appointment today. I'm pregnant, Matt. We're going to have a baby!"

His eyes widened, then he bent and vomited all over the driveway.

Reese and JT enjoyed a leisurely dinner, courtesy of the hotel's highly rated kitchen, then had some wine outside on the small stone patio under the stars. Her declaration that she wasn't spending the night had been all but forgotten. As they sat in the silence, sipping, she realized that she had no idea why she enjoyed being with him as much as she did. The fact that he made love to her as if she were the most precious thing in his world played a big part, but it was more than that. She'd never wanted to know everything there was to know about a man, but she did about Reese. "What do you like to do when it's raining outside?" she asked.

"Go fishing."

Surprised humor filled her voice. "What?"

"Go fishing. You asked, I answered."

"In the rain?"

"Best time to go. Every fisherman knows that."

JT smiled and sipped from her flute.

"You fish?" he asked.

"My daddy took us fishing with him once. Maxie and I were probably seven and eight. We got to fighting and tipped the boat. He never took us again."

"What were you fighting about?"

"I don't remember. Something dumb probably."

"My brothers and I had some dumb fights over the years. Why'd you ask about the rain?"

She shrugged. "Just wanting to know more about you."

The night hid his pleased smile. "My turn, then. What do you like to do when it rains?"

"If I'm not working, walk around the house in my pajamas, curl up with a good book. Play Madden on the PlayStation if D'Angelo or Jason stop by."

Reese stared. "Play Madden?"

"Yes, Reese. You have a problem with girls playing Madden?"

Filled with wonder, he sipped and shook his head with amusement. "No, ma'am. Not at all. You any good?"

"Is Texas big?"

He laughed softly. "Modest too, I see."

"Best thumbs in the West."

Reese's brothers were big Madden fans. "Bryce is the family champion. I've seen him reduce Pops and Jamal to tears with the whippings he gives out, and Pops used to *play* pro ball."

"Really? What team?"

"Chicago back in the late sixties, early seventies."

Something else she didn't know. "Well I'm telling you now, your brother will lose the family belt if he plays me."

"You take him down, and Pops, Jamal, and I will send you to Hawaii."

"Really?" She liked the sound of that. "You all must want him beat bad."

"Boy talks entirely too much yang when he wins. You beat him and Pops may propose."

"Let's not get carried away here, Mr. Anthony. Hawaii will be quite enough."

He grinned. "I already know the perfect place. We can go see Kilauea—"

"What do you mean, 'we'? I thought this was my trip."

"It is, but I own that perfect place and I'm the only one with a key."

Stunned, she turned and stared. "You have a house in Hawaii?"

"Yeah. I'm the VP of a multinational trucking consortium. You're not the only one on this porch with big bucks, Ms. Thang."

JT dropped back against her chair.

He chuckled. "What's the matter?"

"You are so not the truck driver you were pretending to be."

"I wasn't pretending, I am a trucker. I was just being careful. Wanted you to be dazzled by my charm first. That's all."

She never knew she could enjoy one man's company so much. "Then mission accomplished," she confessed softly. "I am dazzled."

"Good," he whispered while imagining the two of them sitting under the stars together until they reached Pops's age and beyond. He knew without question he'd still find her hot. Leaning over, he gave her a humid kiss that let her know how hot he found her at that moment, and she responded in kind. Slowly, one thing led to another. This time they made it to the bed.

The next morning the sun was just getting up when Reese awakened to the sound of the shower. He'd been in so many different hotel rooms in the past few weeks it took him a moment to place himself. Once he did, he turned over onto his back and enjoyed the sounds of her being near and the memories of a very steamy night. He felt as if he were making good progress storming the walls of Queen JT's well-guarded castle, but she was so complicated, who really knew? What he did know for certain was that she was the most uninhibited women he'd ever had the pleasure of pleasuring, and his manhood stirred at the remembered tastes and feel of her lean luscious loveliness.

She came out of the shower dressed in the white outfit she'd had on yesterday and with her hair pulled back. He was admittedly disappointed seeing her dressed. He'd planned on spending the morning making her purr, and it must have shown on his face.

"Morning. What's wrong?"

"You leaving?"

Her amused eyes met his. "It's a weekday, Mr. Anthony. Some of us have to go to work. I also need to stop by my place and change clothes."

"I thought you said you were dazzled."

"Dazzled doesn't mean crazy," she pointed out, stepping into her mules. "Besides, I'm assuming you'll come by the office when your brother gets in."

Reese nodded but he still wanted her back in bed with him. "His flight gets in at noon. You want to meet us for lunch?"

"Can't, got a prior commitment with my accountant, but we can get dinner."

"Okay. We'll swing by your office around three?"

"Sounds good."

He expected her to head out, but she remained where she was, her eyes holding his. His mouth curved up. "What's the matter?"

"I want to kiss you good-bye, but if I do, I know I'm going to wind up with my clothes off again, and I'll be late."

He laughed.

"It's not funny," she scolded, smiling.

"Suppose I promise not to touch you?"

"We both know you lie."

"There is that."

Walking over to the bed, she stood beside it for a moment, letting the sight of him bare-chested and leaning back against the headboard with the bedding covering his waist fill her eyes. The handsome chiseled face and his dark muscled guns made her want to lap him up like cream. Instead she bent and kissed him softly. "See you later."

She wound up on his lap. They lingered over the parting as lovers were wont to do, but she didn't lose her clothes and as a result got to the office on time.

Once there, however, there wasn't much real work she and Carole could do, being unplugged as they were, so Carole spent the morning tidying up the paper files while JT composed counterproposals for Keith Owens's contract using a pen and a yellow legal pad. She missed not being able to scan the Web for the morning's sports news, so she clicked on the TV, let the sports channel play in the background and prayed no one on her client list had done anything dumb last night.

She, on the other hand, had had a fabulous night, and the memories made her look up from the legal pad and ponder Mr. Reese the Fine Anthony. Goodness, his loving was amazing, she thought. A daily diet of that could make a woman want nothing more in life for the rest of her life. Her body was tender everywhere, but it was a good tender, and yes, she wanted more. She also wanted to know more about him. Did he really like to fish in the rain, or was he just messing with her? With Reese it was hard to tell. He was as multifaceted as he was handsome, and who knew he had money? He certainly didn't act like any high-powered men she'd met. Where they were often stiff and boring, Reese was silly. None of them would have been bowled over by seeing whales, or make her almost drive off the road with talk about women melting in their mouths. Reese was a mess, really. Handsome, charming, sexy. Nice too. That quality seemed to be rare in the eligible men in her sphere, but maybe he was that way because of where and how he'd been raised. She didn't know a thing about living in the Midwest, but if it produced men like him, she bet the women didn't mind the cold.

So the question remained: What did she want? The answer was obvious. She wanted Reese. But under what format and for how long? She'd been raised to take care of herself, and she did it well; too well, according to some of the men who'd called themselves having a relationship with her. She thought back on the financial planner from Sacramento who after a few months of being with her stomped off because she refused to let him oversee her portfolio. After him came a Seattle lawyer. He seemed nice enough at first, but one night over dinner declared that her being a sports agent wasn't something he wanted "his" woman to be doing. She dropped him quick. In hindsight, she realized neither man knew a thing about lovemaking. With them sex had been something she'd tolerated, but Reese showed her it could be a volatile red hot sport, and she did love her sports.

By eleven o'clock her eyes were starting to cross and her fingers were cramping from all the writing. Rolling her chair back from the desk, she stood to go freshen up for her noon appointment. As she walked by the television, the announcer on the sports channel said, "This just in. High-powered sports agent JT Blake is reportedly on her way to rehab."

She stopped and stared.

"According to sources, Ms. Blake is seeking help for an unspecified problem, leaving the fate of her agency and her clients up in the air. In other news . . . "

"What!"

She snapped open her phone, got the network on the line and barked to speak to whomever was in charge. While waiting for the secretary to put her through, JT yelled, "Carole! Call Francine!" Francine Ross was her lawyer. "Tell her to break out her lawsuit pearls. We're hunting bear!"

Twenty minutes later the bear was all but nailed to the wall. The network cut into the finals of a poker championship to retract the Blake story, and offered an on-air apology for running the unsubstantiated report. When she got done blistering them, she turned them over to Francine, who, from her Bel Air kitchen, demanded chapter and verse on where the story had come from and the identity of the so-called source. JT bowed out of the three-way call, knowing Francine had her back, and turned her attention to the phones ringing off the hook in Carole's part of the office. It seemed everyone in her part of sports-dom had seen the report. Never mind the network's retraction, all fifty of her clients called over the next two hours to find out what the hell was going on. In reality, she wished she knew.

In his Wilshire Boulevard office, a pleased Bobby Garrett clicked off the big screen and put down the remote. He could only imagine the surprise on Bitch Blake's face when she heard she was on her way to rehab. He laughed. It was just something he'd done to mess with her head. These opening salvos would lay the foundation for the more serious stuff he planned to throw at her later. He also imagined she'd be spending the rest of the day on the phone denying the story, and that was okay too. Pro athletes were notoriously skittish about their money and their futures. Rumors that their agent of choice might not be as mentally or physically fit as they believed could lead to some hard thinking on their part, even if the rumors were false. Too bad he wasn't in the Bay area so he could stop by the office and offer his support. He was out to get her, and by the time he finished his campaign, she would be begging someone to take over her business, and he'd be right there to scoop it up.

Trina's voice came over his intercom. "Mr. Wenzel here to see you, Mr. Garrett."

"Send him in."

Wearing his usual black cowboy boots and string tie, Big Bo Wenzel walked in. Bobby considered him too country to really trust, but he put up with his good old boy ways because he had to. "How was your trip?" he asked, gesturing the big man to a chair

"Relaxing. Nothing like a young blonde to take the edge off. So where are we on this deal?"

"Your son says you want out."

"My son's scared of his own damn shadow. What's your man saying?"

"He wants to wait another few days to make sure the police are done sniffing around then he'll be ready. Your people in place?"

"Ready to roll whenever I give the word."

"Good, but you need to talk to Matt. He's shaky. Real shaky."

"You leave Matt to me. He'll do what I tell him."

"I hope you're right because I'd hate to have to make his wife a widow."

"I said, he'll be fine," Big Bo replied with a soft edge to his voice. "You just handle your part and try not to kill anybody this time around."

Bobby's jaw tightened angrily.

Big Bo didn't seem to care. He stood and his cold blue eyes met Bobby's. "Let me know when your man is ready. You have yourself a good day." And he walked out.

Bo drove back to his office in El Segundo and thought about Garrett. He hadn't liked the agent from the beginning, and liked him even less now. If there was a way to cut him out so he could deal with his man Ham directly, the operation would probably run a whole hell of a lot smoother. An innocent man might or might not be dead either. The night it happened, he could tell by the look on Ham's face that Ham had been as stunned as he was when Garrett blew Pennington away. Ham had left immediately afterward, and Bo wished he'd been able to follow, but the murder had taken place on his home turf, so he had to clean up the mess.

Now, to hear Garrett threatening Matt? He and Matt rarely saw eye-to-eye, and no, they didn't like each other particularly much, but Matt was his son, and as far as Bo knew, his *only* son. That being the case, nobody was allowed to threaten his life but his daddy, and he didn't remember seeing Bobby Garrett's name anywhere on Matt's birth certificate. In spite of the silk suits, fancy speech, and fine manners, Garrett was still a bottom feeding shark from Compton, but he was a big ol' Mississippi swamp gator, and when you toss a shark in a tank with a gator, he thought, the gator always wins.

JT never made it to lunch with her accountant, so Carole went out and picked up burgers in a bag for them to eat. The phones were still ringing, JT's cell in particular as she continued to mop up the mess caused by that morning's erroneous report. Francine was still leaning on the network for a name.

"You know," Carole said, "it's been a pretty interesting last few days."

"No kidding. First the computers and now this. What else is going to happen?"

"I'm not sure, but two of the finest men I've ever seen in my life are crossing the street coming this way," she said, looking out of the window by her desk. "Oh, my goodness."

JT sidled over to take a look. She smiled. "You're getting your first look at Reese the Fine. The younger one has to be his brother Bryce." And they were two fine specimens. Their walks alone were enough to stop traffic.

"That smile on your face says you've been keeping something from me," Carole said, looking up into JT's beaming face.

"Who me?" she responded innocently. "Of course not. Well, maybe a little. Did I tell you the man makes love like a god?"

Carole's mouth dropped. "You already done the horizontal tango with him and you didn't tell me. What kind of friend are you?"

A laughing JT hurried back into her office so she wouldn't be caught staring. "I love you too."

"Liar!"

A few moments later there was a soft knock on her closed door. Seated behind her desk, she took a deep breath, composed herself, and called, "Come on in."

The sight of Reese in her doorway did something to her. She still didn't have a name for it, but it felt good. She stood. "Well, hello."

"Hey," Reese said. "This is my brother Bryce."

JT stepped over to him and stuck out her hand. "Nice to meet you, Bryce. I'm JT."

Bryce was a dreds-wearing, caramel-colored, thinner version of his older brother. "Wow," he whispered, looking her over with appreciative amazement in his light brown eyes. "Nice to meet you. Big brother said you were fine, but man."

Reese laughed. "Would you act like you have some home training," he said to his brother. "Let go of her hand."

JT grinned. "Welcome to L.A., Bryce."

Releasing her hand, he shook himself. "I'm sorry. If Pops were here, he'd've already popped me upside the head." Seemingly recovered, he said sincerely, "Pleased to meet you, Ms. Blake."

"Come on in and have a seat."

Reese was shooting daggers his brother's way, but when he remembered having the same reaction meeting JT for the first time on the 5, he chilled.

JT asked, "How was the flight?"

"Long, but I brought some work, so it wasn't too bad."

"I told Reese you didn't have to come all this way. I just needed you to point me to someone."

He shrugged. "It's no big deal. I needed a break. We Anthony men are suckers for a damsel in distress."

Hearing him use Reese's exact words on the subject caught her off guard.

Reese seemed to have read her mind. He looked pleased. "Told you."

"Okay. I give," she said with a smile.

Bryce looked confused, but before she could attempt an explanation, Carole's voice came over the intercom. "JT. Fran just called. The network said their source faxed over the story on our letterhead."

"Excuse me?"

"That's what they said. She said she'll call back after she smacks a few more people around."

"Thanks, Carole." She could see the concern on Reese's face, and since half the world already knew what was going on, there was no reason not to bring him up to speed. "According to the news this morning, I'm going into rehab for an undisclosed reason."

When confusion creased his features, she explained in more detail. When she finished, both brothers still looked confused.

Reese asked, "Why would somebody plant a rumor like that?"

"You tell me. Between that and the computer problems, I'm starting to wonder if someone's sticking pins in a voodoo doll."

Bryce asked, "You think the two events might be related?"

She shrugged. "I hadn't really thought about it like that, but who knows?"

Reese didn't know either, but the cop in him and the man inside who cared about her were not pleased to think they might be. "Who would have access to your letterhead?"

"Everybody I've ever dealt with. Players, team execs, the media, charity organizations."

"Ex-employees?"

She paused to study the seriousness in his eyes. "You met him." It was a statement. Not a question.

He nodded. "Like you said, he's a piece of work. You think he's capable of this?"

"The phony story, yes. The computers? No. He's

not that tech savvy, or at least he wasn't when he worked for me."

Bryce asked in a dead-on English accent, "You have brigands in your life, my lady?"

JT chuckled. She liked Bryce. "Yes, I do." She saw Reese drop his head.

Bryce added, "Then point me to the computer and a place where I can work. The sooner we banish the bad guys, the sooner big brother can get on with his campaign to win the hand of yon fair maiden."

Reese shook his head again. "And you wonder why I don't let you roll with me?"

Bryce grinned, and an amused JT went to clear space in the conference room so he could get to work on banishing the brigands.

After getting Bryce set up, she and Reese went back into her office. "I like your brother," she told him.

"He's an idiot."

"But a cute one."

"Thought you said I was the cute one."

"You are. He's little boy cute. You're man cute."

"I like that. Wait until I tell him. That'll kill the Einstein playa."

"Leave Bryce alone, at least until he finds out what's up with the virus." She brought the conversation back to an earlier subject. "So you met Mr. Bobby G3?"

"I did. And he told me Quise Chambers won't be taking the anger management class."

"Why not?"

"Because now that he's the agent, the agreement

you worked out is void. Wants to meet with Commissioner McNair to work out a settlement more in his client's favor."

"Said I sold Quise down the river, right?"

"Basically."

"He's the real idiot here. Lord."

"Yes, he is, because he's not getting another agreement." He studied her for a moment and couldn't help but see the stress on her face that hadn't been there when she left his lap that morning. "So how are you really doing with this?"

"I'm pissed. I've talked to every athlete on my list, trying to convince them that there's nothing wrong with me. Some wanted to know if they needed to get a new agent, was their money safe? I understand their concerns. I'd be asking the same questions if I were in their shoes, but it's aggravating to even have to deny some crap like this."

"Suppose it does turn out to be Garrett. What will you do?"

"Try and keep D'Angelo, Jason, and the rest of my children from kicking his gang-banging ass."

"Gang banging?"

"Don't let Bobby's high maintenance look fool you. He's straight out of Compton, and has the rap sheet to prove it."

"Really?"

She nodded. "On the outside he's an American success story—gang member makes good—but beneath the façade is a snake who'll eat his young to get to the top."

"So you fired him."

"With a smile."

Reese now had a better picture of Bobby Garrett, and it wasn't flattering. "Would he get physical?"

She shrugged. "I had a man put me in the hospital before, and I refuse to go down like that again."

"What do you mean?"

She told him the story about being beaten by Lamont Keel.

When she was done, Reese's blood was ice cold with fury. "He's dead, right?"

"Yes. Killed in prison by the babydaddy of another woman he'd beat half to death."

"Karma's a bitch."

"Amen, and I'm never going to be a victim again."

"You took self-defense classes?"

"Yep, and then I got a gun. This gun." She took it from its hiding place and showed him.

He looked surprised.

She thought back on that awful day. "I never felt so helpless. He threw me around in here like a rag doll." It seemed she could still feel the pain from his first punch. It was like her face exploded. "Never again." As she replaced the piece, she gave him a rundown on her injuries, how long she'd been hospitalized, and the surgeries she'd had to have to repair her face.

In spite of all his police training, Reese didn't know what to say. He'd never taken his anger out on a woman and had no respect for any man that did. "Damn, girl," he whispered emotionally.

"It's okay," she offered reassuringly, but added, "If Bobby Garrett wants to get physical, he's going to eat some lead first."

Reese ached inside that no one had been able to help her during the attack. "When was the last time you were on the gun range?"

"Few days ago. I'm a regular, believe me. Max and I were taught to shoot when we were teenagers, but as I got older I didn't keep up with my practice. I do now."

That made him feel better.

The empathy in his eye and voice touched JT's heart. She knew that he thought of himself as a twenty-first-century knight, and unlike Calvin Beard, the man she'd been dating at the time of that attack, Reese would have stayed by her side. When Calvin came to see her in the hospital, he took one look at her face, turned around and walked back out. A few days later he called and gave her a lame excuse about not liking hospitals, but she knew it was because she was no longer beautiful enough to be on his arm. She didn't mind that he never called again.

Bryce stuck his head in the door. "JT, can I talk to whoever does your tech support? Got a few questions."

"Sure, her name's Misha. Carole can run her down for you. You find anything yet?"

"Still doing the preliminaries. These things take time, so you two may as well go have dinner. I'm going to be a while."

They nodded, and he left to talk to Carole about Misha.

Ten

They had dinner at a small seafood café down on the wharf, and Reese spent the whole time watching her and wanting to protect her from ever being harmed again. It was a man thing, he supposed. An armed and determined JT Blake had to be a formidable adversary, yet he still wanted to protect her, hold her, and somehow banish the memories of that ugly day. Trauma of that magnitude wasn't something a person ever forgot. She'd live with the remnants the rest of her life, and he hated the man responsible.

After dinner they walked on the wharf and strolled among the house boats, restaurants, and small shops. He bought her an ice cream cone, which she found endearing. She even shared it with him, and she never shared her butter pecan. They moved on while the gulls soared overhead and the sun began to set out on the bay. Even though they'd been enjoying each other's company, she sensed the silence in him. "You've been awfully quiet."

"Feeling protective, I guess," he replied solemnly.

She stuck her arm in his and enjoyed the warmth of his body against hers. "You're a very special man, Reese Anthony."

"Somebody should have been there to help you."

"I know," she softly responded, "but no one was, and it can't be changed." She looked out over the water for a silent moment while the pain of that day played in her head. "I had nightmares for months." She looked up at him and said, "I'm better now."

He savored the honest face of the woman he knew he wanted by his side for the rest of his life. "If you ever, ever, need me. Call."

She nodded. "I will."

"Promise."

The serious tone and eyes made her heart pound. "I promise."

He lifted his hand and ran a dark finger down her soft cheek. "I will kill the next person who hurts you."

"Reese?"

"They'll have to go through me."

She realized he meant every word, and the intensity moved her. "I'm hoping there'll never be a next time."

Eyes still reflecting his mood, he nodded. "Me too."

This was a bonding moment, and she knew that from this day forward they'd be linked in a way both beautiful and new. The certainty thrilled and scared her at the same time. "When you court a woman, what should she expect?"

The question garnered a small smile. "That I'll buy her flowers and make love to her." He traced her cheek again. "That I'll take her to dinner and make love to her. That I'll take her to my place in Hawaii and make love to her on a black beach under the moon."

She fought off the dizziness brought on by his powerful gaze and the seductive tone of his mahogany voice. "Then a woman would be crazy to tell you no."

"You think so?"

"I do."

Pleased by what her words meant, he nodded. They sealed the unspoken agreement with a slow lingering kiss, then arm in arm continued their lazy stroll.

On the ride back to her office, Reese's phone went off. It was Mendes, calling to thank him for bringing Pennington's missing music player to the attention of the detectives, and to let him know that the grandson had called in the serial numbers.

Mendes added, "Thanks for that too. Mrs. Pennington doubted the grandson would have talked to us about it if you hadn't paid her a visit. The player is one of those new clip-ons all the kids are sporting. The grandson had the word 'Pops' engraved on the face of it."

Reese's pulse jumped. His father's face rose in his mind. "The serial number's gone out?"

"Yep, to pawnshops and secondhand stores all over the area. Let's hope we get lucky. Just wanted to bring you up to speed."

"I appreciate it."

"Thanks again, Lieutenant."

And he was gone.

JT looked Reese's way. She'd only heard his side of the conversation and it sounded innocent enough except for the serious tone of his voice and the "Lieutenant." But she didn't ask about it because one, it was rude and two, she was having enough trouble handling her own business without sticking her nose in somebody else's. If he wanted to talk about it, he would, and if not, that was fine too. "You think Bryce has found anything?" Not wanting to disturb him while he was working, they hadn't called.

"Never know. If there's something to find, the Brain will find it. Might take time, though."

Reese seemed worlds away, and she wondered if it was because of the phone call. "You okay?"

It took him a second or two to respond, then he said, "Yeah. Just thinking about my father."

"Is he all right?"

He nodded. "It's nothing. One of those moments." He had been pondering how he'd feel if his pops had been the one murdered. After meeting Mrs. Pennington, talking with the grandson, and now learning about the engraving, the case was morphing into something bordering on personal. When he looked over at JT, he saw the concern on her face. He couldn't talk to her about what he was working on, and even if he could, she had enough on her plate at the moment. "I'm okay."

"Just checking."

"Thanks."

Back at the office, Bryce and Misha had filled the conference room with enough electronic equipment to do a remake of *Frankenstein*. There were monitors and mother boards and odd-shaped gadgets that she'd never seen before. Both geeks were seated and pecking away on keyboards attached to screens filled with code sequences. Without looking up, Bryce asked, "You two have a good time?"

"We did," his brother answered. "How's it going?"

"Most interesting. This is not your average everyday virus. Not only is it beautifully constructed, it was made specifically for you, JT, and only you. It's coded directly to your computer. Amazing."

"So is this good news or bad?" she asked.

He looked up and the grin he gave her was so like Reese's, she thought it had to be genetic. "Good and bad. Good in the sense that I get to play with it, and bad in that it may take me longer than I expected. Be easier if I was home in my own lab."

Misha talked and typed. "Nothing stopping you from shipping it home."

He met her eyes, then shrugged. "Never thought about that. Want to come along?"

The look they shared was so loaded, JT wondered what the two of them had been doing beside turning the room into a *Frankenstein* set. She glanced Reese's way and saw him shaking his head with amusement.

Not wanting to be involved in whatever was happening between Mr. and Ms. Frankenstein, she said to them, "You two work it out. We'll be in my office."

Once there, she checked the messages left by Carole, then took a seat on the sofa next to Reese, leaned back and relaxed. "I think your brother's going to be surprised by Misha."

"How so?"

"Every athlete I've represented in the past three years has hit on her. Not one of them made it to first base, let alone home plate."

Reese smiled. "A challenge will be good for him. We Anthony men like that."

"Oh really?"

"Can't you tell?"

Their heads were turned toward each other. "Both of you are a mess," she told him.

"Genetic. Wait until you meet Pops and Jamal."

She thought she'd like that.

Bryce walked in. "Okay. We're going to pack everything up and ship it to the house."

JT asked, "Is Misha going?"

"No. Says she has to stay here and do the install on your new computers."

Both Reese and JT could see he wasn't happy.

JT said, "Yes she does. The equipment is supposed to arrive in the morning."

"I told her I'd fly her out later in the week and pay for her hotel, but she still said no."

"Misha is a very focused young woman. She takes her responsibilities very seriously. Can you work on the virus without her help?"

"Of course, but I like her company. I don't get to meet many women with a brain as fine as their face."

JT said, "Not many women tell you Anthony men no, do they?"

They answered in unison. "No."

JT had never met a family like theirs. "Humility is good for the soul." She stood. "What do you need from me?"

"Not a thing. Misha and I will get some shipping boxes in the morning. Once everything is packed, I'll fly home, sometime tomorrow afternoon or evening."

"Okay."

Bryce looked to his brother. "She and I are going to get some dinner and check out a couple clubs. I'll see you in the morning."

Reese nodded.

Bryce threw JT a wink then left them alone.

Reese asked, "So what do you want to do this evening?"

She shrugged. "I have to call my lawyer and see if she left anyone alive at the network, then I just want to sit and do nothing. It's been a long day."

"Your place or mine?"

He loved the sly little smile that played across her lips. "Yours, but I have to be back here early to help Misha hook up the equipment."

"Whatever you say." His eyes were working overtime.

"I mean it, Reese."

"Whatever you say."

She chuckled, then took out her phone and called her lawyer, Francine. While she talked and took notes, Reese went to the outer office and made a couple of calls of his own. He wanted to know all there was to know about Bobby Garrett, so he left one message with the commissioner's office and another with an old friend on the Detroit Police Department who owed him a favor.

It was almost 9 P.M. when Bobby Garrett pulled up in front of his ex-wife Kelly's house. Even in the dark his shiny new convertible stood out on the tired-looking streets. He was so glad he'd moved on with his life and no longer called this part of L.A. home. Being rich was a whole hell of a lot better than being poor.

He stepped up on the porch and knocked. A beat later the porch light went on and Kelly's mechanic husband David Young opened the door. Through the screen, he gave Bobby a long hard look, then called for Kelly. He didn't invite Bobby in, and Bobby didn't expect to be. The two didn't like each other at all. When Kelly came into view, she patted her husband's muscled arm reassuringly, then stepped outside. "You got my money?"

Bobby could see David still standing behind her. " I told you, in a few days. I came to see my son."

David snorted loud enough to be heard.

"Why?" she asked.

"Because. Haven't seen him in a while. You tell me to act like a father, so I'm here."

"It's a damn school night, Bobby."

"I'll bring him right back. I just want him to ride with me for a minute."

"Where?"

"No place in particular. Just ride. See how he's doing."

Kelly's skepticism was plain, but she finally relented. "Okay. Have him back here in one hour. One."

She stepped back inside. Bobby could see the hostility on David's face but he ignored it. Jalen appeared a few moments later. His hostility mirrored his stepfather's, but Bobby ignored it as well. "Hey, Jalen."

"Hey." He was much taller than Bobby had been at sixteen, but according to his grades, just as smart.

"Let's take a ride."

The boy stepped out of the door and followed Bobby to the car.

After the first few moments of silence, Jalen said, coolly, "Nice car."

"Got it a few months ago. I like it."

"What's it cost? Thirty-five, forty grand?"

"About that."

"Must be nice." Jalen didn't bother hiding his sarcasm.

Bobby glanced over at the sullen face looking out of the car window. The young blood had a lot of attitude. On one level, Bobby liked it, but on another, Jalen took after his mother. "Got something for you." He reached into the pocket of his suit coat and tossed the gift over.

Jalen examined the music player skeptically. "What's this for?"

"Just something to make up for not having seen you in a while."

"Why's it say Pops on it?"

"So you'll know who gave it to you."

"Thanks," he said a bit too disinterestedly for Bobby's taste and stuck it into his jeans. "I'm a junior this year. Are you going to help Mom and Dad pay for my college?"

Bobby had expected him to be ecstatic over the gift, not grill him about money. "Sure, yeah."

Jalen turned away. "I need to get back. I have a big trig test tomorrow."

"Okay." A tight-lipped Bobby drove him back.

On the way to the Valley and his home, Bobby thought about his son. Having never had a father of his own, he admittedly didn't know a lot about the role. He'd grown up in a single parent household with a mother who'd gotten pregnant with him at the tender age of fourteen. She died in a house fire during one of his early stints in juvie. He'd been in college before he ran into people who had real fathers in their lives. For them, growing up without their dads was unimaginable. They called on their fathers for advice, when they were in crisis, or just to say hello. He knew nothing about that, and back then, watching them interact with their dads was like watching one of those old fifties sitcoms he and his homeys used to laugh at while downing forties. No, he knew nothing about being there for Jalen, and in reality he didn't have the time, he thought now, and never had. He'd done okay without having a father in his life. Jalen would too.

Setting aside those thoughts, Bobby put in a call to

Ham. Preseason games would begin on Sunday. With the L.A. Grizzlies opening up on the road against Oakland, he wanted to make sure everything was tight. He got Ham's voice mail. "Call me back," he said and ended the call.

His cut for the first delivery would be fifty grand. Not a lot, but enough to pay down his more pressing bills like the mortgage, car note, and his secretary Katrina's salary. In order to maintain his lifestyle and keep up the pricey front at his office, he'd skimmed so much money off the tops of his clients' accounts he couldn't afford to take another dime without raising flags. And not getting the contract with Owens had been a major setback. But Bitch Blake was getting hers. In the meantime, he planned to duck the people that he owed, and ignore the others with their hands out, like Kelly and the car dealership that held his lease. When he got paid, they'd get paid.

Before going to Reese's hotel, they swung by JT's place so she could pick up some clothes for work the next day. She also grabbed her mail, and was in her kitchen going through the stack when an envelope from one of the financial institutions she dealt with caught her eye. Opening it, she read:

> *Dear Bitch! Get out town. Lamont Keel let*
> *you live. I won't.*

Reese walked in from the patio, and seeing her blanched face, hurried to her side. "What's wrong?"

She handed him the letter and then sank to the floor. "Lord," she whispered. She could feel herself shaking.

Reese read the note. A second later he was on the phone with Mendes, who turned him over to the FBI.

The local office sent two agents to view the note and to talk with JT. After she gave them the background on the Lamont Keel incident, she told them about the virus and what Bryce had said about it being targeted specifically at her. In response to the agents' questions about who the perp might be, she shrugged. "The only person on my list is Bobby Garrett," she said, then told them about the history between them, the vandalism to her car and the running feud he seemed intent on waging. "As a lawyer, I know it's all circumstantial, but he's the only one giving me any kind of grief."

One agent, a redheaded woman named Brenda Tate, raised her green eyes from the notes she was taking and agreed. "It is circumstantial, but if he's the one responsible for this letter, he's crossed the line." She then asked about any other people who might also have issues with JT, like old neighbors, former or present clients, old boyfriends. JT answered as best she could.

When Tate seemed satisfied that she had enough information, she and her male partner stood. "Okay, we'll be in touch. In the meantime, you be careful. If anything else happens, or Mr. Anthony's brother gets a line on that virus, call."

"I will."

JT walked them out, then looked over at Reese. His face was set like stone. "Why don't you leave town for a few days while the Bureau works the case?"

"No." Now that the initial shock had worn off, she was angry.

"Jessi—"

"No. I'm not going to be intimidated, at least not yet, and besides, I can't leave. The preseason starts this weekend, and if I don't show up, my people might start believing I really am in rehab."

"What if whoever this is makes a move?"

"I have my nine-millimeter, the FBI, and I have you."

He smiled. "Yes, you do."

"I'm not dumb enough not to be scared, Reese, but I want to know who's threatening me. If I leave town, I might never know."

That made sense to him, but the urge to wrap her in cotton and keep her safe in his pocket was strong. "Okay, but you need to let those mountain men of yours know what's going on so they can have your back too."

That was already on her list of things to do in the morning. She'd call D'Angelo and Jason first thing. They'd pass the word to the others. She yawned and stretched. It had become an even longer day.

"So do you want to go to the hotel or stay here?"

She didn't know, but she did know she didn't want to be alone. "You choose."

"Hotel. Better security."

"Once a cop, always a cop."

"I don't want anything to happen to you, Jessi."

"And neither do I." She lived in a gated community. No one could enter without the proper codes, and there was a valet on duty 24/7, but there were no armed guards patrolling the place. The idea that she might be at risk in her own home was a reality. "Let me throw some stuff in a bag and we'll go."

Reese nodded and with concerned eyes watched her head to her bedroom.

He was angry too. The sight of her ashen face as she'd handed him the letter would stay with him a long time. He never wanted to see her that way again. He also wanted to get his hands on the perp. Could Garrett be behind it? In reality, it could be anyone. But who? And why was the big question. Was the perp just trying to scare her, or intending to go through with the threat? There were too many unknowns for his liking.

She returned with a fancy designer satchel in hand. "When are you flying back to L.A.?"

"Supposedly tomorrow evening."

His reply seemed to catch her off guard. "Okay. Are you taking the shuttle to the airport or do you need a ride?"

Leaving her was the last thing he wanted to discuss. "I don't know. I may stick around for a few more days."

"No. You go on back to L.A. and do your job. I'll be fine."

He walked over and lifted her chin so he could

study her mesmerizing face. "You trying to get rid of me?"

She smiled. "Of course."

He kissed her for a long moment, then held her tight against his heart. "I don't want anything to happen to you, and if I'm not here, I'm going to worry."

He leaned back so he could see her eyes.

"My great-great-grandfather was a Texas Ranger. His brother was one of the baddest outlaws in the West. I have good genes. I'll be okay."

He grinned and eased her back into his embrace. "If you put it that way."

There was silence for a moment as they savored each other. She whispered, "You're a great knight, Reese."

He kissed the top of her head. "Just trying to protect and serve."

They went back to the hotel and made love with a passionate possessiveness that further strengthened their bond, then they slept.

JT told Carole about the threatening letter first thing the next morning, and her secretary and friend was appalled. "Did you call the police?"

"And the FBI. They took the letter and said they'd be in touch."

The worry on Carole's face was plain. "Lord, JT. What next?"

"No idea. Let's just hope they catch whoever it is."

"Amen. In the meantime, we should turn the light back on."

JT nodded. The red light had been installed inside JT's office above the door after the Lamont Keel incident. The switch was located on a small wireless box on Carole's desk. If there was trouble, Carole would hit the switch and the light would blink in JT's office, hopefully giving her time to be armed and ready before the trouble burst in. The light hadn't been needed since its installation, but it was now.

The new computer equipment was delivered, and as JT and Carole began unpacking it, Misha arrived, accompanied by Bryce carrying an armload of folded packing boxes. The two techies said their good mornings then went into the conference room to get the old computer and its parts boxed up. When they were done, they began configuring and setting up the new stuff.

After touching base with her lawyer about the previous night's scary letter, and getting an update on Francine's gelding of the sports network's execs, JT spent the rest of the morning helping Misha and Bryce. The phones kept ringing, however. She'd called D'Angelo and Jason earlier to tell them about the mailed threat, and as a result every athlete she knew, client or not, had called to pledge their support. Some offered to camp outside her office, others volunteered their services as personal bodyguards. All of them wanted the perp's name so they could grind the person into salt. Although she had no name to give, it made her feel good knowing they were willing to be her linemen in this ugly game she seemed to be playing.

* * *

Before taking a cab to JT's office, Reese had spent the morning at the hotel's business center waiting on faxes from various people like Mendes, Commissioner McNair, and his police contacts in Detroit. All the faxes had to do with Garrett. Now, after reading Garrett's rap sheet and reviewing the names of the athletes he represented, he had an even truer portrait of the man, and it was getting uglier and uglier.

As JT had noted, on paper Garrett was an American success story. From gang member to the elite halls of one of the finest schools in the country, he seemingly had the world by the tail, but his client list had thinned in the last two years. His biggest cash cow, former Heisman Trophy winner Jermaine Crane, was serving a fifteen-year sentence for ties to illegal gambling and organized crime, and his big money contract had been voided. Reese wondered how much that had affected Garrett's cash flow. With only six athletes on his roster, and none of them upper echelon, things had to be tight. He knew from talking to Jessi that she and Garrett had been after Keith Owens and that she was now representing the phenom. Had Garrett been angry enough about that to do something as stupid as threatening her life? More questions he didn't have the answers to. He hoped she'd let her clients in on the letter, because the only way he'd sleep at night was if he knew that she had a bunch of gladiators standing between her and danger if he wasn't around.

He entered the office and found it piled high with

boxes. He gave the smiling secretary a smile of his own. "Morning, Carole. Is the boss lady in?" He glanced over at Jessi's closed office door.

"Yep, she's talking to some clients at the moment. She said you were to go on in when you arrived."

Reese was surprised by that. "Okay." He wondered who she was meeting with.

Bryce came out of the back carrying a box. Misha was behind him.

Reese asked, "Hey, you all set to fly home?"

Bryce set the box on the floor. "Yeah. Misha's going to take me to the airport. I'll call you tonight."

"Thanks for your help."

"No problem. JT's great. Probably make an even greater sister-in-law."

Misha grinned, as did Carole.

Reese knew better than to touch that. Instead, he said, "Safe flight," then headed to JT's office.

He knocked, and when she called for him to come in, he did. But when he opened the door, the sight of what had to be twenty-five men big enough to be sons of Atlas packed in the room like a bunch of sardines froze him where he stood. Not one of them looked happy.

"Hey, babe," JT said.

Her smile seemed to free his feet. He closed the door behind him.

"Everybody, this is Reese Anthony," she said. "Take a good look because you're going to see him with me for quite some time, I hope."

Grinning inside, he met the hostile stares of the men. "Nice meeting you."

A few guarded mumbles were offered by some of them in response, and then came, "Doesn't he work for Commissioner McNair?"

She replied easily, "Yes, he does."

Somebody else cracked, "You sleeping with the enemy now, Lady Blake?"

She didn't hesitate. "Yep, but anybody dumb enough to think that'll make me sell them down the river should get a new agent right now." She looked around the room. "Anybody?"

No one moved.

"Good. Reese, these are my clients and my friends. I called them and told them about the letter."

Reese nodded, but inside he was still reeling from the declaration she'd made to them about their relationship. He'd had no idea she was prepared to put her agency on the line for him. "Anything from the Bureau?" he asked.

"No. Reese is a former Detroit cop, everybody. Just so you'll know."

He saw the demeanor of some of the men change. A few stopped shooting daggers his way and others seemed to be checking him out in a new light. The big linebacker D'Angelo Nelson was one of them. He gave Reese an almost imperceptible nod and Reese replied in kind. His buddy, Jason Grant, the blond-haired Viking, did the same, and Reese acknowledged him too. He wasn't naive enough to believe they'd all come around, but he didn't need their approval, and JT had made that clear.

D'Angelo said, "Now that we're all one happy fam-

ily, let's get back to business. I say we throw Garrett
off the Golden Gate and see if he can swim."

"You think he's the one behind the letter?" Reese
asked.

"Of course. Everybody knows he's got it in for
Lady B. Has for years."

There were rumbles of agreement.

"Can we prove it, though?" she asked. "If I was
Garrett's lawyer—and thank God I'm not—I'd argue
circumstantial evidence, because that's all there is."

Reese agreed. There was nothing tangible tying
Garrett to anything other than being an arrogant
jerk, and there were no laws on the books against
that.

D'Angelo countered fiercely, "I still say we toss his
ass off the Gate."

His companions roared with approval.

Eleven

In the end they all agreed that the only sensible and legal course of action was to let the police handle the matter. Her gladiators weren't pleased with the decision, but they knew the spine twisting and head bashing they wanted to inflict would only bring them up on charges.

They were getting to ready to leave when Jason looked her way. "Make sure you check in with somebody three times a day."

"Three?" she protested loudly.

"Be glad it's not every hour on the hour," a big man Reese recognized as pro wrestler Death 2 U told her. "We're worried about you, Lady B. Since you won't let anybody crash at your house, except my man over there—" he gestured brusquely toward Reese.

"Don't hate," D'Angelo cracked.

Death dropped his head. Male laughter filled the room. Everyone knew he'd been hopelessly in love with JT since the day he signed with her. He regained his composure and stated, "My point is, if we can't be with you 24/7, we need to know you're okay."

She nodded. "Point taken. I'm not going to do it three times a day, that's out, but I will check in with somebody a couple times a day until this is over."

"By phone, so we can hear your voice," prompted all-pro defensive lineman Big Daddy McCoy. At six-foot-eight and 325, he was the most imposing figure in the room. "Anybody can send an e-mail claiming to be you."

JT didn't like all this cotton they wanted to wrap her in, but recognized that their hearts were in the right place, and she had no problem with that. She also knew that if she tried to argue, they most definitely would move in with her, Reese or no Reese. "Okay, I'll check in by phone. I promise."

That pleased them.

Now that they were satisfied, she was too, and so took a moment to give each of them a kiss on the cheek for their TLC. As she'd told Reese, the big men were more than clients, they were her friends. "Thanks, you all."

They nodded, then D'Angelo led the troops out.

Once JT and Reese were alone, he told her, "I thought I was going to get eaten when I first walked in here."

"They only eat people on Sunday, so you were safe."

They shared a smile. He added, "Liked the way you stood up for me."

"It's the truth. I hope you do stick around." And

she did. For how long, she didn't know, but she was enjoying taking it day by day.

He walked over and gently locked his arms around her waist. He thought she looked good in the black suit she was wearing. "Whatever the lady wants."

The kiss that followed was soft, potent. When it was over they embraced silently while the unspoken words flowed. He placed a kiss on her forehead above the perfectly arched brows and stepped back. "I have time to grab a quick lunch, then head to the airport. Can you go?"

"Yes."

On the drive to the airport after lunch, JT was already missing him, and he hadn't even gotten out of the car. The threatening letter she'd received flitted across her mind, but she pushed it back down. "When do you think you'll be able to visit again?"

"Saturday afternoon. The commissioner is flying in for Sunday's opening game, and I'm part of the entourage."

She liked the sound of that. "I'll be there too. I'm sitting in the owner's box."

"Really?"

"I've a couple of clients on his team with contract issues, and Kyle's trying to sweeten me up so I'll stop beating up on his GM, Pete Landers."

"Kyle?" he asked, looking her way.

"Kyle Miller. The owner of the Oakland Earthquake?"

Reese knew Miller's name from newspaper articles and from the orientation files Tay McNair had faxed him when he first hired on. "Fifty years old. Owner and CEO of the largest minority software firm in the world."

"That's him."

"I don't remember hearing about a Mrs. Miller."

"Because there isn't one." She laughed and glanced his way as she switched lanes to head into the airport complex. "You aren't one of those crazy jealous men, are you?"

He shrugged. "Never had anybody to be crazy jealous about."

Her eyes reflected her mirth. "Kyle has tried to hit on me, but he's not my type. He's one of those 'want to put a sister in a cage' kind of brothers, and I wasn't doing that."

"Good to know."

She chuckled and merged into the traffic.

A few minutes later she slowed the Lex to a stop in front of his terminal. Because of the security edicts, they knew the airport police wouldn't let her idle longer than a few minutes at the curb, so he leaned over and gave her a kiss good-bye. "I'll call you later. Keep yourself safe."

"I will."

She watched him grab his bags out of the trunk. He waved and she waved back, really missing him now. The policeman whistled her to get a move on, so she took one last look at Reese going into the terminal and drove off.

She was on the highway when her phone rang. It was Reese. "I thought you said later," she said, laughing.

Who knew one man could bring so much delight?

"It is later."

While she drove to the office they talked about everything and nothing, like two teenagers playing at love, until he boarded the plane.

The rest of the week was uneventful; no drama in the mail, with the newly installed computers, or with any more rumors about rehab visits. The FBI called to check on her and admitted it might be weeks before the letter came back from the lab. She was disappointed, but they promised to keep her posted. Neither she nor Misha heard from Bryce, but they assumed he'd call when he had something.

She missed Reese, though, and talked to him as often as their schedules allowed, which was mostly after dark. As promised, she checked in regularly with Jason and D'Angelo, but at the end of the day it was Reese's rich mahogany voice that sent her off to sleep.

Reese was driving in an area of L.A. that could have been any urban neighborhood in the country. The sidewalks were filled with young bloods hanging out, kids on their way home from school, men and women standing at bus stops waiting to go to or from work. Beauty parlors and nail shops shared the blocks with dollar stores, heavily armored dry cleaners, and abandoned buildings that butted next to small convenience stores with signs out front reading, WE CASH CHECKS.

As Frankie Beverly sang about a "Southern Girl," he parked his nondescript rental car in front of the small yellow building that sported the address he'd been looking for and got out. This would be his fifteenth pawnshop of the day. He knew how stretched thin the local police were, so with Mendes's blessing he was canvassing on his own.

The clerk behind the desk was White and wearing a tattered red T-shirt so faded and old you could barely read the slogan: save the whales. He was big enough to be one of JT's clients. Intricately rendered tattoos flowed up his massive arms like living things, swirling around his throat, totally obscuring his skin. The clerk checked him out with wary suspicion in his brown eyes, then asked, "What can I do for you?"

"I'm looking for one of these." Reese showed him the ad he'd downloaded with the picture of the brand of music player given to Gus Pennington by his grandson, Chris.

The clerk glanced at it, then back up at Reese. "You looking to buy one or looking for something specific?"

"Specific. The word 'Pops' is engraved on the front."

"Belong to you?"

"No. My father. It was stolen off his body at the funeral home."

The big man stared. "Damn."

Reese nodded. "One of my nephews is a crackhead."

"Gotcha. Well, nothing like that's come in. You got a number just in case it does? Stealing from the dead is whack."

He slid one of the store's flyers across the counter, and Reese put his cell number on it, saying, "We promised the old man we'd bury it with him so he could take his jazz to heaven, but evidently my nephew had other plans."

"That's a shame."

"Yeah, tell me about it." Reese slid the flyer back. "Appreciate the help."

"Any time."

Reese stepped out into the sunshine and drove to the next address on his list.

By the time he walked into his hotel room at the L.A. airport, he was dog tired. Dropping down onto the sofa, he rolled his head back and just sat. After visiting what seemed like a hundred pawnshops and resale stores, he was no closer to the whereabouts of Pennington's player than when he first set out that morning. In reality, the pawnshops were a shot in the dark. A device as hot as the digital clip music player was more likely to be kept by someone than pawned, but sometimes shots in the dark paid off. Not today.

He walked over to the small fridge and pulled out a cold can of cola. Neither he nor Mendes had been able to get an audience yet with the Grizzlies owner, Big Bo Wenzel. According to his office, he was still out of town. Rather than believe the man was avoiding the interview, Reese decided to give him the benefit of the doubt. Wenzel would be at the game on

Sunday, and so would he. Being part of the commissioner's crew guaranteed that. He wouldn't be able
to quiz Wenzel about the Pennington case, of course,
but he would at least get a good look at him, and for
a cop, sometimes that had to be enough.

He picked up the room phone and ordered dinner from the room service menu. While waiting, he
thought about JT. He wanted to call her and hear her
voice, but she was doing her thing in New York City
at a basketball game and he felt he had no right to
disturb her. One of her former clients was having his
jersey retired during halftime, and she'd flown out to
participate in the celebration.

Although it had only been three days since he'd
seen her last, it seemed like months. The sheer depth
of the feelings he had for her scared him to death.
A man was never supposed to get so taken with a
woman that he wanted to see her every second of
every day, and he definitely wasn't supposed to tell
her. He hadn't, but he sensed she knew. Back in the
day, he'd considered himself seriously in love with his
ex, Suzanne, but in hindsight? Puppy love. Play love.
None of what he felt during his marriage came even
close to his need to have the Lady Blake in his life.

He was eating dinner when Bryce called. "Hey,
baby brother. What's up?"

"You, man. How's your lady?"

"Good."

They talked about what was happening at home.
Jamal and Pops were back from their world travels
and were getting Pops's garden ready for spring.

"I called to tell you that somebody put a hit on JT."

Reese froze. "A hit! When? Give me a name!"

Bryce went silent for a moment, as if hearing himself, then said, "Wait. Back up. Not a gun hit. I'm talking about a virus hit on her computer."

Reese let out a long sigh of relief. "You're killing me here, Brain."

"Sorry."

"Okay, start over."

"I found the info in the Underworld."

"Where?"

"Underworld. It's what we call the underbelly of the Internet."

"The Internet has an underbelly?"

"Yeah, deep down the rabbit hole. Lots of action down there too. Boards full of messages for hacking bounties on unreleased software, patches, corporate data bases. Somebody aboveground contacted one of the trolls and he took the job."

"What the hell is a troll?"

"An underbelly dweller."

Reese shook his head. "I feel like I'm in Middle Earth, but go ahead."

"Trolls make their living hacking, and some of their brains make mine look like yours."

"Excuse me?"

"Just joking," he laughed.

Reese wasn't. "Go on."

"Anyway to make a long story short—"

"Thank God."

"Somebody put out a call for a hit, and a kid in Seattle answered. I talked to him. He said the hit was posted on one of the boards. The customer sent him two hundred dollars up front and another two hundred when the job was done."

"Does he know the person's name?"

"Of course not. Nobody has a real name down there."

"Silly me. So how do we find this customer?"

"We don't. The kid never asked for a name, and the payments were cash. Snail mail. Unmarked envelope."

"You think he's telling the truth about not knowing more?"

"I do. Freaked him out that I found him. I could tell he was scared."

"So JT lost all of her data for a lousy four hundred dollars? How old is this kid?"

"Fifteen, and that's a fortune when you're that age."

Reese sighed his frustration. "Okay. You did good, Brain."

"Thanks. You're not going to tell the FBI about him, are you? My boys and I are trying to seduce this kid over to the light."

"No, Skywalker. He's safe from the emperor's Death Star. At least for now."

"Good."

After they ended the call, Reese went back to his now cold dinner, but his mind was on the threats hanging over JT.

* * *

JT loved the perks of her job, and being able to sit in the owner's box with its plush seats, perfectly chilled champagne, and fancy appetizers was one of the best. Better still was the car Kyle Miller had sent to bring her to the stadium. Not having to deal with the traffic had been a blessing. This was the first game of the World League Football preseason. The regular season ran from mid-spring to late summer. During the first two years of the new league's existence, it tried to compete with the old league by playing in the fall, but it took such a financial beating that four of the original ten teams folded. To save the rest of the fledgling franchises, the games were switched to the spring, with good results for both the owners and players because the upstart WLF teams played old school football, and fans like JT loved it.

"More champagne, JT?"

She looked up at her host and smiled. "No, Kyle, I'm fine."

"Sure?"

"Positive."

As he walked back up the stair to the top of the suite where the sumptuous buffet was spread out, she had to admit that he wasn't a bad looking fifty-year-old man. He had polish, a dry sense of humor, and dressed very well, but he wore a rug on his head that looked like it had been purchased in a back alley at night. How on earth he could believe anyone would think it real never ceased to amaze her because he wore it every time she saw him. He'd even worn it in a photo that ran on the cover of *Forbes* last winter. She smiled to herself and sipped.

"Ah, here comes the commissioner now."

JT slowly set down her flute, took a deep breath and turned around. Reese was standing next to the commissioner but his eyes were on her. Hers were on his too, and then, as if they both remembered where they were and who they couldn't be, at least here, they caught themselves. Kyle led the commissioner's party down to the seats. "Have you met JT Blake, Commissioner?"

She stood and Taylor McNair gave her a kind smile. "I have," he said.

They shook hands. "How are you?" he asked.

"Just fine." She turned to Reese. "Mr. Anthony. Nice to see you again."

"Same here."

Kyle said, "Game's going to start in about five minutes, help yourselves to the buffet."

Tay looked out over the stadium, "Think I'll just stand here a minute and take it all in. First time I've seen your digs. Looks good."

"We're still working on getting it ready. In fact, Bo and his people will be in the box with us for the game because the visiting owner's box isn't finished yet."

Glad to hear he'd get an up-close and personal look at Big Bo Wenzel, Reese left them all talking and went up to check out the food. He grabbed a plate but found himself checking out JT instead. She was wearing a white sleeveless dress that flowed to her ankles. The expensive-looking jeweled sandals on her feet showed off her freshly painted toes. She had her hair up, a style he'd never seen her wear before, and there was a pair of sunglasses pushed into the hair above her eyes. The makeup was perfect, as was the jewelry riding her ears and neck.

"Gorgeous, isn't she?'

Kyle Miller was beside him. Reese had been so busy staring he hadn't noticed the owner walk up. Some cop I am, he noted inwardly. "Yes, she is," he replied, pretending to concentrate on which shrimp he wanted to put on his plate as opposed to the terrible rug on the man's head.

"I keep asking her to marry me but she keeps saying no."

Reese tensed but didn't look up. "You never know with women."

"I mean, it's not like I can wow her with my money. She's rich as Cleopatra herself."

"That's something." Reese picked up a can of iced cola.

"You know what my greatest fear is?"

Reese's greatest fear was that the rug on Miller's head would suddenly start to move and scare everybody half to death, but he didn't say that. Instead he looked his host in the eyes and asked, "What?"

"That all that beauty is going to wind up married to some bumpkin from the Midwest who'll never understand what a priceless piece of art she is."

"That would be a shame, wouldn't it?" he responded earnestly. "Ah, there's the whistle. Game's started."

He moved back down with the others. The commissioner was seated right behind JT, so he took the open seat by Tay's side and sat down with a smile.

The first quarter was almost over when Kyle Miller's second group of visitors arrived. Big Bo Wenzel, wearing the hat, boots, and string tie of a Texan, was accompanied by a perky breasted young blonde with big green eyes. The low-cut, short, white tank dress showed off her tan and her long legs. Bo greeted the commissioner with a smile and a shake and introduced his companion as Brandi.

McNair in turn introduced Wenzel and Brandi to Reese.

Wenzel said to Reese, "Heard you been trying to get on my calendar."

"I have, but it's nothing that can't wait."

"You going to be around L.A. next week?"

Reese nodded.

"Come see me Tuesday morning."

"Will do."

Then it was JT's turn, and Reese was surprised to see a fond look come over her face when the grinning Wenzel said, "Well it if ain't Lady B."

"Hey, Bo."

They shared a light hug.

"How are ya, girlfriend?"

"I'm doing fine."

Bo then announced to everyone within earshot, "Don't ever play poker or Madden with this lady, men. She'll whup ya."

JT dropped her head.

"Whup ya and leave ya naked and cold."

They all laughed, then settled in to watch the second quarter.

There was six minutes left in the first half when JT got up to make a trip to the buffet. Bo was there, piling up his plate when she approached. He gave her a concerned look. "What is this about some bastard threatening you?" he asked quietly.

JT placed some shrimp on her plate. "You heard."

He nodded. "Heard you called the FBI."

"I did."

"Anybody putting their hands on you is going to answer to me."

"Thanks, Bo."

"Damnedest thing I ever heard. That and you going into rehab. What the hell was that all about?"

So she told him, and about the computer virus.

He stopped. "Sounds like somebody's gunning for you."

"Sounds like it."

"You packing?"

"Oh, yeah."

"Good girl." His plate was now as full as it could stand. His eyes serious, he said to her, "If you need anything, call. Keep me posted."

"Will do."

Misha Wells rolled over in bed and reached blindly for the clock on the nightstand: 1:00 P.M. She turned to go back to sleep but saw him standing in the middle of the bedroom, dressed in a crisp gray suit and making last-minute adjustments to his tie in the mirror on the wall.

She sat up, dragging the scarlet sheets up over

her nakedness, and asked sleepily, "Where are you going?"

"Out to take care of some business."

"What kind of business?"

"Not your concern, Mish." He turned to her and asked, "How do I look?"

Propped against the headboard, she surveyed him. "Fine as always."

"Good."

Misha looked at the man she loved and said, "I want to get married, Bobby."

"Let's not talk about this now."

"I mean it, Bobby. We've been together five years. I know you're mad at JT, but let's just leave and go someplace else and start over. You have your degree. I have mine. We can live anywhere in the world."

"No," he said emphatically. "Maybe after I bring her down we can talk about that, but right now? That bitch's ass is mine."

She shook head. "You're going to get caught."

"No, I'm not. Too smart for that."

"She gave the letter to the FBI."

"You told me that," he told her, putting his wallet into his inside pocket and picking up his keys. Ready to leave now, he walked over and stood beside the bed. He looked down at her. "When this is over we can live in Tibet if you want, but I have to do this first." He stroked her cheek softly. "Just a little longer baby, okay? Don't start getting the shakes on me now."

"I'm not getting the shakes, I just . . . " Her words trailed off.

"Don't worry," he whispered. "We'll be man and wife real soon. I promise."

He ran a finger over her dark lips. Lips he never would have kissed had he not needed her complicity and her tech skills. "After this is over, it'll be just you and me."

Misha didn't believe him but gave him a reluctant smile.

"One more thing. I need you to find me a weapons expert. Someone who can build a small bomb." He traced his finger down her cheek again.

She stared. "Why?"

"I want to scare her again, that's all. Make her close her shop. Make her leave town."

Misha knew this had to stop, and thought that maybe if she did this one last thing for him, he would. "What are you willing to pay?"

"Whatever it takes. Do this for me, and I will love you forever."

She no longer believed that either. "I'll see what I can find."

"Good girl. I'll be back late tonight."

He gave her a wink and left the room.

After his departure, she sat propped up in the bed alone with her thoughts. They'd met as summer interns at JT's agency five years ago. Bobby Garrett had been a fascinating mix of street and sophistication. She, the sheltered, twenty-year-old, nerd daughter of a British family with roots in Jamaica, had been immediately drawn to him, but his escalating obsession with JT was beginning to scare her. She'd been okay with the virus and with the letter, but now he was talking bombs, and she wanted out, but she wanted his love too.

Bobby drove away from her apartment with no intention of marrying Misha now or in the future. She was a pawn, and pawns were meant to be discarded. During their five-year hookup, she'd proven very valuable not only between his legs, but in keeping tabs on Blake, who according to Misha was bumping Reese Anthony, the man from the commissioner's office. Sleeping with the enemy. He wondered if her players knew. Misha also told him that Blake wanted to finger him as the source of the virus but had no solid evidence. Yes, Misha had been valuable, but as soon as he had a clear shot at the queen, the pawn would be sacrificed.

At the stadium, he parked, and after flashing his league-issued VIP credentials, made his way to the sidelines where the visiting Grizzlies had set up camp. He threaded his way through the chaos of players, coaches, trainers, and camera people while the crowd in the stands roared in response to a late second quarter touchdown by the hometown Quake. He was looking for Matt Wenzel. He found him on the far end of the sidelines standing with other members of the team's front office. Behind them a high school band in red uniforms lined up in preparation for the halftime show. Wenzel didn't look happy to see him, but he didn't care—they didn't have to be lovers in order to move two hundred pounds of coke.

Keeping his eyes on the game, Matt asked, "What do you want, Garrett?"

"Just came by to say hello."

"Bullshit."

They watched linebackers D'Angelo Nelson and Jason Grant sack the Grizzlies quarterback Brian Jacobson behind the line of scrimmage, negating any chance for a Grizzlies field goal to tie up the score. "And don't send any more of your friends to my home," he added, turning cold eyes his way.

Bobby gave him a shark's smile. "He just happened to be in the neighborhood. Thought you might like to meet the man watching over your wife. To keep her safe, of course."

Hate flashed in Matt Wenzel's eyes.

The ref whistled the end of the half, and the players on both sides headed to the locker rooms.

Bobby said, "We're all set on my end. Where's your old man?"

"Owner's box with the commissioner."

"Okay. I'll see you tonight."

"Go to hell, Garrett," Matt said, and followed his team to the tunnel.

Twelve

When the band marched onto the field, JT and the others in Kyle Miller's box stood to stretch their legs. She kept her manner casual as she met Reese's eyes, when in reality her mind was filled with all the ways she wanted him to make love to her, preferably soon. Having him seated behind her during the first half of the game had made her so aware of his presence, she felt as if his fingers had been softly stroking the back of her neck the entire time. She couldn't wait to get him alone. "Great first half," she said.

Commissioner McNair nodded. "Your linebackers are killing Jacobson."

She tossed back proudly, "They don't call them Shock and Awe for nothing. Am I right, Kyle?"

Grinning, he toasted her with his half-filled champagne flute. "You're always right, my lady, but let's ask our distinguished guest what he thinks of our defense?"

Bo Wenzel smiled. "Just wait. We'll get you in the

second half. Jacobson may be young, but he's good."

On the heels of his boast, the blond Brandi looked up, confused. "You mean the game's not over?"

Bo chuckled, "No, darlin'. There's another two quarters to play."

"What?" she asked in a stricken voice. "You didn't say we were going to be here all afternoon."

The others discreetly excused themselves to replenish their plates while Bo dealt with his pouting date.

Everyone had retaken their seats in anticipation of the beginning of the second half when Bobby Garrett strolled into the owner's box. His history with JT was well known to Kyle Miller, so Kyle's voice was frosty. "This is a private party, Garrett. What can I do for you?"

Bobby took a moment to glance at everyone, noting in particular Anthony, Wenzel, and JT, then said, "Heard the commissioner was here. Stopped by to pay my respects."

McNair stood and shook his hand. "You're Chambers's new agent."

"Yes. Hoping I can talk to you about his suspension. As men, I'm sure we can work out something less punitive."

JT knew a dig when she heard one, and so did everyone else in attendance, and as if to reinforce the verbal put-down, he turned her way and asked, "How are you, Ms. Blake?"

She didn't bother hiding her arctic reaction. "I'm fine, Bobby. You?"

"Can't complain." He then went back to the commissioner. "So, when can we meet? I can come to New York if that's necessary."

"We've nothing to discuss, Mr. Garrett."

"I beg to differ, sir. I—"

"Are you a lawyer?" McNair asked plainly.

"No."

"Then you might want to consult counsel. The agreement Mr. Chambers signed is binding and legal. Now, I'd like to get back to the game. Nice meeting you," he offered politely, then settled back into his seat.

Reese could tell Garrett hadn't cared for Tay's rebuff any more than he himself had cared for the verbal swipe he'd taken at Jessi. When the fuming Garrett met his eyes, Reese's face remained impassive, but his thoughts were not.

Big Bo hadn't liked the swipe either, because he knew Garrett wasn't half the man Lady Blake was. Insulting her in front of the commissioner hadn't accomplished anything except show Garrett to be the arrogant bastard that he was. They were supposed to be meeting later on tonight, and he hoped Garrett had enough sense not to mention it.

Garrett met Wenzel's eyes and nodded. "How are you, Mr. Wenzel?"

"Fine, Garrett."

Garrett then turned cold eyes on Kyle Miller, who by his impatient stance was ready for him to leave. "You all enjoy the rest of the game, and my apologies for the interruption." As he climbed the stairs to depart, he shot JT a nasty smile that nobody missed. She snarled silently in response.

* * *

Later that evening, Michael "Ham" Birmingham set a large Ziploc bag filled with coke on the table and tapped a spoon's worth onto a small flat glass for the buyer to try. The brown-skinned woman wearing a red Cleopatra wig took her time with the test and taste of the glistening white powder. When she seemed satisfied, she looked at Ham and asked, "Did you bring it all?"

"Did you bring all the money?" he countered.

She beckoned one of the tall men flanking her and he set a black briefcase on the table in front of her. She opened it, then slowly spun it around so Ham could see the pile of fresh green bills stacked neatly inside.

Ham glanced over at Big Bo, who gave him an almost imperceptible nod of approval. Beside him stood a silent Bobby Garrett and two members of Ham's crew. Everybody in the room was armed.

The exchange was made, and when the transaction was finalized, both parties left the shabby, pay-by-the-hour motel room and disappeared into the night.

"So, when are you flying out?" JT asked Reese as they lay sated in her bed. They'd celebrated the end of their days'-long separation with a blistering bout of lovemaking that they were just now recovering from.

"Early," he told her. It was now midnight. "Seven-fifteen early." He loved the feel of her long lean body pressed against his and brought her closer. He kissed the top of her very mussed hair. "Bryce called me. He found the virus maker."

"Really?"

Reese proceeded to tell her about the underbellies and trolls and the kid in Seattle. When he was done, she said, "All that grief for a lousy four hundred bucks?"

"I'm afraid so."

"I don't know if I like knowing I was a cheap hit."

He grinned. "If we find out Garrett's behind this, do you want his head on a platter or a pike?"

"A pike so I can plant it on the Golden Gate. It'll serve as a reminder to misogynists everywhere."

"I admired your restraint today."

"I wanted to shoot him. That smug smile he gave me at the end didn't help." She looked up. "Would you really chop off his head?"

"With the rustiest blade I can find."

Smiling, she cuddled back against him, enjoying being held close enough to hear his heartbeat.

Reese thought back over the day. "I didn't know you knew Bo Wenzel well enough for him to call you girlfriend."

She chuckled. "Met him when the league started. We've had some arguments over contracts, but he's mostly okay. Wouldn't turn my back on him, though."

"Why not?"

"He's like a gator. Either likes you or eats you. Seems to like me, though, especially after I won his yacht two years ago playing Madden."

"What?" he said, surprised.

"He bet it and lost it. I told him I didn't want it, but he insisted. Said I'd won it fair and square."

"Do you still have it?"

She shook her head. "Sold it the next day and sent the proceeds to the East Oakland Youth Development Center, a nonprofit run by a friend of mine. Got a real good price too."

"You're amazing."

"That's me."

He slid a magical finger over one of her nipples, which bloomed to attention almost immediately. "You're amazing in other ways too."

He bent and took the nipple into his mouth, and she shimmered like the tea lights lit around the room," You're not so bad yourself," she husked out.

And for the next few hours they dazzled each other with amazing things. Only after they were both too amazed to move did they whisper good night and drift off to sleep.

The following morning it was still dark when she drove him to the airport. The commissioner had flown back to New York after Sunday's game, so Reese was heading back to L.A. alone. He had no idea how long he might be there, but unless Mendes and his detectives turned up something new, there'd be no mandated reason for him to remain in California once he was done interviewing Bo Wenzel. It was his hope that something would surface so he could stay until the threats against JT were laid to rest.

"You take care of yourself," he told her softly,

leaning over from the passenger seat, then kissing her good-bye. He ran a parting caress down her cheek. The last thing he wanted to do was to leave her.

"You too," she said, not knowing why she always missed him when she'd never missed any other man before.

The whistle from the airport police blew shrilly, so a few seconds later he was out of the car and entering the terminal, and she was driving away.

Reese walked into Bo Wenzel's office on Tuesday morning and found the big man waiting for him. "Come on in, Mr. Anthony."

Reese took a seat. The large brown and gold space was far different from his son's office next door. The wealth of antlered heads showcased on the walls and the stretched and cured animal skins draped over the furniture made the place feel like a hunter's den. "Interesting office," he said, looking around at the variety of horned trophies.

"Shot everything in here myself. You see Ursus out by the doors?"

Reese nodded. He'd passed the big mascot coming in.

"Three hundred and sixty pounds of raging bear. Took it down with a bow."

"That's something," Reese admitted. Had to have taken a lot of guts to face a bear of that size with nothing more than a bow. The feat told Reese a great deal about the man.

Wenzel took a seat behind a large wooden desk. "So, how can I help you, Mr. Anthony?"

"Just trying to pull together my report to the commissioner on the Pennington murder."

"Gus was a good man. Hope you catch the bastards that did it."

"You know any reason why anyone else might have been in the office that night?"

"Nope. Place should've been empty but for Gus and his people. Like I told the police, I was in San Diego that night looking over some property."

Reese looked at his notes. "Ah, I see that in the detective's notes, but funny thing. I called every realtor in San Diego and not one of them remembers you."

Wenzel stilled.

Reese waited.

Wenzel gave him a guilty smile. "Did I say San Diego? I meant Santa Barbara."

"Ah." Reese scribbled on his pad. "Can I have the realtor's name?" He looked up.

"Sure. Have to dig it out of my car. Leave your number with my secretary and I'll have her call you."

Reese nodded. "Will do. Well, that should do it for me, Mr. Wenzel. Thanks for taking the time to see me." He stood. "If you remember anything else that might help, give Captain Mendes a call."

"Suppose you're heading back to New York now that you're done here."

Reese shrugged. "Not sure. Are you going to be in town if I have any more questions?"

"I'm flying out with the team on Friday for the Dallas game. Be back on Monday."

"Good to know. " Reese stuck out his hand. "Good luck to your team."

They shook. Reese noted the tightness in the man's grip and in his smile.

"Thanks," Wenzel said.

As Reese drove away, he had to admit that Wenzel had handled being busted well. An inexperienced investigator might have missed the quick flash of alarm in Wenzel's blue eyes when he told him about the realtors, but working the streets with junkies, hookers, and thieves had given Reese all the experience he needed. Wenzel had been scared.

In reality, he hadn't made any calls at all, he'd simply been after a reaction, and got one that put Big Bo Wenzel on the radar. He'd be willing to bet the man hadn't been in either San Diego or Santa Barbara. Did he know more about the death of Gus Pennington than he was saying? Maybe. It was still too early to tell, but one lie always led to another, so he phoned Mendes to see if they could widen the trail.

Big Bo was furious when Anthony left his office, so much so that he slammed his fist down on his desk with so much force it rattled the heads on the walls. "Dammit!"

His son Matt strolled in. He knew about the meeting with Anthony. The anger on his father's face told him the interview hadn't gone well. "Problems?"

Bo looked back at him like he wanted to tear him in half. "You were right. Anthony is going to be a problem."

"What happened?"

Bo told him the story, and when he was done, Matt couldn't enjoy the moment because he was in this mess up to his eyebrows too. "So he caught you in a lie. Great. Thought I was supposed to be the stupid one here."

"Shut up. I'll give him the number of a realtor I know who'll say anything I tell her to say."

"You think that's going to satisfy him?"

Bo didn't know. He hated acknowledging that even to himself, but he was going to play the game as if he still had the ball. There was too much at stake to do anything else. In hindsight, he should have challenged Anthony's accusation and told him to call the realtors again, but with no name to offer to corroborate his alibi, that strategy would have blown up in his face as well. "At this point I can't worry about Anthony. Ham has the deal set up in Dallas for Sunday night."

Matt didn't believe his father was still going to plow ahead. "No. We need to get out of this before we get in so deep that we can't."

"You just get the team ready to fly to Dallas. I'll handle the rest."

Matt's lips thinned, but he did as he was told.

JT thought about Reese on and off all week. It came to her that she had no idea what he was doing on behalf of Commissioner McNair, but she decided it was probably best that she not know, since her involvement with him might well be a conflict of interest.

The telephone calls they shared every night, although wonderful, weren't doing it for her. She wanted him close enough to touch, close enough to look into his eyes. As she lay in bed alone that night, she wondered if she was in love. She could say honestly that having never been in love, she knew nothing about the symptoms other than the ones she'd seen in movies or heard in the lyrics of songs, and she wasn't sure she could trust those. What she knew for sure was that she looked forward to being with Reese no matter how short the time because, not once had he told her who she should be, how to act, or treat her as if she couldn't handle her own affairs. He approved of the world she'd carved out for herself and wasn't forever offering suggestions on how her stuff needed to be changed. Women liked men for various reasons, and she like being left alone. If she needed advice, she'd ask. Reese seemed to sense that in her and didn't appear threatened by it. She was a tall, independent woman from Texas and always would be, but Lordy, she missed him.

At work on Thursday morning, her first call of the day came from Marva Wingate. She and her son Marvin had worked out a truce, and Marva was once again in his life; not in the role of business manager or agent, but as his mother. "I'm chairing the MAMA ball this year. How many tables do you want? There'll be ten to a table."

MAMA stood for Mothers and Mentors of Athletes. "Let's see . . . " JT did a mental head count. "Put me down for two."

"Okay. Make sure you bring that new man of yours."

"What new man?"

"Reese Anthony?"

JT went still. "How do you know about Reese?"

"Our sons, who else? Talk about women not being able to keep a secret. The ladies and I have been talking about it all over the country."

"All over the country?"

"Yes, and we all think it's about time you settled down. Just say the word and we'll start prepping the shower."

"Shower! Marva, hold up."

"Gotta go. If you need another table, give me a call." And she hung up.

JT had her forehead pressed down on her desk when Carole walked in. "What's wrong?"

"Marva Wingate wants to give me a shower."

Carole seemed to ponder that for a moment. "You and Marva Wingate in a shower. That's kinda kinky. Who knew she was a freak underneath those pearls?"

"Not that kind of shower! She's talking a wedding shower, baby shower."

"You're pregnant?"

JT stared at Carole as if she'd never seen her before. "Of course not! What is wrong with you? I feel like I'm talking to—what's that woman's name?—Gracie Allen."

"To tell you the truth, I've been wondering myself. Brad and I did the horizontal tango last night and I think he blanked my brains out."

"Blanked your brains out?" For as long as JT had known Carole, no curse words had ever crossed her lips.

"Yes, blanked my brains out. I haven't been right since I got up this morning. Took me twenty minutes to find my keys, drove off in the wrong direction when I left the house, tried to go into the exit lane at the parking structure instead of the entrance."

JT was laughing. "That must have been some loving he put on you."

Carole fought back a smile. "Quit laughing or I'll make you drink the coffee I made this morning without the filter."

"You're a mess."

"Tell me about it. But I'm surprised you aren't doing the same dumb stuff, considering who you've been tangoing with."

"I'm a lawyer and I know how to plead the Fifth."

Carole's voice turned serious. "You really like him, don't you?"

JT nodded. "Yeah."

"I think you'll be good together."

"We'll see. You know me. I meet these men, they look good at first then turn into lunatics, so I'm taking it day by day."

"This one's gold."

"I'm starting to think that myself, but like I said, we'll see."

Carole nodded her approval, then said, "Now, I'm trying to remember why I came in here. Oh, yes. The mail." She hurried back to her desk to retrieve it.

JT chuckled. Carole returned and handed over the small stack of envelopes and overnight mailers.

"There's a box out front too. Might be more computer equipment."

"Go ahead and open it. If the contents don't look like something we can handle, call Misha."

"Okay."

JT settled down with her mail. Letter opener in hand, she slit open a mailer holding the completed Owens contract and heard a man's voice in the outer office shout, "Die, bitch!" Puzzled, she stood, and just as she did, an explosion filled her ears. Before she could react, time seemed to go into slow motion and she watched in disbelief as the door and wall splintered and the debris come barreling her way. Horror grabbed her when she realized she was airborne. Pain and the sound of her own screams were the last thing she remembered.

When she came to, she was outside on a stretcher. Sirens were blaring. Red lights pulsated from police cars and fire trucks. The smell of smoke was thick. For a moment she didn't understand. Why were firemen racing around dragging hoses, and why was there a bunch of people standing behind lines of police? What were they all gawking at? What was burning? Then everything came back. *Carole!* Panicked, she struggled to sit up. Pain flashed through her ribs, but she didn't care. She had to find Carole!

The face of a woman in an EMS shirt loomed near. "Lie back, please, Ms. Blake."

"Where's Carole?"

"She's on her way to the hospital."

"Is she okay?"

"Lie back, Ms. Blake. She's in good hands."

The medic tried to place a bandage on the huge gash in JT's forehead, but she slapped it away. "Answer me, dammit! Is she okay?"

"She's alive. That's all we know for sure."

JT laid back and prayed the woman was telling the truth. She needed to talk to the police. She knew she had something to tell them but was drifting in and out of consciousness and couldn't remember what it was.

"I'm going to give you something for the pain. Probably put you to sleep."

"No!"

But the woman had already injected her, and a few moments later JT was being hoisted into the back of an ambulance and then was on her way to the hospital.

Reese's phone rang. He was in the middle of a meeting with Mendes. He glanced down at the caller ID. Seeing D'Angelo Nelson's name puzzled him, so he excused himself and took the call outside.

"Reese?"

"Yeah?"

"JT's been hurt, she's in the hospital. Jason is on his way to pick you up."

Reese forced himself not to panic. "What happened?"

"Police say a mail bomb."

Reese's eyes widened and his heart began to pound. A thousand questions clamored to be asked all at once, but he kept it together. "Where do I meet Jason?"

"Airport. He's flying down in his plane. Should be there within the hour." D'Angelo gave him instructions where to go.

Reese went back into the room and quickly retold the story to Mendes and his detectives. After promising to keep them in the loop, he ran to his rental car. Driving to the airport, he did the only thing he could. He prayed.

Misha was crying. The explosion at JT's office was all over the news. The police wouldn't speculate as to the cause, but Misha knew. So far she hadn't heard anything on JT's condition but Carole was reportedly critical. As she watched the firefighters battle to save the gentrified old building, she knew he'd lied to her. He hadn't wanted to just get back at JT, he wanted her dead, and she was appalled that she'd been the one to put the means to do so in his hands.

At that moment, Misha grew up. For years she'd refused to see Bobby with the rational mind she proudly applied to the rest of her twenty-seven-year-old life. She thought that if she wished hard enough and made herself available to him whenever he wanted, he would love her as much as she loved him. But this? To her discredit, she'd overlooked the computer virus and the threatening note, but not even a woman deranged by love could pretend to ignore bombs that sent people to the hospital. She'd been a seventeen-year-old senior in high school when she

began working for JT part-time. And after she en-
rolled in college, JT always had an intern position
waiting for her when she came home for summer vacation so she'd be able to earn enough money to pay
for tuition and books when the fall semester started
up. "And how do I pay you back?" she said aloud to
herself.

She was sick inside. She'd paid her back with an
act of betrayal so heinous and vile she could wind
up on Death Row. All because of her obsession for a
man who didn't care about anything except getting
to the top, even if it cost Carole's life. *What else have
you lied about, Bobby?* Determined to try and make
this right somehow, Misha opened up her laptop and
began to type.

Reese and Jason were striding urgently down the
halls of the hospital. Both men were so worried, it
took all they had not to run, but they managed to
keep walking. They entered the waiting room to find
D'Angelo and a number of other athletes on JT's client list inside.

Reese stuck his hand out to D'Angelo. "Thanks for
calling me. What are the doctors saying?"

"She's going to be okay. Busted her left arm in
two places. Has a few broken ribs and some internal
bruising. Carole's in real bad shape, though. She took
the direct hit, but they're pretty sure she's going to
pull through."

He relaxed for the first time since receiving
D'Angelo's call. "What are the police saying?"

"The box had an incendiary device inside along with a lot of glass shards and metal shavings."

"Meant to maim and/or kill," Reese stated angrily.

"That's what the police said."

"Have you seen her?"

"Yeah, but for just a minute. They originally told us only family, but after we politely explained that we either see her or tear up the place, they gave in."

Reese understood. "Has anybody called her mother or sister?"

"Not that I know of. I don't have a number. I don't think any of us do. Carole probably does, but . . ." his words trailed off. "Her husband's with her. He seems to be holding up pretty well."

Reese wondered how he'd be doing were Jessi the one in critical condition. "Who do I see about getting in?"

"Nurses at the station down the hall."

Reese turned to Jason. "Thanks for the ride."

"No prob. D and I thought you needed to be here. I'll go in and see her after you're done."

Reese saw the seriousness in their eyes. "Appreciate it." And he did. He left the waiting room and went in search of the nurses' station.

With no celebrity and less muscle to throw around, he had more trouble getting past the nurses. "Ma'am, please," he finally said, "that's my lady. I have to see her."

Something in his face and voice much have touched her because relented. "Okay, but the police outside her door have the final say."

"Thank you!"

To Reese's relief, the lady FBI agent who'd interviewed Jessi about the letter was by the door to her room, talking with a small group of agents wearing windbreakers that read fbi and atf. Upon seeing him, she broke ranks and walked over. "Mr. Anthony."

"Special Agent Tate. How are you?"

"I was doing okay until I got the call that someone tried to blow Ms. Blake and her assistant to smithereens."

"Me too. Any leads?"

"Not yet. We put a rush on that letter, though."

That was good news. "Can I see her?"

"Sure. I heard Jason Grant flew down to L.A. to get you."

"Yes."

"Go on in. Docs don't want her tired out, so not too long. When you come back we'll talk."

Reese went in. He was pleased to see a policewoman seated inside. She nodded a greeting and he walked over to the bed. Every beat of his heart was moved by the sight of JT lying so still. There was a huge bandage swathing her forehead and a fat cast on her left arm. He couldn't imagine how he'd have coped had she been killed. They were just beginning to explore what it might be like to be with each other long-term. He gave thanks that she would recover. As if JT sensed his presence, her eyes fluttered opened and she gave him a weak smile. "Hey."

"Hey yourself."

"Why aren't you out chasing down the bastard who did this?"

He smiled. "Wanted to make sure you were okay first."

"I'm pissed but fine. How's Carole?"

"Surviving, from what I'm hearing."

"Good."

"Do you want us to call your mother?"

JT shook her head. "No. She'll just worry. I'll call her soon as I can stay awake long enough to talk."

"Glad you're okay."

"Me too. D and Jason didn't trash the hospital trying to get in to see me, did they?"

"No."

"Worried about that."

"You go on back to sleep. I'm right outside."

"Thanks, Reese."

"You're welcome."

Her eyes closed and she drifted away.

Grateful for her life, he placed a soft kiss on her cheek and quietly left the room.

Thirteen

The meeting with the FBI and ATF lasted over an hour. Everything was discussed, from the nature of the bomb and who might have constructed it to the threatening letter and Bobby Garrett.

Agent Tate stated, "I want to take a hard look at him. We don't have enough to call for a warrant, but let's put him under surveillance and see where he takes us." She looked to Reese and added, "And you can't have any official role, Mr. Anthony."

"I know. I'm working in a nonofficial capacity on another investigation down in L.A."

"What's going on there?"

He told them the story.

When he was done, one of the ATF agents cracked, "For a cop who's supposed to be retired, you're awfully busy."

"I know, and I'll help out here too, if you need me. The sooner this person is caught, the better."

"We agree," Tate said. "For now, though, once

Ms. Blake is released we're suggesting she rehab somewhere away from the city. Might be safer."

Reese thought that made sense, but the question would be how she'd feel about it. His phone rang. It was the tattooed clerk at the pawnshop. The music player had come in a few moments ago.

"What did the person look like?" Reese asked, trying not to get excited over what could be the first big break in the case.

The clerk described a typical teen.

"Okay. I want you to call Captain Mendes—his detectives are handling the case." He recited the number but the clerk wasn't buying it.

"I hate cops. Only person I'm giving this to is you, otherwise I sell it noon tomorrow."

"I'm in Oakland right now."

"I'll hold it until tomorrow at two. Best I can do."

Reese cursed inwardly. "Okay. I'll be there before two." Ending the call, he told Agent Tate, "Somebody just pawned the music player tied to the Pennington case I was telling you about earlier." He glanced at his watch. It was almost four. He didn't want to leave Jessi, so decided to hole up in the Bay area overnight then catch an early flight back to L.A. in the morning. He took a moment to call Mendes and explain the situation. Mendes was pleased with the news and agreed to wait for Reese to return so the player could be retrieved. He didn't want to send a detective to the pawnshop and have the clerk go dummy on them, and maybe sell the thing as a result.

Reese stayed at the hospital until late into the evening. The Fed agents and the athletes had all gone, so that left him and the policewoman inside JT's room as her only visitors. The nurses were nice enough to let him look in on the sleeping JT once an hour, and as he sat in the waiting room eating a burger bag dinner, he got the opportunity to meet Carole's husband Brad. As D'Angelo had noted earlier, the high school history teacher appeared to be holding up under the weight of his wife's injuries. He told Reese it would be a few more days before the docs could determine if she'd actually turned the corner. Some of the glass and metal from the bomb had penetrated her eye and they were afraid she might lose it. A surgical evaluation was scheduled for the next day. Reese's heart went out to him.

After leaving the hospital, Reese entered his hotel room, tired, angry, and again grateful that both women hadn't been killed. Once he had a shower, he felt better but was no less concerned. He called Bryce and told him of the day's event.

Bryce sounded stunned. "A mail bomb?"

"Yeah."

"Oh, we need to find this person in a hurry. I'll lean on the Seattle kid again. Maybe he knows more."

"Do that because we need to get whoever it is off the streets."

"I'm on it. How're you doing?" his brother asked with concern.

Reese shrugged. "Mad, but okay."

"You know, if the Feds want her to recuperate someplace else, you should bring her here. We'll watch over her. No problem. We've got tons of room, and nobody is going to mess with her with all of us here."

Reese hadn't thought about that, but it sounded like a damn good idea. "I'll run it by her and see what she says. Let me speak to Pops."

Bryce put Pops on the phone, and Pops immediately barked, "Is Bryce right? Did somebody try and blow up my future daughter-in-law?"

Reese chuckled. "Let's not go there yet, Pops."

The two of them talked for a few minutes about Bryce's idea to bring Jessi to Michigan. Pops said, "We can help. She can recuperate here with no drama, and I dare some bastard to try and blow her up on my watch."

"Thanks, Pops."

The call ended a short while later, and Reese put down his phone. He didn't know how JT would respond to the suggestion, but thanks to Bryce, at least they had a plan.

The next morning, Reese had the taxi driver run him by the hospital before driving him to the airport. He wanted to make sure she hadn't developed any complications overnight. The nurses said she'd slept well, and that was like music to his ears. When he tipped in to see her, she was asleep. He was torn between letting her sleep and waking her so he could look in her eyes, but he knew that was purely selfish, so he opted for the former. Lord knew, he didn't want to leave her, but he had a job to do and he needed to get going. She'd be in good hands. The medical staff was stellar, and Special Agent Tate would be keeping an eye on her as well, so he gave the sleeping Lady Blake a soft smile and left the room.

Matt Wenzel's only concern was the welfare of his wife and their unborn child. He didn't care about the team operations, his greedy father's perverse plan to get them out of debt, or what might happen to him personally because of the crap he was in. Melissa's safety was all that mattered. To that end, he'd used part of his cut from Sunday's drug deal and sent Melissa, her two sisters, and their mother on an all expense paid trip to Europe. Ostensibly it was to celebrate his mother-in-law's fifty-fifth birthday. He'd always liked her, if only because she'd welcomed him into her family in spite of meeting Big Bo. In reality, though, the trip was his way of putting Melissa out of Garrett's reach. The verbal threats and the man on the roof of his garage had scared him badly. They'd be gone for a month, touring Britain, France, Spain, and Rome. By the time they returned, he hoped the situation keeping him awake at night would be resolved somehow.

Why couldn't Garrett have been the one blown up by the package bomb sent to JT Blake? As far as he knew, the Lady Blake was just that, a lady, and the Grizzlies organization had sent her a large display of callas to show they cared. Why were the innocents preyed on while scum like Garrett were allowed to go their merry way? The fantasy of reading about Garrett's death in the paper put a cruel smile on his face.

He'd never been the type to wish death on anyone, but he did for Garrett.

According to the pawnshop's records, the music player belonging to Gus Pennington had been pawned by a kid named Jalen Young. The tattooed clerk even had an address and a phone number. Whether the information was truthful or not, the clerk didn't know, so after Reese brought it to the police station, Mendes sent a squad car to Compton to pick up Jalen Young for questioning. Reese and Mendes watched the interrogation from the other side of the glass. Jalen's parents were with him, and Reese did a double take, remembering where he'd seen the mother before. *Babymama drama*, Garrett's secretary had whispered. What in the hell was going on? How did Garrett's kid wind up pawning Gus Pennington's music player?

The young man's voice came through the speakers in the room where Reese stood.

"I told you, my father gave it to me. I pawned it because I don't have a credit card or the money to buy more songs and the music on it now is whack. Pawnshop gave me fifteen dollars for it."

The detective then asked about the date and time of the gift. Jalen's reply placed it after the date of the murder. As the interrogation continued, the anger on Kelly Young's face was plain. Who or what she was mad at, Reese didn't know, but she looked like she wanted to hurt somebody bad. She cut in and said, "For the record, his father is Bobby Garrett, and whatever he's mixed up in, Jalen has nothing to do with it. He's seen Bobby once in the past six months."

"Bingo!" Reese whispered, pleased.

Captain Mendes nodded with satisfaction.

Reese wanted Garrett under the lights now. He couldn't wait to hear his explanation as to how he came to possess a murdered man's property.

Before bringing the player to the station, Reese had stopped by the Pennington home. Both his widow and grandson verified that it was Gus's. The serial numbers matched, as did the music files Chris said he'd downloaded into it. Reese's mind was humming like one of Bryce's prototypes. If it could be proven that Garrett had been in the Grizzlies offices that night, who'd been with him? The elder Wenzel? The younger? Both? Matt Wenzel didn't impress him as a killer, but it was well known that his old man was. Ursus and all the other dead animals hanging on the office walls proved that. But did Big Bo also hunt people? He was still waiting for Wenzel's secretary to call and give up the name of the realtor Big Bo had supposedly been with the night of the murder, so he assumed Wenzel had no real alibi. Reese added that piece of the puzzle to the mix and turned his attention back to the proceedings on the other side of the glass.

The interrogating detective got up and excused himself. As he entered the room where Reese and Mendes were, he told them, "I think we have everything we need."

Reese and Mendes agreed, then the captain added, "Let's bring Mr. Garrett in for questioning and get his story. Kick the kid loose. He seems clean."

The detective went back into the room with the Young family and thanked them for their cooperation. He had one last thing to say: "We advise you not to contact Mr. Garrett about what we've discussed."

"Don't worry," Kelly replied. "Whatever Bobby's done, I hope he fries for letting whatever this shit is splash on my son."

And they left.

Reese pulled out his phone and made a call to Agent Tate to tell her about the surprising developments.

"Wow," she said. "Okay. We're already ramming through the paperwork so we can get started on this end. We'll find out how busy Garrett's really been, and who he's been getting busy with. Thanks, Lieutenant. I looked in on Ms. Blake this afternoon. She's doing just fine."

"Thanks. I'll have Mendes call you."

"Do that. Take care."

JT awakened and felt like she'd been run over by one of those giant asphalt pavers. Every inch of her body was sore. Thanks to the nurses, she knew why. They'd told her the extent of her injuries, and that it was going to be a while before she felt like herself again. In the meantime, they were pumping her full of pain meds in order to keep the discomfort levels down. Usually, she hated being doped up, but in this case, she didn't mind.

Memories of the explosion and the aftermath brought Carole to mind. It scared her to know that she'd almost lost her friend. *God is good.* It was what her mother always said. Speaking of whom, JT had called her last night. The chat had been brief because she kept drifting in and out, but it was long enough to convince her mother that she didn't need to cancel her long-awaited trip to South Africa, scheduled to start in two days, in order to fly to California to see about her eldest child. JT assured her that the docs had everything under control and promised to e-mail her as soon as she could with progress reports.

The thought of almost losing Carole scared her, but something else scared her too—the idea that somewhere out in the world there was a person who hated her so much that they wanted her dead. It was hard to fathom a hate that deep, especially when she had no clue as to why, but told herself Reese and the police would figure it out. Her thoughts drifted to him. She hoped he wasn't worrying too much. She had a fuzzy memory of seeing him after they brought her to the room, but wasn't sure if it had been a mirage courtesy of the drugs or if he had actually been there. She opted for the latter. He was her knight, and she knew he wouldn't be very far away, no matter what.

A few minutes later Carole's husband Brad stuck his face in the door. "Come on in," she invited softly. She was glad to see him. "How's my girl doing?" What with the painkillers they'd given her, it was hard for her to stay focused, but she wanted news and to make sure Brad was doing okay.

He walked over and stood by her bed. "She's hanging. The surgeons are going to operate again tomorrow." Carole's lower jaw had been shattered by the blast and the surgeons were slowly trying to piece her back together.

"Send all of the bills to me," she said.

"That's not necessary. I've got insurance, and Carole has a good health package through you."

"True, but they're not going to cover everything she's going to need."

"Let's wait and see."

"I don't want you going broke."

"Neither do I, but I'd sell my soul if it means having her whole again."

"No soul selling allowed," she countered with quiet amusement. "That's why you have me and my bottomless checkbook." She looked into his eyes. "I love her too, so let me help."

He nodded. "Thanks, Jess."

"Welcome, now go back to your wife because I'm going back to sleep."

She closed her eyes. A moment later, she felt his brotherly kiss on her cheek. Smiling, she surrendered to her dreams.

Wearing latex gloves, Bobby Garrett counted out the bills and stuck them in an envelope, sealed it, then stuffed it into another envelope addressed to the post office box of the bomber Misha found for him. It was late, the sun had gone down, and he was in his office alone because he didn't want anyone to know what he was doing. Luckily, he had the money from his cut on Sunday to cover the payment, because from all indications, the bomber had done a hell of a job. He was disappointed that Carole Marsh had taken the brunt of the explosion and not Bitch Blake, but he heard she was pretty messed up too, so it was all good. He grabbed his keys. Before heading home he wanted to take the envelope to a post office drive-up box. He didn't want the envelope going out with the office mail. No one needed to know his business, and handling it himself would ensure that.

With his music thumping and the top down on the red Mercedes, he drove through the dark streets of L.A. Thinking about how he'd jammed JT made him smile. Pulling out his phone, he brought up Misha's number and waited for her to answer. She didn't. Although the connection rang and rang, her voice mail didn't kick in either. He shrugged and cut the call. He'd catch up with her later.

Bobby pulled into a post office near UCLA and dropped the envelope into the box. He was stripping off the gloves and about to drive off when a cop car appeared behind him seemingly out of nowhere. Taking in a deep breath, he slowly and smoothly dropped the gloves to the floor at his feet and hoped the cop now advancing on him wouldn't see them.

"Problem, officer?"

"Registration and license, please." Bobby kept his annoyance in check while he dug out the IDs and handed them over.

"Back in a minute."

Bobby didn't have any tickets or warrants, so when the cop returned and said, "I need you to come to the precinct," he asked, "Why?"

"Questioning in regards to a case."

"What case?"

"Not sure. You're not under arrest, Mr. Garrett, but the department would like your cooperation."

"I'm calling my lawyer."

"That's fine. Let me know when you're ready to go. I'll follow you." And after telling him which precinct to drive to, the cop walked back to his cruiser.

Reese was watching the interrogation from behind the one-way glass, and he had to give it to Garrett, he hadn't cracked; not in temperament, body language, or intonation. He'd remained calm and smooth throughout the session, and gave the same answers no matter how many times the detective rephrased the questions.

Garrett's story was that he'd bought the player off of a kid on the street and had no idea who it belonged to previously. He'd didn't know Gus Pennington. Never heard of Gus Pennington. And was in Houston with a lady friend the night of the murder. Reese knew of Garrett's gang past and could tell by the way he conducted himself that he'd played this game dozens of times. Add that experience to the polish and veneer he'd acquired in the years since, and he became a hard nut to crack. But he didn't believe a word Garrett was saying. Granted, that could be because he wanted Jessi's nemesis to be guilty, but his cop sense was blaring from all speakers, and he'd learned to trust it.

In the end, Garrett was allowed to go. The detectives had no real evidence tying him to the murder, and they all knew it. This had been nothing more than a meet and greet that also served to put Garrett on notice that he was under the microscope. They also advised him not to leave town. If he was guilty—and Reese was convinced that he was—it would only be a matter of time before he tripped up and allowed the detectives to prove it.

With that in mind, Reese thought he could step away from the twin investigations for a while, go up to the Bay, check on his lady's welfare, and then fly back to New York for a couple days and set up the office he'd yet to see because he'd hit the ground running. Staff had to be hired, and no matter how much he preferred to hover over Jessi, he had an obligation to his job and to the old friend who'd hired him. If she agreed to go to Michigan so his family could keep an eye on her and keep her safe, he'd be able to handle his job and not worry about her 24/7, even though he knew he would anyway. He planned on keeping close tabs on the investigations, though, not only because of the league's interest in the outcome of the Pennington case, but because of his personal interest in the bombing.

After Garrett and his lawyer departed, the detectives conferred on what would happen next, and Reese reminded them of Garrett's possible ties to the bombing investigation being handled by the Feds up in Oakland. Neither Mendes or his men wanted the Feds around, but they were willing to contact Agent Tate to see if she'd dug up anything that might pertain to Garrett's L.A. doings.

When Reese left the precinct, it was past ten. He wanted to call Jessi, but guessed she was asleep, and even if she weren't, was in no shape to be talking on the phone. He'd grown accustomed to their late night phone calls and missed the sound of her voice. Missed her, as well. The urge to see her was so strong, he thought about just jumping on the 405 and taking the 5 north to the Bay area, but decided against that because of how dead he'd be by the time he finished the long drive. Instead, he drove the rental car to his airport hotel room, had burgers for dinner, and booked another flight to Oakland. His last act of the day was to send Tay an e-mail detailing the day's events, then he went to bed and dreamt of the Lady Blake.

At seven-thirty the next morning Bobby was banging on Kelly's front door. He was boiling after being grilled by the police. Somebody had given them the music player and he wanted to know who.

His thundering summons was answered by David Young, pistol in hand. "What the hell you doing knocking on my door like you the FBI or somebody! Get the fuck off my porch!"

"I want to see my son!" Bobby yelled at him through the screen, wishing he hadn't left his own piece in the car.

Kelly, dressed for church, appeared at David's side, and her anger was plain. "What?" she snapped at him coldly. "What the hell do you want?"

"You raising my son to be a snitch?"

"You got a lot a damn nerve coming here. The police pick you up?"

His eyes flashed.

"They did, didn't they? I'm glad, because if they ever drag my son in again because of you, you won't have to worry about David shooting you. I'll kill you myself. Close the door, David."

He did, with much force.

Bobby slammed his closed fist against it. "Kelly! Kelly! Open this damn door! Kelly!"

She didn't.

He ranted and cursed until the neighbors started looking out of their blinds. Stalking back to his car, he snatched open the door and yelled out furiously, "I'll get you, bitch!" Grim, he sped off, tires squealing.

Bobby had problems and he knew it. If the police had him figured for the killing, they were getting ready to get knee deep in his life. With the new antiterror laws on the book, the Feds could do just about whatever they wanted, from tapping his phone to confiscating his computers. For all he knew, they could have had him under surveillance for weeks. He wanted to bust Kelly in her face for bringing this down on him. He'd get her, though, he promised himself again. But that didn't help with the now. Ham would have to be told about the police, and so would Bo Wenzel. Both conversations were going to be ugly, so he put them off until later. Instead he put in a call to Misha again. He wanted to know how long it would take to download all of his personal computer data so the Feds wouldn't find anything. But just like the last time, no answer, no voice mail. Wondering what the hell was up with her, he snarled and cut the connection.

Even though he'd been told by the police to stay put, leaving town did cross his mind. There had to be at least one country in the world that didn't have an extradition treaty with the United States. Barring that, if push came to shove he could go underground. He still had gang contacts, but the idea of living the rest of his life as a phantom in the urban jungle he'd spent the last decade trying to leave behind wasn't anything he really wanted to do, so, what were his options. Right now, he had none.

If Bitch Blake hadn't fired him way back when and then bad-mouthed him so no other agency would take him on, he wouldn't have been in the conference room that night the janitor walked in, and there wouldn't have been a shooting. As always, his troubles began with her. No matter what happened, she had to go down permanently because that would be his only consolation if he wound up on Death Row. To that end, he pulled out the pay-as-you-go phone he kept for private transactions and made some calls. He needed somebody to keep an eye on Bitch Blake.

Bo Wenzel paced the large confines of his Dallas hotel suite and pondered the future. He'd just gotten a call from Garrett's man Ham. Seems Mr. BG3 was questioned last night by the LAPD. Ham had no idea why, but a cop on his payroll saw Garrett and his lawyer being escorted into one of the interrogation rooms. Supposedly, the session lasted about an hour, then Garrett and the lawyer left. Ham promised to get back to him as soon as he had more info, and for Bo it couldn't be fast enough.

For all of Bobby Garrett's faults, Bo couldn't see him as a snitch, so what the hell had he been doing there? Having his lawyer in tow ruled out dropping off a check for an LAPD charity, he thought sarcastically, but it could mean Garrett was involved in something no one else knew about, and that's what worried him. He knew next to nothing about the man, and Garrett could be mixed up in who knew what. If that were the case, would it splash on the operation he had set up? He also wondered if the commissioner's man, Reese Anthony, was involved. Still smarting from being caught in the lie about the realtor, he knew that the former cop had interviewed Garrett. Had he found something damning? Too many questions and no answers. He couldn't wait for Ham to call so they could get to the bottom of this.

Maybe Matt was right, he thought. Maybe it was time to cut bait. But the lure of such easy money was hard to walk away from. On paper the setup was perfect: He got the drugs from an old friend down in Mexico who had a high-tech lab in a barn on the grounds of an orphanage outside Tijuana. Neither the people running the place nor the local law cared as long as they got their cut. Once the bags were loaded into his small two-seater plane. he flew the drugs back over the border and landed at a tiny municipal airport whose strip was nothing more than two ruts in the road.

His old friend was a disgraced Texas politician who'd fled the country ahead of a drug indictment for selling coke to other highly placed politicians. When word got out about his dealing and a grand jury convened, the clients realized they were looking at some serious jail time, so they turned on him like pit bulls in a cage and he ran for the hills. Federal law agencies, Interpol, and the rest looked for him for over a decade, but must have given up.

Because Bo had run into him on the streets of Tijuana last year. They'd had a few drinks, and when Bo asked him what he'd been doing, he told him, then asked Bo if he wanted a slice of the pie. All Bo had to do was find a connection to handle the distribution and he could set up his own network. The coke was lab coke, the kind made in Europe before the big bust made famous in the movie *The French Connection*, and not the swill being made in barrels filled with who knew what and cooked over crude outdoor fires. The money Bo was promised had more of a kick than the tequila they were drinking, and he'd said yes.

But because Bo didn't run in those circles and knew nothing about finding a connection, he turned to a Grizzlies cheerleader he'd been sleeping with who had a roommate who loved coke like he loved big breasts. As fate would have it, her connection was BG3, who was doing some discreet dealing for Ham on the side. Garrett had been all ears when Bo approached him, and Bo met Ham a few days later. The partnership was formed, and now everything might crash like the stock market in 1929 all because Pennington had walked in while Ham had been explaining the ins and outs of dealing, weighing, tasting, and Garrett killed him.

What a mess, Bo thought. The idea had been to use the team's away schedule to shield his and Ham's movements as they dropped off coke in the cities they traveled to, because Ham had connections all over the country. The deal in Oakland last week had gone down nice and smooth. The Dallas deal was scheduled for after today's game at yet another seedy hotel. He hoped it would be easy too, but he kept his passport and other necessities handy because if the situation got sticky and the cops came a'calling, it would be every man for himself.

JT was sitting up in bed Sunday afternoon when Reese came striding into her flower-filled private room. She didn't know what was more gorgeous, him or the huge bouquet of white callas in his hand. The choice was no contest, he could have walked in with a bag holding last week's garbage and she would've still been mesmerized by all that he was. The policewoman on duty had seen him before but made him open his coat, which revealed his holstered weapon strapped against his gray silk polo, then she patted him down. It was the reception every visitor allowed into the room was given. When the officer was satis-

fied, he pulled two of the callas free from the bunch
and handed them to her with a flourish.

She gave him an amused skeptical look. "You
know bribing an officer of the law is a felony, Mr.
Anthony."

Reese feigned innocence. "Bribe? Me? I wouldn't
bribe an officer of the law just so Ms. Blake and I
could have a few minutes alone."

She smiled and then, as if the thought suddenly
occurred to her, told them, "I think I'll go see if the
nurses have a vase."

Once she was gone, JT cracked, "You are a mess,"
hoping she sounded a lot less banged up than she
knew she was. "And where the hell have you been?
Took you long enough to come see me."

He didn't speak, he kissed, slowly, tenderly, breath-
lessly, until the only drug in her system flowed from
his lips. She fell so deeply under his spell, a soft moan
of grateful welcome slipped out before she could stop
it. Next she knew, he was sitting on the edge of the
bed and she was in his arms. Her cast was in the way,
and because her busted ribs hurt, she couldn't hold
him like she wanted to, but the lazy kisses, oh my, the
sweet lazy kisses were like manna from heaven.

"If you don't get off my patient, I'm going whip
your Denzel-looking behind!"

They both jumped.

It was JT's nurse, Lena Sanchez. The Spanish
beauty had been sending JT's male visitors into
fits. "Back off," she said. "This is a hospital, not a
pay-by-the-hour motel."

Looking as guilty as two teenagers busted necking on the front porch, they couldn't help but grin.

She shook her head. "I came in to take her vitals but everything will probably be off the charts now, thanks to you."

"Me? She's guilty too," Reese said, defending himself.

"Yeah, yeah. That's what they all say." The nurse shot JT a grin and started to the door. "I'll be back in fifteen minutes, and you," she pointed at Reese, "keep your hands and those lips to yourself, or you'll have to sit in the corner."

"Yes, Nurse Sanchez."

"Say my name," she demanded, and made her exit.

Fourteen

He pulled up a chair and, straddling it, spent a few silent moments just enjoying the sight of Jessi alive and well. The makeup was gone, the face clean and beautiful. He assumed she hadn't been near a mirror because her hair was a mess and she was going to have a fit when she saw it, but he loved every breathing gorgeous inch of her. "So, how you doing?"

"I'm here, and that's a good thing."

His voice softened with the affection he felt inside. "Yes, it is."

"How are you?" she asked, searching his face as if it would give her the answer.

"I'm good, and glad to look in your eyes, hear your voice. Miss our phone calls."

The memory of his mahogany voice in her ear while she lay in the bed with the drapes flapping in the midnight breeze made her smile. "Me too."

"Want me to break you out?"

"I wish. These ribs hurt so bad, we'd have to take

the pharmacy with us. Nurses said the pain should even out in a few days. Right now it's rough."

The man in him wanted to ease her pain. "Any idea when they'll release you?"

She shook her head on the pillow. "Another four, five days, I'm hoping? I hate hospitals."

"The FBI wants you to recuperate somewhere outside the city."

"Why?" she asked with irritation. "I want to go home, to my own bed, my own shower. No." She looked over at him, and the patience she saw reflected there made her ask, "What?"

He shrugged. "Didn't say a word."

She rolled her eyes. "Spit it out."

"What if there's another attempt? You want the bomber to get it right next time?"

Her lips tightened. "No," she replied grudgingly. "But where am I supposed to go? I'm not holing up in some spa or rehab facility, and I'm definitely not going home to Texas and maybe bring this drama to my mother." She was glad her mother was out of the country. She didn't want her anywhere near this madness. "I suppose yon knight has an opinion?"

Humor lit his eyes. "You know I do, my lady."

"And it is?"

"It's really Bryce's idea."

"Why does that scare me?"

"It might. It might not. My family would like you to come to Michigan."

She studied him and then asked, "Really?"

He heard the skepticism. "We could get a visiting

nurse if we need to, and Pops said he dares anybody to blow you up on his watch. You'll be safe there, Jessi."

Hearing her name on his lips made her as loopy as the drugs. "And where will you be?"

"Wherever the commissioner sends me."

She tried not to sound disappointed. "Is there enough room for me at your dad's?"

"Plenty. Since I won't be there, Pops thought we'd move you into my place."

She paused. "Your place? Is it is a condo? Apartment?"

"No, it's a house. Four bedrooms."

Nurse Sanchez returned. Right behind her was the policewoman, who retook up her position in the chair by the door.

Sanchez asked JT, "Has he been behaving himself?"

She looked his way and smiled. "Unfortunately, yes."

"Good. He gets to come back later."

Reese got the hint and stood. "How late is later?"

Sanchez didn't look up. "This evening."

He didn't like it but there was nothing he could do. Her health took precedence over his desire to be by her side.

"Where are you staying?" JT asked as the nurse wrapped the blood pressure cuff around her right arm. The fragrance of the bouquet of lilies lying across her lap wafted to her nose.

"Hotel," he said, again not wanting to leave, but resigned to it. "Think about Bryce's idea, okay?"

She nodded.

Sanchez silently cautioned JT to stay still while she took the readings. The departing Reese threw her a wink. She threw back a mock pout of disappointment and then a smile. A second later he was out the door and gone.

For the next three days, through sheer force of will, JT cut back on the amount of pain medication she needed. The ribs were still sore as hell and she was adjusting to the limitations posed by having a cast on her left arm, but each day she was able to get by with less of the pharmaceuticals. Reese made twice daily visits, and the nurses let him stay a little longer each time because JT was getting stronger and because, she thought, they loved looking at him. He rewarded them by bringing them ice cream, flowers, and on a couple of occasions lunch and dinner, depending on which shift received the benefits of his largesse. He brought up Bryce's idea to her a couple of times, but she invariably changed the subject, so he decided to leave it alone.

The stalemate broke on the fourth day when Special Agent Tate paid her a visit and said, "Someone torched your car last night."

"What? Aw, hell." The car had been chilling in a city parking structure since the day of the explosion. JT sighed loudly.

"Preliminary reports say an accelerant was used. The plates on the burned vehicle came back as being registered to you."

Reese was in the room and the news tightened his jaw.

JT asked, "Is it related to the bomber, you think?"

Tate shrugged. "No solid proof yet, of course, but it's a distinct possibility. We found a ski mask and a pair of gloves in a trash receptacle inside the garage. Not sure if they're related to the fire but we sent them for testing."

She sighed again and looked over at Reese. "Tell your father I'll be on my way. I may be stubborn but I'm not stupid. Damn," she added. "I've only made two payments on that Lex."

He gave her a faint smile. "I'll hook it up."

She said to him, "And I'll call Kyle Miller. Maybe he'll let me use his plane. I can't see me flying commercial. I'm not steady enough yet. I'd ask Jason, but he's busy with the team."

Reese knew she didn't want to leave, but he was glad she wanted to be safe.

JT asked Tate, "So has your investigation turned up anything?"

"We're taking a real close look at your Mr. Garrett. Something's come to our attention that might be key, but we have to wait and see. All the more reason to get you out of town. Whether he or someone else is tied to the bombing, we want you out of reach."

JT agreed that made sense, but she wasn't happy.

Tate wrote down JT's phone number and numbers where Reese and his dad could be reached and said her good-byes.

JT looked over at him. "Guess I'm going to Michigan," she said, offering him a small smile.

"Beats having to call in all the king's horses and all the king's men to put you back together again."

"True that." She thought about all that had happened in the last week, and it gave her a real bad case of the blues. Technically she was out of business. Her building had burned to the ground, taking with it ten years of hard work and a large chunk of her heart. She'd built her business from scratch, and it had been decimated in an instant because of some crazy. "It's scary knowing somebody wants me dead. And poor Carole . . . all the operations she's facing?" She heard her voice wobble and saw him move toward her side, but she quickly put up a hand. "No. If you come near me I'm going to cry, and Blake women don't do that."

He stopped and watched her with tenderness, amazement, and what he felt for her in his heart. "And why not?"

"We just don't."

"I see."

She took him in, all six-foot-plus glorious inch of him. "We're not weak women."

"Having somebody help you with the weight doesn't make you weak, Jessi."

Lord, she knew if he called her by her name again she would bawl. "I'm okay," and upon seeing his skeptical face, added, "I am."

Weak was not a word Reese would've used to describe the Lady Blake. Hard-headed, yes. Weak, no. The hard head was part of her charm, though, and the urge to offer her the shelter of his arms was still strong. The lack of light in her eyes showed that this nightmare was wearing on her. Add to that her concerns about Carole's condition and he saw a woman he wanted to whisk away to a place where worries and fears wouldn't be allowed to follow. "We'll get you to Pops."

She nodded. "Okay."

With the help of her lawyer, Francine Ross, JT prepared to move her life temporarily to the Midwest. Francine packed clothes, replaced all of JT's personal electronic equipment, like her laptop, BlackBerry, and phone, all of which had been eaten by the fire, and handled miscellaneous chores like canceling her mail and taking over payment of her bills.

By the sixth day the internal bruising and her overall soreness was beginning to subside. Her doctor figured it would be two weeks before she could move around comfortably, but he saw no reason why she couldn't recuperate at home, which in this case meant Reese's place in Michigan.

Kyle Miller graciously volunteered his plane and pilot, so that afternoon, after saying good-bye to the slowly recovering Carole and her stoic husband Brad, JT and Reese were winging their way across the country.

Because JT had been lying in bed for the last week, she didn't have as much strength as she'd hoped. By the time they landed at the Detroit airport, she was hurting and exhausted. A skycap met the private jet with a wheelchair that had been arranged for before they left Oakland, and once she was seated, it took all she had to stay upright and awake. She must have dozed off because next she knew, she was outside the terminal and Reese was helping her out of the wheelchair and into a car. A large older man who had Reese's eyes and coloring was in the front seat. Seated next to him was Bryce and another man, who she assumed to be Jamal. All three appeared very concerned.

"I'm okay," she told them. "Thanks for the invite." She gingerly settled herself in against the backseat, then closed her eyes in an attempt to keep body and soul together. The pain meds she'd taken right before landing hadn't kicked in yet and she prayed they'd hurry. Her ribs were yelling like they were on fire. Reese got in on other side and closed the door. A worried-looking Pops drove them home.

She awakened in a bed. Not her own, though, that she knew. This one was bigger, and the room's decor was very Afrocentric, with beautiful carved masks hanging on walls painted in rich warm hues of brown and tan. She sat up slowly and noted that she felt a world better, but where was she? she wondered. Was this Reese's house? And how long had she been asleep? He walked in then, carrying a bed tray. He'd traded in his corporate clothes for jeans and a T-shirt. He looked like the Reese she'd first met back on the 5, and as always, her heart skipped when she saw him.

"Evening, Jessi," he said in that low sweet voice. "How ya feeling?"

"Much better." And she was. She felt human again. "How long have I been asleep?"

He shrugged. "Almost four hours, but who's counting? You obviously needed the rest." He placed the tray across her lap. "Pops sent you some eats."

She eyed the small spread with glee. She was glad she'd broken her left arm and not her right so she could eat without any problems.

"There's roasted chicken, sweet potatoes, broccoli with cheese sauce, and his homemade French bread."

"Your father makes bread?" She bit into a small piece and groaned her pleasure. It was still warm. "Oh, this is good."

He chuckled. "I'll let him know."

She looked up. "And tell Bryce thank you. Coming here was a good idea."

"I think so too, but I'll tell him."

"Did you eat?"

He nodded. "Yeah."

"Will you stay with me while I eat?"

The words filled his heart. "Yeah baby, I will."

So she ate and they talked, about nothing really. The feelings blooming between them had gotten off track, what with all the drama thrown her way, and they both needed to reconnect.

After dinner she felt even better. "I like this room," she said, looking around while he took the tray and set it aside. "The sitting area is real nice. It's like being in a hotel suite only homier."

The sitting area was on the far side of the big room where a chocolate leather couch faced a big fireplace surrounded by beautiful black marble tiles. Comfortable-looking leather chairs anchored the couch. There were a couple of lamps with dark gold shades placed atop Moroccan-inspired end tables, and more African-influenced framed art and masks adorned the walls. Above the fireplace there was the big dark rectangle of a flat screen TV. "I'm liking your flat screen too. This is NBA playoff time. Isn't Detroit playing tonight?"

He grinned. "You are so the woman after my heart."

She grinned back. "Just doing my job."

They moved to the couch and he hooked up the game. Setting down the remote, he saw her shiver. "Cold?"

"Little bit. It's chilly here for a California girl."

He opened a wooden chest and withdrew a flannel blanket. She wrapped herself up and cuddled close. He draped an arm around her and she used his warm body as support, then settled in to watch some ball.

Detroit was playing Chicago. Both teams were noted for their defense, so the scoring during the first quarter was low, but it didn't make the game any less exciting. Reese noted to himself how perfect it was being with her and that he could easily sit with her this way until the end of time when his brothers walked in and messed up the fantasy. "What do you two want?"

"Good evening to you too, big brother," Bryce responded cheerily. "We come bearing ice cream and cake."

Jamal, shorter but thicker than his siblings, was pushing a serving cart that bore a huge chocolate cake and big green bowls of ice cream. He stopped and pointed at the desserts. "Ta da."

JT turned and her face lit up at the delicious sight.

Seeing her interest, Reese said, "Don't encourage them."

But Jamal had already placed a slice of cake on a paper plate and brought it to her along with a bowl of ice cream. "Butter pecan, right?"

A bit stunned that he would know that, she looked from him to his older brother and back again, but took the offerings. Bryce magically produced a TV tray and placed it in front her, and she set it all down. More than a little overwhelmed, she shook her head. "Thank you."

"We aim to please," Jamal told her, then asked Reese, "You want dessert, Your Excellency?"

Reese muttered something unintelligible, and JT grinned around the best tasting ice cream she'd had in a long time. "Your Excellency?"

Reese didn't respond to her, but told Jamal, "Just give me a damn bowl." He'd planned on spending the evening with her, alone. He loved his brothers, but this was supposed to be *his* night, and he saw nothing wrong with being selfish.

The younger Anthonys got themselves plates and bowls, but when they sat down in the leather chairs, Reese asked, "What do you think you're doing?"

Jamal said around a mouthful of cake, "Watching the game. What do you think?"

Reese wasn't happy, but they grinned because they didn't care. They'd come to check out JT.

Bryce responded philosophically, "Look at it this way. You were going to have to share her sooner or later, so it might as well be now, right, Lady Blake?"

She smiled around her ice cream, but instinctively knew not to get in it. "I'm just visiting."

Pops strode in with the aid of his cane, asking, "What's the score? What did I miss?"

Reese dropped his head.

Pops took one look at his eldest and asked his two youngest, "What? Did he think he was going to have her all to himself?"

Bryce raised a spoon. "Give the man a cigar."

Pops shook his head. "He can forget that."

And as JT tried to keep from laughing out loud, Pops took a seat on the couch and settled in too.

JT had a ball. Being with the Anthony men was like watching the game with her athlete friends, except there was a whole lot less cussing. She got the impression that if she hadn't been there, the air would have been blue, but she appreciated the respect they were showing her. Even Reese eventually stopped his mock sulking and got into the game. Although Pops had lived in Detroit most of his adult life, he was a Chicago native and thus the only Anthony in the room rooting against the home team. His sons gave him grief as his team went down by six, then eight, and then twelve. When the game-ending buzzer sounded, Detroit left the court with a ten-point victory. Chicago was now officially eliminated from the playoffs, and Detroit had earned the right to move on to the next round.

There was a second game on next but JT was as whipped as Chicago. She tried to yawn discreetly but everyone seemed to have seen it. Ignoring his family's pretense of not watching her, Reese asked quietly, "Sleepy?"

"Yeah."

Pops stood. "Okay, buckaroos, grab your plates and let's let the little lady get some rest."

She eyed him fondly, "Thanks for a great welcome."

"Our pleasure. Did you like the ice cream?"

"I did."

"Wasn't too salty? It's been a while since I made ice cream. Hoped I hadn't lost my touch."

JT was dumbstruck for a moment. "You made the ice cream?"

"Yep. I do most of the cooking around here. They won't let me chase women, so I have to do something to stay busy."

She liked Pops a lot. "I'm surprised the women aren't chasing you."

"Oh they are, but I'm still pretty fast."

Unable to hold it in, she laughed. She was looking forward to having a good time in exile. "I see where Reese gets it now. It's genetic."

"'Fraid so," his father confessed. "You get some rest. Blueberry pancakes in the morning with your name on a stack. See you then."

"Good night, Mr. Anthony."

"Night, Ms. Blake."

Jamal and Bryce were standing but hadn't moved.

Both were staring at her as if mesmerized. Neither had ever met a woman with her sports knowledge. The comments she'd made during the game had been awesomely on point, and they were wondering if they were in love. Their father snapped his fingers in their faces. "Wake up! Let's go."

As they jumped, Reese laughed inside and wondered if he could sell them to the circus. As Jessi was fond of saying, they were a mess.

They finally exited, closing the door behind them, and JT and Reese were alone. She cuddled closer to him on the couch. "You have a nice family."

"I agree."

"Your brothers are a trip."

"Wait until you really get to know them."

"They call you 'Your Excellency'?"

"And the Great Dictator, King Arthur, His High Ass, and if they really want to push my buttons, Kingfish."

JT's burst of laughter shook her ribs. "Oh, you're going to make me hurt myself."

He grinned. "They are something, and so smart they give me headaches sometimes just being around them. When we were growing up, I wanted to kill them every day, but can't imagine life without them now."

"I'm glad you let them live."

He kissed her forehead. "Me too."

Not wanting to move but knowing she was two seconds from being dead on the couch, she asked, "Are my bags in here somewhere?"

"Oh, sorry. They're still downstairs. Carried you up here and forgot about them."

"You carried me?"

"I did. You were out when we pulled up. Tried to wake you, but you were gone. Did I make you break a Blake family rule?" His eyes were filled with humor.

Enjoying their time together, she shrugged. "I don't know. But if you did, I can't be charged because I was asleep."

He placed another kiss against her forehead. "Spoken like a true lawyer. I'll go get your stuff."

"Thanks."

When he returned, she was asleep. He placed her bags by the door to the connecting bath then walked over to the couch. He watched her sleep and his heart was full. There was peace in her face, but a weariness too. Dressed in her gray sweats, with bare feet and unpainted toes, she looked like a sister from around the way; maybe one who worked for the post office, or taught school and had two kids and a man who loved her. Nothing about her resembled the powerful woman he knew her to be. That woman had legions of gladiators ready to take on her battles, big money admirers who lent her private jets and pilots, and a family of men named Anthony who'd never seen anyone like her before. He wanted this woman to be his from now 'til now on, as his grandmother used to say, but rushing her would only scare her off, and besides, he liked the slow, leisurely pace at which they were moving because it seemed to make everything richer, more sensual somehow. Pops called it slow hand courtin'. When Reese and his brothers were growing up, their father was always offering advice on how to woo the ladies. "Take it slow," he'd say. "Give her some space if you really want to get next to her."

And in this instance his father was right. Getting next to Jessi T. Blake was exactly what he wanted to do. At the moment, though, he needed to get her over to the bed. He picked her up and moved across the room. Her eyes opened. "Hey," she said softly.

"Hey."

"You carrying me again?"

"Yep."

"Where are we going?"

"Putting you to bed."

"Are you coming too?"

"You have three broken ribs and a cast on one arm, remember?"

"Oh yeah, that's right."

He smiled and gently laid her down.

"I promise to be gentle," she told him.

Reese tucked her in. "Go to sleep, woman."

Leaning down, he kissed her so potently and so well her eyes closed again and she murmured, "I need to hurry up and get well."

"Amen," he whispered. He stood up and committed her sleepy face to memory. "Get some rest."

"Thanks for everything."

"You bet."

She snuggled down beneath the covers and was asleep before he doused the lights and quietly left the room.

His father was waiting for him downstairs in the living room. Even though the calendar said May, it was Michigan, and in Michigan the name of the month meant maybe spring, maybe not. There was a coolness to the air that held the last vestiges of winter, and he was pleased to see the fire Pops had started in the fireplace. Having been in California, the chilly weather was noticeable. To beat back the cold, he grabbed a sweatshirt out of the closet by the front door and pulled it on.

Taking a seat, he looked over at his bear of a dad sitting on the couch in front of the fire. "Well?"

"Like her," he responded in a pleased tone. "Like her a lot. Pinky and the Brain are probably over in their lab trying to build something just like her right now."

"Probably."

"She's a nice lady. Emphasis on the 'lady.'"

Reese agreed with that too. They spent an hour or so catching up. Reese brought him up to speed on the cases out West, and his father's anger was plain. "So, this one guy might be responsible for the whole mess?"

"Maybe not by himself, but he's the person everybody's looking at now."

"Give me a picture or something, so I'll know to blow his ass away the minute he steps on the property."

"I'll get you one."

"When are you heading to the Big Apple?"

"Monday, I need to get this job off the ground."

"I understand. We'll take good care of her."

"I know. I'm not worried." Reese suddenly remembered something important. "Pops, everybody in her crew says she's a killer Madden player. Won a man's yacht."

Pops's eyes lit with excitement. "You think she can beat Brain?"

"According to her, blindfolded and standing on her head."

"If she can take him down, I'll make her ice cream every day for the rest of her life."

"Knew you'd like hearing that."

"Then let's get her well so she can kick some Brain butt!"

Reese couldn't wait either, but the games he wanted her to play had nothing to do with a PlayStation.

Bobby made the drive to the Bay area in record time. He had no way of knowing whether he'd been tailed from L.A., but if he had, he hoped the police enjoyed paying the high gas prices.

Now, however, he was driving away from the hospital Bitch Blake had been in. The woman in the passenger seat beside him worked in the kitchen. Her name was Tiara and he'd just picked her up from her shift.

"So, she's in Detroit somewhere?" he mused aloud while mentally moving pieces around on the chessboard in an effort to get to the queen.

"Yeah. The police and the nurses like to think they got everything on lockdown, but there's no such thing as secret in that place. People even know she flew out on a private jet."

"You got an address?"

She passed him a yellow sticky note. "Had an orderly I cop weed for get it for me. He's bumping one of the nurses up there. Told her the maintenance guys wanted to send Ms. Blake flowers—her being connected to sports and all that. They had it in the computer. Needed it for insurance, aftercare, something."

It didn't matter to Bobby. "Thanks, baby. Where can I drop you?"

"I thought you said we were going to dinner?"

"Have to take a rain check. Got a meeting with a client back in L.A. first thing in the morning."

She scanned him for a moment, then said with a bittersweet chuckle, "Stupid me. Here I was thinking you called because you really wanted to hook up again, but you haven't changed a bit, have you, Bobby?"

"Sure I have. How many of the brothers we grew up with drive something this fine? Those that are still alive. My suits cost more than they make in a year."

"You're shit, Bobby, you know that? Always have been, always will be. Still don't care about any fucking body but yourself. You just wanted that address. Why?"

"My business."

"Would that business have anything to do with why she was in the hospital in the first place?"

He didn't answer.

"Let me out," she snarled.

He eased the Mercedes over to the curb. Tiara got out and strode off angrily.

He merged into the traffic and with a cold smile headed back to L.A. Bitch Blake couldn't have picked a better place to hide. He had family in Detroit, including a cousin named Po-Boy who had enough gangster in his blood to do anything, as long as the price was right. Picking up the phone, he made the call, and when it was over the price had been cut, the address given, and an agreement struck to talk again once the matter was handled. It was the last trick up his sleeve. If she escaped this time, he didn't know what he'd do.

Fifteen

JT awakened the next morning to the sun pouring in through closed blinds and the smells of food cooking in the air. Sitting up made her ribs ache but she was healing. It wasn't fast enough by a long shot, but she'd take what she could get. Walking into the bathroom, she took one look at herself in the mirror and shuddered. Turning away from the scary reflection of her hair, she concentrated on brushing her teeth instead.

Being one-armed didn't impact taking care of her morning hygiene needs, but getting dressed was something else entirely. She struggled into clean panties, and after a frustrating few minutes managed to drag on a fresh pair of sweatpants, but a bra was impossible. Francine had packed an assortment of shirts and tanks, all of which were designed to be pulled on over her head. Sighing with frustration, she picked up her phone. When Reese's phone went off, he was downstairs in his kitchen frying bacon. The name on the caller ID made him smile. "Morning."

"Hey. Are you anywhere close?"

"Yeah, I'm downstairs in the kitchen."

"Can you come up a minute?"

"Sure. Be right there."

He looked over at Jamal seated at the table reading the paper. "Hey. Take over his bacon. I need to go up and see what JT wants."

Pops was throwing together pancake batter and Bryce was whipping up eggs. Both said in unison, "Don't be all day."

Sunday breakfast was always an event in the Anthony household, and this morning was especially so because they were feeding a lady.

When he walked into the bedroom, he was torn between looking into her freshly scrubbed face and being aroused by the sight of her bare breasts teasing him from behind the halves of her untied blue robe. "Morning."

"Morning," she tossed back in a voice as sexy as her smile.

His arousal was instantaneous.

As if knowing that, she slowly walked over to him, raised up on her toes and kissed him in warm welcome. "Missed you beside me last night."

It was all the encouragement he needed to gently ease her closer and respond in kind. The last time they'd been alone seemed like a lifetime ago, so the kisses only fed more hunger. "I need help getting dressed," she whispered as his mouth moved over her jaw and made her head drop back.

"In a minute."

It turned out to be a long, leisurely minute, and when he finally pulled back, her lips were kiss swollen and her nipples tight and damp.

"Now," he said softly, "how can I help?" What he wanted to do was lay her down and offer help until she begged for more, but then she'd never get dressed.

Very distracted by his morning greeting, JT fought off the haze so she could think. "All of the tops Francine packed for me have to go over my head."

"I have some old flannel shirts you can wear." Unable to resist, he brushed the open halves of her robe back and took a nipple into his mouth. It didn't take long for her groan of pleasure to float over the silence, then he backed away again. In another second or two they were going to be late for breakfast, so to keep that from happening he forced himself to move away. Crossing the room, he opened the door to a walk-in closet that put her own huge closet back home to shame. She stared around in awe. The dressers, built-in storage cubicles, and paneled walls were a deep mahogany. There had to be at least two hundred suits, sport coats, and trousers lined up as neatly as in a men's store. Then the lightbulb went on in her head. "I thought you were putting me in a guest room? This is your bedroom, isn't it?"

"Yep. My house. My bedroom. My bed."

She shook her head. "You are such a man."

"And you are such a female."

She scanned the space. "I feel like I'm in a store."

"I get it from Pops. We both like to look good." He

opened a drawer and withdrew a long-sleeve black flannel shirt. "Let's see if this will go on."

She extended her left arm as much as she could, and he worked the sleeve up and over the cast, then she bent her right arm into the other sleeve and Reese straightened her up. Looking down into her face, he did the buttons. "How's that?"

"Can I hire you?"

He was kissing her again. "Depends on what kind of benefits come with the job."

"I can make it worth your while."

He ran a finger over her lips. "Can you?"

"I guarantee."

His phone beeped. He looked at it and tried not to grin. Raising it, he said before his father could start fussing, "We're on our way." He closed the phone. "Breakfast's ready."

JT wanted to make love to him as soon as it was physically possible. The short interlude they'd just had made her achingly aware of how much she missed his magic. "Then we should probably get going."

"One more . . . "

He kissed her until she melted like butter, then led her out of the room and downstairs.

Breakfast at the Anthony table was truly memorable. There were so many selections they could've put a sign out front and called the place a restaurant. Pancakes, waffles, scrambled eggs, hash browns, orange slices, bacon, sausage, spiced fruit, and more lined the counter like a five-star buffet.

Because she only had the use of one arm, Reese put her choices on her plate and carried it to the table for her. When the men finished piling up their plates, they took seats and bowed their heads while Pops blessed the food. Once the amens were said, everyone dug in.

Later, a stuffed JT sat outside in an aged rocker positioned in a corner of the big old-fashioned porch. The men were inside cleaning up. She'd offered to help but she and her cast were told to go sit on the porch and relax, so that's what she was doing, and enjoying both the warmth and the scenery. Unlike California, Michigan was green, and it reminded her of her home in Texas. Mature trees lush with the first leaves of spring towered over the expansive property. Off in the distance were two houses. One appeared to be brick and older, while the other, with its boxy metallic design looked like it had been transplanted from Malibu or South Beach. She was willing to bet the older place belonged to Mr. Anthony and the other to either Pinky, the Brain, or both. The Frank Lloyd Wright influences were apparent and seemed suited for Reese's designing and engineering siblings. She knew that the two had a lab somewhere but didn't know if it was on the premises or located elsewhere.

Having lived most of her adult life in big cities, the silence was going to take some getting used to though. There were no sirens, car horns, or the cacophony of noise associated with the hustle and bustle of a million-plus people handling their business. The Anthony compound was supposedly located near Detroit, but the silence surrounding her made her think otherwise.

When Reese stepped out to join her a few minutes later, she asked how far away they were.

"We're about twenty minutes from the city line," he told her.

"It's so quiet."

"Nice, though."

"Jury's still out on that. Not used to silence you can almost touch. When does it start turning cold?"

The corners of his mouth lifted. "End of October if winter's early. No time soon, though, so you can relax."

That was good to know. "Is that your father's house over there?"

"Yep, and Bryce and Jamal share the other one. Jamal is building his own behind those trees to the left of Pops. He'll move in when it's finished."

"Why do you all have your own place?"

He shrugged. "Probably because economically we can, and because sometimes you need privacy."

She understood.

"I'm flying to New York in the morning."

She kept her disappointment hidden. "Be back when?"

"No idea. Soon as I can, though, believe me. Bryce will run me to the airport."

She'd hoped to have more than one day with him. "Okay. I'm probably going to spend the week on the phone trying to put my shop back together. I need to find a new building. Keep tabs on Carole."

"Just remember you're supposed to be recuperating too."

"Don't worry, the ribs will keep me honest." They felt better but she knew they wouldn't be fully healed for a while. She looked at her watch. "Pregame shows starts in a few minutes. Where are we watching?"

"Probably here, with the whole crew."

"I don't mind."

"I do."

"That's because you're selfish."

"And the problem is?"

Her eyes sparkled with amusement. "Does your daddy know how spoiled you are?"

"I didn't start acting this way until I met you."

"Right, and your brothers call you Kingfish, why?"

"That's cold."

"You're still cute." And he was. The slope of his shoulders and those gorgeous guns paired with his dark chiseled face made him a man usually reserved for a woman's dreams.

"Always knew you wanted me for my body."

"You got that right."

Jamal stuck his head out of the door. "Pregame!"

"We're coming."

When Jamal's eye lit up at the unintentional double entendre, Reese said warningly, "Say it, and I'll kill you."

Laughing, Jamal disappeared.

JT cracked, "Real off the hook family you got here, Reese Anthony."

"It'll get better. Just wait."

Enjoying herself, she followed him inside.

* * *

"You lied to me," Misha said coolly.

Bobby looked across the table at her angry face. She'd called him out of the blue last night saying she was in L.A. and wanted him to meet her for breakfast this morning. She wouldn't explain why she'd been out of touch, but at this point he didn't much care. With all the stuff he was looking at, he didn't have time to meet her, but figured it was the least he could do in honor of their last meeting. Thanks to a young female student he was cultivating at one of the community colleges, the data on his computer was downloaded and in a safe deposit box, so he didn't need Misha anymore. "Lied to you about what?"

They were seated outside at a table in an otherwise empty section of a café.

"About hurting JT."

He sipped coffee. "Not my fault if the man *you* found couldn't follow directions."

Misha snarled softly, "Carole could have died!"

He shrugged. "I hear she didn't, so what's the big deal?"

"The big deal is, have you lost your damn mind? I hear JT's car was torched too. One of your homeys?"

It was, but he didn't respond.

"It's all about you, isn't it? You don't care what happens to anybody as long as you get what you want."

"Yep."

Misha couldn't believe she'd deluded herself into thinking he cared about her. For five years she'd worn blinders, made excuses, but no more. "I hacked into your life, Mr. Garrett."

He looked startled.

"Thought that would get your attention. I looked into all the little dirty corners of your life, and you know what I found?"

His eyes were cold.

"You don't have a dime and neither do your clients. You've been tapping into their accounts and they're just as broke as you. What do you think'll happen when they find out?"

"Are you threatening me, bitch?"

"I got your bitch because now, Bobby Garrett the Third, it's all about me, and if you're thinking about doing me like you did Carole and JT, think twice. Everything I know is on a disk sitting on the desk of a friend of mine who works for a top dog lawyer. Anything happens to me, my family, or anyone else I know, you're going down."

He looked like he was going to explode, but she didn't care.

"I also know about the woman in Houston, the one in Miami, and the ho in Santa Clara. I got you by the balls, Bobby, and I don't ever want to see you again. Don't call me, don't e-mail me, don't come near me. You do, and I'll drop a dime so fast you won't know what hit you!"

When she stood and stormed off, Bobby slammed his hand down on the table so hard the glassware fell to the pavement and broke. The waitress hurried over, but he snarled, "Just give me the damn check."

She backed away and went to do his bidding while he simmered and contemplated Misha's death.

Across town, Big Bo and Ham were sitting in Bo's stadium office also contemplating death: Bobby's.

"He took Pennington's music player?" Bo said, incredulous.

Ham nodded. "Yeah. Like a damn raven going after something shiny. Gave the thing to his son and the kid pawned it. That's how the police found out."

Bo cursed. "What the hell was he thinking?"

Tight-lipped, Ham shrugged. "Stupid muthafucka. I'm cutting him out of the loop."

"You think the police have him under surveillance?"

"Of course, so he's got to go. Willingly or not."

Bo met Ham's eyes. "You think he'll rat us out?"

"Not if he wants to keep breathing. Bobby knows I don't play. Not about business."

Bo was in over his head now, and could feel the noose tightening. "So what do we do about tonight?"

"We keep the date because it's already lined up and I have a reputation to maintain. We'll deal with BG3 afterwards."

Bo nodded. He'd let Ham take the lead on this, but in the meantime he planned to make sure his rabbit hole was ready, because the way things were looking, he might need to run.

Bobby was in his office clearing out his files. He added Misha's name to the list of bitches screwing up his life. Even though he took her threats seriously, he didn't see her turning snitch, because then she'd have to implicate herself. She was the one who arranged for both the virus and the bomber, but with a big-time lawyer having her back, a plea could be worked out. If she was offered immunity from prosecution in exchange for what she knew, he was screwed. So he was contemplating heading underground, but not until he finished shredding everything that could be used against him. If he could find a place to hole up before the Feds tied him to the music player, or Misha started singing like Mary J. Blige, he might be able to disappear long enough to figure out his next move. His phone rang.

The caller ID showed it was Ham. He let it go to voice mail. It was the third call this morning. He didn't know what Ham wanted but his gut said let it ring.

He was in the middle of feeding some of his clients' financial documents to the shredder when his phone rang again. He didn't recognize the number, so he let voice mail take it then punched the button so he could hear the recording in real time. The voice sounded foreign. Jamaican. Sinister. "I'm still waiting on payment, Garrett. You asked me to send Ms. Blake a surprise. I did. I'll call back in one hour. If you don't pick up so we can talk about this, the surprise will be on you."

Bobby stared at the machine, puzzled. Replaying the message, he listened carefully this time, and at the end surprise widened his eyes. Was that the

bomber he'd hired? It was the only logical conclu-
sion, but how had the man found him? Panic wanted
to grab him, but he took a deep breath and forced
himself to think. Was Misha already singing? What
had the caller meant about wanting money? The payment had been put in the mail last week, the same
night the police picked him up.

Bobby stilled and got a sick feeling. Had they somehow intercepted the payment? Had they already tied
him to the bombing? With effort, he calmed himself.
If the message had been from the bomber, more than
likely the man was just trying to shake him down for
more cash, and he wasn't going down like that. He'd
paid him once, he wasn't paying him again. To that
end, when the man called back precisely one hour
later, Bobby didn't pick up.

JT decided it was a good thing she'd been laid up and
had lost a few pounds because at her regular weight
she'd never be able to fit into her clothes the way the
Anthony men ate. Sunday dinner was a barbecue,
complete with some of the best ribs she'd ever tasted.
There was also chicken, coleslaw, baked beans, corn
on the cob, and more of Pops's French bread. She
laughed as much as she ate at the antics of Pinky and
the Brain. They poked fun at Reese, threw napkins
and plastic forks at the screen in response to the terrible play of the hometown team, and treated her like
a queen. They fetched her food, brought her second
and third glasses of her favorite grape Kool-Aid, and
spent so much time just looking at her that all she

could do was smile and shake her head. By the end of the second game she was exhausted. This was the first full day she'd spent on her feet since the explosion, and her body was letting her know it was time to pull up. "I need to lie down for a little while," she told them.

Concerned, Pops said, "We didn't mean to wear you out. Reese, take her upstairs."

JT tried to reassure him. "It's okay, Mr. Anthony. I'm having fun. Just need to pace myself."

His concern was still apparent. "Come on, Brian and Jamal. Let's go watch the postgame show at my place."

JT hated being the one to break up the party. "You all don't have to leave."

Reese countered, "Yeah, they do."

Pops chuckled. "Cramping your style?"

"I am leaving in the morning, remember?"

Bryce rubbed his hands together and cackled like a mad scientist, "Which means we get to have her all to ourselves."

Jamal added his cackles, and JT couldn't help but laugh. They were something. "I'll be up later, so you're all welcome to come back for the Sunday night game."

"No, they're not."

Pops shook his head at his eldest's response. "Okay, Mouseketeers, let's leave Kingfish in peace. JT, I'll send you over some ice cream later."

JT tried to decline. "I can't eat another bite."

"Maybe not now, but you might want something

later. If Reese doesn't have the force field up, I'll leave it in the freezer, and see you tomorrow. By the way, one of my neighbors is a retired nurse. She'll stop by in the morning and help you out with whatever you need."

"Thanks." JT was glad he'd arranged for some assistance.

"You're welcome."

So Pops and Pinky and the Brain headed across the field to Pops's house, and she and Reese were left alone. Reese could see the weary slump in her shoulders. "Want me to carry you?"

"No. I can make it."

"Want some company?"

"Sure."

"Want a kiss?"

"Is Bret Favre going to the Hall of Fame?"

Looking down into her smiling face, he bent to kiss her, and afterward followed her upstairs. Climbing, she turned and said, "When I wake up, I want to take a two-hour bubble bath, and then you're going to make love to me."

"Oh really?"

"Yep. Now, if you're not interested, I can call your brothers."

He popped her on her lovely behind. "Quit playing."

She laughed. "I knew that would get you."

Lying in his bed, she took some meds and washed them down with a glass of water then handed the glass back to him. He was seated on the bed. "I'll probably have nightmares sleeping, with all this food in my stomach. Where did your father learn to cook so well? He's amazing."

"Our gran owned a small restaurant on the south side of Chicago. Pops says he was about nine when she first put him to work."

"I'm impressed. Do you all cook?"

"Yes, but none of us can come close to Pops. He is the kitchen king. We used to love it when he came off the road because we knew we'd feast."

"When he was playing ball?"

"No, when he was driving rigs after mama died."

"Who kept you when he was gone?"

"Sometimes my aunt would drive over from Chicago if he was going to be gone more than a week, but most of the time I was in charge."

"Really?"

"Why do you think they give me such a hard time? Back in the day, when Pops wasn't around, I ruled."

"The Great Dictator."

"Yep. I did the cooking, the cleaning, laundry, and made sure they got their homework done."

"How old were you?"

"Twelve."

"Lot of responsibility for a twelve-year-old."

"I know, but Pops trusted me, and I didn't want him worrying while he was away, so I made sure everything was okay here at home. Jamal and Brain gave me fits, but they helped out a lot too."

She could imagine him at twelve telling his brothers what to do, taking care of the house. After the death of his mother, she bet he'd had to grow up fast, and that probably accounted for the serious undertone she sensed in his personality.

He bent and placed a kiss on her forehead. "No more stories. Get some rest. I'll be across the hall in my office. If you need me, just yell."

"Okay."

Reese knew she was healing but he still worried. "You sure you're okay?"

JT found his concern touching. "Yes, Reese. Just did too much, that's all. I've never had to pace myself before. Takes a bit of getting used to. Wake me in three hours if I'm not up, please."

He nodded and placed a parting kiss on her lips. "Okay. I'll see you later."

She snuggled beneath the lightweight quilt and closed her eyes.

True to his word, he awakened her later and began running the water in his big tub for her bubble bath. She had him dig through her bags until he found her soap and oils, and once he added the liquids to the streaming water, the scent of sandalwood and almonds permeated the air. Reese looked at the bottle. "So, this is why you always smell so good?"

"You like it, huh?"

He set it down and began undoing the buttons on the shirt she was wearing. "Very much."

"Good to know."

When the buttons were all freed, he slid his hands into the open halves and settled them on the warm skin of her waist. "Need help taking off your pants?"

The mischief in his eyes made her grin. "Think you can handle it?"

He smoothly worked his hands into her sweats, filled each big palm with a soft hip and squeezed suggestively. "You mean like this . . . ?"

"Yeah," she tossed back.

He tugged them down, took care of the thong, and she stepped free.

Naked but for his black shirt, her beauty was all his eyes could see. The truth be told, he and his rising manhood wanted her there and then, but the prospect of exploring her scented loveliness at his leisure once she was done was enough of an incentive, so he said instead, "Hold onto my arm so you don't slip getting in."

A few seconds later, using him as support, she was standing in hot frothy water. "I think I should sit backward, that way I can put my cast on the edge and it'll stay dry and out of the way."

He thought that sounded like a good plan but held onto her until she was submerged to her waist. The cast made the process awkward, but once she was settled in, she sighed with pleasure. "I may be in here forever."

"Let's hope not. Making love to a raisin could be tricky."

She laughed. "Sounds freaky."

They were both smiling. She looked up at her gorgeous knight. He'd been such a blessing. "Thanks for everything."

"My pleasure."

"No, that's later."

"Call me when you're ready to get out," he said, chuckling. "I'll be on the couch watching the game."

After he left, closing the door, she soaked and relaxed.

An hour or so later when she called, he came in with a large fluffy towel and helped her out of the tub. "That was wonderful," she gushed. He wrapped her up and then surprised her when he bent and lifted her into his arms.

"You're carrying me again."

"Yep."

He walked her out of the bath and into the candlelit quiet of his bedroom. The flames undulating in the fireplace gave off both light and heat, which was where his steps took them. She saw a thin mattress set out on the floor in front of it, along with a couple of pillows and blankets. The soft jazz playing in the background added to the very romantic setting. She was impressed. "More of your courting technique?"

"Yes. Is it working?"

"Oh, yeah."

He set her on her feet. "Let's get you dried off."

The towel was used so gently and erotically that when he was done, she was left throbbing everywhere; her nipples, between her thighs. "Are you sure I can't hire you?"

He began kissing her slowly, passionately. "What kind of man are you looking for?"

"One who's good," she whispered heatedly.

The kiss deepened before he trailed kisses across her throat and filled his hands with her yielding breasts. Teasing the nipples with his thumbs, he looked down into her lidded eyes. "How's this?" He flicked his tongue against first one nipple and then the other before treating them both to a lingering welcome.

She shimmered in response. "That's very good."

The heat of desire flared like the dancing flames of the fire. Mindful of her injuries, he loved her gently and was careful to touch her softly so he wouldn't cause her pain. He treated her as if she were as rare as she was precious; awing her with his technique and making her croon in response to his exploring hands and lips. The clean fresh smell of him and the faint dampness of his skin told her he'd showered too, and she wished she had two good hands to caress him with instead of one.

He undressed and they both knelt on the mattress to resume their play. When she grasped his straining manhood, his eyes closed and she didn't think he cared that she only had one hand; one seemed to be more than enough. Moving her palm over him wantonly, she teased her tongue against his flat nipples. He groaned in response and she smiled, savoring the power she held.

To keep from exploding, Reese backed away. Eyes glittering with desire, he had her lie down then worshipped his way down her body from her lips to the shrine between her thighs. He conquered her, teased her; made her spread her legs so shamelessly for more that a few intense moments later the powerful orgasm buckled her and she shattered, screaming.

When she came back to herself, he whispered, "Come, ride."

So she impaled herself on his condom-sheathed

staff, loving the slide of his hardness as he filled her to the hilt. Reese wanted to stroke her like a madman, but mindful of her injured ribs, forced himself to go slow and let her set the pace. The rhythm was hot, seductive. He guided her with gentle hands on her waist and thrilled to the sight and feel of her moving above him and with him. He fondled her breasts and the tiny temple at the apex of her thighs. She came again and the heat and contractions of her sheltering flesh made him roar and grab her hips as his exploding orgasm sent him tumbling after.

JT had no idea what time it was when he finally carried her over to the bed, but because he slid in beside her and held her close, she went to sleep without a care.

Sixteen

She awakened the next morning to the sounds of rain and thunder. Struggling up, it took her a few moments to remember where she was. *Reese*. She looked around but she was alone. There was a note on the pillow beside her: *I'll call you later. Rest. Reese*. He'd written his father's phone number on the bottom.

Disappointed because she'd wanted to see him off, she laid back against the pillows and stared at the ceiling. She was in love with Reese Anthony, and if she were being truthful with herself, had been for some time—maybe since that first meeting on the 5. She wasn't sure she was supposed to tell him, though. To hear her girlfriends tell it, men changed once declarations were made. Relationships went from fun, easy and equal, to one where the man decided he was in charge and called the shots. Would Reese change if he knew how she felt? She had yet to meet a more caring, considerate individual. If he remained true to that person, there would be no problems, but if he started trying to manage her, they as a couple would implode. She wanted things to stay as sweet and as hot as they were, and she wanted him in her life, but she didn't want to create a monster either, so she decided that keeping her feelings to herself was probably best.

She went into the bathroom to brush her teeth. When she finished, she ran water in the tub. After last night's marathon loving, she needed to soak, and since taking a shower was out, another bath seemed the only logical solution.

She was pouring bath oils into streaming water when her phone went off. It was Special Agent Tate calling to give her an update on an envelope Bobby had placed in a post office pickup box the night he was interviewed by the police. "What was in it?" JT asked. Reese had told her about the interrogation but hadn't mentioned an envelope.

"Five thousand, cash."

"Cash. Who sends cash in the mail?"

"Apparently, Mr. Garrett does. Cash that tested positive for cocaine, I might add."

"Really? Who was the envelope addressed to?"

"A P.O. box number in Cleveland that turned out to be one of those mail services you can use if you want to mask your real address."

"So where was it supposed to go to next?"

"Funny thing. We tracked it from Cleveland to a similar service in Orlando where it was forwarded to another service in Boston."

"Somebody's really trying to cover their tracks."

"Correct, and they did it well because from Boston it went to a private service in France, and that's where the trail ends. The French are refusing to let us follow it without official red tape. By the time the Bureau does the paperwork, the envelope will be on to its next stop, which could be anywhere."

The news was disappointing. "Do you think the money was for the bomber?"

"We've been listening to Garrett's phone and we think it may well be."

"So what do you do next?"

"We keep watching and listening. I'll let you know if anything turns up."

JT had just set the phone down when it rang again. It was Pops. "Morning, Mr. Anthony."

"Morning, Ms. Blake. I'm supposed to check on you and make sure you're not trying to get into the tub by yourself."

She smiled. Reese knew her well.

"I'll take that silence as a yes you were."

"I plead the Fifth."

He laughed. "Mrs. Boggs, my neighbor the nurse, is here. I'm going to send her over."

"Thanks, Mr. Anthony."

"The last thing either of us needs is Reese taking bites out of our butts."

JT chuckled. "True that."

"She'll be bringing your breakfast too."

"Okay."

"I'll be over later."

"I'd like the company."

"So would I."

* * *

At about the same time on the West Coast, law enforcement agents and canine officers affiliated with the L.A. offices of the FBI, Transportation Safety Administration, and Homeland Security were conducting routine security checks on some of the state's small airports. Because most of their focus had been on larger facilities like LAX and the ones in the Bay area, little airports had been given low priority. The airport targeted for inspection that morning was a tiny postage-stamp-size operation with a landing strip that was little more than two tracks in a field. The corrugated metal hangar sheltered four small planes. The uniformed dog handlers walked their canine companions around the first three aircraft without encountering any problems, but when they neared the fourth plane, Lucky, a drug dog, let the humans know to call for a warrant. After tracking down the airport's manager, an aging gray-haired hippie named Doyle, they were given the name of the owner of the plane in question.

"Name's Bo Wenzel," the nervous looking Doyle said.

The FBI agent took out his phone and called it in. The remaining agents went with Doyle back to his office to take a look at the records of Wenzel's flight plans and to await the arrival of the tech teams.

Three hours later the techies had come and gone. They'd found traces of coke on the plane's controls, floor, and seats. The flight plans showed Wenzel making a series of trips to Tijuana. The agents placed a call there, but the airport there couldn't provide verification that Wenzel ever landed or had taken off from there.

Reese was in New York only one hour before he had to grab a flight back to L.A. The commissioner had received a call that morning from the FBI about Bo Wenzel being brought in for questioning on cocaine smuggling, and someone from the commissioner's office needed to be on site. Reese was that someone. Neither he nor Commissioner Tay McNair had any idea what the investigation might turn up, but the commissioner wanted to have all the facts firsthand, in case it became necessary for the league to step in and take over the running of the team. Matt Wenzel had proven to be a competent GM, but if he was involved too, no one would be in charge.

Reese was hoping this might shed some light on the Pennington case. He also hoped the answers would come quickly because he was missing Jessi. Last night's lovemaking had been incredible, and even though they hadn't been able to swing from the light fixtures because of her injuries, he added the sensual evening to a growing list of memorable JT moments. Before leaving for the airport that morning, he'd wanted to wake her and kiss her good-bye, but she'd been sleeping soundly. One day hadn't been nearly enough time for them to be together, and now he was on a plane touching down at LAX.

After deplaning, he called Mendes. The captain had been notified about Wenzel, and said that the Feds were on their way to pick him up even as they spoke. Mendes gave Reese the address of the office and told him one of his detectives would meet him there. Reese grabbed a cab.

Bo was on the phone talking to Ham. No one had seen Garrett. Ham wanted to shut down the operation until he was found. There was no indication that Garrett was being held by the police, which led Ham to believe that he'd either left town or gone underground. Bo was about to respond when a man and a woman in dark suits appeared in his doorway. "Got visitors," he said cautiously into the phone. "I'll call you back." Closing the phone, he looked at the man and woman, who he thought had to be FBI, and asked, "Can I help you?"

He was right. The woman identified herself as Special Agent Brenda Tate and asked him, "Are you Mr. Bo Wenzel?"

"I am."

"I ask that you come with us, sir. We have some questions about your plane."

Inside, Bo shook, but he held it together. "Has something happened to it?"

"We'll talk about it at our office."

"I'm calling my lawyer."

"That's up to you, sir, but for now you have to come with us."

A grim Bo grabbed his keys, phone, briefcase, and hat, then walked to the door. Matt was standing off to the side. He looked ashen.

"Call my lawyer," Bo snarled as the agents escorted him out.

At the Federal Building, Tate led the questioning as
Reese, behind the one-way glass, studied Bo Wenzel's
expression and movements. Wenzel didn't look particularly nervous except for unconsciously tapping
his fingers on the table where he was seated. Tate was
walking him through the trips to Tijuana.

"Now, you say you flew down to drop donations
off at an orphanage?"

Bo nodded. Since his lawyer had yet to arrive, he
was being cautious with his replies. He knew that by
law he could've refused to answer any questions, but
he didn't want to appear uncooperative and maybe
piss the lady agent off. He also wanted to know how
much, if anything, the Feds had on him.

"And your contact down there?"

"A padre named Gabe Lawrence."

"Are you aware that Mr. Lawrence is a federal
fugitive?"

Bo paused and weighed his answer. The lady agent
was looking into his eyes. "I knew him years ago in
Texas. No idea he was wanted."

She gave him a small smile. "He's a Mexican citizen now. We've been trying to bring him back to the
U.S. to face charges for years."

"Didn't know that either."

The questioning continued, and in response, Bo
spun a tale about how he'd run into Lawrence on the
streets of Tijuana and been asked to help the orphanage. In his mind, he thought his story sounded innocent enough; he was simply a man trying to do a
good deed. But it was understood that Tate hadn't

dragged him in just to chat, so he braced himself for whatever might be coming next.

"What can you tell us about the night of April third?"

Bo responded with a perplexed look, but inside the panic bells were screaming. "That's the night Gus Pennington was killed. Have you turned up something?"

She offered him another small smile. "Where were you that night?"

"Looking at some property."

She glanced down at her notes. "Ah, that's right. Says so here. You were going to provide Mr. Anthony from the commissioner's office with the name of the realtor you were with." She met Bo's blue eyes. "I'm not seeing any indication that you did."

"Got busy and forgot."

"Can you provide it now?"

He froze. Her manner was pleasant as she waited for his answer. He gave her the name of a realtor who owed him a favor. "Carson Adolph."

She picked up a sheaf of documents and began to read through them. "This is a list of all the realtors in the state of California, and I see Mr. Adolph's name here at the top." She pulled out her phone and made a call. When it went through, she said, "This is Special Agent Tate from the Federal Bureau of Investigation." She paused for a moment, then stated, "Yes, ma'am, the FBI. I'm trying to reach Mr. Adolph."

Tate looked Bo's way. "Good. Adolph's secretary says he's in."

Bo wanted to shit.

She began questioning Adolph, then turned toward Bo as she stated, "So, Mr. Wenzel wasn't with you that night? I see." She listened for a few moments more, then responded, "I appreciate your help in this matter, Mr. Adolph. I agree. Mr. Wenzel must have been gotten his dates mixed up. Thank you." She closed her phone.

Bo didn't move for a moment and neither did Tate, until finally she said, "Let's leave that part of your story for now, shall we?"

He nodded curtly.

"You're aware that the forensics done on the conference room in your offices where Mr. Pennington was murdered turned up traces of cocaine." It was a statement, not a question.

"I—I'd heard rumors."

"Did you know that cocaine has a signature chemical compound, depending on how it's manufactured?"

Bo shrugged and shook his head. "No."

"The chemical makeup of the cocaine found in your conference room is an exact match of the cocaine found in the interior of your plane this morning, Mr. Wenzel. How do you explain that?" Her eyes were steady, serious.

Bo swallowed inwardly. He was a cooked goose. "I don't know, so I'm not saying another word without my lawyer."

She nodded. "That is your right. We'll continue at that time."

On the other side of the glass a pleased Reese nodded. Stick a fork in Big Bo Wenzel. He was done.

Pops's neighbor, Mrs. Boggs, turned out to be a godsend. Not only did the woman help JT in and out of the tub, but she'd brought along a shower chair and a plastic sleeve with elasticized openings that she could pull over her cast to keep it dry. To her further delight, she learned that the retired nurse did hair out of her home to supplement her pension and social security checks, so later that morning, JT got the works: wash, relaxer, and a trim. When Mrs. Boggs was done, JT was a bit tired out from all the activity, but she looked good.

So much so that when Pops brought over lunch, he checked her out and said, "Wow."

JT was seated on the rocker on the porch, enjoying the warm May day. She shook her gleaming cut and said, "Looks good, doesn't it? I think I'm going to kidnap Mrs. Boggs and take her back to California with me."

"And the ladies around here will walk there to drag her back."

"I wouldn't blame them. She's special. Thanks for asking her to come by."

"No problem. Brought you a turkey sandwich, some chips, and some raw carrots."

He set the tray on a wire café table in the center of the porch and began to unload it. "Brought my lunch too."

"Good." She walked over and sat down in one of the chairs. "I'd like the company."

They ate and talked. She told him about her family and its Old West roots, and he told her about his family's links to Louisiana.

"We are descendants of the House of LeVeq. They were *gens de couleur libres*."

She did the translation. "Free men of color?"

"Very good. We have African, Spanish, and French blood in our veins. The free Black citizens of Louisiana were pretty wealthy in the years leading up to the Civil War."

"How interesting. The House of LeVeq? Do you have a crest?"

"I'm sure there was one back then, but it's been lost through time."

"We still have our Granny Loreli's derringer. She was a gambling woman."

He grinned. "A derringer? So you come from a long line of tough women? If she was a gambler, she had to be able to take care of herself."

"The stories said she was something else. Gave up gambling to marry a pig farmer."

He laughed. "A pig farmer?"

"Yep. Grandpa Jake Reed."

"She must have been seriously in love to marry a man with pigs."

"Yes, she was. They were married over fifty years, and according to the family Bible, died two days apart. Mama said her mama told her that Loreli died first and he died of a broken heart."

Pops looked off into the distance for a silent moment and said solemnly, "When I lost my wife, thought I'd die of a broken heart too. Never remarried because I didn't want to let go of her memory."

"And now?"

He shook his head. "Nothing's changed. I'll be her husband until they put me in the ground beside her."

"Didn't mean to make you sad."

He waved her off. "It's not about that. She was just the love of my life. Always will be. Not many people get to have that."

JT thought about her mother. "My mama never remarried after Daddy died either. I think she feels the same way. In fact, the two of you would probably get along real well. She loves to cook, loves ball."

"She tall?"

"And fine."

He grinned, "I already knew that."

Jamal drove up in a golf cart and stepped up on the porch.

"Thought you and Brain were working today," Pops said.

"We were, but he's doing some trolling on the computer for Reese, so I thought I'd come see if JT would like to take a tour of our Ponderosa."

The reference made her smile. Her mother was a big *Bonanza* fan. "Sure." She'd finished her lunch and felt pretty good physically, so why not?

Pops thought that a good idea. "You two go on. I'll clean up here. Good talking to you, JT."

"Good talking to you too, Mr. Anthony."

She got into the cart, grabbed the seat belt with her good hand and strapped herself in. Once she was ready, Jamal gently put the petal to the metal and they were off.

The Anthony's Ponderosa was impressive. Jamal drove them past his father's house and then Bryce's place. Up close, the Brain's cubist-inspired crib was pretty spectacular. They then drove to see the home Jamal was building for himself, and like Pops's and Reese's, his house was more traditionally designed. Next, he took her to see the orchards that were filled with trees that would bear apples and pears, an outdoor half court paved with asphalt, gardens where Pops grew everything from collards to roses, and a good-sized pond stocked with koi.

The open air, the lush green, and the quiet made it seem as if she'd stepped into another world. A world where bombers didn't exist, Carole didn't need surgery, and she wasn't afraid to let Reese know she loved him. While they drove around, Jamal asked her about her job and some of the athletes, and she answered as truthfully as she could. She liked Jamal. He was quieter and seemingly more introspective than his brothers, but she supposed his temperament was needed to balance off the vivid personalities of the other two.

The highlight of the afternoon was the tour he gave her of the labs. First of all, the facility was underground, which rocked her.

"Keeps out those pesky spies," he explained as he took out what appeared to be an electronics remote and pointed it at the door of a building resembling a small Quonset hut. The doors opened and he drove them inside. When the doors closed, the floor beneath the cart began to descend. JT looked around with surprise and a bit of apprehension.

He smiled. "We're fine. It's like a mine shaft. It'll take us down a couple hundred feet."

The walls of the shaft were made of black metal, with recessed lighting embedded into them that gave off enough illumination so she could see. When the platform stopped, the wall in front of them parted and he drove them into a brightly lit area that made JT stare like a country girl in the big city. Large glassed-in rooms held what looked to be prototypes of engines, brake systems, and truck cabs. "We have our own world down here."

He drove on while she stared around in amazement. "Looks like a top secret government lab."

"We do some government work here. Sometimes grad students at the universities need a clean lab to test a prototype and we'll let them come in and run their data."

"What's a clean lab?"

"Sterile."

"Ahh."

They passed more sealed rooms containing works in progress. There was even a kitchen. "We each have bedrooms down here for when we're too busy or too tired to crawl home."

"And just you and Bryce work down here?"

"Yep. This is our underground tree house."

"Can I ask how long it took to dig this all out?" The area seemed cavernous.

"Not long. This part of the state has underground salt mines. Some are still working, others like this one were abandoned when they stopped turning a profit."

"We're in a salt mine?"

He gave her the Anthony grin. "Yep."

"Wow!"

That evening, she was relaxing up in Reese's bedroom when he called. "How are you?" she asked, beaming in response to his familiar voice. Who knew she could miss a man so much.

"Doing okay. How are you?"

"Just fine. I toured the Ponderosa and the lab today." And she was still wowed by all she'd seen.

He chuckled. "Really? You must be special. Pinky and the Brain never give tours."

"I was very impressed."

"My brothers, the mad scientists. How are you feeling? They didn't wear you out, did they?"

"Oh no. In fact I'm in here chilling and taking it easy. Besides, you did a bit of wearing out yourself last night if I'm not mistaken."

"That's different."

"I like different," she teased back in a sultry voice. "A lot."

"I noticed. Man likes a responsive woman."

"Woman likes a man who can make her responsive."

"Then we're even."

"Oh yes sir." Her senses had come to life. Was this how people became addicted to phone sex? she wondered, smiling. "How's the weather in New York?"

"I'm in L.A."

She was confused. "I thought you told me New York?"

"I did, but something came up this morning that put me on a flight back here."

The idea that he was even farther away than she'd thought was disappointing. "How long will you be there?"

"No clue. Bo Wenzel's been charged with cocaine smuggling. He made bail and the hearing's scheduled for a month from now."

She sat up. "What?"

"Yep, you'll probably see it on the news. Traces were found in his plane."

She was stunned. "Goodness. Is his son involved too?"

"Not as far as I know, but the Feds are still collecting evidence."

"That's a shocker."

"The league sent me here to make sure the team's front office keeps rolling."

She was still trying to wrap her mind around Big Bo being charged with smuggling cocaine. Who knew he was mixed up in something like that, and she wondered about the ramifications on her clients if the team went belly up.

"Agent Tate headed up the questioning."

JT told him about the call she'd had with Tate that morning concerning Garrett's money and the post office boxes.

"There's so much going on with this," he said.

"I know, but if anybody can unravel it, I'm putting my money on Tate."

"Me too. You should have seen her interviewing Wenzel. She cooked him with a smile."

"Bo and cocaine. I'm still trying to process that. But the bomber's at the top of my list. Be nice if they caught this fool so I can stop looking over my shoulder."

"Yeah, it would. Did you get any business done today?"

"If you call talking to fifteen different clients business, yeah. Everybody and their mama called today to check on me. Jason, D'Angelo, Death."

"They worry."

"I know, but I told them I was fine. I did get a chance to talk to Francine a couple of times, though. She's scouting out new locations for the office. Talked to Brad. Carole's doing well. She has a few more surgeries left before they'll let her go home, but they've reconstructed the bones in her jaw and he said it looks good."

"Great news."

There was silence over the connection for a moment, then he said softly, "Miss you, girl."

"Miss you too. Makes me want to grab a flight to L.A."

"Would be nice, but you stay put and heal up. I'll be back soon."

She knew he was right, but it didn't keep her from wanting him near.

"I should let you go," he said.

"Okay" she agreed reluctantly. "Keep me posted on Big Bo. He signs some of my clients checks. If I hear anything from Tate on our bomber, I'll call."

"Fine. Keep healing so I can really wear you out sometime soon."

She laughed. "I'm going to hurt you when I get well."

"I dare you."

"Good-bye," she said, still laughing.

"'Bye, Jessi."

She closed the phone, held it against her heart and smiled.

She heard a knock on the door. "Come on in."

It was Bryce. He looked pensive.

"What's wrong?"

"Something I need to talk to you about."

He looked so serious. "Okay."

"Found the ID of the person who paid for the virus that took out your equipment."

"Who is it?"

For a moment he didn't respond.

She peered into his face. "Bryce?"

He looked at her, sighed, and finally said, "Misha."

"What? That's crazy. I've known Misha since she was in high school. I helped pay her tuition. I took her with me to South Africa for her twenty-first birthday. There has to be a mistake."

"I thought so too, but no. It was her."

She felt like he was speaking in a foreign language. "I don't understand."

"I don't either." He told her about the kid in Seattle

who'd created the virus and how he'd found him.

"This is the same kid who got the four hundred dollars for wiping out my computers?"

"Reese told you?"

"Yes."

"Same kid. I offered him some incentives if he found the name of the person who'd taken out the contract. Took him about a week to hack into all the ISP servers but he found her."

JT supposed she should have been awed by the kid's tech skills, but she was still in shock over Misha's involvement. "Why would she do this? Why?"

"Gets worse."

She looked into his eyes and instinctively knew what he was about to say next. "She hooked up the bomber too."

He nodded.

Furious, she unthinkingly slammed her arm down on the arm of the couch, and the pain reverberated with such intensity her curses turned the air blue.

He came quickly to her side. "You okay?"

She was still wincing and cursing at her own carelessness. "Give me a minute." She closed her eyes. Teeth clenched, she waited for the aching to subside. It finally did. "Carole was almost killed!"

"I know."

"Damn that girl! What did we ever do to her to make her think blowing us up was okay?"

He didn't answer.

She snapped open her phone and hit Misha's number. "I'm going to find out." The voice mail kicked in. Keeping her voice level, she said, "Hey, Mish. JT. Give me a call back. 'Bye, babe." She closed the phone. "Wait till I get my hands on her ass."

"I have a camera on my computer, and I know that she does too, because we talked after I got back from Cali. I'll try and contact her by e-mail and maybe you can get some answers face-to-face."

"That would be good." She was angry and, yes, hurt by the betrayal. She wanted answers and wanted them now. "And if she doesn't want to respond to us, she can respond to the police."

Seventeen

Early the next morning JT heard a knock on the door and called out sleepily, "Yeah?"

"It's Bryce."

She'd had an awful night. She'd tossed and turned the entire time, dreaming of explosions, and blood, and Bobby riding a broom and cackling like the witch in the *Wizard of Oz*.

"Come on in." She dragged herself up to a sitting position and pulled the blankets up out of modesty and to keep from freezing in the chilly room.

He entered carrying an opened laptop. "Misha."

The one word rendered her instantly awake. He set the jet black machine on her lap, and there on screen was Misha, crying. "I'm sorry, JT. So sorry."

JT had no sympathy for her. "Just tell me why. That's all I want to know."

"He said he wouldn't hurt you. But my God, Carole almost died."

"Who said?" JT could see her hesitate. "Misha,

I am mad enough to reach through this screen and strangle you! Who, dammit!"

"Bobby," she whispered.

JT was dumbstruck. For a moment she couldn't speak. She searched Misha's wet tearstained face and yelled, "Bobby? Bobby Garrett!"

Misha's face told all.

"You did this because of Bobby Garrett?"

"I didn't know!"

"Misha, how could you!"

"I thought he loved me!" she wailed from her heart. She put her face in her hands and wept.

Tight-lipped, JT looked over at Bryce's stony face before returning to the screen. This was the ugly side of love, the awful kind of love that sent women to jail, made them leave their children and forget their true worth. Most of the time the men responsible weren't worthy enough to scrub their toilets, and in this instance it was especially so. "How long have you been seeing him?"

Misha raised red eyes. "Five years."

JT threw up her good arm. She didn't believe this. There wasn't a woman on the planet who hadn't done something stupid in her life because of a man, but this was beyond anything she'd ever heard of or seen. She now understood why Misha gave the clients the cold shoulder—she already had that weasel Bobby in her bed.

Misha blew her nose. "I put him out of my life after the explosion."

"A little late.'

"I know, but when I woke up, I hacked around in

his life to see what else he'd lied to me about. He's got women all over the country, and he's broke."

That was the best thing JT had heard all morning.

"He's been stealing from his clients and they're basically broke too."

She wasn't happy hearing that. She sighed in response. "You have any proof?'

Misha held up a small USB drive. "All here."

"Okay. I want you to call Francine and tell her I said to get you the best criminal lawyer in town, and then call Special Agent Brenda Tate with the FBI. Fran will have the number. Tell Tate everything. Everything. She'll take it from there."

Misha stared across the miles. She looked stunned. "You're going to help me? Why?"

"Not you, your parents. Because this is going to kill your parents when it gets out, and I don't want them hocking their future to pay for your defense. And two, Carole didn't die. If she had, Misha, I would have called Tate last night when Bryce told me you were involved in this mess, and by now you'd already be in custody."

Misha dropped her gaze.

"So call Fran."

She was crying again. "Thank you."

"Just be thankful Carole's alive."

She nodded.

JT handed the laptop to Bryce.

He cut the transmission and took in the anger on her face as she lay propped up against the pillows. "You're forgiving her?"

"No. Truthfully, I want to chop off her head, but

it's Bobby Garrett I really want. When they throw his skank behind in jail, then we'll talk forgiveness."

He offered a small smile. "Remind me to stay on your good side."

"Be glad I'm busted up. Otherwise I'd already be on a plane going home to find him. Silly girl. I'm so mad at her I could scream."

"How about breakfast instead? Pops was up when I left the house."

"Sounds good. Maybe it will take my mind off garroting Garrett."

"I think that's a great idea."

"Your big brother would probably tell you not to encourage me."

Bryce waved her off. "Nobody listens to Kingfish."

He left grinning, and JT went to brush her teeth. When she finished, she called Agent Tate, and after telling her about Misha, offered to put up a $10,000 reward on Carole's behalf to anyone with information leading to Garrett's arrest. After the conversation ended, she called Reese.

Later, Francine accompanied Misha to Agent Tate's office, and by noon L.A. time a federal warrant was issued for the arrest of Bobby Garrett the Third in connection with the bombing of JT's office.

Bobby drove to Watts. Over the years the neighborhood had had its share of ups and downs. It appeared to be on another down cycle, if all the boarded-up homes and deserted stores and strip malls were any indication. It was heavy gang territory, and he and his red Mercedes were drawing lots of attention from the young bloods on the streets, but as he passed them he threw the proper hand signs and they seemed to relax. The car would be one of the first things to go; he'd already resigned himself to that fact. He would be needing something with way less bling if he wanted to stay out of the police's sights.

The house was where he remembered. The blinds were drawn, as they'd always been. He stepped up onto the porch and hit the button for the bell. He hoped she still lived there. She did.

Upon opening the door, she took one look at his face on the other side of the screen door and said coolly, "Well, if it ain't Mr. Got Rocks. What the hell do you want?'

It angered him to have to ask for help, but he spit it out. "Need a place to stay."

"Really?" She hadn't changed much; still over-weight, still wearing wigs—this one blond—and her eyes still had the power to reach into his soul. "Police must be after you if you had to break down and come crawling to your grandma."

His jaw tightened. She was his late mother's mother. Her name was Irene. "Yeah. Bad." Rather than be subjected to more ridicule, he pulled out his wallet and extracted four crisp fifty-dollar bills. "This ought to make up for the inconvenience."

"Add another five hundred and you got a deal."

"Five hundred!"

"Take it or leave it. It's not like you've been family

since you went off to that fancy school. I charge you just like anybody else off the street."

Fuming, he showed her the bills. She smiled and opened the door to let him in.

That night JT couldn't sleep. She supposed it was due to all the day's drama. From Misha to Big Bo and back to Misha again, she was too wound up to drift off. Every time she closed her eyes, she saw Misha's tearstained face. At home when she had sleepless nights, she'd simply get in her car and drive, but her car was in California and she was here with a cast on her arm.

Tossing aside the covers, she saw by the glowing numbers of the clock on her nightstand that it was 3 a.m. She padded to the window and looked out into the darkness. The other houses on the property were dark so she assumed the Anthony men were all asleep, unlike her. Deciding to go downstairs and get a glass of Kool-Aid, she was about to turn from the window when a shadow outside caught her eye. A lone figure was heading toward Pops's house. It didn't look like Jamal or Bryce, but whoever it was was doing his best not to be seen in the beam of Pops's porch light. Probably so the gun in his hand couldn't be seen, she thought, and grabbed her phone to call Pops, but it went straight to voice mail. Cursing because she'd lost sight of the intruder, she got Bryce on the phone.

He answered sleepily. "What?"

"There's somebody sneaking around your dad's house."

"Stay put," he ordered, yelled for Jamal, and ended the call.

But she was worried something might happen before the sons could get there, so she quickly found her purse and pulled out the new 9mm Francine had gotten to replace the one lost in the explosion. With only one hand at her disposal, she held the gun against her body and used her right hand to snap in the clip. Heart pounding, she forced her bare feet into her sneakers, stuck her phone in her robe pocket, and headed out of the room.

She was going down the stairs when she heard glass breaking. Stopping, she froze and listened. The sound came again, and her head swiveled toward the kitchen. There was a glass pane in the back door. Quickly and quietly, she pulled out her phone and whispered to Bryce, telling him what was going on.

"We're almost there!" he said.

Gun at the ready, she had no intention of letting the intruder catch her unawares—been there, done that, with Lamont Keel—so she eased down the steps and hid next to the sofa, where she would have a clear view if the person entered the room.

She didn't have to wait long. It was a man, short, and he was looking up the steps when JT snapped on the lamp. He startled, but by then she'd already squeezed off the first two shots. The lead exploded in his knee. He screamed and grabbed his leg. Fury replaced the pain in his eyes when he saw her, and he raised his gun, but her second volley was already on the way. Two more bullets caught him in the other leg, and with a demonic howl he went down, in too much agony from his shattered kneecap to care that his gun had rolled away.

Then the Anthony men came barreling through the front door. The man writhing and moaning on the floor at their feet took them by surprise. JT was standing on the far side of the room with fire in her eyes and her gun pointed their way. Seeing this, all three Anthony men slowly dropped their hunting rifles and raised their hands. Shaking with adrenaline and reaction, she drew down, then collapsed bonelessly onto the arm of the sofa.

The intruder was moaning, but otherwise you could hear a pin drop. Pops eyed JT and whispered, "Damn."

Jamal and Bryce appeared frozen.

Pops asked, "Are you okay, girl?"

She nodded. She wasn't really, but was damn tired of folks trying to take her life. "Somebody should probably call 911."

Bryce got on his phone.

An angry Pops looked down at the intruder and asked, "You come here to rob us?"

"Fuck you, old man."

Before Pops could react, JT strode across the room, planted her foot firmly on the prowler's waist inches from his genitals, leaned down and stuck the gun in his young face. His eyes went big as Frisbees.

"Apologize!" she growled. She was so sick of this, she wanted to shoot him right then and there, and to hell with the consequences.

He could see that she wasn't playing. "Okay! Okay! I'm sorry!"

She kept her gun in his face and her weight on her foot. "Now, answer his question. What were you after?"

His face was mutinous. "A woman named Blake."

JT shook her head. *Lord, now what?* "Why?"

"A hit."

"Who sent you?"

When he didn't answer, she kicked him hard in the leg. He screamed, but because there wasn't a sympathetic person in the room, he confessed with a whimper, "Bobby Garrett! My cousin, Bobby Garrett. Get this crazy bitch away from me!"

So the crazy bitch backed off and sat down, to await the arrival of the police.

They roared up a few minutes later. The young man's name was Desmond "Po-Boy" Barker. He had a rap sheet a mile long and myriad outstanding warrants for everything from carjacking to armed robbery. The paramedics patched his leg and took him away on a stretcher. The police took her report, promised to touch base with the LAPD and the FBI, and left her and the Anthonys alone.

Pops said, "Having you around sure makes life interesting."

JT gave him a small smile. "Nothing like a little target practice to cure my insomnia."

"I told Reese we'd keep you safe, but you don't really need us, do you?"

Jamal and Bryce flanked him, and they still looked amazed.

She said to them, "One of my great-great-grand-mothers was a gambler. The other organized a wagon train of mail order brides back in the 1880s. A great-great-grandfather was a Texas Ranger, and an uncle was an outlaw. No. We Blakes can take care of our-selves, thank you very much."

"Then all I can say is: Who wants ice cream?"

Three sets of hands shot up.

Pops nodded. "Now that's what I'm talking about."

When Bobby turned over in the bed, he cracked open his eyes a bit, saw daylight through the small attic window, and moved deeper into the thin lumpy mat-tress with the intent of going back to sleep, until he noticed Ham seated in a chair right beside the bed. He was so startled, he sprang up and smashed his head against the attic's low ceiling. As the pain thud-ded through him, Bobby fought off both the ache and the embarrassment brought on by Ham's cold grin.

"Why the hell are you here?" Bobby asked.

"I could ask you the same question, but I already know the answer: You're here because you're stupid!" he yelled.

The forceful reply made Bobby jump again, but he tried to play it off. "Fuck you." Ignoring Ham, he turned over and pulled the blanket back over himself, only to have Ham stand and snatch it away. Bobby flipped over to confront him but froze when he found himself staring at a silver gun with a bore the size of walnut.

"Stupid piece of educated shit!" Ham growled angrily. "I ought to blow you away right here, but that would be disrespectful to Miss Irene's house. Do you know how much money you cost me because you had to steal from that dead old man? Do you?"

Bobby was trying not to shake but couldn't stop.

"Big Bo's been charged with smuggling. The popo's probably going to link him to the murder, and he's gonna have to sing to save his own ass, and you know what? I can't be mad at him because I'd do the same damn thing!"

"What do you mean he's been charged?"

"Oh, you're deaf now too? Charged as in the FBI, muthafucka! He made bail, but he'd have to be stupid as you not to make a deal, and we both know he ain't that."

Bobby's brain was trying to make sense of this, but Ham was throwing so much shit at him at once it was hard to focus so he could think.

"We want you out of the neighborhood," Ham stated flatly.

Bobby glared contemptuously. What do you mean 'we'? Who's 'we'? You don't even live up here."

"'We' is everybody who makes their living on the low low, and that means Watts, Compton, and South Central. You're a liability. We don't need the extra police patrols your being around is going to bring."

"Nobody knows I'm here."

Ham threw up his hands, gun and all. "Everybody and their cousin saw you driving through in your fancy ride. A kindergartner could give you up."

"Nobody's going to snitch."

"Why, because you're such a stand-up brother? You're a fuck-up, Bob. Nobody's going to protect you. Not around here, not nowhere. Word's out."

Bobby seethed.

"If you cared about somebody other than your own damn self, things might be different, but we want you gone. Be out of here by this time tomorrow or you'll go out in a box."

Ham saw the anger flashing in Bobby eyes, but he didn't care. "Be glad I gave you a day. Some folks wanted you out last night."

That said, he turned and walked over to the steps that led down to the floor below. He descended, and when Bobby heard the door slam at the foot of the staircase, he knew Ham was gone.

He cursed and planned to take all of those twenty-four hours, fuck Ham, his grandmother, and the rest of the haters. He wasn't leaving one minute sooner. They could all kiss his black ass. He'd collect his car that he'd stashed with a guy Irene knew and then head for parts unknown. He didn't need Ham or anyone else.

Satisfied with his plan, he pulled the covers over his head, but getting back to sleep took a long time.

Reese was riding with the detectives who were turning over rocks looking for Garrett. Hearing from Jessi and his family about last night's visitor had left him so infuriated he wanted to get his hands around Garrett's throat. He was glad that Jessi had taken care of herself, but what if the encounter had turned

out differently? What if the cousin had been success-
ful? JT had barely recovered from her first brush with
death, and now this? He couldn't wait to find Mr.
Bobby G3 so the LAPD could throw his cowardly ass
in a cell. Garrett had so many charges hanging over
his head now, he'd be dead before he became eligible
for parole, if a jury didn't send him to Death Row
first. The idea that Barker had come to kill Jessi while
she was staying at *his* house only added to his mood.
How Garrett had found the address was something
law enforcement and the hospital was looking into,
but he didn't care about that now. Finding Garrett
had become his one mission in life, and if he got
the chance to get Garrett alone, he was sure he'd be
going to jail because he planned to kick his ass until
the snow fell.

But so far Garrett was nowhere to be found. They'd
ridden out to his home in the Valley but found it as deserted and cleared out as his office had been. They'd
flashed his picture in strip clubs, grocery stores, and
fast food outlets all over the city, to no avail. Having a man tied to a bombing loose in the community
wasn't good for the community, so the media outlets
had gotten involved by plastering his face on TV and
in the newspapers. His name had been added to the
no fly list, and his face would be displayed in post
offices all over the country as the newest member of
the FBI's Most Wanted. Everybody from L.A. to the
Bay area knew Garrett was wanted by the police, and
because they did, Reese didn't fret. It would only be a
matter of time before he was caught. Jessi had upped

the ante with the $10,000 reward. It was a lot of money, and eventually somebody was going to drop a dime to collect it.

And the sooner that happened, the sooner he could go back and propose to the Lady Blake. He wanted her to be his wife. Although he had no idea how she'd respond, he was ready to take the relationship to the next level. He'd kept his heart under lock and key since his divorce, but like the lyrics of one of Frankie Beverly's tunes, Jessi had given him a reason to love one more time.

Big Bo Wenzel decided he wasn't doing time; he wasn't taking the fall for Garrett, and he certainly wasn't going to trial. He knew that middle-age White men like himself didn't fare well behind bars. If Bobby Garrett were to walk into his office, he'd choke him to death with one hand. Had Garrett not acted like a Compton grave robber and taken Pennington's property, he wouldn't have found himself cooked under the interrogation lights of the Feds, or be facing charges for dope smuggling. He and Ham agreed the operation was over, but he hadn't made contact with his supplier to let him know what was going on for fear his phone was tapped. To shake the monkeys off his back, he was on his way to the rabbit hole. The Feds had confiscated his passport to make sure he didn't leave the country, but he didn't care. They could keep it. Where he was heading, he wouldn't be needing it anyway.

He left his office and walked into Matt's. "I think

I'm going to run down to Santa Monica this evening and take the boat out. I want to see if I can find that oil leak in the motor. Maybe it'll relax me, take my mind off things."

"Okay," Matt said and added, "Sorry about all the mess. The courts. The media."

The commissioner would be holding a press conference later that afternoon announcing Bo's relinquishment of his duties as owner of the Grizzlies until after the trial.

Bo told him, "'If you can't do the time, don't do the crime.' Isn't that how the old saying goes?"

"Yeah. It does."

"I'm not going to jail, bet the bank on that. Garrett is still on the loose, though, and just in case something happens to me, give this to the police." He tossed Max a CD.

"What's this?"

"My testimony on what happened the night Pennington was killed. According to that, the only people in the conference room that night were Garrett and me, and Garrett did the shooting."

Matt stared. "But why?"

"You'd last half an hour in prison, Matthew."

Matt couldn't remember the last time his father had called him by his full name. "I know, but you'd take the fall for me?"

Bo didn't answer that. Instead he said, "You're going to be a father. You need to be here for that. Who knows, maybe you'll be better at it than I've been."

Matt's jaw dropped. He searched his father's weary-looking face. "What's going on with you?"

"Tired, that's all."

"You sure?"

"Yep. In fact, I think I'm going to go on home. Spend the day puttering around the house, think about some things. Wait and see what the commissioner tells the press, then see about the boat."

Matt was looking at him like he'd never seen him before. "Sure, go on ahead. I'll take care of things here."

Bo nodded. "I'll see you later."

In fact, Bo knew that more than likely it was going to be the last time they'd ever see each other. As he went back into his office to grab his keys and briefcase, the reality of that coupled with never seeing his unborn grandchild left him surprisingly melancholy. When had he gotten religion? he wondered.

JT was watching the afternoon edition of *Sports Center* and waiting on the press conference the commissioner was supposed to be having when her phone rang. It was Special Agent Tate calling to let her know that the federal prosecutor was prepared to offer Misha immunity in exchange for her testimony against Garrett. He was already being charged with a plethora of felonies, and now solicitation for murder had been added. Garrett hadn't been found so far, but Tate was sure it wouldn't be long. She promised to keep her up to date.

Now, JT turned up the sound on the flat screen

as the commissioner's press conference began. Reese was standing behind him. He was dressed in all black and looked so delicious, she could have lapped him up. Instead she opened her phone and called her mother, who'd gotten back from South Africa a few days ago.

When she came on the line, JT said, "Hey there, Mama."

"Hello, baby. How are you?"

They chitchatted for a few moments, then JT told her about Garrett's latest attempt to get her. Her mother was appalled. "Am I going to have to send your sister and my granddogs after this bastard? Glad you capped him before he could hurt anyone."

"So am I. Do me a favor, turn on *Sports Center*."

"I have it on."

"Do you see that man in black standing behind the commissioner?"

"The fine chocolate one?"

"Yes, the fine chocolate one. That's the one courting me."

"Shut up! Oh, he's gorgeous. I thought you said he was a truck driver?" Michele asked, sounding confused. "What's he doing with the commissioner?"

"Long story."

"I'm all ears, especially about Mr. Fine."

They talked for nearly an hour about Reese, the ongoing investigation, Misha's perfidy, and last but not least, Carole. JT had talked to Brad earlier, and he reported that she was still making good progress.

Her mother was pleased by that. "Give them both

my love, and tell Brad I'm putting her name on the prayer list at church."

"I'll tell him."

"Talking to you, I didn't hear a word the commissioner had to say. Guess I'll have to catch the tape of the press conference later."

"And I was too busy staring at Reese."

Her mother laughed. "He is a fine one."

"That he is." And she hoped he'd be back sometime before the snow fell. "His father is a widower. Wants to meet you."

"Oh really. He as fine as his son?"

"Yep, and he makes homemade butter pecan ice cream, Mama."

"Do tell?"

"Should I hook you up?"

"We'll see. Let's let the dust settle around you first, then I'll see about Mr. Fine's butter pecan daddy."

JT grinned. "Okay."

"I'm going to let you go," her mother said. "Take care of yourself and keep me posted, please."

"I will. Love you."

"You'd better. Love you, baby."

Big Bo looked around his study to make sure everything was in order. He had no regrets. After it was over, Matt might have problems getting the insurance company to pay up, but he was smart, he'd figure out a way to handle them. Bo grinned, thinking about how disappointed his ex-wives were going to be when they found out there'd be no more alimony.

But it was about time their gravy train ended anyway.
Greedy whores.

He drove to the marina where his small speedboat was docked, and a few minutes later he was out
on the open water. The engine was misfiring but he
didn't pay it any attention. He wouldn't be needing it
in a little while. When he was far enough away from
land, he cut the engine, prepared himself, and waited
for the end.

The explosion and the resulting fireball could be
heard and seen for miles by the people gaping on
shore. Many of them grabbed their cells and called
911, but the boat and whoever was on it appeared to
be toast.

Matt Wenzel stood on the dock of the marina and
waited for news from the police divers. It had been
three hours since he'd gotten the call from the marina's panicked owner. Matt had dropped everything
and driven like a madman to get there, but he didn't
hold much hope. Neither did the divers. The explosion had been so powerful, only pieces of the boat remained, floating on the surface like flotsam. He was
told it could be days, maybe years, before the body
was found, if ever.

It was now too dark to see and the police were
calling off the search. They promised him they'd be
back first thing in the morning. Matt thanked them.
Reeling from the shock, he went home to grieve.

Once he walked into the silent house, he began to
cry. For the first time in his life, his father had acted
as if he'd actually cared about him. Matt remembered

how he'd gleefully wished for Garrett to get blown up, and he could only wonder if he was being punished for the cruel thoughts. There was certainly no glee in him tonight. He washed his face then picked up the phone. He had to call Melissa and give her the terrible news.

JT was watching the late edition of *Sports Center* on Reese's flat screen when the news about Bo Wenzel's boat accident was announced. It was yet another shock in a series of shocks for her, and she shook her head sadly. Many people had issues with Big Bo, but he'd always been kind to her. His coke dealing notwithstanding, she'd miss the old gator. She made a mental note to send condolences to Matt and the family in the morning.

The manner in which Bo died brought to mind her own explosion. As far as she knew, the police were still trying to locate Bobby Garrett. No tips had come in yet, but word had gone out about the reward money, and she was confident that it wouldn't be long before the law enforcement agencies received something they could use.

In the meantime, she was missing home. She enjoyed being a guest of the Anthonys, and they were treating like she owned the place, but she wanted to go home; she had a million things to do in order to put her work life back together, and it was difficult trying to do it from half a continent away. Carole was also a concern; even though she knew her friend was in good hands, JT wanted to see for herself. By the end of the week, she planned on being physically up to the challenge of flying, so she'd already booked her flight. The Anthony men weren't going to be happy, but it couldn't be helped. She was ready to go home.

She also missed Reese something terrible. She knew he was knee deep in the search for Garrett, which forced them to communicate sparingly, but she missed his mahogany voice and his presence. It was a given that he'd try and convince her to stay put, but she needed to go home so she could sit and think and attempt to make some sense out of all that had happened, then gather herself and move on. She understood that nothing would be truly settled until Garrett was found, but didn't think that would be much longer.

She also needed time alone to think about what kind of relationship she wanted to have with Reese. Part of her was ready to toss caution to the wind and be with him from this day forward, amen, but other parts were still wary of how being with him might impact the independent life she'd carved out for herself. Maybe after she got home and Garrett was found, she'd fly to Texas for a few days to see her mother and try and integrate the warring parts of herself. Her mother Michele always gave good advice, even when JT didn't like hearing it.

Eighteen

It was early evening when Miss Irene climbed the attic stairs. Her girth and age made climbing difficult, but Bobby's face was all over the television. Because he was her grandson she'd give him one last chance to leave her house before the police dropped down on him like Godzilla on Tokyo, because she knew they were coming. "You gotta go," she announced flatly.

"Ham gave me until the morning."

"Well, this ain't Ham's place. I want you gone. Now."

Bobby was seated on the bed. In reality, he had no place to go, but he wasn't telling her that.

"Your damn face is all over the television. The police are offering ten grand in snitch money, and it won't be long before somebody gives you up, so get your shit and get out."

"I'll leave when I'm ready."

"Did you hear me?"

The doorbell rang.

"Go answer the door," he ordered contemptuously.

Miss Irene stood with hate in her eyes. The bell sounded again. "I'll be right back."

"Take your time," he tossed out sarcastically.

Downstairs, she turned on the porch light and looked out of the peephole. Cracking the door cautiously, she asked the policemen standing on the other side of the locked screen door, "Can I help you?"

"Looking for Bobby Garrett."

She opened up. "He's in the attic. This way."

When Bobby heard his grandmother's footsteps on the stairs, he yelled, "Old bitch, I told you I wasn't leaving, so take your fat ass back downstairs and leave me the fuck alone!"

When she rose into view, he opened his mouth to cuss her out, but stopped. The two men in the dark suits had to be the police. The third man was Reese Anthony.

One of the detectives said, "Robert Garrett, you're under arrest."

The other cop cuffed him while his partner read him his rights.

They turned him toward the door.

"Call Ham!" he said to his grandmother. "Call my lawyer!"

Miss Irene looked confused. "I know you're not talking to me. I'm taking my fat ass back downstairs and leaving you the fuck alone. Just like you asked."

And she did just that.

One detective stayed with Irene for a moment to

give her his card while Reese and the partner took
Bobby to the car. When they reached the curb, the
detective opened the door. Bobby slammed his foot
against the man's knee and took off running. It happened so quickly, Reese was stunned. He was torn
between helping the cop and chasing the suspect.
Yelling for assistance from the detective inside, he
took off after Garrett.

With his hands cuffed behind him, Bobby couldn't
run fast, but he managed to make it halfway down
the street before Reese caught up to him and tack-
led him hard. When he hit the pavement he cried out
in pain, but it fell on deaf ears. A grim-faced Reese
snatched him up and threw him forcefully into the
side of a parked car. Garrett's face met the metal and
it broke his nose. Blood spurted out and he screamed,
"Police brutality!"

Reese slammed him against the car again. "This is
a citizen's arrest. That's for JT, you piece of shit!"

He slammed him again, barking, "That's for
Carole!"

Reese wanted to slam him again and again, but by
then a slew of squad cars were on the scene, sirens wail-
ing, and uniforms were spilling out with guns drawn.

The detective who'd been with Irene came up huff-
ing and puffing. "Thanks," he said to Reese. "We'll
take it from here."

"Bastard!" Bobby screamed at Reese. "You broke
my nose!" Blood streamed down his face.

Reese snarled, "Be glad that's all I broke."

Bobby was spared further vengeance at the hands

of Reese by the detective who escorted him back to the car. One of the uniforms held a towel to his bleeding, busted nose, and this time when the detective opened the door to the vehicle, Garrett got in without a fight.

As they drove away, if Bobby had been able to look back he would have seen his grandmother standing on the porch and shaking her head over what her grandson had become. In her hand was the detective's card, and in her head plans for how she was going to spend that $10,000 reward.

While the detectives took Bobby to the hospital to get his nose looked at, Reese drove to the precinct to speak with Captain Mendes. Now that Garrett was captured, he planned to head back to Michigan, but first he wanted to thank the captain for his help.

The two shook hands and Mendes said, "If you ever want to put the badge back on, we'd be glad to have you."

Reese grinned. "Thanks, but no thanks. I've had enough excitement to last the rest of my life."

Mendes nodded. "You're a good cop, Lieutenant."

"Thanks, Captain."

"Heading home?"

"Soon as I can book a flight."

"Keep yourself safe."

"You too."

Mendes's phone rang. Reese took that as his cue to leave, but before he reached the captain's door, Mendes yelled, "What do you mean you can't find him!"

Reese turned.

"Find his ass! Now!" He slammed down the phone and said to Reese, "They lost Garrett at the hospital. A uniform escorted him to the john and they both disappeared."

Reese stared.

The captain grabbed his suit coat. "Let's go."

"Shit!" Reese snarled.

They ran for the exit.

Bobby was in the backseat of a police cruiser. He knew the uniformed officer driving wasn't really the popo but an old friend of Ham's, so he was ecstatic that Ham had somehow gotten him sprung. He didn't know the other two men flanking him in the backseat, but that was okay. "Hey man, thanks." All the cotton the E.R. doc had stuck up his nose to stop the bleeding made speaking and breathing difficult, but he knew it would only be a temporary discomfort. What mattered now was that he was free.

"No problem," the driver replied.

The other two men seated on either side of Bobby hadn't said a word, but he could see them eyeing him. He knew he wasn't looking his best. "What the fuck are you all looking at?"

"You, my brother," the taller one said.

Bobby froze. The man had an accent. A Jamaican accent. One that sounded eerily familiar. "Who are you?" he asked.

"You didn't return my calls. I was starting to think you didn't wish to speak to me."

Terrified, Bobby looked to Ham's man and saw that he was smiling. He yelled, "Let me out!"

Of course he didn't, so Bobby was forced to turn back to the bomber's reptilian eyes to try and explain. "I paid you your money!"

"You sent me an empty envelope."

"No! The police must have—"

"The word 'police' in any sentence tied to me is not something I like hearing," he warned in an easy but deadly voice.

Bobby turned panic-filled eyes to the driver. "Call Ham!"

But of course he didn't do that either. Bobby's heart was thumping like a boom box. "Where are we going?"

"Some place private, so we can talk."

"Look, I can give you your money again. Just drive me to an ATM."

"It's way too late for that, Mr. Garrett, way too late, so just settle back and enjoy the ride."

It was four in the morning, Michigan time, when JT heard frantic knocks on her door. "What!" she yelled sleepily.

Bryce, Jamal, and Pops came hurrying in. She could see by the light from the hallway that Bryce was carrying his open laptop. "Sit up!" he said to her. "Jamal, get the light!"

As Jamal clicked on the lamp on her nightstand, she asked, blearily, "What's going on? Has something happened to Reese?"

The computer was placed on her lap and she found herself looking at a man on the screen. He appeared to be tied up. Two other men with their faces covered by bandannas were with him. Confused because she didn't know what she was looking at, she asked, "What is this?"

Bryce said grimly, "I think the guy tied up is Garrett. Reese left us pictures of him so we'd know his face."

She focused on the man slumped in the middle of the picture. The battered and bruised face was indeed familiar. Heart beating fast, she stared. "Oh, my lord."

Jamal said quietly, "They already chopped off one of his hands."

Her hands went to her mouth. Sure enough, blood was pooling from the stump at the end of his arm. The severed hand was lying on the floor next to him. She thought she was going to be sick. She couldn't tell if he was alive or already dead. "Where is this coming from?"

"No idea, but somebody on scene is uploading it and feeding it via e-mail to ISPs everywhere. Been on about ten minutes."

Jamal added, "The ISPs are probably scrambling to shut it down, but not having much luck by the looks of it."

One of the hooded men was talking, and JT yelled. "Sound!"

Bryce brought up the volume and they all heard a Jamaican-accented voice say, "Always pay your debts, boys and girls. Or this could happen to you."

Bobby could be heard moaning in the background.

The man said, "Let's put our guest out of his misery, shall we?"

He walked over and put a gun against Bobby's temple. Bobby began screaming and pleading. JT cut the volume and handed the laptop back to Bryce. She didn't want to see any more.

But in L.A., Reese and the rest of the investigative teams didn't turn away. They'd been alerted to the grisly scene by their in-house tech groups, and so, like millions of other cyber watchers across the globe, were eyewitnesses to the final frame of what the pundits would call "the Shot Seen Around the World." The man put the gun to Bobby's head and fired. Bobby Garrett was dead, murdered, and all Reese could say was, "Karma was a bitch."

Nineteen

Reese caught the red-eye and touched down at the Detroit airport at 3:17 A.M. Jamal and Bryce were there to meet him in baggage claim. He gave each a brotherly hug of welcome, but it was Jessi he was craving to hold. He'd spoken with her earlier, after Garrett's surprising death, but he hadn't told her he was coming home. He'd wanted to surprise her.

Hearing Reese's plan, Jamal shook his head. "You know she's armed. You'll mess around and get shot sneaking in on her this time of morning," he warned as Bryce drove them home.

"I'll take my chances." And he would. His plan to ask her to marry him was still on the top of his list. Like any man, he was hesitant to put his heart out there, but he wanted her, no ifs, ands, or buts about it, and the only way to find out if she felt the same was to pop the question.

The sound of voices outside the open window woke JT out of a dead sleep. She sat up, picked her gun up from the nightstand, and moved to the window to look out. What she saw under the moonlight made her grin. Reese. He was talking to Pops, who was wearing a big gray robe. She watched the two embrace then saw Pops head back to his place.

She got back in the bed, stuck the gun in the drawer, and when Reese came creeping in, she called out softly, "Hey, sailor."

He chuckled. "Hey, you."

She sat up, and he fed his eyes on her in the moonlight.

"You going to stand there all night or come and give me one of the thousands of kisses you owe me?"

He moved toward the bed. "Thousands?"

"At least."

Standing over her now, he reached down to gently caress her cheek, and all she felt for him rippled inside as she closed her eyes.

The kiss that followed was slow enough to stop time. There was longing, eagerness, hunger. His need for her drew him down to the bed so he could hold her in his arms, and she wound up on his lap, comforter and all.

"You're warm," he whispered, lips against her throat. There was something about a sleep-warmed woman that always aroused him, and with Jessi it was even more so. The weight of her breasts in his hand, the soft skin beneath her ear, all contributed to making him iron hard and ready.

"Do you mind if we skip the prelims and go right to the game?" she asked.

He smiled. "A woman after my own heart."

So Reese shed his clothes, slid into the warm bed, and filled her while she sighed. "Oh my, I've missed you."

He was already moving, and she fed herself on those long, hard, slow strokes until she couldn't say another word. His hands guided her hips and she let him set the pace because this was what she'd been waiting for all the while they'd been apart. The feel of him filling her, loving her, taking her to a realm where there was just the two of them; a realm of searing sensations, unbridled passion, and no inhibitions. It didn't take long for her to explode from the orgasm, and as he watched her arc and twist and ride out the wave, he came too, with a force that rocked his soul.

Later, when they were sure they'd had enough of each other, at least for the time being, they slept.

Bobby Garrett's body was found two days later floating facedown in the cement ribbon that was called the L.A. River. Law enforcement agencies and ISPs worldwide were still hunting for the people responsible and the place where he was killed, but they turned up nothing. Matt Wenzel had contacted Tate about a CD his father made detailing how and why Gus Pennington had been killed, so there had been closure for the family and that made Reese feel good.

Only after the Pennington case was closed did Reese tell Jessi about Garrett's ties to that case.

They were walking in the woods on the Anthony compound, and she stopped. "He killed an old man?"

"Yep, and stole the man's music player. That's how we broke the case. Garrett gave the thing to his son and his son pawned it."

She shook her head. "Bobby was a piece of work."

"You told me that the first time we met. Do you remember?"

"I do. I thought you were the cutest thing walking," she confessed.

"I thought you were pretty hot your damn self."

"Great minds think alike," she whispered, enthralled by every glorious inch of him, still.

"Apparently."

Reese decided to ask her to marry him. "Jessi, I—"

But his phone rang before he could say anything else. It was Bryce. "What?" Reese snarled.

"Damn! What did I do? Just calling to say Madden is set up and if JT is ready to get whipped, now's the time."

Reese said, "We'll be right there."

"What's up?" she asked.

"Bryce wants you to beat him playing Madden."

"Really?" she said with a smile.

"That's not what he said, but that's the outcome I'm looking for."

JT studied his face. "What were you going to say right before he called?"

"Nothing. It can wait. Just whip his butt. It'll make me feel better."

Sensing something was on his mind, she asked, "You sure?"

"I'm positively sure I want you to beat him like a rug."

She slipped her arm around his waist and they headed back to the house. "Whatever my baby wants, my baby gets."

He smiled, and she did too.

JT whipped Bryce like he stole something, as the old folks used to say. Even though she had the cast on her left hand, she'd regained enough dexterity in her fingers to beat him so badly, he was staring at her with his mouth open.

The jubilant Jamal and Pops gave each other fives, and Jamal crowed, "And she beat him playing with Arizona!" The Cardinals were one of the worst teams in the NFL. They didn't win on the field and they certainly didn't win in Madden football.

Pops gave her a big hug and a fat kiss on the cheek. "I'm going to make you enough butter pecan ice cream to start your own ice cream parlor."

She grinned over at Reese and he grinned back.

"Get the belt!" Pops cried ecstatically. He'd lived long enough to see Bryce get his Brainiac behind kicked, and now he could die in peace. "Get the belt!"

The still stunned Bryce left the house and returned a few minutes later carrying the Anthony version of a championship belt. It was made of wide black leather and there was a large medallion in the center that read t he gr eat est! Circling the medallion were a bunch of beautiful red stones that to JT's eye looked real.

"Are these rubies?"

Reese answered, "Yep. He was born in July and the ruby is his birthstone."

She was amazed by the belt's beauty. "How come only rubies?"

Pops cracked, "Because he designed it, and nobody's been able to take it away from him since."

Bryce countered, "Not my fault you all don't have any skills."

JT told him, "Well, I'm a September baby, so the next time you see this," and she held up the belt, "there'll be sapphires all over it."

Jamal, Pops, and Reese cheered.

Bryce knelt and kissed her hand.

Later that night, as JT and Reese lay in bed after a long session of making love, he looked down into her face and said, "Marry me."

JT closed her eyes. She'd been anticipating this moment and dreading it all at the same time. "Can you give me some time to get my life back together first before I answer?" She saw his jaw tighten and knew that was not the answer he'd been seeking, but for now it was all she truly had.

"Sure," he said quietly.

She knew she'd hurt him, so she tried to explain, "Reese, I—"

"We'll talk when you're ready," he told her, adding, "But I'm not going to wait forever, Jessi."

"And you shouldn't have to, so just give me a little time."

The atmosphere in the room had changed, they could both feel it. He pulled her against him, kissed the top of her head and said, "See you in the morning."

She bit her lip and closed her eyes, but sleep took a long time for them both.

Reese took her to the airport the next morning, and there was a distance in his eyes that didn't need any explanation. "Call me when you get home, so I'll know you made it," he said to her.

"I will. Reese—"

He leaned across the seat and kissed her softly. "Have a safe flight, baby."

She took the hint and got out of the car. He got out too, and carried her luggage over to the check-in station. When that was done, he gave her a wink, then walked away. As he drove off, he didn't look back or wave good-bye.

When she arrived at the airport in San Francisco, she called him, but got his voice mail, so she left a message and hung up.

She spent the next week pulling her life back together. Francine found a great location for the new office on the edge of downtown San Francisco. The rent was high, but well within her budget. She flew down to L.A. to attend a memorial service for Big Bo Wenzel. There was no casket, only a huge life-size picture of him smiling, because his body still hadn't been found. The docs gave her a new lightweight cast, which allowed her to drive, and she visited Carole every day. The jaw had been reconstructed to the satisfaction of the surgeons, and the teeth they'd implanted to replace the ones she'd lost in the explosion were also binding well.

The only speed bump in JT's life was Reese. He hadn't called at all, and when she called him, she always got voice mail. She supposed it was what she deserved, but it was maddening just the same because she missed him more than she missed Pops's homemade butter pecan ice cream.

So a few days later, she got on a flight and headed home to Texas, hoping the visit would clear her head and help her finally find the courage to do what she knew she wanted to do, which was say yes to Reese.

Her mother met her at the airport, driving a brand new, emerald green Navigator. Now that her cast was gone, JT dumped her bags in the back and got in. She and her mother exchanged a long welcoming hug.

"So good to see you," her mama whispered emotionally.

"Good to see you too."

They shared a grin, and Michele drove them away from the airport. JT looked out at the familiar landscape and was glad to be home.

Over dinner, she caught her mother up on her new office, Carole, and Misha, who was with her parents, visiting relatives in England and trying to make peace with herself over the anguish she'd caused.

Michele asked, "So how are you and the chocolate man doing?"

"I'm not sure, Ma." She told her the story.

Her mother listened without comment, and when JT finished, said sagely, "I understand your concerns, baby, men will change your life, but the only question you need to ask yourself, is: Can you live without him?"

As the next two days passed and Reese didn't return her calls, she began to wonder if he'd answered her mama's question with a yes.

Her mood was lifted by the arrival of her sister Max and her highly trained rottweilers, Ruby and Ossie. Michele called the rotties her granddogs, and JT wasn't sure who her mother was happier to see, Max or the dogs. Max worked for the government in a secretive and shadowy capacity, which meant the family never knew where she might be in the world and, more important, if she was alive. She was taller than JT, a Marine, an ex-cop, and so well-trained in martial arts and weapons, nobody in their right mind would mess with her, not and live.

That afternoon, JT and the shades-wearing Max were lying around the pool. Max was having man issues of the heart too, and after hearing the story, JT asked her with surprise, "This is *the* Dr. Adam Gary, the inventing brother who was on the cover of *Time* magazine last year?"

Max nodded.

"Since when did you start hanging around with men with IQs?"

"Shut up," her sister said, chuckling from behind her shades. "It was a job at first. Now?" She shrugged.

"Now you're wishing you'd read more than just *Fanny Hill* in school, I'll bet."

Max snorted. "I will shoot you, you know."

JT yelled to Michele, who was inside the house with her granddogs, watching a DVD of *For Love of Ivy*. "Mama! Maxie said she's going to shoot me!"

Michele yelled back, "Maxie! Only plastic bullets. Okay?"

"Okay, Mama!"

The sisters laughed, then Max tossed back, "From what I'm hearing, I'm not the only one with manly issues."

JT sighed, and Reese's face filled her mind.

Max turned over on the warm tile and propped herself up on her side. Looking at JT through her shades, she said, "Spill it."

JT's brown eyes met her sister's green ones. "I think I'm in love," JT said.

The wonder and surprise on her face made her sister start to laugh. "Really?"

"Yeah, I think so."

"I thought I was in love too, twice, remember? Sure it's not the flu?" Max had been married and divorced twice.

JT grabbed one of the pillows off the chaise and threw it at her sister.

Max yelled out, "Mama!"

Michele hollered back, "Interrupt me with 'Mama!' one more time and you're both going to your rooms!"

They fell out.

Once they regained some sense, Max asked seriously, "Why do you think it's love, Jess?"

"Can't eat, can't sleep. Think about him all the time. Dream about him."

"Then why are you here instead of where he is?"

"I don't know. Scared, I guess."

"Of him?"

"No, of me. I've been by myself for so long. What am I going to do with a man?"

"He treat you good?"

"Always. A little arrogant, though, but hey, so am I."

"Then what's the problem?"

"I suppose I just need to figure out what I really want." And as she'd told herself before, she already knew. Silence settled between them for a moment before she asked her sister, "What about you?"

Max rolled over onto her back and sighed with the same frustration JT had a moment before. "I don't know either. He's so smart. He's kind, nice, and fabulous in bed, by the way."

"Then I'll throw your question back: Why are you here instead of where he is?"

"He wants me to give up the Life."

"I ain't mad at him. Mama and I worry about you all the time. Where you are? Are you alive?"

"I know," she replied softly.

Because JT and her mother loved Max, they rarely expressed their fears about what she did for a living, but JT could see fear in her mother's eyes every time she spoke about Max having a new assignment; a fear that maybe their last good-bye would be the last ever. "Even Pam Grier got too old to play Coffy, Max."

Max smiled beneath her glasses.

"So what are you going to do?" JT asked. She would love not having to worry about her sister's safety.

Max gave a minute shrug. "Who knows, but if I turn in my stuff, it'll have to be because *I* want to, not because somebody else does. I do that and I'll be letting folks chip away at my soul for the rest of my life."

JT had never known her sister to be so philosophical. "Deep."

Max tossed back a smile. "Thought you'd like it."

That evening, JT admitted to herself that not having Reese in her life was the thing chipping away at her soul. Lord, she missed him. She stepped outside to get some air and to look at the stars and saw her sister slowly closing her phone. "You okay?" she asked.

"Yeah, " Max replied solemnly.

"Was that him?" JT wondered if she'd get to meet her sister's famous scientist love.

Max nodded.

JT shook her head and said softly, "We're a mess, you know that?"

Max smiled.

"I'm going back to Cali in the morning. You want to come? We could do some major shopping and call it retail therapy."

Max grinned. "Nah. Think I'll hang here with Mama for a little while longer."

"Okay."

"I'll take you to the airport in the morning, though."

"That'll be cool."

After a few moments of silence, JT said, "I'm going to bed. Don't be out here all night." Max had been a night owl since they were young.

"I won't. Good night, Jess."

"Night, Max. See you in the morning."

At the airport, JT decided she wasn't going to California after all. Going up to the agent at the ticket counter, she changed her itinerary, paid the additional fees, and walked to the gate to await her flight.

Reese and Pops were sitting on Reese's front porch. The afternoon air was finally starting to feel like summertime. Pinky and the Brain were underground working on a new design, while Pops and Reese enjoyed lunch and each other's company.

Pops said, "I hear she's been calling, but you won't talk to her. How long you planning on punishing her?"

"Frankenstein and Igor talk too much," Reese groused. "And I'm not punishing her. She wanted space. I'm just letting her have it."

"Uh-huh. You're in love, Reese, and we men hate putting our hearts out there for some woman to take an axe to. Suppose she's been calling to say yes?"

Reese had told his father about her response to his proposal. "She's not."

Pops shook his head at his stubborn eldest. "And you know this, how? Have you talked to her?"

Reese sighed. "No." Mainly because he didn't want to hear her say no. Too painful.

"Your brothers and I love her a lot, and we really wish you'd hurry up and get this fixed."

"I'm trying, Pops. I just don't know how. I can't drag her to the altar by her hair."

"True, and she'd probably shoot you afterward."

"No shit."

They both stilled as a cab pulled up in front of the house. Pops asked, "Who's that?"

Reese didn't know. Both men stood.

JT stepped out dressed in one of her killer designer suits and her signature heels. Her hair was fly, and gold was around her neck, wrists, and in her ears. She looked good.

"Damn," Pops said softly, torn between staring and grinning.

"I second that." To Reese, she looked so good she made his heart ache.

While the cabbie took her bags out of the trunk, she stood looking up at Reese. "You promised me a trip to Hawaii if I beat Brain at Madden, so I'm here to collect."

Reese grinned. "You don't look like you're dressed for the islands."

"I'm sure you can fix that," she tossed back saucily.

Reese's arousal was instant.

She paid the cabbie and gave him a fat tip. After he drove away, she said softly, "Hey, Pops."

"Hey, you," he called back affectionately. He turned and looked at the happiness on Reese's face and said, "I think this conversation might be too much for an old man, so I'm going home and make butter pecan ice cream." He gave his son a pat on the back, then walked down the steps. As he approached JT, he said, "Knock 'em dead."

"I plan to. Oh, here's my mama's number. She said call her."

JT didn't see his startled smile because her eyes were locked on Reese.

"I'll do that," Pops said, and hurried off to his place.

They were left alone. They stood motionless for a moment, savoring the sight of each other, then he left the porch and she started up the walk. They met in the middle and no words were needed.

They flew to Hawaii the next day. A car met them at the airport and whisked them away to one of the islands' small private enclaves where a few high-priced condos were nestled on the ocean. She'd never seen such a gorgeous place. There were wall-wide windows to let in the view of the water and the breeze, and the space was furnished in his signature Afrocentric style. There were three large bedrooms and a matching complement of baths; a fully stocked, beautiful kitchen and a key-shaped in-ground pool.

"You know," she said, turning to him, "you're probably going to have to throw me in a bag to get me to leave here. This is fabulous."

He walked over and settled his arms loosely around her waist. He gazed down at her happy and very beautiful face. "Glad you like it. Now, we need to change clothes so we can get lunch."

"Where are we going?"

"It's a secret."

"Hmm. What should I wear?"

"If it was up to me, you'd wear that little black number you had on last night."

"The one you ripped to pieces?" she asked with a grin. They'd been so eager to reconnect, her black bustier and tap pants had been rather tattered by the time they finished making love.

"Oh, that's right," he said as if suddenly remembering. "Guess I'll have to buy you more, but jeans and a top are fine for lunch."

She leaned up, gave him a soul-stirring kiss, then whispered, "Be right back."

A shiny black SUV driven by a young man picked them up a short while later. She'd been to Hawaii numerous times for the NFL Pro Bowl, held the week after the Super Bowl, but because of all the activities tied to it, she'd never had a chance to see anything other than the hotel and the game. Looking out of the window as the SUV rattled over the unpaved road, she had no idea where they were, but the raw beauty was unlike anything she'd ever seen. It was a tropical paradise complete with hidden waterfalls, lush green foliage, and a breeze that soothed.

Reese reached into the back pocket of his jeans and took out a blue bandanna. "I'm going to blindfold you."

"Oh really?" she asked, looking at him. "Sounds kinky, but there are children in the car, babe."

The driver chuckled.

Reese grinned. "Behave yourself. Hold still."

He covered her eyes with the soft clean cotton and then tied it at the back of her head. "Too tight?" he asked.

She touched the fabric. "Nope. Feels okay."

"It'll only be for a minute. It's part of the surprise."

JT knew that he was the only man she'd ever allow to do this, which meant he was the only man for her. A few moments later the road beneath the SUV grew even more bumpy, and she assumed they were now off-roading. They tossed and bucked for just a bit longer and then the vehicle came to a stop.

Reese said, "I want you to keep the blindfold on while I help you out and get you seated."

"Reese?" she said, laughing. Her curiosity was piqued and she was eager to remove the blindfold.

"Just another few seconds. It'll be worth it, I promise."

She could feel the ground under her feet and the soft breeze on her face, so they were still outside, and she didn't hear the hustle and bustle usually associated with a restaurant, so where were they?

"Okay. Here's your chair. I'm going to guide you down."

She sat. Her fingers played over the edge of what felt like a table, and then the bandanna was taken away. She gazed around and what she saw made her jaw drop. They were outside on what appeared to be a plateau so high up in the mountains that she could see the dense Eden spread out before her for miles. "Wow!"

"Like it?"

Words failed her. She felt like a goddess overlooking a world, one unsullied by the works of man and as pristine as it might have looked at the beginning of time. Between the silence, the beauty, and the sheer magnificence of the surroundings, she didn't know what to say. "Where are we?"

"A little piece of property controlled by the developers who built my condo complex. First time they brought me out here I was blown away."

She understood why. She'd been all over the world but had never seen a vista as stunning. "And this is where we're having lunch?"

He nodded.

The table was beautifully set for two, with gleaming gold-rimmed china, ornate silverware, crystal wine goblets and water glasses. "Is this more of your courting?"

He simply smiled and took his seat at the table.

Another SUV drove up, and out of it stepped a uniformed waiter. Assisted by the young man who'd driven Reese and JT there, he unloaded their prepared lunches and served the three-course meal with an elegance befitting the surroundings.

JT couldn't get over her amazement, and as they ate and talked, she realized just how much she loved him. She knew of no other man who would go to such lengths to give her a gift of such magnitude. She would never forget this lunch. Ever.

To her amazement, he wasn't done. After lunch, they got back into the SUV and were driven to a small airport a short distance away.

"Ever seen the inside of a volcano?" he asked as they walked toward a helicopter sitting on a pad a few yards away.

She stopped. "Volcano?"

"Yep. Volcano. The copters fly as close as they can get and the view is wild. You game?"

Of course she wasn't, but she was willing to try anything once. "Yeah," she said enthusiastically.

He grinned. "Then let's go."

It was the ride of her life. Kilauea, home of Madame Pele, the goddess of fire, was so scary and beautiful, JT found it hard to breathe. According to the pilot, the present eruption began in the late nineties, and she'd been spewing red and gold lava since. He got them as close to the main cone as safety would allow and she looked down into a pit of glowing magna that was indescribable. It was like being on another world. Plumes of smoke rose from the rims of one of the major vents, known locally as Pu'u O'o. It was the most active at the moment, and located on Kilauea's backbone. From the air, it could be seen moving over the landscape like a fat red snake. Next, the pilot swung over the Martin Luther King vent, named for the great leader because of the flow that began bubbling from it in January 2004, around the day of his birth. She marveled at the lava in all its shapes and forms, particularly the veins that slid off high cliffs and exploded into the Pacific Ocean below, creating the island's signature black beaches and huge clouds of hydrogen sulfide gas. She wanted the trip to go on forever but they had to land when the tour ended, and she added yet another memorable moment to the day.

* * *

On a different part of the Pacific Ocean, thousands of miles south of Hawaii, Big Bo Wenzel looked out from the veranda of his beachside estate in New Zealand and savored his new life with Brandi. He supposed he was going to have to marry her; after all, her plan for faking his death had worked like a charm.

It had been Brandi's idea to use scuba gear to mask his escape. Her small sailboat had been positioned a few hundred yards away from his speedboat. The fuse on the explosive had been long enough for him to light it and swim away. With all eyes on the explosion, no one had seen him slip aboard the sailboat and hide himself belowdeck. As far as the United States government was concerned, Big Bo Wenzel was dead, but in New Zealand his name was Carson Paget and he was very much alive. Trips to a plastic surgeon in Spain had altered his face just enough to blur his features, but of course it hadn't altered his memories. He wondered how his son was doing. Brandi said she might have a way for Matt, Melissa, and the coming baby to visit, so he was holding her to that. In the meantime he was enjoying life.

That night, Reese and JT had dinner outside by the pool. The condo management supplied the elegant meal, and they'd dressed for the occasion; he was in a nice suit, and she wore a skinny black sleeveless dress that brushed her ankles and a pair of jewel-encrusted sandals.

When they were done eating, they took a stroll

in the moonlight along the black sand beach. Filled with the memories of the beautiful day and her feelings for him, JT said, "After we get married I'd like to live here a couple of months out of the year. I love this place."

Reese's heart began to pound but he played it cool. "We're getting married?"

She looked up at him in the moonlight. "Yeah. We are."

"Really?"

She stopped, got down on one knee in her very expensive designer gown and said against the sound of the waves, "Will you marry me, Reese Anthony?" Because she loved him more than she loved breathing, and because she couldn't live without him, now or ever.

Reese thought this was the absolute best day of his life, so in response he got down on one knee too. "Only if you marry me, Jessi Teresa Blake." He loved her more than life.

He extended his hand and they both stood. He eased her close. She ran her hand down the dark pane of his cheek.

"I think I fell in love with you over the cherries."

He smiled. "I was a goner by then myself."

"You know what I want to do on our honeymoon?"

"We're having one of those too?"

"Yep, and I want to ride cross-country in a big rig."

He laughed. "What?"

"Yep, and as your bride, you cannot deny me."

He leaned in and kissed her softly. "I love you, Jessi."

She kissed him back. "And I love you, Reese."

They sealed their agreement with more kisses under the Hawaiian moon, then he picked her up.

"You're carrying me again," she said.

"Yep, taking you to bed."

She placed her head against his chest, and in his mind Reese heard Frankie Beverly singing:

I knew you were meant for me.
Right from the start,
It was like destiny.
You've given me a reason to love one more time . . .

And she had.

Author's Note

I am a huge sports fan. How huge? Well, when I went into the final stages of labor during the birth of my daughter, it was the first day of the 1980 NFL season, so I put off going to the hospital until halftime of the *second* game of the day because I knew there'd be no football shown in the delivery room. My poor husband!

JT's character has been with me for over a decade. Originally, I'd toyed with the idea of hooking her up with Mayor Drake Randolph, aka His Fineness, and having her be the heroine of *Black Lace,* but I'm glad I didn't. Making her the sister of Max Blake from *Sexy/Dangerous* and putting her with Reese Anthony proved a much better fit. Authors will tell you that sometimes stories morph in ways only the characters seem to understand, and this was such a case. I had no idea the Anthony men were the descendants of the House of LeVeq until the story began to unfold. The realization put a smile on my face, and I hope all of you LeVeq lovers smiled as well.

I've never had a story come to me complete with its own unique soundtrack, but *Deadly Sexy* did. Frankie Beverley and Maze. When I first began sketching out the story, one of the local radio stations played a song by Maze titled "Reasons" that I'd never heard before. I've been a Maze fan for over thirty years, and in my mind and in the minds of many others this iconic group has never received the industry awards or accolades they've so richly deserved. The song blew me away. It said everything Reese felt for JT. I know that many of my readers reread my books, so before you do that second read, download "Reasons" into your MP3 or iPod. Start with "Reasons," add "Golden Time of the Day," "Traveling Man," "Love You Much too Much," "Can't Get Over You," and listen to "Reasons" again at the end, and you'll have your *DS* soundtrack. In my fantasy world this book would have shipped with a customized Maze CD, but this is the real world, ☺ so you'll have to compile your own. Many thanks to Reve Gipson, Maze's publicist, and their lawyer, Mr. Bernard Fischbach, for helping me get permission to use the "Reasons" lyrics.

For the readers who've recently discovered my work through the romantic suspense titles, all of the characters in these books are descendants of characters in my historicals. If you enjoyed *Deadly Sexy,* then pick up *Topaz, Always and Forever,* and *A Chance at Love* to read about Grace Atwood Blake and Loreli Winters Reed, the fiery great-great-grandmothers of JT and Max Blake.

In closing I want to send a few shout outs to: Lawan

Williams, who's over in Kuwait helping our soldiers; Rene Motley, in Lansing, Michigan, for her continued support and love; Sarita and the Songbird, whose six degrees of separation hooked me up with Maze's people; Detective Sharon McCalop of the Dallas Police Department, for answering my questions about police procedure; my crew in Beverlyland and our newest bundle of joy—Marisa Haynes—who just happened to be born on my birthday! And last but not least to all my readers old and new. Stay blessed everybody. Keep reading and I'll see you next time.

B.